The Dark
ELUDING
Nirvana

To Justine,

Thank you for your support

Much ♡

V.L Brock
xx

V.L. BROCK

Copyright
Eluding Nirvana:
(The Dark Evoke Series, #2)
By V.L. Brock
Copyright© 2014 V.L. Brock
Licence Note

This book is licensed for your personal enjoyments only. This book may not be sold or given away to other people. If you would like to share this book with another person, please purchase an additional copy for each recipient. If you are reading this book and you did not purchase it, or it was not purchased for your use only, then please return to your favorite book retailer and purchase your own copy. Thank you for supporting and respecting the hard work of this author. This is a work of fiction, names characters, businesses, places, events and incidents are either the products of the author's imagination or used in a fictitious manner. Any resemblance to actual persons, living or dead, or actual events is purely coincidental.

This book is licensed for your personal enjoyment only.

The author acknowledges the copyright and trademark owners of any brands/stores/establishments, which are used in the book, and that I do not claim ownership to.

Cover Design by: Sprinkles On Top Studios.
https://www.facebook.com/SprinklesOnTopStudios
http://sprinklesontopstudios.com/
Formatted for paperback by: Cassy Roop at Pink Ink Designs.
Edited by: Brittani Pritchard.

__Dedication__
To my Nan:
16 years without you
and yet it still seems like yesterday that I was holding your hand, listening to stories of WWI and WWII, alongside married life in the olden days, while eating a chocolate animal bar.
You were the first strongest woman that I knew and loved; I was and still remain in awe of everything you had experienced. My love for you is unending.
To my mother:
You were the second strongest woman that I know and love.
You're a Stevens…you're your mother's daughter. You're a fighter… you got out while you could. I love you.

Gratitude unlocks the fullness of life. It turns what we have into enough, and more. It turns denial into acceptance, chaos into order, and confusion into clarity. It can turn a meal into a feast, a house into a home, a stranger into a friend.
—Melody Beattie

Acknowledgements

Firstly, to my readers. They say that a writer merely begins the story; the reader is the one to finish it. Without you, these stories would be left incomplete. So from the bottom of my heart, I thank you. I thank you for journeying alongside the characters, experiencing the emotions which come hand-in-hand with that journey, and taking the time to get engrossed in a world in which I have created.

To my fellow IEZ ladies. Where do I even begin? We laugh alongside each other, we cry alongside each other, we twirl and pick each other up if we get a little dizzy and fall, and for that, I thank you. The IEZ isn't just a group of Indie Authors, it isn't just a group of friends…it's a family, and I'm honored to be a part of that. I don't know where I would be without our chats, videos, or words of encouragement. I love you, all. You ladies rock!

My besties and beta readers: Samantha Ulysses, Charlie Chisholm and Brittani Prichard (who is also my kickass editor). The amount of faith you have in me, and the amount of times you have shaken some sense into me is bountiful. I can't thank you enough. When I've doubted my abilities, you were there, when I doubted the direction of the story, you were there, and when the emotions ran too high on certain scenes, you were there to reason with me. The love I have for you all is out of this world. You were my first angels, my first readers, my first fans, and I thank you for that.

To my Street Team, Vic's Angels: Justine McFadyen, fellow

author S.M. Phillips, Lora Lynch, Renee Craycraft, Sam Pixiebelle O'neill, Karen Shenton, Angie Cooper-Jenkins, Lorraine Lilly Wickson, and all the other members, thank you for your pimping skills and spreading the love of not only Walker and Kady, but also Hayden and Samantha from Impulses. Let keep it up. #WalkerLove #Impulses.

Kaprii Dolphin and Lorraine Lilly Wickson who make up the fabulous Two Ordinary Girls and Their Books, I have two simple words: **you're amazing!** Your continued support and enthusiasm towards The Dark Evoke Series will always warm my heart. Thank you for hosting Eluding Nirvana's Cover Reveal alongside the Release Day Blitz. And not forgetting the many other blogs which participated in the event also: M&D's have you read book blog, Sarah and Kirsty's Book Reviews, A Girl Who Loves Books, Best of Both Worlds: Books & Naughtiness, Ms. ME28, My books and Me, Author Sandra Love, Books and Friendz, This Girl Loves Books, 2 Girls a book & a Glass Of Wine, Just Another Girl and Her Books, Naughty Girls of Romance, Sassy Southern Book Blog, Beautifully Broken Book Blog, S.M. Phillips, We Stole Your Book Boyfriend, Bookland, Bad Boys Bedtime Stories, Book Nook Nuts, Words Turn Me On, Little Shop of Readers, Steamy Book Momma, This Mommy Loves to Read, Eye Candy Bookstore, Confessions of a Book Whore, Cover to Cover Book Blog, Musings of the Book-a-holic Fairies, Inc. Randy Raunchy Romantic Book Blog, My Book Inspired Ramblings, Glass Paper Ink, Sweet N Sassy Book A Holics, Girl with Book Lungs, Book Blogs For Book Lovers, Fictional Mens Page for Book Hos, LBM Book Blog, Fictional Boyfriends, The Literary Gossip, Literary Lust, BJ's Book Blog and Luscious Literature.

To all of my reviewers: thank you for taking the time to read, rate and review. I know family and life can interfere with reading schedules and I am so thankful that in between those commitments, you could read something new by someone new.

Lastly, to my husband and my munchkin. You see me at my best and at my worst. You see the downside and my upside, but regardless of that, your support is unending. The ample times of doubt are cast into oblivion when you restore my faith. You bolster me and my vision, you remind me of what I want to achieve, of why I am doing this. You help remind me that anything is possible when you fight and work toward it. For that, I can never repay you. I love you both until the end of time...The moon and back is a no-go.

PROLOGUE

Spying through the bay window, Liam was pacing in the living room, the phone to his ear as he flexed his free hand.

Two weeks I had been seeking clarity, enlightenment… nirvana. And right then, Walker's words haunted my mind. *'If it's the last thing I do, I'll make damn fucking sure you remember'*.

As I stood staking out my home from the safety of the sidewalk like some abused little woman, I felt myself spiraling rapidly down the rabbit hole without any brakes. The quandary which I came to accept back when I was laying in the hospital bed, about the doctors and medical personnel being unable to hook me up to some device like in a sci-fi movie, and travel the tunnel of past memories, was now very much tangible.

And it took Walker and everything I had seen and felt that night to instigate it.

Sparks fired. Memories unlocked. Nirvana was found.

Fuck…

CHAPTER
one

December 2010.
Two and a half years before the accident…

The warmth and softness of the velvet backrest left my body feeling cold as I shifted to the edge of my seat, practically folding myself over the romantically dressed, table for two. I was staring at the man before me, a man who was fiercely passionate in both work, and his relationship. A man who was never dealt his cards; he was the one who dealt them.

He was pretty much as haughty and as confident then as he had been, the night I agreed to go on a date with him. And so there we were sitting, in the heart of the most romantic Italian restaurant in Boston, amongst high-class lovers swathed in golden flickering candlelight, in the exact place, right down to the exact table, where we had our first date, celebrating our two year anniversary.

I drew in my lower lip and clamped my teeth down gently. He knew my game. He saw it in my eyes. The way they glimmered and darkened as I held my head low and coquettish, casting him with my scandalous, 'I want you to fuck me, and I don't care if you take me over this very table with the clientele watching', look.

Liam DeLaney could read me like a book.

It was a shame the skill wasn't mutual.

"Happy Anniversary, Kady baby," he muttered on a small smirk. His tie was held flush against his black shirt when he swiftly rose from his seat opposite to avoid catching the flickering, golden flame of the candle in-between us. Bestowed with a chaste kiss on my lips, Liam left me humming in both profound appreciation and objection, when he drew his skillful lips away from me.

"Happy anniversary, Liam," I whispered back. I could feel the creases fanning out from the corners of my pale blue eyes as my once demure smile, broadened with the merging of his warm, soft hand as he tenderly cradled the side of my face.

If I had known that the moment he lowered himself back into the seat opposite, that my stomach was going to free fall and the smile on my face was about to vanish with the husky, deep beckoning of a certain name, I would have kept Liam him there for a little longer.

"Raven?"

Craning my head to the source of the voice, I was met by a tall, coffee-skinned man, whose head was reflecting the muted, romantic glow of the restaurants lights, making a beeline to our table. "Jerome," I gasped. What the fuck was he doing there? Damn fucking timing.

When a warm, friendly hand lightly crashed down onto my shoulder, Liam did a fantastic job of making damn sure everyone knew he was pissed. Looking at him wasn't necessary. I could feel his green and blue speckled eyes hardening into emeralds and hear his jaw tightening with the shadowed sound of grinding teeth. The gust of air he ousted in an angry sigh, pasted itself to my forearm.

"Hey, girl, I didn't expect to see you in here."

Although my head was caught somewhere between cursing the rich punter to Hell and praying he would leave us alone, I found myself smiling politely. "It's our two year anniversary, so we're celebrating."

"Oh, wow," he sounded stunned and he looked it, too, with his black eyes widening and, well, I would have said his eyebrows meeting his hairline, but he was bald as a coot. Extending an arm to Liam, he offered his congratulations. Silent and making no attempt in reciprocating the gesture, Liam simply responded with a glare, and I swear if he was telekinetic, he would have strangled the poor man with his ruby colored tie. Jerome turned his attention back to me. "I was wondering if you're working Friday night."

"That I am, Jerome. That I am." I took a sip of the pink champagne which left a lingering taste of strawberries on my pallet and bubbles tickling my nose.

Black eyes glistened like black sapphires, while his mouth curled into a knowing and satisfied grin. "Great, I'll come in for my usual." I nodded my acknowledgement as he turned on his heel and muttered, "See you, Friday, girl." And I was left pondering whether the tall, muscular black-man could have made that statement sound any seedier.

Emotions I felt that night sitting opposite my lover, in the most notable restaurant in town, losing myself in his loving gaze as we celebrated this monumental bridge in our relationship, and which would hopefully bring about a climatic result when we got home, took a nosedive. Love, joy and excitement curdled into embarrassment and anxiety. I hooked my hair behind my ears. Liam glowering at me was something I couldn't fare with. Not if we weren't having angry sex anyway. And sex was something, angry or not, that we hadn't had in several weeks. And I was sexually frustrated beyond all comprehension.

"Liam, please. Stop looking at me like that." With a crumpling brow and my lips forming a firm line, I eventually surrendered to a full-on, sullen pout before taking another sip of the fizzy liquid, in an eager attempt to drown the additional serving of guilt which was flooding my system. He was making that night so perfect, spoiling me rotten, being as loving as Liam DeLaney could be, and one of my punters had just gatecrashed it.

"I've had it, Kady. I can't keep doing this."

I lowered the flute onto the white linen cloth, while shaking my head and shrugged my shoulders, completely baffled.

"Kady, the first time a guy approached you regarding work, I was fine with. The second, third and fourth, I'll admit, I found a little hot, knowing that they could only look and I was the lucky bastard that got to touch. But enough is enough."

"What does that mean?" I gasped, slighted.

Focusing his livid gaze on the empty plates before us, he scoured his hand over his mouth. "Kady," he peeked up, holding me with hard eyes. "We haven't had sex for weeks because I am feeling physically sick knowing that all those men, including that Jerome guy, are going home and knocking one off while fantasizing about *my* girlfriend's ass grinding up against them, and her tits being shoved in their face, counting down the fucking days until they get to actually, *physically* experience *my* fucking girl doing that to them."

I was sitting overlooking the table where we'd begun a life together and journeyed through two years side-by-side, and I was completely dumbstruck, flabbergasted by his omission. I didn't know what to say. I didn't know he was being affected that badly. Two years, and I still continued to work Red Velvet without any regard to how he felt. A part of me felt terrible.

"I'm done with it, Kady," he flailed his head and spoke in earnest. "You can't expect me to continue like this."

"Liam," I murmured over the violins which were being played a few tables over. "Am I ashamed of what I do? Yes, I am." The nodding of my head swiftly became a faint shake. "But I can't just quit. I make more money in a night than what some people make in a week."

"For the love of fucking, God, Kady," he reprimanded and I instantly recoiled at his harshness. God he was severely pissed at me. I swore I could see his breath rising in steamy clouds as he blew out of his nose, his mouth hard. I'd never seen him so angry before. He looked like a raging bull in a china shop. I knew in that moment, it was something I wouldn't care to see again. "Fuck the money, Kady. Do you want us to go back to how we were?"

"Yes," I replied without hesitation, because if there was one wish I could've had granted, it would be to reclaim the passion which had bound us since the beginning.

"Then choose." I watched his mouth upturn scornfully and the power behind his voice had my brow, once again, creased for what seemed like the hundredth time that night, as he presented me with his ultimatum. "Come on, baby," his tone softened as he rose from his seat and drew it to my side. When he lowered himself back into the velvet, my hands were promptly clutched in a clam-like grasp. His eyes softened substantially, matching the timbre of his voice. "Remember the passion? The need and want?" Dropping his head, his breath tickled my face as he resumed his, DeLaney Persuasion. "I miss taking you however I can get you. The moans and groans I can draw from your lips."

His words were gradually killing me and my resolve. The rasping vibrations which penetrated my flesh, connecting with me on a deep, needy level, made me squirm in my seat and cross my legs.

"I miss making you come, knowing that you're mine, knowing that I'm the only one who gets to see you vulnerable *like that*, and knowing I'm the one *to make* you vulnerable like that." My eye were searched, my silent contemplations hunted by the intensity of his gaze. "We can have it all back, Kady baby. Just say the word. Make me happy."

Make him happy? He was my boyfriend; I wanted nothing more than to do just that. I drank in a breath before slipping my hand from his and taking a mouthful of liquid courage, disguising itself as a $300 bottle of pink champagne. "And we go back to normal? If I do this, we go back to how we were?" I questioned after swallowing, my upper lip curled slightly.

The grip around my lingering hand tightened. Smiling, he nodded his response.

"Okay," I resigned. "Okay, Liam. I'll quit Red Velvet."

My hair was fisted as his hand threaded through my large, bouncing curls, holding the back of my head as he wrenched me closer. His mouth crashed down onto mine, his tongue cool from the alcohol and slightly bitter from the Key Lime Pie, as he swept it through my mouth and over my lips. A groan was torn from my throat as he pulled his lips away, and braced our foreheads against each other. "Those groans I draw from you…" he breathed, an element of desire and approval went unveiled in his tone, while tightly screwed eyes enhanced the faint creases from their corners.

"I hope you'll draw more from me tonight, Liam," I flirted.

Cool air eradicated his warmth and bonded to my brow, when he freed himself from me, leaving me feeling somewhat bereft while his large hand cradled my face. I leaned into his caress, while his eyes bored a fucking void in my mind. "You have no idea, baby…" He shook his head shrewdly, his mouth giving way to that haughty, conceited smirk that I loved so damn much. "You have no, fucking idea."

After settling the bill, Liam proffered his hand, and with a beam to rival the Cheshire cat, I unthinkingly slipped my hand into his warm possession, our fingers locking as he led us out into the chilly nightly breeze. The weight of the world had seemingly been removed from his shoulders as he gazed down at me. I suppose, in a way it had. My conceding to his wishes had made him happy, and regardless of losing sometimes anything up to $900 a night, knowing that it was my answer and my decision to grant his wish, had me feeling like I was in Seventh Heaven.

Smooth flesh of his mouth united with the back of my hand when he planted a kiss on my knuckles. Into his body I stepped, and despite the fact I was in heels, I rose onto my toes to eliminate the good five inches which was looming above me, to meet his lips. "Take me home, Mr. DeLaney," I requested with seductive purpose.

I didn't need to ask twice.

The hard muscle of his burly thigh was warm and tempting beneath my hand. Fingers roamed subtly into his inner thigh, tracing his inner seam, and up to the decadent bulge which lay beneath his black suit pants. "Eyes back on the road, Mr. DeLaney, you'll get us both killed," I chided with a roguish arch of a perfectly threaded eyebrow, when he shot me a hungry stare.

"Yes, Ma'am," he sighed, turning his attention back to the busy road ahead. "How about we go to the movies tomorrow night?" he asked on his next breath.

Tomorrow would be Thursday. I knew I told him I would quit Red Velvet, but even so, I couldn't just walk out. I had to give Benny notice. I'd worked there for three years, built relationships with the workforce, and the man who gave me a chance, deserved the level of respect which I was going to reward him with.

"I've got work tomorrow, Liam."

The growl which left him as he whipped his head to face me, in conjunction with slamming on the breaks, had me both recoiling and being thrown forward, the seatbelt burning as it tightened against my neck. "What?"

"Liam, I am quitting, I just need to hand in my notice. I can't leave them hanging high and dry."

"What, like the sleaze balls who go to those places to be left hanging after my girl cock teases them?" he berated, regardless of my recoiling or the reasoning of my answer.

My stomach sank to the deepest depths of the sea, and the crease in my brow had followed suit. "Liam, please, I'm being reasonable—"

"Reasonable? Fucking reasonable?" he yelled. I didn't appreciate how fast his tone of voice and demeanor, was making my heart beat in…well, in something I didn't wish to consider my boyfriend baiting in me. "Do you even have a fucking heart in that chest, Kady?" His pointed finger climbed from my chest up to my temple. "Do you even have a fucking brain in there? Hello?" I battered his assaulting hand away from my head and rubbed my temple in an attempt to sooth the pressure which lingered on the surface. A rushed stabbing, sensation shot through my head thanks to the brute force he issued with his reproach.

"Liam, please, stop this," I implored, all the while the click of the seatbelt buckle release sounded through the BMW. His arm stretched across my middle as he pulled the release for the door. What the fuck was he doing? "Liam…?" I drew his name out with greatest caution.

"Get out."

"Liam, please,"—my hands made their way to frame his

gorgeously handsome face which was rapidly being taken over by The Devil himself—"We can talk about this." Nevertheless, my supplicant, peacemaking hands were hit away as he shouted repeatedly for me to get out. It was him, finally shoving me from the car that had me forfeiting to his outlandish demand.

"And you will stay out there until you can respect me and my requests, and learn to have some fucking empathy," he pointed a disdainful finger out of the opened window, like he was scolding an untrained puppy. The bystanders of Dorchester launched their quizzical, prying stares upon hearing his escalating voice booming from the car.

"But, Liam—" I wrapped my arms around my chest in a feeble attempt to shield my inappropriately clothed body of the December chill. I sniffed back my tears and choked on a sob. "I'm cold."

Head held high, eyes wide with a loose grin on his smoothly shaven block jaw, he looked almost satisfied, while he shook his head, insensitive. "I don't care, Kady," were the last words spoken before the window went up, and the black BMW pulled off at speed, the tires screeching as he fled.

Cars darted past, inquisitive people stopped to stare, and one even walked into a streetlamp as he gawked at the spectacle. Being physically ejected from Liam's car had made me feel like a cheap whore, and I would have bet my life that any viewers would have strung the, 'whore with an unhappy punter' assumption, together.

Overlapping my right arm across my body, I grasped the top of my left arm, as it hung tensed, down the span of my body, pressing my floating black mini skirt against my legs to stop the breezes intention of whipping it up and exposing me physically. I already felt exposed emotionally.

For a Wednesday night the streets of Dorchester were

surprisingly bustling. I meandered on autopilot, taking my time to deliberate in my dazed state, what exactly had just happened, through the masses.

I found what hurt the most, was his lack of humanity. Who in their right state of mind, would repeatedly and brutally, press against their partner's temple in anger just to prove a point? Dammit, who the fuck would physically shove them out of the car, in the middle of December, wearing a miniskirt and knee-high boots, without a fucking jacket, to walk home at night, alone? The fire which burned in the depths of his eyes and mounted to the surface, the tensing of his jaw, even the disgusted glower he aimed at me, it all revolved around my mind as I made my way through the streets, passing a guy sitting on a wall corner muttering in hushed voices to, who I could have only have speculated, was a man who needed his nightly fix.

My musing was cut short as I became aware of a car slowing beside me. "Hey," a deep voice boomed through the window, and at that moment, I cursed Liam DeLaney and his anger to the fifth Circle of Hell. "Hey," the voice repeated again. Unenthusiastic, I stopped mid-stride and craned my head to come face-to-face with a black and silver pick-up; the man's left arm rested across the steering wheel, a black flat-cap on top of his head had cast a shadow across his face. "Can I give you a lift, darlin'?"

A lift? Yeah okay, I inwardly scoffed. I knew what 'a lift' meant, and realizing that I'd been approached by a random stranger, who boldly propositioned me, made me realize the degree of how shameful, and how much of an indecent person I was, especially with my clothing choices. God, no wonder Liam's parents hated me.

It was in that moment, the mental fog lifted. I didn't need a pole tattooed on me to indicate my profession. I blatantly had stripper/whore marked all over me, and men could smell it like a bitch in heat.

"No thank you. I'm fine," I replied with an enforced smile.

"You sure, darlin'? These streets can get a little rowdy after nightfall. It's no place for a lady to be walking around without a chaperone." I couldn't see his face, but my God, he was a smooth talker, and that accent...

I smiled. "No, honestly. Thank you, but no."

"Very well, darlin'," he began to pull away. "You have a good night." He beeped his horn, and then he too, was gone.

Parked in its designated space in the parking lot, was the BMW. Thank God, Liam was already home. I didn't have my keys, and I didn't relish the idea of being locked out in that weather much longer. My arms were like ice blocks attached to my torso, the painful tensing of every muscle in my body from shivering, made me feel nauseous, and I swore my lips were turning blue.

Stepping under the porch, the hallway light which beamed through the glass entranceway lit up the buzzers on the right-hand wall. I pressed for 8c and waited.

"Hello."

"It's me. Can you let me in please?"

"That depends—" he countered, totally unconcerned for the risk of me catching hypothermia.

"Liam," I whined, tossing my head back with my hands concealing my face. "Please, this is no place to talk. Just let me in."

His sniffling was rough and husky as it vibrated over the telecom. "Cold out there is it, Kady baby?" His lack of fellow feeling made everything clear. And it was driving me crazy because he never acted this way. Ever. How can you know someone for so long, wake up next to them every day for years, laugh with them, and cry with them, feel whole and content with them, and then out of the blue, they do something that strips a portion of that contentment and trust away?

That being said, if I'd took more consideration to his feelings, if I didn't push it with saying I'd quit, and then on my next breath, say that I had to go back for a few more days, none of what happened that night would have happened. I was the one at fault. I was responsible for his outburst. I made him do this with my sheer lack of empathy. I couldn't blame him. I brought it on myself.

"Liam, please. You've made your point. I understand now. I'm sorry. I'll call Benny and Liv in the morning."

"I want your word that you won't go back there, Kady."

My head dropped forward on an exasperated sigh, as my body continued with its incessant vibrating and my teeth chattered. "You have my word, Liam. Please," I lifted a numb hand to hastily swipe a falling tear. And to think I used to laugh at Brittany for crying and hiding under the stairs when a thunderstorm hit. I was stood surrounded by darkness. The already cold air, cooling furthermore as the nightly temperature plummeted, and triggered the stabbing of knives all over my body. My tears weren't only ones of remorse. I was crying because of the cold. I was crying because to prove a point, Liam had deliberately put me in pain. "Liam, I'm freezing. Please, let me come in."

After a few excruciating moments, the welcomed sound of the loud buzzing echoed down the speaker, the heavy glass door before me, unlocked.

That night, I was taught a lesson.

That night, a lesson was learned.

CHAPTER
two

Upon reaching the summit of the steps, I turned to the apartment to see the door open with Liam resting his shoulder against the frame. He teased me with the sliver of hard flesh on display as his black shirt hung open. Had it been any other occasion, I would have run into his arms and finished the job he had begun with my teeth.

But it wasn't any other occasion. It was the night that I was made to feel utterly vulnerable. And that was how I felt.

He hung his head, focusing his gaze on the scuffing movements of his shoe against the hardwood surface of the hallway. "I'm sorry, Kady," his apology was barely above whisper. But, he had the decency to at least look contrite.

Shivering from head to toe, I fought to eject my words through the chattering of my teeth and quivering of numb lips. "Don't worry about it, it's alright, Liam." My gesture was mirrored as I took a fragile step toward him and before long, I was swathed by warm, burly arms.

The usual tickle of his chest hair was absent as I was scooped up and held against his chest. Still, the iciness of my cheeks was thawed by his warmth, and for that I was grateful. Shuddering incessantly, I gasped when he pulled away, his soft hands framing my face as he tipped my head back to hold my gaze. "I didn't want to do that, Kady. But you had to learn your lesson."

I nodded and licked my lips. The warmth of my tongue burned at the frozen flesh. "I understand," I muttered simply.

"Do you?"

"Yes. I want to make you happy, Liam. I'll do anything to make you happy."

Lips slanted over mine, the heat of his breath collided and eradicated the iciness in my mouth and on my face as he swept his tongue against me. However, the coldness of my body and mind, proved impossible for me to respond while matching his fervor. Lips were numb while my jaw continued to quiver, and I swore I almost bit him. "Kiss me properly, Kady."

"I can't. I'm so cold."

Restrained once again by hard, demanding eyes, his hands made their way into my hair and fisted painfully. I winced and screwed my eyes as tightly as I could, scared to witness the expression which lingered before me. "Open your eyes." When I failed to comply immediately, he hissed his command again, making me jolt and his hands fisted even tighter in my curled masses.

Apprehensive, my long mascaraed lashes pulled away from the arch of my cheekbone slowly…hesitantly. His mouth was trembling, but unlike mine, I knew it wasn't because he was cold. Held by a menacing stare, I saw the gradual bubbling of anger rising through his blood, his block jaw taut as he spoke through clenched teeth. "I already feel guilty enough; I will not have you making me feel worse."

"I'm not trying to make you feel guilty. I'm really not, Liam. It was my own fault." That, I could actually understand. He was left with no other option. The tables were reversed, and because of that, I had a fundamental grasp of what it must be like to share your life with someone who lacked empathy.

His eyes unstiffened, along with his jaw and hands "You said you want to make me happy. You have." I offered him a tightlipped smile. "Now, let me make *you* happy. Come to bed with me, Kady." And with his words, the chills and shuddering that had me at its mercy, and the blood which turned to ice in my veins, were thawed and purged, only to be replaced with a sensuous trembling of anticipation, and my blood was wildfire through every blood vessel.

He led me into our apartment, and started down the hallway to the left of the entryway. My heels clicked hollowly on the flooring, before he quickly turned and pinned me against the wall. His hand caught me behind the knee and my leg was drawn up and hooked over his hip. Hard, masculine body pressed against the span of my slim form and resting between my legs, I groaned eagerly as his hips dug into me, circling and grinding against the most sensitive part of my body, while his adept tongue invaded my mouth with luscious sweeps.

I couldn't feel the cold any longer, his touch alone left trails of burning desire coating my flesh. He grasped me beneath my ass and hauled me up, the wall scraping my back as he did so. Locked around his hips were my legs, and I whimpered unreserved into his mouth before my head was lulling back, granting him access to take my neck and throat after pulling away from my lips.

"Liam, I need you," I groaned, while his hips briskly grinded into me again, his hand clutching painfully at the back of my thighs.

In a daze, he stumbled through the corridor with our mouths sealed against one another. My frantic hands framed his face then fisted into his long, dark, slicked-back hair, as my legs naturally tightened around him. I refused to let him pull away when I was lowered onto the vast bed, which sent his body crashing down atop of me, pushing me further into the mattress. My neck was the first station for his hands caress. Once they began their torturous decent, and his hands journeyed down my body, a tiny whimper was torn from throat. Slowly dragging the wall of muscle from my writhing form, my panties were hooked by his thumbs and peeled down my legs and over my boots.

I watched enraptured with a lustful throb striking between my legs as he unbuckled his belt. The sound of the leather whipping through the hoops of his pants ricocheted around the bedroom, sending a slight breeze in my direction once the belt cut with precision through the air. "I think you can keep those on," he suggested, eyeing up my knee-high, black heeled boots, all the while, divesting himself of his pants and boxers. "Top and bra off," he ordered.

I complied instantly, tossing both garments onto the flooring beside the bed.

"Now the skirt," he added, and that quickly meet the heap, too.

Eyes which betrayed the degree of his greed ignited my body. The distance between us may have been miles, instead of feet. His breathing caught during the moments he studied my naked body, with the exception of my boots, as I waited in anticipation, while he tantalized me with the vision of his cock growing before my very eyes.

Proceeding to stroke his very substantial length at a leisurely pace, he rasped, "Touch yourself, baby." An immediate smile spread across my face. I like that game. I didn't know if it was a stripper thing or not, but I loved knowing that I could tease him just by having him watching me. So I did as I was told.

Shifting onto my knees, I cupped and hoisted my tits up to practically meet my throat, giving my nipples a tiny squeeze between my thumb and middle finger. My lip found its way under my teeth as my hands dropped over my body, my hips thrust forward and circled briefly when my hand fell between my thighs. I was impelled by the growl which left the man at the foot of the bed as he watched the action of my finger stroking up the slick coating of my core.

The echoed noise of him getting wet while dragging his fist back and forth at the same time as observing me, was making me even needier. I sighed and tossed my head back momentarily, releasing a wanton groan and circled my hips brazenly. "Look at me, Kady." I did as I was told. We reflected each other's obvious hunger as our eyes locked. And I was floored.

He'd freed his heavy cock of his grasp and pulled out a foil packet from the unit. As soon as he rolled the condom over his length, he pounced on me. He licked his fingers and without warning, plunged them inside of me. My hips bucked as I bore down onto his assaulting hand, urging him deeper.

"God, you're so warm, Kady," he breathed, his fingers circling me, opening me, readying me for his remarkably thick, steel length, while my own feverish hands worked over his body. It was like a chain reaction. Each muscle my hand skimmed and dipped over, whether it be his pecs or his six-pack, sent them tensing and rigid beneath my touch.

Only a hairsbreadth away from my goal, I grazed through his pubic hair, only to have his untamed hand batter me away. "I want to touch you," I pleaded, but the only answer I received was my own protesting feral growl as his fingers hastily left me high and, not so dry.

"Don't you growl at me, woman," he ordered, and without warning, I was flipped onto my stomach. Potent hands firmly clutching my hips drew me back so my ass was in the air, ready an exposed just for him.

"I'm sorry."

"Shut the fuck up, Kady," he commanded, pulling my hips back farther, and I was instantly consumed by the wet heat of his mouth as it crashed down onto my pussy from behind. Hands fisted into the sheets, the side of my face was buried in the mattress as I called out his name on a pleasure enthused cry. His tongue orbited and flicked over and across my clit before sucking at my core. I pushed back onto his teasing mouth when his tongue traced my entrance before ruthlessly plunged into my void.

"Fucking Hell, Liam," I called, before being pulled back onto his mouth by the increasing forceful grip on my hips. Ending the shallow thrusts of his tongue, he resumed lapping up the sinuous juices he induced, from the warmth of my core.

With his mouth bound around me, his hum of appreciation vibrated against my clit as he swept across the swelling of nerve endings. And before I knew what hit me, my looming release was being drawn closer and closer. My legs tensed, my back arched further until I was thrusting back onto him with desperately grinding hips, goading him to eat me faster.

On the cusp of my climax, I was left stranded. I felt and watched it fade into the distance. His cool breath bonded over my center, as the man with an expert tongue behind me, blew lightly on my swelling, parted lips. My body wasn't the only thing left to throb painfully. "Liam," I whined.

"God, you taste so fucking sweet," he countered while his fingers massaged the area between my glazed thighs. "You are more than fucking ready for me now." And just like that, I was impaled by his cock on a savage yell. My head rolled back on an impassioned cry when he hit the ache, which had been burdening me for weeks, head-on.

The absence of his right hand on my hip was felt after I peeled my face away from the sweat coated sheet beneath me. As quick as I'd noticed its absence on my hip, I was reminded of its presence all over again, this time, at the back of my head. He gathered my hair, and my neck was tugged back when he wrapped it around his wrist. With each brutish yet exquisite, demanding thrust of his hips, the tugging grew harder and harder, while each strike upon the ache at the very tip of my void, had my hands growing tighter and firmer into the sheets.

Fuck anniversary lovemaking. This was sheet clawing, fuck me like you hate me sex, and I loved every damn fucking second.

"Damn, Kady, you got one tight fucking pussy." He pulled back the stringent hand which my hair was wrapped around, causing my neck to be hauled back so the ceiling was in my peripheral vision as he pummeled into me. The weight of his body along with the sweat which coated it, when he leaned into my back, had me frantically forcing myself onto his mammoth cock, swallowing him to the root as I met him thrust for thrust. Heated breath and a grating voice in my ear asked, "Who does this pussy belong to, Kady baby?"

He expected me to answer fucking questions? All I could think about was how damn good it felt finally feeling his hardness inside of me, how deep he was getting, each nerve he was sweeping against as he dragged his cock from me, then rammed it back without hesitation, and how he was pushing me to my release.

"Fuck, Liam. Harder, please—"

My neck was snapped back further so it was near impossible for me to swallow comfortably. "Who…does…this…pussy…belong…to?" he punctuated between every decadently, ruthless lunge.

"You!" I screamed. "It belongs to you."

Hair finally loosened, my neck drooped forward, causing me to bury my face once again into the rumpled sheets, and influential hands were set back on my hips. "Damn right it fucking does," he muttered with a gravelly voice, and I knew his teeth were clenched. "Hold the fuck on."

So I did. I squeezed those sheets so fucking hard, that I could feel my nails digging into my palm between the material, while he continued circling and grinding his hips, before mercilessly carrying out his assault and battering my cervix with the swelling crown of his erection. Feeling his pulsating steel inside of me as I cinched around him, made my body strain and every muscle from my neck, down to the tips of my toes were tautening and compressing, as he roughly struck me back onto the weapon which never failed to have me screaming.

My orgasm was no longer on the horizon; it was right there in front of me, goading me with the need of only a few additional wild, dynamic lunges from my man. My head was spinning. My vision blurred as I was fucked like there was no tomorrow. And if there wasn't, at least I knew I could sail into my afterlife sated.

"I'm going to come, baby," he gasped between each laborious breath. His drives were more insistent. His grip was painful yet enflaming, as his nails dug into the void above my hipbone.

Pounding, panting, slapping, grasping, shuddering… everything was so intense, so wild, as together, we frantically raced to climax. And when we finally crossed that finishing line, my walls clenching and pulsing around him, as his dead weight crashed down onto my back, I knew that if that was the kind of fuck I would receive if I complied to his requests, I would quite happily comply to every outlandish demand he made, for the rest of my life.

CHAPTER *three*

June 2011.
Twenty-four months before the accident…

It was 8:45 p.m. when the familiar buzzing sound rebounded around the apartment. Sitting on the cream leather sofa, Liam's arm uncurled around my shoulders, prompting me to grudgingly tear my head away from the warmth of his chest. Al Pacino resumed mumbling about something or other from the surround sound system while the buzzing sounded again in two rapid short bursts. Suspicion and anxiety formed in my chest as my heartbeat hastened under his leery stare.

"Who the Hell would be calling at this time of night? Are you expecting anyone?"

With a frantic flail of my head, I quickly answered, "No. Are you?" The shake of his head advised me that he wasn't, and with his ticking jaw and progressively toughening eyes, I knew I needed to unpeel my ass from the butt imprint, and find out who was disturbing our night, before he assailed the poor person responsible for the interruption.

Padding through the double glass and oak doors at the end of the living room, I picked up the coms. "Hello?"

"What are you playing at, chick? Open up, I'm wet."

I noticed Liam was already resting against the frame of the door when I turned my head to the direction of the living room. The grey T-Shirt smoothed and molded to the shape of his body as his arms folded across his chest. "Who is it?" he asked.

Although the speaker was covered by my hand, my voice was nothing more than a guilt laden whisper. When I told him it was Liv, his arms were instantly thrown into the air on an exasperated groan. If I thought his jaw was working a moment ago, I was very much mistaken.

"Did you hear me, chick? Open up. I have wine."

Mouthing that I was sorry to the wall of intimidation over my shoulder, I was rewarded with a brusque nod of leniency before he turned his broad, muscular back to me and headed for the couch.

"Sure thing, Liv; come on up," I muttered, before pressing the button release then unbolted the apartment door, leaving it ajar for her to walk straight in.

A hand towel was tossed at the drowned rat when she made her way through to the living room. "Lovely, thank you," she gasped, catching the cloth and setting the bottle of wine down onto the coffee table in the center of the room, just ahead of the chair and couch. Like a second skin, the leather biker-girl jacket was shed from her body then hooked over the door before she set about toweling her hair. You could tell the eight flights of stairs had taken its toll on her, when she breathlessly questioned, "What took you so long?" and dropped her ass into the leather chair to the right of the sofa with an appreciative sigh.

My mouth opened to speak, however the words were taken

from me. "We weren't expecting visitors tonight, Liv." Liam's voice was dripping with hostility, while the TV ahead remained the focal point of his attention.

Golden eyes shone like clear honey as her eyebrows rose. Liv darted her finger between Liam, who was sitting back in the couch, his left arm outstretched along the backrest, his right braced on my knee as a blatant display of affection, and me as I nervously gnawed on my fingernail. "Oh, you two were…" her hand scurried straight to her mouth, shocked and apologetic.

"No, Liv," I interjected, bringing some clarity to her assumption, and then motioned toward the fifty inch flat screen. "We were watching a movie, that's all."

Sensing rapid daggers stabbing me at the side of my skull, I craned my head. An angry, accusing pair of emeralds was glaring back at me. "Just watching a movie? I thought we were having a romantic night?"

Discomfort and apprehension chilled through my bones before swiftly surfacing, sending every hair follicle standing to attention. Although I was shifting unnervingly, I strove with everything I had to mask my uprising concerns, while being choked by my words. "Yes, Liam, th–that's what I meant." Unlike me, the movie was lucky enough to receive his calm focus as he stared back at the screen.

"Anyway," Liv piped, dropping the cloth in her lap. "I haven't been out with my girl in a long, *long* while, too long, actually. So…" her laugh lines were carved deeply into the sides of her mouth, and her eyes glimmered as she lightly, yet animatedly bounced on the edge of the seat, totally unashamed that her hefty chest was enjoying the ride, too. I swore she was going to knock herself out one day with those things. "I'm calling a girls' night. What do you say, chick? Dancing pants on for Ecstasy tomorrow night?"

Instant unease and panic inundated my system, the kind you get when you need a shot, but you're scared shitless of needles. "Um…" A prickling sensation took place of words which were still yet to be thought, and radiated from the center of my brow to my temples.

With a masking worthy of an A-star, a wince was successfully contained as the once affectionate caress became a powerful hand on my knee, squeezing firmly upon the joint. The sharp burning bred by the tips of his fingers bruised my flesh, and began its unpleasant course up my thigh. Incapable of anything other than listening to his voice, I remained motionless and rode out the discomfort in hope it would be alleviated once his words were spoken. "I thought we could go to the movies tomorrow night, and see that horror movie you wanted to see."

"Horror movie?" Liv stared at me dubiously with her brow knitted, head cocked. "Since when does, Kady Jenson like horror movies?"

I sought to move, however, Liam's subtle death-grip was tightening with every indirect persuasion and each skeptical question delivered from Liv's lips. I blinked back tears, and with everything I had, I pleaded that she would put an end to her interrogation and stop provoking him. "Well, um…I've seen two or three that Liam likes," I shrugged. "They were okay. I handled the gore really well, didn't I, Liam?" I whipped my head to face him. The delight and self-satisfaction in my voice was palpable, like a little girl passing her dancing exam. Even through the pain he was inflicting.

"You did, baby," he smiled and moved to place a chaste kiss on my lips, the leather gripping under his weight as he shifted. "I was so proud of you," he breathed and I felt his lips forming the words against my mouth. After what seemed like an eternity, the death-grip finally came loose, and the tender area was granted a soothing rub before he retracted. Being told he was proud, or comprehending the degree of it, was unnecessary. I knew he was proud by the smile and praise he gave me after I faced something which I'd found insufferable and loathed, just for him. And knowing that I was making him happy was the best feeling in the world.

Focusing my attention back on the brunette to my right, her expression betrayed her judgments. She didn't look too impressed. She didn't look proud. She looked…suspicious.

Liam pushed himself to the edge of the couch, his hand crashing back down to the area above my knee. I set my hand atop of his and gazed longingly into his sparkling eyes. "As Liv's here, would you mind if I went out for a beer with the guys?" he queried. Unprepared for the return of his grip, I channeled all my strength into looking unaffected for our visitor, while the power behind his fingertips insisted that the breath in my lungs was to be held prisoner. "I flipped them off because I thought we were having tonight for us, but…" How he maintained his even, unsuspecting tone was beyond me. A soft whimper fled my throat. Lucky enough, the combined volume of the movie and Liam talking, shadowed the pained groan and was obviously inaudible to Liv's ears.

I smiled sweetly through the burning bruising in my flesh which seeped into the muscle and tissue beneath. "Absolutely, don't worry about us. You go and have fun."

When my leg was freed, his damaging hand lifted to frame my face, and I finally released a slow, concentrated breath. "Good girl," he praised me and sealed our lips before retreating to the bedroom to make himself presentable.

Before he left for his lads' night, I was pulled into his arms and bestowed with a passionate kiss that made my head spin. The roving journey down the span of my back came to an end as Liam parked his hands on my ass, and without a second thought, I was drawn against his muscular physique. A small suggestive chuckle vibrated low in my throat when his hips lunged into me.

"Liam, will you put the damn girl down for a second?" Liv teased, making her way to the kitchen with the bottle of wine clutched by the neck.

He flipped her off with an unimpressed snigger, and once she was out of sight, and singing out of tune in the kitchen, Liam's blasé demeanor switched, and I was instantly pinned with a stern expression, one I knew not to dare argue with. "Do not fucking drink, do you understand me?"

"Yes, Liam," I nodded.

"Do not let anyone in, do you understand me?"

"Yes, Liam," I nodded again.

"Good girl." The quick, uncaring kiss cast a shadow on his words, and then he was gone.

Entering the kitchen doorway, I was bombarded by a fraught voice asking, "Where's the fucking wine glasses, chick? They're not in the usual cupboard," and the sight of Liv frantically pulling every cupboard door open in a desperate search. She could continue rummaging until her face turned blue, she'd never find them. Liam hated me drinking without him. He worried too much about the way alcohol lowered inhibitions, and he didn't want people to take advantage. So, I slowly found myself only drinking if he was at my side.

"Wouldn't you prefer a coffee instead?" I posed, rounding her curvy body and heading straight for the coffee pot.

She glared at me with her dark eyebrows meeting her hairline.

"Coffee?" she sighed like it was some ghastly word. The bottle of red was lifted clear off the unit by its neck and pressed against her chest like a child clutching their favorite teddy bear. "But I have wine." Watching the twenty-seven year old woman whine like a sullen child chipped away at my resistance, making me giggle.

Lips rolled free from over my teeth with a pop. I shook my head faintly and wrinkled my nose. "No thanks, Liv. I–I think I'll stick to coffee. Would you like to join me,"—I retrieved two red mugs from their hooks and held them by the handles, swinging them enticingly—"or poison your liver?"

After a beat, the bottle gently met the surface of the counter. She folded her arms across her chest and huffed, "Damn you, Kady Jenson."

With a muttering of, "Very well," I placed the mugs on the surface, and poured the coffee from the pot while my best friend made her way to sit her ass on a dining chair. "Okay, he's gone. Give it up, Jenson. What's going on?" her words were spoken in the most serious tone I had ever heard come from her.

"Excuse me?"

"You quit Red Velvet months ago without warning, you haven't come back. You hardly ever answer your phone and when you do you're terse and guarded. I've barely seen or spoken to you in almost five months. You're not even interested in coming dancing anymore, let alone having one measly glass of wine. For us, this is alien, Kady. Now what the fuck is going on?"

I spooned two sugars into her mug and stirred before taking our nonalcoholic drinks to the dining table. "Liv…" placing a coaster in front of her, I set her mug onto the table and took a seat.

"Don't, 'Liv', me, Jenson!" she chided. "You're not 'allowed' out, but he can go gallivanting? I don't like this, Kady. A–and what's all of this," she stumbled over her words with a derisive upturn of her lip, while reaching across the space between us and fumbled with the high neck, filigree blouse tie, flicking it in my face in an attempt to prove her point. I battered her away. "You look like you're going to the funeral of, Queen fucking Victoria."

Her words hurt, I wouldn't deny it, but I was learning fast not to bite back to such derision, so I simply pursed my lips into a surly pout and frowned. "Liam likes me wearing this."

Hands which were both gentle and supportive reached out and swathed my own as I wrapped them around my mug. Eyes swarming with profound concern, were staring back at me. "Too much is changing, chick," her opinion was expressed in a pacifying timbre. "You're not the Kady I was in the company of a few months ago."

No, I wasn't. That would be because I was putting the one important person in my life, first, something I should've done a long time beforehand. I sighed. "Liv, I was a menace—"

"WHAT?!" Freed by her hands as they fell away from my own, she pushing herself back into the leather-backed seat in a fit of pique. If she wasn't sitting already, I swore she would have collapsed on the spot. "Where the fuck did you get that assumption?" she grumbled.

"I didn't pay any consideration to how Liam felt about my actions, the way I dressed... Liv,"—I peached myself on the edge of the seat, my shoulders gathered at my ears as I leaned into my forearms, eager to demonstrate my point—"To see the look in his eyes and how happy he is when I fulfill his wishes, is the best feeling. Knowing that I am making him happy..." Even her hard, disbelieving eyes couldn't wash the lunatic grin I had plastered over my face.

As I trailed off rummaging through my brain to find a word expressive enough to describe how deliriously happy making

Liam happy, was making me, Liv delved into her bag. A moment later she sighed, "Here." I seized the tube she handed me with caution. Removing the lid, I twisted the bottom to raise the cherry red lip stick.

"Liv, I don't think red is my color."

"No, neither do I, but if you're altering yourself to become a Stepford Wife, which gesturing by your attitude and poor, poor taste in clothing, it's blatantly obvious that you are, you might as well go the whole nine yards."

Stunned by her rebuke, my eyes flared. There were no words in the entire human language which I could've used to describe how utterly insulted I was. How dare she think she could talk to me, not only in that tone, but with those harsh speculative words aimed at *my* relationship? I had to give it to her, Liv had a tongue like a razor, and I had just come to realize that I never wanted to be on the receiving end of it again. I hung my head as the ungainly silence sifted around the area, only to be ruptured by affronted gasps.

"I'm sorry, chick, that was—"

"You know what, Liv?" I lifted my head to stare into contrite, gold dusted eyes, her lips rolled over her teeth, and it would benefit her if she kept them there. "Until you enter a long-term relationship and learn the value of compromise and empathy, and to know that you are making your partner happy by doing those things,"—head shaking faintly, my eyes tightened while my upper lip curled in distaste—"then don't think you can give *me* relationship advice."

"You know what, chick," she said pointedly. Even over the distance across the table, I could feel her pointing finger jabbing at me, albeit not physically. "You should never change for a man. No offence, but if doing all of that means you'll end up like this,"—

her point became a wave of her hand as she motioned down my body—"then I will quite happily remain single for the rest of my Goddam life."

Taking a sip of coffee, I muttered my final words on the topic over the brim of my mug, "And that's your choice."

The best thing about mine and Liv's friendship was, we could have our moment of expressing differing opinions, and yes, we would get into a debate about it, and something's may be said which could easily be taken out of context. But, we were educated enough to understand that not everyone shares the same values and the same views of life, so we never let our words dictate the fundamentals of our relationship. It was a verbalized expression of our differing opinion. And it wouldn't be taken any further.

She crossed her legs and raised her mug to her lips. "And swiftly moving off that topic, have you had any thoughts about his birthday?"

"Nope. I am completely stumped. He has everything, and I wanted to do something amazing for him, he deserves it, especially for the big three, zero. Still unemployed and I'm feeling like shit because I'm living off my boyfriend. I can't use his money to buy him a gift, what sort of idiot would do that?"

"Bet you wished you saved up some of those tips now don't ya," she grinned like a cat that got the cream, and I couldn't help but mirror at her attitude with an agreeing nod of my head and rolling of my eyes. Yes, she was damn right. I did wish that, it could have come in handy right about now.

"Thirty…what would a man love for his thirtieth birthday?" I mused, mostly to myself while gazing into thin air.

A gasp from across the table had drawn my attention back to the brunette. Her mouth agape, while mischief twinkled in her hazel eyes.

That expression was a traditional 'Brainwave Liv' expression. Damn, we were in trouble.

CHAPTER
four

October 31ˢᵗ 2011.
Twenty months before the accident…

"I cannot believe you actually invited someone without passing it by me first. Liam's going to have kittens." The feisty brunette may have been donning a kinky Devil costume, damn; she could have been The Devil herself for all I cared. Either way, nothing was going to halt my scolding. Things had been going smoothly between Liam and me since his birthday several weeks ago, and if Liv's infamous running off at the mouth was going to rock that boat, the large bowl that I was pouring potato chips into, would be flying across the room to meet the coffee and cream painted wall.

"Oh, come on. She's been living above you for a few months now and"—she jumped down from the chair, taking a step back to admire her draping web in the living room doorway—"you still haven't spoken a word to each other. It'll be fun."

I was just about to begin my sardonic probing into who it

would be fun for exactly, when a shriek followed by a clattering of bags resonated from the hall. "Sis!"

I turned to face the direction of the squealer, and was suddenly attacked by a broomstick and a mass of green hair. "Brittany," I opened my arms to give my little sister a not so little hug. "I love the wig."

"Wig?" By the quizzical sound of her voice, something was about to tell me that this was yet another mishap for, Brittany Jenson. Both the world and the people in it were lucky that she strayed from beauty school. She pulled me away and held me at arm's length, shaking her head. "This"—scornfully pointing to the masses, she continued— "is supposed to be cosmic blue. That's what the box said, I double checked. Does it look like cosmic-fucking-blue to you?"

Liv propped her hand on my sister's shoulder and offered a sympathetic caress through her tears as we fell into loud fits of guffawing. I was sure that if her hand wasn't braced on my sister's shoulder, The Devil would have been rolling on the floor like a turtle trapped on its back. "It'll fade soon enough, but at least it goes with the costume." Liv always knew how to make someone see the upside to their downside, and by the grin on my baby sister's face, she found comfort in the words of my best friend—the best friend who also suffered many a mishap in the hair and beauty department over the years.

"Speaking of costumes," Brittany turned her attention back to me. Blue irises, which were a darker hue than my own, combed over the length of my ivory satin and lace high neck blouse with filigree shoulders, and a pair of simple black pants. She eyed me warily. "What are you supposed to be, sis?"

"Oh, haven't you heard," The Devil interjected, sweeping her hand in a downward motion over my body. "This is the new wardrobe—"

"And I think she looks just as beautiful as the first day I met her," Liam countered, brushing the doorway web out of his face and strolled toward me. His hands were being loosely stuffed into his pants pockets.

"Hey, big man," my sister raised her arms in defeat and in the process, nearly whacked Liv on the head with her broomstick. "I'm not one to judge. You hear all the time about past fashions making a comeback. Who's to say we won't all be wearing the Victorian ensemble within the next year, eh?"

His eyes were ablaze as he snared my chin between his thumb and crooked index finger, tipping my head back to gain eye contact. "The Victorian's, if I remember correctly, had a lot of class," he muttered, just before sealing his soft, warm lips over mine. As I was drowned in Liam's arms, a sweet smile tiptoed across my face.

He loves me. And he thinks I have class.

By 9:15 p.m., the apartment was heaving. I didn't realize we invited so many people. Well, when I say we, I meant Liam and Liv, considering the only unrelated person I knew *and* invited amongst the throng, was the only friend I hadn't cut from my life…Liv.

Liam/Dracula, was mingling with a group of rowdy lads near the couch with a beer in hand, Liv was somewhere or other, and don't get me started on Brittany and her man-obsessed brain. I wouldn't have been surprised if I found her in the bathroom with her ass in the sink and Casper between her legs. Her public demeanor would have Daddy far from impressed. But the only time she got to let her hair down, be it cosmic-blue, green or purple, was outside of D.C. and with me. I found pleasure in knowing that she was able to have fun with her big sister. And especially in knowing that she knew she was safe enough with me to let her hair down.

I made my way to the kitchen for another drink. Regardless of him being at my side, I didn't want to embarrass myself or embarrass him, if something should've happened in an alcohol induced state. So, under Liam's orders, I was limited to water or punch...punch was more favorable.

Lifting the silver ladle from the glass punch bowl, I poured a generous volume into the red plastic cup, when I overheard my name being called. Attention drawn away from the center of the dining table, I lowered the scoop and was met by The Devil with her red glittery lips turning up into a tempting smirk.

"Kady, this Laurie, she lives just above."

Swapping hands, I grasped the cup in my left while extending my right. "Hi, it's nice to meet you."

"You, too," she smiled. She was only a slight thing with glossy black hair sitting just beneath her shoulders, her bangs block-dyed purple. She was donning black jeans and a white turtle neck, and in that moment, a part of me was thankful that I wasn't the only person at a Halloween Fancy Dress Party, without a costume.

By the time I had offered the pale, round-faced woman, who merely stood at my chest, a drink, The Devil had disappeared back into the swarm of strangers ransacking my home.

Sitting down at the dining table in an awkward silence, our hands dipped every few minutes into the bowl of potato chips and pretzels. I used to love meeting new people and establishing new friendships. Yet, over the months, since I had cut a generous number of people from my life, I found that being in the company of very few people, with Liam at my side of course, was my comfort zone. Sitting at my dining table, in my kitchen, in my apartment, I felt completely out of my depths. I felt like a stranger to my surroundings.

Eventually, the deafening silence was too much to withstand. "So what is it you do, Laurie?"

She cleared her throat and took a swig of punch. "I'm actually in between jobs at the moment; it's so hard out there at this time. But usually, I love being in the kitchen."

"What, you're like a chef or something?"

Amusement shone in her hazel eyes and she released a girlish, innocent giggle. "No, I'm no good with actual meals, but more like baking."

"As in cakes?"

She nodded her response.

"Wow. That's amazing. Even if I knew where to begin, I wouldn't have the patience to complete it."

Her hand was buried in the center of the bowl of potato chips as she spoke, "It's really relaxing. And it saves on family birthdays," she laughed quietly, removing her hand and popped the nibbles into her mouth. "What about you?" she added around her food.

At that point in time, I think it was more embarrassing for me to admit that I was unemployed than a stripper. But, through my humiliation, I fessed up, and did so with a very deep pleat scoring my brow.

"There's nothing to be ashamed of, Kady," she rubbed my forearm in a gesture of reassurance. "My cousin has just been laid-off from some steel factory place that he's worked at for about a year. It's really hard out there at the moment."

Being laid-off and quitting of your own freewill was two entirely different things. Although a stranger, I felt sorry for the poor guy. "I'm sorry to hear that."

"Ah," as she waved off my compassion with a gesture of her hand and an eye roll, an idea struck me. One I was sure killed two birds with the same stone, and one that Liam was going to love me for.

"Steel factory you said?"

With her lips caressing the plastic cup, she peeked over the brim, "Mmm, hmm," she sounded on a swallow.

"I'm not sure if I should be saying anything, because it's still in the pipeline,"—Laurie mirrored my movement as I inched forward on my seat and doubled over the table with my elbow perched on the edging—"Liam, that's my boyfriend, he owns his own architect and construction company, DeLaney Constructs. Now"—I peeked over to the doorway, making sure we were indeed on our own—"do you know the old Williamson Estate a few miles from here?"

"Sure."

"Liam's drawing up a contract with someone or other, to have it demolished and have a new, up and coming estate of luxury homes built. He's going to need more construction workers. If your cousin would be okay with construction…" I must have been addicted to making people happy. Watching Laurie's eyes light up and sheen like toffee triggered warmth to radiate through my chest. It was the same elated expression I had been addicted to seeing, and being the cause of, on Liam.

"Really? Oh, my, God that is fantastic. My cousin will do about anything, he's so passionate and he always puts in two hundred per cent at whatever he does. Do you think Liam would do that?"

As if he knew he was the topic of conversation, Liam sauntered through the kitchen door. "Hello, ladies." He was swaying. He was beaming. He was tipsy. "Kady baby, your sister is a menace," he slurred and waved his arm with an over exaggerated, drunken flare. "You give that Wicked Witch of the West a few drinks, and off she trots, pinching everyone's asses and cackling loud enough to wake the dead."

That wasn't news, at least, not to me. That was typical Brittany and something I was used to seeing. So, I simply brushed off his remark and drew out his name like a child who's about to ask for a pony off her parents, as the chips were invaded by his large, merry hand.

"Yes, baby."

Laurie and I both broke into a smile as he mimicked my persuasive tone, kissing my head between crunching and swallowing.

I motioned a wave to the petite woman opposite. "This is Laurie. She lives upstairs."

"Well, hello, Laurie." Her pale cheeks flushed when he captured her hand and placed a chaste kiss on the back of her knuckles. Yeah, he really was drunk. "Welcome to the party."

"Thank you, you got a wonderful girlfriend."

"I know, she is wonderful," he smiled down at me through his drunken haze, "and she's all mine." With his upper lip rolled to showcase his fake vampire teeth, he released a playful growl and lunged at my neck. The warmth of his mouth, alongside the sensations of his teeth and lips upon the tendon running from my neck to my shoulder, had me in an uncontrollable fit of laughter.

As I playfully battered him away and gasped for vital breath through the small stitch in my ribs, I began to talk. "Liam, Laurie's cousin used to work at the old steel factory, but he's just been laid-off."

He craned his head. "I'm so sorry to hear that, Laurie. See, that's why it's more fulfilling being your own boss."

He was getting way off track, and that haughtiness of his was sure to make a bad first impression. "Yes, well, you know what they say, 'it's not what you know; it's who you know'?"

"Yes..." he drew out his word with interest.

"And with this next project being as huge as it is you're obviously going to need more construction workers, aren't you?" Motionless, I watched as Liam gradually sobered with each word I freed, and as realization dawned at which direction I was intending to steer this conversation...okay, persuasion. "And Laurie just stated that he always puts in two hundred per cent, and is very passionate about his work."

I knew just as I had finished that that was Liam's final straw. His drunken, fun-loving state was a past moment and the ticking jaw was making a brutal appearance once again. Somehow, I began to realize that pitching ideas obviously wasn't my forte.

"He wouldn't let you down, Mr. DeLaney," Laurie bolstered.

A weighted sigh in addition with the daggers he was firing at me, had me shrinking in my seat and nervously gnawing on my thumbnail. Setting about the opposite side of the kitchen with heavy strides, Liam tore some paper from the notepad and scribbled something down before rejoining us and handed it to my new friend. "It won't be for a few more weeks just yet, but you can give him my number. Get him to call me." Laurie was still nodding when hard emeralds turned to pin me in my chair. "Kady, can I have a word with you a moment, please."

By the elbow, he pulled me up and marched me out of the quiet kitchen into the hallway. The brusqueness of his movements had the air trapped under his black shimmering cape causing it to billow, while the rowdiness emanating from the throng in the living room was enough to drown out any words. Risking a glance, I peeked up and recoiled at once when I sighted his lifting hand. He tucked my hair behind my ear, and I found myself somewhat indebted that his touch was light and caring.

When he proceeded to trail it across my neck and held my nape, and as he leaned in with his head intimidatingly low, the bitter smell of beer on his breath spiraling and pasting on my flesh, I was immediately aware that this wasn't caring Liam at all...

"I would appreciate it if you allow *me* to decide who is on *my* payroll in the future, do you understand?" the underlining fury in his voice was poorly masked. My body began to shake nervously while the sickening, weighted sphere of anxiety in my gut had the small contents of my stomach rolling.

"I'm sorry, Liam. It just seemed like a logical idea. You need more workers, and the woman in there knows someone who is in desperate need of work. I tho—"

"And don't you think there are hundreds of people in Boston looking for the exact same thing?" he hissed in disdain, the profound guilt I felt was revealed with a drooping of my head. I overstepped the mark. Liam was right, DeLaney Constructs was *his* business, I had nothing to do with it, yet here I was offering a job to someone, when I was in no position to do so. *What was I thinking?*

"I'm sorry. It was wrong of me to do that. I promise I won't do it again."

"Damn right you won't, because you seem to be forgetting one significant factor in this relationship, Kady. *You* are unemployed. *I* am keeping *you*. Without me or my money, you would be on the streets. Do you understand?"

Barely a whisper, my voice was deep and cracked with remorse. "Yes, Liam." I muttered, our brows braced against one another.

"If he isn't worth his salt, his pay-packet will be coming out of what I spend on *you*. No cosmetics, no nice new clothes, nothing. Do you understand?"

A sob had to be stifled, I nodded with regret. "Yes, Liam."

Slipping his hand from the nape of my neck, his warmth and tender palm cradled my face while his lips slanted over mine, bestowing me with a lingering kiss that I just couldn't reciprocate. "Good girl," he mouthed, pulling away. "You're looking tired. You've had such a long day preparing this. You've done such a great job on the decorating."

I didn't have to study my reflection to know that my eyes were promptly alight with delight at his encouraging words. "I have?"

"Oh, Kady," he smirked down at me and cocked his head, his thumb skimming over the arch of my cheekbone. I pressed myself into his palm. "You really have. You've blown me away." Each verbalized degree of his approval had me beaming further. Nevertheless, my stomach quickly sank when he suggested, "Why don't you go to bed. We can tidy up in the morning."

I may have looked tired, but I didn't feel it. Regardless of lacking familiar terms with most of the people in our apartment, I didn't want to not be at my own party. "But, Liam, I don't want to go to bed yet, I'm not sleepy," my statement was underlined by a small awkward giggle. "And what sort of hostess would I be if I left y—"

"Baby," searching my eyes I didn't doubt for a moment that he was endeavoring to hypnotize me with his Dracula-like enthralling eyes. "You're looking drained. I don't want you making yourself ill. You need your beauty sleep."

He was right, I suppose. I had had a long day, and I most certainly didn't want to make myself ill. It wouldn't be fair on Liam for me to burden him with cooking and chores after everything he has done for us. "Maybe you're right. It is getting quite late," I resigned.

"Go on, you go to bed and I'll keep all these quiet so you can rest."

I reached up on my toes, and set my hand on the side of his face. "You always take such good care of me, Liam. Thank you."

After a kiss goodnight, I headed to bed while my boyfriend, sister, two friends, and a whole lot of strangers continued to party in my living room.

He really did care if he was going to put up with all of those on his own, just so I could sleep.

CHAPTER
five

I rolled over to drape my arm over Liam, only to be fully awoken by the absence of his body as my fingers grazed the cool bedding. The covers pooled at my waist whilst I pressed my hands into the mattress, sitting myself up, and listened intently to my surroundings.

No music. No raucous party noises. Just…silence. Well, near silence.

Once I shrugged on my robe and removed myself from the blissful comfort of the empty bed which was calling out to me like Lucifer himself, beckoning me to return, the smell of coffee and sounds of cutlery clattering traveled through the door.

The gold doorknob was cold in my grasp…cold and immovable. I twisted and shook the handle frantically, nevertheless it wasn't shifting. It was jammed. The door was fucking jammed? We'd lived in the apartment for years and never had any of the doors gotten stuck.

"Liam…" I called at the same time as jiggling the knob fiercely and repeatedly, panic apparent in my hasty attempts. "Liam, can you help me please?"

From the opposite side of the barrier, I heard heavy footsteps approaching. "Kady?"

"Thank God, Liam." I pressed my brow against the white wood. "The door is jammed I think. I can't get out."

"Hold on. Stand back okay, baby. I don't want you getting caught by the rebound. Tell me when you're at safe distance." Oh, good grief, he was talking like he was going to test some kind of military defense weapon.

The bed was touching the back of my legs when I gave him the all-clear. A little click followed by Liam's body charging through the now opened door, had me sagging with relief. The first words from him were, "That was new," which was trailed by his eyes following his hand as he ran it up the frame speculatively, giving it the once over in a nonchalant approach to detect the cause.

"It's okay, you got it open." I meandered sleepily towards my knight in shining armor. Hands which displayed my gratitude rose and were quickly pressed against his powder blue shirt, sweeping and clawing over the body which I loved, a body which I would do anything in this world for no matter how obscene. "Thank you for rescuing me, Mr. DeLaney," I murmured with a flirty grin and was awarded with a soft, delicate kiss. Hmm…he tasted like strawberries.

"Thank you for needing rescuing, Miss Jenson. I'm glad my work here is done. Breakfast?"

Breakfast? He was going to cook? Inwardly scoffing at the thought, I however, managed to see past the undomesticated ways of Liam DeLaney and gave myself a stern pep-talk. I should've been thankful that he was exiting his comfort zone and making the effort. I nodded my agreement and told him I was going to wash up first.

With a morning kiss to send my world out of orbit, he left me to do my thing.

I'm not going to lie; I half expected to see the apartment looking like a bomb testing site when I stepped out of the bedroom. As I tread down the hallway, I was beyond amazed to see everything gone. No red plastic cups, no spider webs, skeletons or ghouls. No empty snack bowls, or bowls full of slime, no pumpkin heads or hanging witches, just everything how and where it should be. I smiled and sighed with profound appreciation at the zero amount of workload for yours truly.

Pulling free my blond locks through the black turtleneck, I spluttered after being whipped in the face by the flicking tips of my hair and I continued to tread lightly to the kitchen, when I overheard hushed voices.

"She is my sister. Don't think I won—"

"Oh, Brittany, would you really risk stooping that low? Get over it."

"Good morning," I piped, sending the pair jumping back and out of their skin when I entered. I giggled to myself. "You know, it's customary for the party to say 'good morning' back, not leave a fucking crater in the ceiling," I teased, heading for the coffee pot which was obscured by my sister's curvy form. Her arms were folded across her ample chest, her legs crossed at the ankles as she rested the small of her back on the edge of the counter. She was peeking down at her feet. For Brittany Jenson, she appeared somewhat abashed.

The clashing of vibrant colors from her bright green hair and thick purple pantyhose with a small red tartan-like skirt was doing nothing for my eyes. I was half tempted to dial for the fashion police myself. That being said, Brittany had always been in a league of her own. She was a shepherd not a sheep, and I admired her for that.

"Morning, sis," she sounded on edge. It wasn't until she finally wrenched her head back, that I noticed how pale she was.

"Hey…" concerned, I instantly set the pot back on its stand and turned to my usually vivacious sister. "Britt, you don't look so good."

"She was drinking last night. She's probably got a hangover." Liam's husky explanation came from behind my shoulder as soon as I lifted my hand to her forehead.

"Is that all it is Britt, just a normal hangover?" I sounded far from convinced. She may have been an adult, but she was still younger than me, so technically, she was in my care. And if there was something wrong with my sister, then I wanted to know.

Fidgeting as she gazed over my shoulder, a spell passed in silence. Shifting into her line of sight with widened-eyes, I urged her to speak. She finally opened her glossy lips. "Yes…no…I don't know…maybe—"

"For the love of God, Brittany, 'she used to be indecisive, now she's not so sure'?" I quoted Mom's motto for uncertainty. My usual sense of humor aimed toward my sibling would have gained me a small niggle of her knuckles in my ribs, before hauling me into a hug, at the very least. But she just remained standing there, ashen, trembling and soundless…everything that's very un-Brittany-like. "You're worrying me, Brittany."

I watched on as her focus dwindled from me, to the man behind me. Her sapphire eyes were welling up with every peaceful second that past and she looked…repentant? I don't know, but I didn't care for it. As though she couldn't bear to look at me, she hung her head again.

"Kady baby, if Brittany isn't well, surely it's not fair for us to keep her here. Maybe she'd like to go home. You know what it's like when you're ill, you want your own bed." I couldn't disagree. Who doesn't want their own bed when they're ill? Then again, the selfish part of me wanted to keep my sister around a little while longer. We very rarely had those times anymore, and it had only been a day for God sake. Actually, no, it was less than a day I got to spend in the company of my sibling.

Her head was coaxed up with my finger under her chin. A tear fell from her eye and rolled its way unhurried down the side of her face. Cooing her in my 'big sister' like fashion, I brushed it away with my thumb. Seeing her ill was something I hated. I hated seeing her cry, but most of all: I hated seeing her crying because she felt so damn ill. I framed her face with my hands and swept my tongue over my drying lips.

"I'm sorry, Kady," she mumbled on a sob.

"Hey, hey, hey, come on, come here, Britt." Sisterly arms wrapped around each other, I held her close as she snuggled into my neck and surrendered to her tears. It was my action to mimic Mom's pacifying strokes through her scalp that finally had her sniffles ebbing. "It'll be okay, Britt. Do you want to go back D.C.?" I asked in her mass of green hair, that self-centered part of me still hoping that she would say 'no'.

"No, I don't," she pulled away and once again, her eyes subtly drifted over my shoulder. She licked her lips, the tip of her tongue capturing a salty droplet which lay peacefully on her lip. "But I think it's for the best if I do."

Squashed and disappointed, I simply rolled my lips over my teeth, sighed heavily and enforced a nod. I couldn't tie her up and command her to stay. "Okay. Let Mom and Dad know about the change of plans. We'll take you to the airport." After a short kneading stroke of her upper arms, my hands fell to my side with the weight I felt baring on my shoulders, the weight of disappointment. My coffee was retrieved from the unit on my right before I turned and headed to the living room.

"What about breakfast?" Liam called when I was halfway down the hall.

Feeling deflated, I simply retorted, "I've lost my appetite."

By the time I dropped myself into the cushion of the leather couch, feeling the cold, protesting material seeping through my beige Capri-pants, Liam was already storming through the glass and oak door with a plate in his one hand and silverware wrapped in a napkin in the other. Finishing adjusting a coaster and setting my coffee on the table ahead of me, I peeked up.

Liam stood like a God. No, scrap that, he loomed over me like The Devil compelling you to give into temptation. Unfortunately, the temptation which I was seeking was opposing the one which I sensed.

"You will eat, Kady," he commanded. His eyes reflected the rise of the sunlight from the window behind me before turning hard and obdurate. His freshly shaven block jaw was taut, and the spikes from the spider's web tattoo on the left of his neck were throbbing and strained.

"Liam, please, I am not hungry. I don't feel like I—"

"I allowed you to sleep in, Kady. I didn't wake you to help clear the mess which was left here after the party. I wanted to surprise you. Are you really going to be that ungrateful?"

I was contemplating an excuse worthy of The Devil aside me, when Brittany craned her head around the door and informed us that she was nipping to the store to pick up some milk and her weekly glossy magazine. For a brief moment, I felt a surge of guilt at the unnerved knot in my gut at the mere notion that she was going to be leaving me here alone with the affronted, raging bull, whereas I should have been worried about my ill sister going to the store on her own.

Once the door was shut securely behind her, Liam kneeled down at my side. The squared red plate was set on the table to join my coffee. He proffered me the cutlery after slipping it from the paper napkin. "Eat."

A full fried breakfast waited before me. So much fried food, I was sure my cholesterol was going to have a fit. "What's that?" I asked cautiously and pointed to the black lump in the middle of the plate.

"Blood sausage."

At the mention of blood, my head lifted straight to the man on his knees at the coffee table. "Blood?" Repulsed, my lips curled. There was no way in Hell I going to eat that. I didn't want to eat anything on that plate, but I would have if it meant I could've had the black stuff removed from it—the black stuff and the mushrooms.

I was silently marveling at the extremes Liam had gone to with cooking breakfast, but my appreciation retreated as I considered the mere fact that, we had been together for nearly three years, he knew full well that I wasn't a huge eater, especially of fried food. He knew damn well I despised mushrooms and would never touch anything like blood sausage. Why would he go through all of this effort to do something nice, when he was aware that I wouldn't eat half the contents on it?

"Liam...I–I..." I faltered.

As I smoothed the napkin over my thighs, his eyes combed my torso to meet my gaze. Dark eyebrows rose in mute question. "Kady, you will eat this. I am going to stay right here, just to make damn fucking sure." When he offered the cool silverware to me again, I hesitantly took it from his possession. "Do you understand?"

Nodding, I began to work my way through the parts I didn't mind eating, like the bacon, sausage and eggs, and steered clear of anything that was touching the parts which I detested.

"Eat the mushrooms," he charged with a voice not to be dared with.

I swallowed my mouthful, shook my head faintly and apologetic. "I can't."

What would I prefer to eat? I questioned myself after the stern words which passed Liam's lips were repeated again. Would I favor the dark, slick shapes which looked somewhat like slimy bugs, and used to have nightmares about as they slipped back up from my throat? Or would I prefer the seasoned blood in a sausage casing? There was no comparison. I could force myself to eat the three handfuls of mushrooms, if it meant I could leave the additional, disgusting thing which was goading me on the red surface and making my stomach pole-vault to my throat.

The fork dove into the mass, scooping and raising it to my mouth as hasty as possible. Screwing my eyes shut until dancing, colored spots swept across my lids, I held my breath and chewed like there was no tomorrow.

Ignore the sensation, Kady. Ignore the sensation... I repeated my mantra while striving to disregard the slug-like texture on my tongue.

With each swallow my throat was becoming less and less compliant. Halting my reflex to pass it down my gullet, the food was left loitering in my mouth while my shoulders hunched, my ribs ached from heaving and my eyes watered.

Finally, after what seemed like a lifetime, I got through the pile of food I'd always averted, set the fork on the plate and concentrated on not having the food making a return.

"You haven't finished."

Gaping at an insulted looking Liam, he fisted his hands back through his slicked-back, brown hair as I drew in a deep breath. "Liam, I don't like mushrooms, but I forced myself to eat them. Please, I really can't bring myself to eat that," I gestured to what looked like a clump of coal in the center of the red square.

"Kady," his mouth curled almost unhinged. An intimidated step was taken towards me while on his knees. "If you were to go to the emergency room to have blood taken and then later fainted, what would the first thought in your head be if you were to have blood taken again?" he spoke in a soft, appeasing tone.

I knitted my fingers together in my lap, feeling as though I was about to get graded on my answer. "Th–that I was going to faint," I faltered once again.

"Exactly," he nodded with a derange grin spanning his face. "Although the results may have come back clear, you'll always remember the negative element of the action…"

"I don't understand what that has to do with you cooking me breakfast, Liam." The crease in my brow had become more of a chasm.

A worrying void of unhinged intention stared back at me. I could see it as clear as day, and I was tumbling down into it. I knew I was going to be broken when I landed. "This is your punishment, Kady, for your insolence last night."

My punishment? Wait. So he didn't cook me breakfast as a loving gesture and from the freewill of his heart, he did it to prove a point? He did it for revenge?

"Liam, I apologized to you last night for offering Laurie's cousin that job when I had no right to." Eyes locked as I jetted my words, I outstretched my arms and encased his hands in mine. "You said it was okay, that I was forgiven. Please, don't do it this way," I begged.

"If an animal shits on your upholstery, you punish it—"

"But I'm not an animal, Liam." And I didn't like the insinuation.

His eyebrows lifted in the Liam DeLaney-like way, daring me to be defiant. "No? Are you sure? We are all animals, Kady. And you shit over my business last night. That is something I. Will. Not. Tolerate." he punctuated clearly and I hung my head like a schoolgirl getting rebuked by the Principle as my arms fell away from him. "Eat!" he directed.

Sullen and teary, I inched to the very edge of the couch and recollected my fork.

"At least next time, you will remember this negative, this consequence for your actions, and you won't be so inclined to tread that line again, will you, Kady?"

"No, Liam." I breathed distantly, all the while picking at the coal in the heart of the dish with the prongs of my fork. When a diminutive gathering was settled on one of the silver prongs, I risked a glance at the man in front of me, watching me intently like some wild cat waiting to pounce. Tears tumbled down my cheeks, splattering and dampening the paper napkin covering my lap.

You can do this, Kady. You can do this. Once it's done, it's done. Not even the mere contemplation of how happy Liam would be if I did what he wanted was able to penetrate the only thought in my mind, which was: this was too damn cruel.

"EAT!" he bellowed causing my tears to stream quicker. I jolted and promptly wrapped my lips around the fork. All my energy went on blocking out all taste. It was the sheer fact that I had pigs blood in my mouth that was making my stomach roll and lurch.

Dry heaves came again, inundating my body with compressing muscles and a tightening ribcage. It was when the fork was hastily snatched from my grasp and the edge was used to slice chunks out of the single item which remained on my plate, that I felt the contents of my stomach claw its way back up my throat. The butterflies and repulsion made itself known, and the evil, commandeering look in his eyes told me that there was no way out of this.

He held my jaw in a grave and sturdy grasp. "Open," he charged. For the first time ever, I was scared. I felt undiluted fear. And it was my boyfriend, someone to which was supposed to love and protect me, that made me feel it. A potent arm hurtled forward, and without time or the ability to protest, the fork was instantly in my mouth. I wrapped my lips around it as he retracted. Yet, his grasp didn't fall away from me. My mouth was held firmly shut with his left hand while he repeated his earlier motion, and used the edge of the cutlery to hack off a little extra than what he just stuffed in my mouth, with his opposite hand.

I was choking. My throat wasn't allowing me to swallow the contents force fed to me, and my stomach was begging to be evacuated as the bitter, grainy taste of the pudding tickled my gag reflex. My ribs strained, my shoulders lurched and my throat opened to allow the fillings in my stomach to be ousted.

Regardless of the lingering food which my gullet refused to accept, he forced another forkful into my mouth. "Don't think that being sick will get you out of this, Kady, because it won't," he cautioned while my parched lips were caressed by my tears, leaving a salty tang coating them like gloss.

Diminutive sprays of food and a garbled rendition of 'please', traveled on a sob. But he was unrelenting, he was callous. He was stern and my God, this was by far the most sadistic thing he had ever put me through. A punishment? That was no punishment. It was barbaric. It was inhumane.

I lost count of how many heaves my body spawned. I lost count after four attempts at convincing him to stop with the ways which were causing me nothing but sheer fear. I lost my fight and conceded to his demands, purely to get the rough treatment over with.

Once my body was cooperative and accepted the final mouthful, I removed the napkin from my lap and curled myself up like a snoozing feline in the leather couch, as I fought through the heaves my body was still succumbing to.

Through the muffling of my ears, I heard the distant sound of the buzzer, informing us of Brittany's return from the store. "You won't pull a stunt like that again, will you?" he asked, seeking clarification, his tone and expression completely impassive.

Shaking my head and sniffling back my tears, Liam trudged with his head held high and a perfectly uncaring posture, through the glass and oak doors into the hall to let my sister in.

In that moment, I knew that was one punishment I was never going to forget. I knew that the look, the taste and the texture, in conjunction with the power behind his pressurizing ways and demands, would haunt me until my final day.

He was right. I would never push him to deserve that level of consequence again.

CHAPTER
six

The journey to Logan Airport was made in utter silence. You know the awkward, disturbing silence that loiters in the atmosphere because you had been made to feel inferior when getting punished by someone of authority.

Inferior…it's an ugly word, a word that no human should be made to feel. We're supposed to be equal, aren't we? Never in my life had I experienced such sensation. Each time I opened my mouth in a vain attempt to slice through the stifling atmosphere, Liam would divert his focus from the road ahead, to me and just gape, as though I didn't have two IQ points to rub together which would result in saying something worth hearing.

And so the journey continued in a near stillness.

A red light brought us to a halt. Sobbing and sniffling echoed from behind me, so I turned in the leather seat and peeked over my left shoulder. Brittany's head was hanging down. The mass of green hair was separated into braided pigtails. Although her profile was somewhat obscured, I, however, was able to discern the tiny crystal droplet trickling down to settle on the tip of her button nose before relinquishing its grip and splattering onto the back of her knuckles.

The light was still red. Cars behind us bleared their horns, causing Liam to shake his head in exasperation. Not a single word passed my lips as I unbuckled my seatbelt and pulled the door release.

"Kady, what the fuck are you doing?" I heard Liam ask, his voice becoming fainter as I slammed the door behind me, placing that barrier between us.

Just as the light turned green, I opened the back passenger-side door to slip in beside my sister. I overheard Liam's heavy sigh and saw his head flail, but I didn't care. I may have been made to feel substandard compared to him, but I was the rock for my baby sister.

As soon as I clicked the belt into place, my arm instinctively crashed around her shoulders, her head went lax and fell into my bosom. "It'll be okay, Britt," I reassured her while swaying softly. My fingers gently brushed over her scalp.

Brittany may have been younger than me by only three years, but I had always been there whenever she needed it. I was her rock, her protector in some ways. I was the one who she cried to if she was hurt or had been hurt, I was the one who always fought in her corner. I wasn't only her sibling, I was her best friend. I was my sister's keeper, and the mere fact that I felt she was concealing something from me…it hurt. It really, really hurt.

"I don't like the idea of you flying in this state, sis," I voiced my concern between each rocking motion.

My name was called from the seat ahead. Familiar green and blue speckled eyes met mine in the rearview mirror. "She has made her decision, Kady. She told you herself she wanted to go back home. Stop making an issue."

Yes, she did say that. Nonetheless, I didn't appreciate being told not to voice my concerns to someone who was my blood. Then again, I didn't want my concern to spawn a form of guilt in her fragile state. So I shut up and continued to be there to offer support and sympathy to my poorly, green haired, tearstained faced sister.

Brittany didn't once leave my side at the airport. If I went to the bathroom, she was with me. If I moved to the window, she was with me. If I changed seats, she did, too.

The air was thick between both Liam and her. I didn't know why. But I couldn't help quash the secret deliberation that it could have something to do with the reason behind her melancholic bearing.

I inwardly slapped my palm against my forehead and groaned. Maybe she hooked up with one of Liam's friends and she's feeling the shame which often follows a one night stand. Liam did after all mention her man-obsessed brain last night, with the pinching of many asses.

Oh, Brittany, Brittany, Brittany…what am I going to do with you?

A husky voice crackling over the system calling the flight to D.C., brought my back to the land of the living, instead of aimlessly searching for road signs in Marvel Land. Thrusting myself out of the cold, hard metal seat, I swallowed her up in an enormous embrace which I hope reflected how I felt about her early departure. I didn't want her to go. If I could have, I would have tied her up and took her back home for the rest of her intended stay.

"I love you, Kady. I'm sorry," she mumbled into the crook of my neck, and although the striving to recapture a form of strength which Brittany Jenson always had was evident, I still heard her words catch in her throat. I heard the sob and splatter of her very unladylike snot bubble against my turtleneck, and just like that, we were kids again, comforting each other in a midnight thunderstorm.

Unsure as to when I would get the chance to be in her company again, she gradually drew her body from my arms and I took a moment to study her. Her sapphire eyes were red and sore. Her usual A-list glossy lips were withered and cracked. Her button nose looked raw as she glided the back of her hand over the flesh, catching her sniffles.

I extended her a tightlipped smile. "It's not your fault you're ill. You have nothing to be sorry for, silly." I rubbed the tops of her denim clad arms. "I love you, too, Britt."

Turning her back to me gingerly, she began to walk away when I called out to her. Head craned over her shoulder, her weight being passed through her hip, she gazed under hooded, puffy eyes. "Doesn't Liam get a hug?" I asked bemused. She's always so tactile, especially with Liam. She always has been, those two bounced off each other.

Before giving her a chance to respond, the husky voice called her flight again. Liam was already at my side, his warm arm around my waist. "Don't worry about it, Britt," he said, saving her the time to either reply or make her way back to us. "I don't want to risk getting ill myself, not with work at the moment."

The arm around my body, and the buoyant voice of my boyfriend had flicked something in her. I could see that. It was unmistakable. Her eyes had turned as hard as priceless gem, and her lip curled with palpable distaste. She shook her head. Well, I think she shook her head. If she did, then it was so faint I barely noticed.

"Call me when you land," I ordered.

"Okay. Speak to you soon," she answered, and continued to make her way past the gate, while I stood stock-still and watched my baby sister until she was out of sight.

Hand in hand, Liam led me to the BMW in the lot. Considering what had happened during the prior four hours, the connection made me uncomfortable. How he failed to recognize it, I'll never know. In spite of everything, his hand frequently squeezed and clutched upon my loose grip, while my gaze remained on the grey flooring of the lot as we made our way back to the car.

Lights flashed as he pressed the fob. My hand had begun to worm its way from his clutch to open the door. When his own hand made contact with the release and he pulled the door open for me, it was fair to say, I was relatively surprised. "After you," he gestured with a gallantly tip of his head and a smile like butter wouldn't melt.

"Thank you," was all I could bring myself to say within my lingering state of inferiority. Body folded, I lowered myself into the protesting leather and reached back to fumble with the belt before drawing it across my body and clipping into place. The door was already slammed shut and narrowly missed colliding with my elbow upon impact.

Liam slipped in beside me, turned on the ignition and began to back-out of the space.

It was as though my jaw wasn't connected to my body the way it kept falling open to free words which I rehearsed in my mind. Rehearsed…stupid I know, but I didn't care. I wasn't going to say or do anything stupid to prove to the man beside me that I needed another punishment dished out. No pun intended. Even the mere concept made my stomach lurch and my head become fuzzy.

In the midst of focusing on the road, he murmured, "What is

it, Kady? You look like a fucking goldfish."

My lungs filled themselves to capacity with a deep inhalation, and while I picked my fingernail in my lap, I bit the bullet and rubbed my measly two IQ points together and hoped that I didn't sound whiny and made a mediocre of sense. "Do you know whether Brittany hooked up with anyone last night?"

A cautionary yet puzzled expression flashed across his face when he chanced a glance as my fidgeting form. "How would I know? Why do you ask?"

"Her typical vivacious, crazy chick attitude, compared to what she was like this morning…" I shook my head in the midst of my musing, and rolled my lips over my teeth before relinquishing a sigh of defeat.

"Kady," an unanticipated tender hand lowered to my beige, linen-clad thigh. "She's a big girl. She doesn't need some third degree. If she did hook up with someone, then that was her choice. Nothing in this world is done without cause, Kady. Every attitude, every action, every approach, it all has an underlining motive."

A moment of clarity formed as those words were given. He was right. Each action in this world is done for a reason. His actions that morning were harsh, cruel and barbaric, but they were needed. They weren't some sadistic ploy to cause distress. They wouldn't have been needed, had I not have overstepped the line and interfered with his business. It didn't occur to me at that time that it was a two way street, and that my actions of overstepping the mark, also had an underlining reason, which he obviously could see or just wouldn't regard.

No longer feeling inferior, the air between us became thinner and clearer. "You're right," I nodded, and as my musings was given a voice, his hand tightened with a degree of affection on my thigh. I repaid him with setting my own understanding hand over his and locked our fingers together.

Dilapidated buildings passed by at speed as I peeked out of the window. "No matter what it is, she'll tell me eventually. She always does."

"What on Earth are you doing?" I giggled after big, strong, powder-blue shirt-sleeves whipped me off my feet as we stood in the small hallway of our apartment building. Yet, my question was left unanswered as Liam focused on carrying me up each flight of stairs like he was carrying a gym bag in his arms instead of a fully grown woman. I would have objected, kicked my legs and swat him away until he set me back on my feet. *'God gave me legs for a reason'*, as my Nan would say. Despite that, my arms came up to lock at the nape of his neck; the tips of his locks tickled at the edges of my fingers, while the pulse in the left of his neck caused the spider's web to throb. Held against the hardness of his chest, I breathed him in and allowed myself to be carried.

Somehow, he successfully managed to dig into his black pants pocket for the apartment key and slip it into the lock without releasing, or accidentally dropping me. I was quite impressed.

Kicking the door open, he took us over the threshold and again, kicked the door shut once we were inside. The solidity of the ground beneath my feet was greatly missed. I squealed for him to please put me down. Then again, Liam DeLaney, being Liam DeLaney, didn't take nicely to orders or requests. He did as he wanted, and if you were on the receiving end of what he wanted, there was no room for opposition.

The apartment was filled with the sounds of my lighthearted chortle. Burnish orange coated the walls as the sun was beginning to meet the horizon. It must have been about 4:30 p.m. and the nights' rolling in earlier and earlier was a factor I held a great hate towards.

Into the bedroom we went. A shriek tore from my throat as I was tossed on to the black and red satin adorned bed. Feeling like I had just walked through some web, my hands immediately flew up to hastily brush the sensation left behind as wayward tendrils tickled my face. Before I could even attempt to push myself up, I was pinned back down by a heavy body, his head hovering above mine.

"Good evening, Miss Jenson," he purred. Just the simple use of him calling me, 'Miss Jenson' had me squirming, not to mention the husky intonation which the two words traveled along. My legs fell open farther, allowing him to be cradled against me. Circling and grinding hips caressed my core, sending my eyes fluttering as I savored the sensation of his hinting motives.

"Good evening to you, Mr. DeLaney," I breathed back, all the while my hips were propelling upward to meet the tantalizing use of his gyrating hips.

He pulled away and slithered down my body where his fingers proceeded to sink beneath the waistband of my Capri's. When the button was popped, he continued to lower the zipper and peel them, along with my underwear, down my legs, slipping my heeled pumps off just before divesting the material from my flesh.

"What are you doing?" I asked as the hard body and hungry eyes glided back up my half-naked form. My arms were grasped insistently in his hands then I was hauled up and stripped of the remaining clothing, which was acting like an unwanted and unnecessary barrier.

Naked, with the exception of my bra, he laid me back down, nuzzled my neck and streamed loud, wet, sweet sensuous kisses down the curve to meet my shoulder. "I was thinking," he began then paused for a second while his tongue slithered across my collarbone. "We could go to the movies tonight and see a movie of your choosing."

My body responded immediately with my head rolling to the right, offering greater access to devour the area. My eyes widened, and my words caught, "Me? You're going to let me pick?"

"This is my way of apologizing." His words were ice water on my libido. Apologize? There was no need. I understood. I accepted it. Why was he rehashing it?

"There's no need, Liam. I understand. Please, let's not talk about it."

His hips rolled sending my back into an arch and tipping my head back. "Okay. I thought we could get something nice after the movie, come back home and have a nice meal."

"Meal?" God only knew what time that would be. There was no way was I going to be cooking that late at night! "Liam, by the time I cook and clean, it will be far too late."

My neck felt cold and bare as he drew himself away, his forearms resting on either side of my head. Fingers grazed through my hair and I gazed up, watching as ravenous eyes glimmered shrewdly and the corners of his lips tipped. "Whose saying I meant cook, and eat off a plate?"

Huh? My brow furrowed and eyes narrowed.

"It's lucky neither of us has aversions to dairy because I was thinking, whipped cream…" I thought my eyes were going to pop out of their sockets; my body suddenly shuddered as my mind was tantalized by one single thought. Down my body he slipped, his lips maneuvered over my throat and the swelling of my breasts which were rising and falling rapidly. A groan vibrated through my chest as my breast spilled out from the cup of my bra as he tugged it downward. "Maybe a little raspberry nipple sauce?" he flicked my nipple with the tip of his tongue, the cool air pasted onto the peaking flesh before he took it into the wet heat of his mouth. "I meant, raspberry ripple," he clarified after a small nip of his teeth.

"Of course you did," I gasped, my pelvis pushing upward as finally, sweet friction was made along the substantial, growing bulge in his pants.

Each perfectly placed kiss which was spread over my body had my squirming and trembling in sweet anticipation. The sound of his voice as he spoke low, husky and in innuendos, alongside his teasing ways of informing me what I was in for, had my thighs glazed with desire.

"But first," I studied him as his head got further away and sank between my parted thighs. Before he had me lying back, panting, wanton and splayed, my legs were hooked over his shoulders, while my core was held with his scissoring fingers. I could feel the throb taking my body over like a lustful demon trying to break free. "I fancy eating a little pussy."

His tongue took one long sweep up my exposed center before orbiting and sucking gently. Head tossed back, my hands clawed into the bedding, my groan of pleasurable approval vibrated from my throat.

As I was lost to Liam and his expert tongue, the events of the day were incinerated, never to be remembered again.

CHAPTER
seven

December 2011.
Eighteen months before the accident...

Where does time go?
I remember when I was a child; a year passing would feel like an eternity. The interval between each Christmas would feel like twelve long years, instead of twelve short months. It's bizarre how as you get older, you become more aware of how quick time actually passes. It goes by in a blink of an eye. Is it because life as an adult is significantly more boring than that in childhood, and the days all seem to meld into one long journey, which makes it feel so? I don't know. All I know is: one morning I'm waking up and red and golden leaves are snapping from the trees, spiraling down to the cold ground without a care in the world. The next, I'm waking up and every tree is bare, their leaves crumpled on the freezing ground and dusted with what looks like icing-sugar, making them stiff and crunch under your weight.

I was standing in the living room, wistfully pursuing the area which had been our home for three years. It wasn't totally empty, the coffee table and rug were still in their designated space, but it felt so…bare.

Memories, both good and bad, had been created in this very apartment, and now we were leaving. We were moving from Dorchester to somewhere called Bricksdale. I didn't care for it. I hadn't even seen the property. Liam went ahead, called all the shots like DeLaney does with his high-strung ways and simply told me to trust him and his judgment.

Having connections in all the right places makes things a whole lot easier. In saying that, having a boyfriend with those connections, makes things twice as difficult for the person who is less inclined to follow through with his requests.

It was simple: I didn't want to leave. I especially didn't want to leave a place I felt comfortable, a place I could call my home, for some random place that sounds like it should have a spot on some paranormal television show.

I was told that the move was to be kept a secret, which meant not spilling my guts to my parents or to Brittany. I couldn't have told Brittany anyway. Since she left us at Logan Airport over seven weeks ago, I had barely spoken to her. Each time I called her cell there was no answer, so I would call Mom and Dad but there would always be an excuse as to why she couldn't talk. Feeling as though she was avoiding me for some reason, made my heart ache in my chest. The last encounter, I gave up on attempting to make conversation. It was too challenging with her grunts and monosyllable answers, while the sounds of feeble giggles, as though she was attempting to satisfy my humorous side, spawned nothing but agitation.

Sighing deeply, my attention fell to the crimson stain on the cream rug at the side of the coffee table. I was shaking my head to myself as I studied the imperfection, silently wondering how one person can be so damn clumsy, when a nudge at my shoulder pulled me from my hypnotic trance. "Hmm," I sounded from my throat while turning my attention to Laurie. Her purple block-dyed bangs, was now a thing of the past. Orange was apparently the new color of the season.

"Still couldn't get it out?" she asked, flicking a quick glimpse to the focal point of my attention.

I shook my head sadly and my voice was just as wistful, "No. I don't think it'll be coming with us, that's for damn sure."

"Kady…" On the tops of my arms she set both hands and stared at me as though she was attempting to read my mind. Her hair piled into a knot atop of her head, her face had a natural glow, even without makeup. "I'm your friend. I may not know you as good as Liv, but I *am* your friend. You can tell me—"

I knew where this was going. The same persuasion tactic had been used every day for the previous five days, and I was getting somewhat jaded in having to continually repeat and defend myself. Through clenched teeth I simply grunted, "He didn't hit me Laurie. He wouldn't lay a hand on me in that way."

"Then why have you got sticky strips holding that gash above your eye shut, and blood on the carpet?" Her hazel eyes were like mud-covered stones as her face screwed up and hardened.

At her words I lifted my left hand, wincing before my fingertips even settled on my flesh. My stomach churned and pain shot through my head when my hesitant fingers delicately caressed the area which was swollen, and looking pretty damn ugly with the purple and red marking outlining it. "I've already told you, Laurie," I muttered and let my hand fall from my head to clutch my right shoulder. "I told him I wasn't happy with the way he sprang the news that we were moving on me, and only a week before the actual move itself. The fact that he kept something so damn big a secret for so damn long, I..." my words waned as the image of that block jaw tightening and his dark eyebrows knitted as he glowered at me that night, prowling toward me, his finger pointed... "I pushed and pushed on wanting to tell my parents. It's my own fault, I shouldn't have pushed him—"

"That's what they all say, Kady. 'It was my fault...I should have known better...I walked into a fucking door...'" she derided.

Rolling my eyes, I was hyper alert of the anger gradually increasing in my stomach, causing my blood to overheat and butterflies to flutter and sweep the walls of my gut. I wasn't going to stand for anyone insinuating that my boyfriend was abusive. He wasn't, he was protective. He wanted to look after me. Defensive, a surge of adrenaline decided to join the party, rendering me a quivering mess. "He shoved me. I lost my balance and cracked myself on the corner of that fucking table. He wouldn't physically hurt me, Laurie. I know Liam. He just wouldn't."

She filled her lungs steadily while shaking her head as though the words I was speaking were anything but truths.

"He was right though—"

Incredulous, her hairline was met by her eyebrows. "What?! To physically shove you?" she squealed in profound disbelief.

My eyes rolled once again and I made a noise of 'don't be so silly'. "He was right for insisting that I didn't tell my parents. They would have done exactly what Liam said they would've done: take over. We already have you and Liv to help us. It would've been the, 'too many cooks in the kitchen' scenario, and no one would have been happy with that."

"Are you sure?"

A grin spread across my face as I nodded. "I'm sure. Now, help me tape up these boxes." I held up a roll of duct tape and with a relaxed smile, we went to work. "That reminds me," I piped over the loud tearing noise of the tape being unraveled. "You never told me if your cousin got in contact with Liam. And Liam won't tell me anything work related anymore," I pouted.

"He did and fair play to Liam, he's made him the happiest man alive," she grinned, closing and sealing the box ahead of her.

"Why do you say that?"

I watched her shoulders visibly droop. "Because he's a hard fucking worker, Kady," she drew her focus from the next box and peeked at me. "That man would go to the end of the world and back just to make sure he wasn't a person who would be labeled as sitting on their ass all day. Actually, he has done. Liam made a good choice in taking him on. And you,"—with her small hands on her knees, she hauled herself up, framed my face in the heat of her hands, and planted a kiss on the top of my denim bandana—"are a star for planting the seed."

Half an hour had passed in a blink of an eye. We spoke about the normal shit which Laurie and I had seemingly fallen into. She told me about the pink pony, birthday cake she just made for her niece's second birthday. It was heartwarming witnessing the passion emanated through her features as she spoke about her fine pieces of edible art. Suppressing a smile was not an option.

"I'll have to teach you one day," she baited, stacking the boxes which were ready and waiting to be moved.

Studying the accumulation of packages gradually piling higher, the silent wonder of where the Hell Liam and Liv were was unavoidable. They had been gone for about an hour. I wasn't going to be happy if this new house was an hour's drive away. With that, I could be certain.

"Teach me what?"

"Baking and decorating."

My eyes flared and my brain was vibrating with each vicious shake of my head. "Nope, I don—"

She bounded toward me like an over enthused puppy bringing a premature end to my refusal. "Come on, Kady, it'll be fun. We can pick at bits of the icing, lick the spoon…make pornographic molds out of fondant…what do you say? You might understand why it's so relaxing."

"Pornographic molds?" It felt like an era for those two words to be out in the open as I freed them at a snail's pace. Glittering puppy dog eyes mutely pleaded from over the frames of her red specs. "Okay," I conceded, "But only male pornographic molds."

The apartment door being swung open drew an end to our giggles. I rolled myself back from my knees into a standing position and strolled to the hallway to be met by a flushed and sweaty looking Liv and Liam. I was secretly grateful that it was insisted upon that I stay here and finish packing the remaining little pieces, instead of carrying boxes up and down eight flights of stairs.

I felt my heart swelling.

He knew how to keep me safe and healthy.

"You two look terrible. We still have a few glasses left unpacked, do you want a drink? You both look like you could do with one." I flipped a glance to my left through to the kitchen. I was going to miss this place.

Liv flipped her perfect sleek brunette hair behind her shoulders then rubbed my shoulder. How she could be that sweaty and not have frizz-ball hair, I have no idea. I envied her. "That'll be brilliant, thanks, chick," she panted, bypassing me to get to the living room.

Liam's presence was consuming as he trailed behind me into the kitchen. I swirled out the high-ball glasses, before filling them with icy cold water. Feeling that familiar hole being burned into my back with his intense scrutiny, I lifted my head. I swear I heard a low, carnal growl travel along the unspoken rift between us. When I turned around with the glasses in hand, Liam's gaze visibly scoured up my skinny, faded blue jeans and cowgirl-like blouse which was screening a white camisole.

"Something like that,"—he gestured with a tip of his brow toward my body—"shouldn't work with that thing you have on your head."

My head low, I focused on my feet and silently chided myself for disappointing him yet again.

God, Kady, what the fuck is wrong with you, it shouldn't be hard to keep your man happy.

He took slow, deliberate steps, his hands loosely resting inside the pockets of his dark grey pants. His hair slicked, his jaw clean shaven, he looked just as delicious as he did the first day I saw him, the day when he watched me—appraising me—as I danced for him in a room of twenty other people. And that approving expression he wore just over three years ago was being honed again.

My body spawned exhilarating shudders as his hand left his pocket and enticingly swept down the side of my neck, to the curve of my shoulder. "But it does," he whispered, his tongue caressing his liking, before lowering himself and slanting his lips over mine. He took what he wanted, with tongues delving into the other's mouths, sweeping and caressing as they spiraled around one another in sweet, agonizing torment. Each time he kissed me like that, I'd be catapulted back to the many decadent times where he would ravage my core with that skillful tongue. The flicks, the twisting, the gentle sucking which he was performing on my tongue sent messages of desire and familiarity through my entire body.

Candy being taken away from a baby was the only way I could describe it when he pulled away from me, allowing me to softly pant and gasp for air after his tongues invasion. Slowly, his hand rose, resembling the cautiousness of reaching out to a timid animal. I winced and screwed my lids closed as his fingers softly brushed around the wound above my left eye. It was the grunt-like noise which vibrated from his throat which prompted my lashes to leave the arch of my cheekbone and flutter open. When I did, I was greeted by firm lips set in a line and a lifetime full of remorse in his green and blue speckled eyes. Hand falling away from the wound, he cradled the side of my face. "You still look, sexy as fuck, baby."

His tender words were what encouraged my smile. But almost immediately, the smile of appreciation broadened into a megawatt beam as he accepted my hand and, with interest, granted me the action of brushing my touch up and down his torso. "Thank you," I breathed, and even I could detect the profundity of need coating my shaking voice. "What's happened here?" I asked when my fingers unexpectedly slipped through a gap in his black shirt. Applying space between us, I arched my back over the unit which harbored the kitchen sink, and glanced down the length of his body.

Not one button, but two buttons he fumbled with threading through the clasp, as he explained, "Those damn boxes. They must have hooked beneath and popped them free. I didn't even notice." Once the task was complete, he lifted his head to gaze at me dead on, his lips twitching in the corners. "It's lucky you're wearing a camisole under that. I wouldn't be impressed if the new neighbors caught a peek at my woman's body." His hands roamed the outline of my figure, cinching my waist. "This body is all mine to do as I please, and I plan on pleasing a lot tonight…"

I cocked my head. "Tonight?" I asked meekly.

"We have a living room, dining room, enormous kitchen—with an island—two bedrooms, an en-suite and a flight of stairs to christen, baby. I hope you're ready."

With that deep, weighted anticipation that was bubbling away at high heat in my gut at those words, all apprehension dissolved. I found that I was suddenly feeling very excited about the move after all.

CHAPTER
eight

I knew it. I just knew it. The name was a giveaway and the eerie quietness of the streets, on a Monday afternoon as we drove through Bricksdale, had my speculations confirmed. And at that point, my inner high school cheerleader was waving her pompoms and flouncing about like an idiot. I cringed. Dear God, did I really used to look like that?

With the blender on my lap, I gazed out the window, and in silence, studied the area rapidly passing by. The road was divided: either continue straight ahead or turn right into a square. A white chapel with a bell-tower stood in the center dominating the enclave, whilst the assortment of edifices outlined the vicinity. It seemed quiet, but it also seemed to…happy. I half expected one of three things: 'Mr. Sandman' to begin playing from one of the diners that had a human-size ice-cream cone figure, topped with pink swirly ice-cream waiting beside the entrance, women to stroll along wearing tiny sweaters, silk neckerchiefs' and flared, high-waist skirts with poodles on them, or, the residence to turn all crazed when the bell hanging in the tower, chimed at a specific time. For a fleeting moment, the latter of my imagination had me feeling somewhat indebted to Liam for making me watch those horror movies. At least now I knew that if the new house was to be invaded by possessed lunatics, to run out of the house instead of up the stairs.

Five minutes later, we were ascending a tree-lined street with various different colored detached houses. We began to decelerate, and within passing a few more houses, Liam soon turned into an inclined driveway alongside a large white, detached property with bay-windows on both levels, and a round window at the attic.

An attic? A shudder paved its way from my scalp to the tips of my toes. I'd never taken kindly to attics. There's something sinister about them which I could never quite shift.

Shifting the car into park, Liam turned off the ignition. "Ta-da," he sang, waving his arms towards the property like some Game Show host revealing the grand prize. "So, what do you think?"

What did I think? I was thinking I really didn't want to move in the first place. I especially didn't want to move somewhere where it felt like I was in some kind of fifties horror movie, and I most certainly didn't want to move somewhere where there was a fucking attic with a round window, I'd seen *American Haunting*. I really wished he'd have talked to me about this first; we could have done this *together*. Instead, I felt like a sullen teen, my thoughts and feelings irrelevant as I got ripped from the family home and high school to be thrown in somewhere new.

"Well?" he pressed again. I clutch my blender like it was a comfort blanket, and when I twisted my head to face him, his eyes were bright with expectant enthusiasm. My knee was eclipsed by his hand. "Kady, will you please say something? This is *our* house; I bought a house for *us*. Doesn't that say anything to you?"

Dried lips were moistened by a sweep of my tongue. Yet again, he was dead-on. He did this enormous gesture, he gave us stability, he gave us a promise of a future—he bought a fucking house for God sake. He surprised me with the physical promise of a future together, in the shape of our family home. Furthermore, he successfully kept it a secret regardless of the excitement he must have felt towards knowing what his intention signified.

I finally rewarded him with a smile. "I'm just so shocked, Liam. I...I..." frustrated with stumbling over my own words, I sighed and tried again. "It's just going to take me a while to get familiarized with the area. Something like this—moving away—it's a daunting step."

"I understand that. But there's nothing to be nervous or scared about, baby. I'm here, I'll keep you safe." Leaning over the console, the chaste kiss which was placed on my lips was torn away by the sound of Laurie's Honda pulling up alongside the house. "Come on, out you get. I can't wait to show you this."

Out of the car I got, with my blender still clutched to my chest like it was Aladdin's lamp. I found my comparison somewhat amusing and lightly sniggered. Liam met me on the opposite side, and with his arm draped around my shoulders, he pulled me into his side and steered me from the driveway. The steep steps which led to the dark wooden front door, was studied from the safety of the sidewalk. It really was a beautiful house, aside from the round window looming above me from the triangle structure. I half expected to see a silhouette or something gazing out of the damn thing.

"And it is the only white property on the block," his deep, whispering voice stroked my ear as he added to my silent musing.

A loud din of Laurie's car doors slamming from behind

made me jump. I turned to face the mischievous twosome who was fetching boxes from the back seat. As they passed us, Liam handed the key to Liv and they advanced up the six steps to the door before letting themselves in.

Protective arms were dropped from my shoulders and we both turned in unison as a voice called, "Coo-ee," from my right. The voice was trailed by a stumpy middle-aged woman with a mass of red hair cut to her jawline, shuffling along the sidewalk. It wasn't the hair which seized my attention; it was the mere contemplation that she was going to give herself a black eye with how her hefty chest was flailing around. Just watching made my boobs and back ache. "You must be the new neighbors?" she gushed, her tone rather shrill.

I felt his warmth as Liam's arm came back around me, draping over my shoulder, pulling me under his arm once again, "Yes we are,"—the denim bandana on my head was caressed by his lips before he continuing his introduction—"Liam DeLaney," politely holding out his hand, the woman accepted while repeating his name. "And this is my girlfriend, Kady Jenson."

I wasn't so lucky to escape with the simplicity of a hand shake. Instead, she grasped me by the shoulders and pulled me down to plant a kiss on my cheek. "Kady," she tested my name, "it's so very nice to meet you both. You're arrival is the topic of discussion along this block. We haven't had anything this exciting for quite some time; well, apart from old Mr. Rogers copping off with his PA…" Oh, my God, was this woman for real? We'd only been on the block for ten minutes, and I already knew I wasn't going to be looking at this poor Mr. Rogers without knowing his dirty laundry. I studied her mouth rapidly moving, but her words were a simple gathering of high-pitched muffles. "It's lovely meeting new people, building friendships and what-not. And you seem like a lovely couple."

Liam and I merely smiled at one another. By the expressions we were honing, we were obviously on the same wave-length.

"I'm Mrs. Steinbeck and I live just next door," she pointed to a chocolate-colored house with a swinging sofa on the porch. Before either of us could reflect her hospitality, she stumbled on. "We're a very tight-knit community here in Bricksdale, Mr. DeLaney, so if you have any questions or you need any help, no matter what, please feel free to pop around and ask." Her enthusiasm was giving me a bastard headache. Still, a part of me couldn't help but find her slightly amusing.

"Thank you, Mrs. Steinbeck; we'll keep that in mind," he grinned his polite grin, the one which is typically used to dismiss people. However, she didn't seem to catch on and remained stood stock-still on the sidewalk as we approached the house.

I was being steered up the steps when she called, "Like I said, day or night, my door is always open."

"Thank you, Mrs. Steinbeck," Liam retorted over his shoulder.

"No, *thank you*, Mr. DeLaney. This is very exciting; I am going to bake some banana bread. I'll pop some over later for you both." And she shuffled away as we stepped over the threshold.

"She's going to be one of those nosey neighbors, isn't she?" Liam questioned, his back firmly pushing the barrier shut.

"Liam," I hissed, "Don't be too quick to stereotype people."

He gazed at me pointedly, his eyebrows meeting his hairline.

"But yes, I think she might be."

CHAPTER
nine

January 2012.
Seventeen months before the accident…

Three weeks. That's it. Three short weeks, or twenty-one long days, refer to it as you will, it's all the same.

Three weeks ago, we moved from Dorchester to Bricksdale. I sat in Liam's BMW cuddling my blender like it was going to save me from taking the next gigantic step in my life. Terrified, I was led up the front steps and into a house that was cold, empty and far from a home. I was led into a shell of bricks and mortar with such weighted anxiety that Liam had to end the grand tour because I couldn't do anything other than cry. Regardless of how many pep talks I gave myself, I knew this was a big deal, and I should have been ecstatic with the gesture. I knew buying a house was huge, and Liam jumping in feet first to offer me this filled my heart with unconditional love, and made the wad of guilt in my head and stomach punch its way to the surface.

Warm, loving arms came around me as I cried in the room

which was to become Liam's office. Soft, cajoling sounds emitted and vibrated from his throat as my head nuzzled into his chest. "Shhh. I'm happy and overwhelmed, too, but I'm not crying," he murmured against my scalp.

I couldn't bring myself to tell him that I was mourning the loss of the apartment—the place where we created three years of memories. Unfortunately, unlike physical possessions, we couldn't withdraw each memory from the walls and place them in their very own box to move with us, and free them in the shell I found myself standing in, to make it feel more like home. Home was what you made it, and in that moment, as I softly swayed in Liam's generous arms and listened to him pacify me, breathing in his Godly scent and feeling the warmth of his chest beneath his shirt, I made a silent promise to him and to me: that I would do everything I could to make this a happy home.

I was standing in the heart of the living room while I thought back to the barrenness of the property only a while ago. Three weeks prior, I had only been surrounded by that of hardwood flooring and cream walls. It was the same throughout. It's astonishing how much you can change and achieve in such short time, if you put your mind to it.

Thick, luxurious cream carpeting now rests where the hard floor once took place. The surrounding walls coated in vibrant creams and gold. I never knew how cream could be considered a vibrant color, but it was. A Grecian theme flowed throughout the entire property—apart from Liam's office of course. I was even now, perplexed with the insistence I shown with selecting a neutral pallet. I had always opted for darker, warmer colors. Yet, I think subconsciously, I was considering the lengths someone would go to, to ensure that a shade so bright would go unsullied.

I had hoped that being surrounded by such pristine valuables and upholstery would be a hushed reminder to stray away from ungainliness. I silently hoped it would remind Liam how clumsy I can get, and therefore, avoid actions which could prompt me to soil what his hard earned money was spent on.

Even so, within the melded twenty-one days past, the fresh, unblemished canvas that was our home, had begun to slowly fill and pattern with new memories. Through the bottom archway I strolled with a faint smile on my face, and surfaced in the conjoined dining room and kitchen. The new glass surfaced dining table with six, white leather high backrest seats and a crystal chandelier hanging in the center of the table governed the room, with the white and oak surfaced island blatantly dominating the kitchen.

After a somewhat heated discussion while I perched myself on the kitchen island, the memory of Liam wedging himself between my thighs before slipping me off and lying me down on the cold, tiled flooring alongside to the range, and took me for his pleasure while dinner was cooking, tantalized my mind.

I remembered the gasp that passed my lips as he lunged into me with momentum. I was a moth to the flame as the heat waves radiated from the large black door alongside my left, my thighs fell open farther, and my flesh momentarily stuck to the broiling door. Although it hurt like a bitch, it did something to me…for me…I felt something that I'd never felt before. One thing was for certain: I felt confused and to some extent, ashamed by the mere fact that a part of me…reveled in it…needed it.

The concoction of feelings which simmered inside my head as we bickered over my entitlement to inform my family that we no longer lived in Dorchester was fogging up my mind. I hadn't spoken to them for so long, and in that moment, I couldn't see or think clearly.

Frustration, desire, longing, anger, dejection…it was too

much.

The inability to focus on one solitary emotion was ripping my mind and heart to shreds, and for the first time ever, Liam fucking me into realization wasn't going to help defog the shit in my head. It was the pain, shock and tenderness of the wound which was my anchor and guided me through my aimless moment.

With that memory and the freeness I felt warming my blood, I held the edge of the towel which was wrapped around my dripping tresses, before pressing the lower half of my short satin robe against my thigh, and peeked down at my left knee. The flesh, once red and shining thanks to that night, had turned into a dimmer hue and lost its sheen-like surface.

Surprisingly, even the stairs were a catalyst to add a smile to my face, as I recalled him taking me on them on our first night. My hand coiled around one of the wooden beams, my legs bound around his waist, while each forceful thrust had the edge of each stair burrowing into my back.

And then there was the front door, which had been knocked on by Mrs. Steinbeck so many occasions in such a short time, I was sure the wood was weakening.

Steinbeck…where did I even begin with that woman?

Thanks to her and her constant disruptions, and the one occasion she took it on to let herself into *our* home, Liam was growing beyond conscious. Ever since that happening, each morning as I saw him off to work, he'd kiss me and mutter the same thing, "Lock the door behind me. Don't open it to anyone." And I did.

The only time his instruction went unheeded was when Liv decided to pop by at lunch in a desperate need for advice. Apparently, a guilty conscience is a bitch. After I told Liam that Liv had stopped by, he fired question after question, statement after statement. And once again, I was left to feel like a scolded child and inferior.

So, on the morning that I remembered and examined the colorful memories newly embedded into our new walls, as Liam leaned down to place a soft goodbye kiss on my forehead, he had asked for my keys.

My brow furrowed as I pulled away and studied his calculating eyes. "What? Why do you need my keys, Liam?" I asked with great caution.

"Because, Kady baby," he set his briefcase on the hardwood floor of the hallway and cradled my face, the tips of his fingers burrowed under my towel attached to my head ever so slightly. "I have told you time and time again not to answer the door for your own safety."

I scowled. What did he mean, 'for my own safety'? I thought this neighborhood had the lowest crime rates in Boston?

The spikes of the spider's web peeking from his collar, strained as his tendon flexed in the left side of his neck, while green and blue speckled eyes hardened. Not a day went by anymore where I wouldn't be halted and restrained by those uncompromising gems. His clean shaven jaw tautened. "Do not scowl at me, Kady. I'm looking out for *you*. I'm keeping *you safe*. I'm not going to start my day off with your cheek. Now, be a good girl." He held out his hand and there it remained until I eventually conceded on an overthrown sigh.

Twisting around to the sideboard along the balustrade of the stairs, I fished my keys out of the bowl and turned back to Liam. "I'm sorry," I whispered, setting my key into his waiting palm.

"Thank you. That wasn't hard now, was it?"

I shook my head and as the warm soft pad of his thumb came down to caress my lower lip, I couldn't help but smile.

"Now I can work without worrying about where you are and if you're safe." His thumb was replaced by his lips.

Pulling away, he informed me of his expected delay home from work…again. That was the sixth late night in two weeks. Nevertheless, I smiled like any dutiful partner would when she saw her significant other off to work. And as the door closed behind him and I heard the key twist in the lock, I hugged my arms around my body, silently screaming at the four walls for holding me prisoner.

CHAPTER
ten

It was pointless sitting in the house, enclosed by four walls and moping. I trudged from the dining room back through the living room and up the stairs, the padding of bare feet seemingly loud throughout the stillness of the house, to get myself dressed.

Turning the corner on the landing, I stepped through the first door on the right, and was engulfed by sun beams as it seared through the large bay window opposite the door. It made the four-poster, satin adorned bed, shimmer and glisten. The heavy satin embroiled drapes were drawn back perfectly, offering a view of the cushioned bench in the bay.

It was a bedroom worthy of a luxury hotel. One I was overjoyed that I created.

If it wasn't for the swift tightness I felt upon my brow, I would have forgotten about the towel wrapped and twisted upon my head from my morning shower. Strolling around the foot of the bed to the dresser, I unraveled the fluffy material and set to work, quickly blow-drying my locks. I wasn't expected to be anywhere to need looking presentable anyway, not with my keys in Liam's pocket, so with bouncy, shiny blond hair, I opted for an old pair of denim shorts and a red camisole.

The bedroom door was closed behind me when I exited the room. I was shuffling along the upper passageway in my fluffy slippers when someone knocked on the front door. My throat was introduced to my stomach before freefalling back into position. Uneven and ragged, my breathing came in short pants while sweat began to bead down the crevice of my spine.

Steady and silently, I lowered myself onto each stair as if the person on the opposite side of the door would think no one was home.

When the knock sounded again, I was halfway down the stairway and found myself lowering my body to take a seat on the cold smooth surface, like a young child creeping down the stairs in the middle of the night after hearing her parents arguing.

"Kady?" I was summoned after another impatient knock was issued. "Kady, its Laurie, open up."

The sag of relief which passed through my body was all but fleeting. My hackles rose, my back stiffened while I realized: I had no key to open the damn door, even if I wanted to. Slipping myself from the step, I held the balustrade with a fierce grip of my right hand; my left hand slowly skated over the cold, painted wall to my left as I warily descended. "Laurie—"

"Kady?" she responded. "What's taking so long? Come on, I have something. People are looking at me like I'm a fruit loop out here talking to a bloody door."

I wanted to giggle at her disposition. But I couldn't. Nothing about this situation was funny. Liam's constant fear for my safety was vastly becoming my own. I knew damn well Laurie was a friend, and there was no way she was packing chloroform and handcuffs in her purse, with some plan to abduct or harm me. But I was still paranoid. For what, I don't know. I think a part of it, was the likelihood of questioning and interrogation to which I didn't have the answers, and anxious of anybody's tarnished opinions of my relationship. I suppose most of it, was the fear that *I* would be the one to cause that tarnished opinion.

Lowering myself from the last step, I took four strides to the barrier that was holding me prisoner and set my hand on my cell door. I muttered the first thing that sprang into my head. "Laurie, there's something wrong with the door."

"What do you mean, something wro—"

Please sound believable. Please sound believable. Please sound believable. "It keeps jamming. I think the wood is swelling too much for the frame. Liam's going to get it fixed; I can't open it until the handyman comes out."

Vibrations journeyed through the wood to caress my palm, and I knew Laurie had just tossed her head against the surface. "So what am I supposed to do, Kady? Go all cat-burglar and climb in through the window?"

I smiled. "No, just..." words faded as I exhaled a crippling, defeated sigh. You'd think I'd be used to being on my own by now. "Just go home and I'll see you another day."

A loud snort of protest was promptly followed by, "Hell no. I got a bag of shit here; I thought we could have some fun and relax."

"You want to relax with a bag of shit?" That was a line in which I couldn't stifle the amusement in my tone, and it felt so good to laugh. Laurie did have a way with words.

"Is the patio key still under Mr. Pointy?" Mr. Pointy was the garden gnome that she had gifted us when we moved in. Apparently, every backyard needs a freaky little dude with a fishing rod. Laurie had taken it on to name him Mr. Pointy thanks to his pointy nose.

I shrugged to myself. "I don't know. Maybe…"

"Okay," she said, and I heard a bag rustle. "I'm going around the back. Thank the heavens you don't have a freaking guard dog."

While I heard her scurrying down the front steps, I made my way through to the kitchen and set two mugs on the counter. Next thing I know, the pale, petite woman sporting loose fitted, faded jeans, a pink hoodie and black ballet pumps was skipping down the pathway, swinging her bag and waving frantically at me as I stood observantly in front of the window at the sink. Amused by her degree of enthusiasm, I shook my head and sniggered. Dorothy and her wicker basket eat your heart out; Laurie and her bag of shit were just as entertaining.

A small hand was lifted in the air and beams of sunlight caressed the silver metal keys as she swung them in a form of triumph. Before I registered what was happening, the double glass doors along the right wall of the dining room were sliding open, and a very lively Laurie, who decided that purple work best for her bangs, was stepping inside.

"I did it!" she bellowed victoriously, sliding the door closed and rounding the dining table. "I broke in, and didn't even chip a nail."

Eyes rolled heavenward, I shook my head. "You are completely off your rocker."

"That's the best way to be, girlie. You only attract your own kind, that's when the fun really happens."

With her bag set down on the island, I asked if she wanted coffee. The tipping of her lips along with dark eyebrows meeting her hairline was my soundless answer.

Onyx liquid was poured into the waiting cups before the pot

was placed back on its stand. The steam swirled weightlessly as I slipped the beverage across the island, prompting her to take possession of the caffeinated goodness almost immediately, and an overly dramatic sigh of approval, unfettered from her throat. The bag of goodies, or using Laurie's selection of words, 'the bag of shit', was gestured towards with a light tip of my brow as the warmth of the liquid radiated through the ceramic, heating my fingers. "What's in the bag then?"

She swallowed her mouthful and lowered the cup back onto the wood. "Here,"—her hand dipping inside caused a loud rustling—"we have a combination that, when added together, helps relax and can be used for comfort."

Okay, now I was scared.

Each time she drew a new item out of that bag, my stomach knotted. Finally, my gaze drifted from the assortment of ingredients that sat on my counter, up to the round faced woman sporting a grin, which to be honest, looked too big for her face. Her hazel eyes sparkled with zeal.

I was sure the amount of air I had sucked into my lungs was tiptoeing on bursting point. Eyes narrowed, I asked, "Call me dense, but wha—"

"We're going to bake a cake," she replied matter of a fact, and my once narrowed eyes were now wide with alarm. No way was I doing that. We only just moved here, there was no way was I going to put myself into a position where I could be responsible for turning the place into a pile of ashes.

I shook my head frantically, while my tiny skittish sniggers emitted along my exhale. "Laurie, I can't."

The ledge of the island was gripped by her small, firm hands. She studied me carefully with unrestrained wisdom radiating in waves from her encouraging gaze. "There is no such word as 'can't'."

"Okay. I cannot." By the stern expression carved into her face, my sarcasm wasn't going to help me escape this hole; it was just going to dig me in further.

"Just try. I'll be here; you'll see how relaxing it can be."

I didn't believe that another chore could be deemed as relaxing. This was a bad idea. The fisted apprehension worming its way through my system and choking me was my confirmation of that.

As she drank in a liberal breath, her face softened and her shoulders dropped when the death clutch on the edge of the island loosened. As if she knew exactly how my mind worked, she incited me with, "It could be a surprise for Liam."

Me surprising Liam and making him happy is all I wanted. I wanted to be a good girlfriend. I wanted to do something nice for my man. He looked after me. He deserved it. An unexpected surge of enthusiasm and excitement floored all negativity, and I was soon smiling at the thought of his praise.

"Okay. What do I do?"

Standing side-by-side, Laurie walked me through each step, from measuring out, to mixing. When the mixture began to curdle, my system was overridden by instant panic. If I was on my own, I would have been terrified and disheartened by failure, but Laurie continued with words of encouragement, and told me to spoon in a little flour if it began to curdle again. Somehow, with a little faith, I managed to save Liam's surprise.

Taking extra care and making sure all the coconut flakes were mixed in properly and evenly, the yellow substance was then equally poured into two sandwich tins. Before putting them in the oven, I smoothed over the surface with the back of a spoon, making a little dip in the center, just as instructed. When I turned back around, Laurie was gazing at me with an approving smile; it was like she was proud of me. Damn, I was proud of me. I just hoped Liam would be, too.

"See, I told you there's no such word as 'can't'," she mocked before lifting her hand in a silent gesture of a high-five, but I ignored her gesture, and beaming like the Cheshire cat, I stepped into my tutor—one of my *best* friends…one of my *only* friends—and wrapped my arms around her shoulders.

"Thank you, Laur. I couldn't have done this without you."

Her shoulder shifted as the warm, soft hand was lowered from mid-air then gently patted against my back. "You are more than welcome, girlie. I told you it was relaxing." Holding me at arm's length after pulling away, her head tilted back a fraction to look me in the eyes. "How do you feel now?"

I perused the area which was my kitchen. I didn't like the mess which came with this baking malarkey, but I felt somewhat… achieved? Accomplished? I couldn't remember a time I'd felt that way without shame overshadowing it. Let's just say, you couldn't generally feel accomplished by getting the most tips in one night when you were stripping to get them.

I grinned and answered candidly. "I feel like I've accomplished something."

My smile was reflected. "You have."

It was 6:35 p.m. and I was standing, rooted to the spot in my kitchen, gazing at the platter in the heart of the island, adorned with the simple masterpiece I'd created. Yes, okay, I had guidance, but I did everything myself. I even topped the cake off with a layer of raspberry jelly and sprinkled extra coconut flakes on top like they were snowflakes.

Liam could never get enough of coconut. It was his guilty pleasure.

Minutes passed swiftly as I smiled at my success. Drawn from my moment by the ringing, along with a loud buzzing, of my cell phone I raced to the dining table, rummaged through my purse, and without a glance at the flashing screen, I pressed the green button.

"Hello."

"Kady?" a sniveling, hesitant voice whispered down the speaker.

"Brittany? Is that you? Thank God you're alright. Each time I called, Mom and Dad said you were busy," I rambled, my words desperately needing liberation after so many weeks of zero contact. And I was thankful to hear her voice.

"Yeah, I've been up to my eyeballs."

"So have we, what with the move—" I bit my tongue and cringed as soon as I realized my slipup. Damn me and my big fucking mouth.

"You moved?"

Shit, shit, shit. "Yeah, umm..." internally scolding myself, I was interrupted before I could continue digging myself a bigger hole.

"Kady, I need to talk to you." She sounded serious. Brittany never did serious. "But I'm scared to—"

"What?!" I didn't know whether to feel annoyed or hurt. "Britt, you are my sister—my baby sister. Have I ever given you reason to feel scared?" I screwed my eyes shut before holding my breath. "God, are you pregnant?" Waiting for her answer, air was finally ousted when she hissed 'no' down the speaker. *Thank God for that.* I loved her to death, but Brittany could hardly take care of herself, let alone a baby. "Then what is it?"

With the handset resting against the side of my face, I strolled back to the kitchen.

"Kady...Liam made a move on me."

The world stopped moving as did my steps. The room span mercilessly on its axis, while my ears rang. I had to force a swallow before I choked on the two simple words which I could only just push passed the lump in my throat. "Excuse me?"

"On Halloween..."

"No. No. No..." the monosyllable words journeyed down the speaker on a suspicious snicker, while my hand found its way into my hair. "It was *you* and your man obsessed brain that was going around pinching everyone's asses. You had a lot to drink, Brittany. You must have been mistaken."

"Kady, I'm not mistaken, *he hit on me*. I told him no, but he wouldn't let up. He was the one who jammed the bedroom door shut the following morning, and near enough forced his tongue in my mouth when we in the kitchen."

There was nothing there in my head to absorb what she was saying; her frank words merely rebounded against my skull, making my head throb. This couldn't be right. Liam wouldn't do that. Not to me. Not after everything we had been through. I felt my blood go from a simmering to boiling point, almost immediately. "Brittany, I suggest you stop with this nonsense right now. Liam wouldn't—"

"Kady," she interrupted me with a stern and urgent tone, a tone very un-Brittany-like. "He forced me up against the Goddamn wall, I tried to push him away when he grabbed my ass, but he wouldn't budge. He told me it was a thrill to live in the moment, to do things which should be forbidden. I wanted to tell you, Kady, I really did. It's been killing me keeping it to myself, but he told me that it would be useless because you would always believe him. Please, Kady, you have to believe me."

Standing in the center of the kitchen, the void in my skull was filled by her echoing words. My body shook, my breathing was ragged and my head was pounding, as I unintentionally allowed myself to be devoured by so many haywire emotions. "I–I have to go," I muttered in a daze, ended the call and dropped it on the unit as though it had just burned me.

Each anxious breath, alongside my mouth gaping, caused my lips to wither. The walls, the floor, everything around me faded into oblivion. Liam and my sister? Brittany and Liam? No. It was lies. It had to be.

The degree of my denial came to run short. I sensed and familiarized myself with the intensifying rage and collective emotions bubbling and steaming in my body—confusion, misunderstanding—I felt cheated and betrayed. I didn't want to believe it; you name me one person in this lifetime who wants to believe that the two people they trust more than anything in the world would participate in some immoral, treacherous act such as that.

Blame, however, seeped and trickled through my veins melding with my upsurge of adrenaline. I blamed myself. If Brittany was telling the truth, then I was certain more than anything in the world, that it was me that had forced him into someone else's arms—me and my Goddamn insolent habits. Why didn't I ever listen to him? I should have treated him better.

Trudging through a conflict-ridden storm, it was impossible to focus on one particular emotion and work through it before diffusing the next. Everything, the feelings, my reaction, along with the words of my sister, obstructed my natural ability to neutralize each emotion and come out the other side with reason, and a greater understanding of the situation as it stood.

Next thing I knew, an intense sensation of hurt overcame me, but with hurt should come pain, right? Yet there was no pain; there was no shock, nothing to make me feel human. It was as though my brain was registering the hurt, but it couldn't register that the hurt wasn't physical, the hurt was in my heart. I was hurting emotionally and on some inexplicable level, I didn't and couldn't deal with it. I didn't know how to. I just wanted it to end.

My heart was shattering, and in a way, I needed to feel that way, too.

I have no idea why, but in a daze, I yanked open the dishwasher which had just finished its cycle. I just needed something... something to help me focus—something to concentrate on and help defog my mind. I needed to somehow send a message to my brain, a message where it could decipher that my hurt *was* due to the act of physical pain.

As bizarre as it sounds, I ran on my pure instinct. An instinct which had never presented itself before.

One of the middle-sized silver spoons was fetched from the washer, and even with a cloth shielding my fingers, I could still feel the heat of the metal scorching through the weave of the fabric. When I braced my right foot up onto one of the barstools, I closed my eyes while heaving each labored and shaky breath, and tossed back my head. My arm felt as weighty as lead, so I let it drop and called out in pain as the hot steel pressed against my inner thigh. The natural reaction to withdraw from the heat of the implement was fought against with every ounce of strength I had. Every muscle in my face bunched together and I felt warm tears falling from my eyes to trickle down my cheeks.

I concentrated on nothing more as I slipped into my own little world, my own very dark place in my psyche where there were no walls holding me captive, no misunderstandings and most importantly, no blame. With each few seconds that passed by, the wounded flesh beneath, and surrounding the hot steel, which lay against my inner thigh, became less sensitive. I was becoming familiarized with it, and in that moment, I was free. I was getting what I needed alongside what I deserved. I needed that time to escape into my mind; I needed that moment of discomfort to bring me a form of detachment. I needed to fight through the form of physical pain, to quell my emotional pain.

"What the fuck are you doing?"

By the time my eyelids had fluttered open, Liam's briefcase was already set on the dining table and he was charging toward me like a bat out of Hell. Nonetheless, I pressed that slowly cooling metal further and further into my skin, desperately seeking complete numbness, not physically, but emotionally. And I was nearly there. I was only a moment away from emotional numbness. I just needed that moment, that one measly moment.

"Kady?" Liam shouted in a bid to get my attention as he rounded the island in haste. I watched as his eyes fell onto my right thigh and the back of the silver spoon which was flattened against it. Embarrassment should have bred from the situation, but I was consumed in the moment of knowing what I needed, that I just didn't care. I was helping myself because only I knew what I needed.

Control.

Wrenching my hand away from my leg as his forceful hand circled my wrist, I protested during his attempt. "No, no. It's mine; I only need a minute, just a minute, please—" I writhed, sounding like a pathetic crack addict begging for her latest fix, but I was shameless. During the months, I felt everything had been taken away from me, some for good reason, I could understand that. But living in the constant fear and anxiety which I felt while inside that house as I strove not to push my boyfriend's buttons, along with the level I went to in a bid to make certain I had a constant reminder not to fuck up, and the feelings which had stirred inside me, whether it be due to feeling like a prisoner under my partner's hold, or because of the words and actions of disloyalty that my sister had entrusted me with, I no longer felt in control of my life.

And I hadn't for a while.

With that small circle of torrid steel on my body, I had regained what I felt was no longer my right. I could *control* the heat by having it hover above my surface and feel the relaxing warmth, or hold it down tight and allow the intense burn to take hold of me. I could *control* the duration, the way in which it was placed, the area which would be taken next, and how much area would be affected. It was mine, and mine alone.

"Kady, give me the fucking spoon!"

"No," it was a futile attempt to pull away and fight him off, but I tried anyway with a flailing of my head as tears of desperation and the need to have him understand, took ahold of me. "It's mine. It's mine. It's mi—"

Clattering upon the tile sounded as the steel spoon was relinquished from my grip, and my head whipped ferociously to my right as the back of Liam's heavy, authoritative hand collided with the side of my face. I stumbled and fell backward, my lower back cracking onto the title, the legs of the barstool griping before being kicked over. Cradling the side of my face, my cheekbone throbbed and I was certain my eyeball was going to explode. Yet, I found that the shock of his assault completed the sequence that I craved, the progression that I had sought after the initial control: shock and unresponsiveness. He halted my intention to gradually seek that mental state, but the shock of his strike, was just another method to free myself from the clouded, overrunning feelings in my head.

I was literally shocked into reason…I was shocked into

numbness.

From the floor, I tipped my head back to peer up at the man which was looming over me with an array of differing emotions in his eyes. He raked his hand back in his slicked brown hair and lowered himself into a crouch. "Kady," my name was a rapid sound journeying on a conflicted gasp. The back of my left hand, which was cradling my face, was encased by his warmth when he settled his hand above it. Lips curled with worry and eyes thawed with apologetic assertions. "I am so, so sorry, baby. I don't know why…" his voice was lost to silence while he hung his head and slowly removed his hand from my cheek.

"Did you do it?" I asked, breaking the deafening silence and feeling somewhat serene and levelheaded.

His head shot up. "Did I do what?"

Blinking slowly, for that brief moment, I felt as though nothing could harm me. I felt blissfully at peace, totally uncaring… detached. I just wanted honesty. "Did you make a pass at Brittany on Halloween?"

I studied the crumple of his brow and the slight presence of his laugh-lines as his face tensed into a perplexed scowl. "What? No, of course I didn't. I would never do that to you." His opposite hand lifted to comb the hair back from my face and set it behind my shoulders. "What would make you think such a thing? What's been said?"

The screaming red blemish on my inner thigh was stealing my attention. When my thumb grazed around and over the area of the wound, after falling from my face, tingles shot through my body. The flesh was still heated, and in the light the wounded surface appeared to shine.

"Brittany called," I began mindlessly, staring into a void that was becoming my life. "She told me you made a move on her.

That it was you that locked me in the bedroom the following morning. She said you near enough forced your tongue in her mouth." I stopped to sniffle, my rapt attention remaining on my leg. "She said you told her that if she told me, I'd never believe her anyway."

In my peripheral vision, I saw cautious, gentle fingers approach my own on my thigh. I should have winced when his fingertips skimmed over the ugly red mark, but I felt...restful, near untouchable. Things felt and appeared more vivid.

"And because of what was said, you decided to do this to yourself?" his tone was borderline on pitiful, but I knew differently. I knew what it was to me, I knew how it helped. I didn't think Liam would ever come to understand the extent of how something like this *could* help. Some would call it attention seeking. That's not me; I had never been an attention seeker. To me, it was an escape. It was a way to have control over a situation. To me, as the temperature of that metal began to gradually lessen, the overwhelming collection of thoughts in my mind lessened, too. Like a graph. The pain is the peak, it starts out high, but it pulls you back from the anger and rage once you become familiar with it, and as the temperature is reduced, the compressed sphere of burdening emotions is unraveled and clarity, levelheadedness and detachment takes place.

This was my form of emotional numbness.

This was my anchor.

When I failed to answer his question in knowing that he wouldn't understand, he muttered, "Kady. Can you see how Brittany's words have affected us today? Can you see what has happened? Because of her, a line has been crossed, a line that we never thought..." wavering, he inhaled deeply and exhaled loudly through his nose before resuming. "Kady, it's nothing but lies. I love you, but I'm sorry, I'm not going to allow anyone to worm their way between us and rip us apart, or turn us into people that we don't recognize."

I heard his words, but they were just that: words—a raspy, deep voice blanketing everything in my mind and holding me there in reality before I slipped further into emotional stillness. I had to do this. I had to do it now while I was still in my realm of detachment.

"Could you please pass me my cell, Liam? It's on the island."

When he came to squat down before me again, he handed me the handset and asked what I was doing.

"I'm drawing an end to this," I mechanically replied.

"Did you tell her about the move?" he asked as I pulled up my contact list.

I just wanted to overcome the hurdle that was standing in front of me, so I shook my head and muttered 'no' while I selected 'little sis', in my contacts then selected the option to send a text message. I typed everything which needed to be said:

I can't believe you would stoop so low.

I'm done.

We're done.

I have no sister.

CHAPTER
eleven

The following morning I woke to an empty bed. My head pulsated while my eyes felt tight and raw. For the first time in years, I'd cried myself to sleep. The recollections of the crazy times I had with Brittany, all the sad times and downright annoying times had my grief-stricken body weeping harder. In spite of everything, she was my sister.

I remembered her tiny hand clutching my pinkie finger the day Mom and Dad brought her tiny innocent body home from the hospital, and each and every pinkie promise we made to each other as we grew older. I remembered her laughing when I pulled silly faces behind our parents back and the very first fight I got into, as I stood protecting her from some bully in school.

Brittany was my right arm. Nevertheless, she had crossed a line as my sibling, and I hacked her out of my life because of it.

I was pushing myself up in the heart of the bed, gathering the edge of the comforter and stretching it across my chest when Liam spoke from the doorway of the walk-in-closest at the foot of the bed. "Good morning, baby," his voice was soothing yet strained as he continued fixing his black tie into place.

"Morning."

Steadily making his way toward me, he asked, "How are you feeling this morning?" When he took position on the edge of my side, the mattress dipped.

"Hurt." I sighed, although I found the strength to force a nervous, tightlipped grin through my blatant honesty when his hand gradually lifted.

By some means, I mustered the strength to combat my body's natural response and not recoil from him. Liam's degree of guilt was discernible not solely by the look on his face, but in his velvety enriched voice as he breathed, "Oh, Kady," while his fingertips smoothed over the arch of my left cheekbone. His handsome, clean shaven face contorted in blatant shame when he witnessed me striving to restrict a wince at the faintest of connections. Had I not the strength to suppress the full extent of my pained reaction, I was certain it would've added to his guilty disposition. I couldn't do that to him. He shouldn't need to feel guilt. He hadn't forced Brittany to fabricate the bullshit which resulted in our actions.

"It's okay. It doesn't hurt." It did. It stung and throbbed like a bitch.

Immediately after withdrawing his hand from my injured cheek, he dove into the back pocket of his suit pants. It was when his wallet was opened and one of his credit cards was being held out to me, that I couldn't mask my confusion any longer.

"Here," he thrust it at me once more. My perplexed scowl remained fixed on my face as I accepted his offering with caution. "Treat yourself. Get your hair done, nails, feet the works."

I shook my head, dubious. Where was this coming from? "What about me staying inside? I don't think I can go—"

"Baby, will you please listen," he interjected with hooded eyes, in that instant, I shut my mouth and a tender hand came down to rest on the comforter covering my thigh. He continued, "I want you to get your hair done. Get your nails and feet done. Buy a new outfit, something that will stun everyone at the Hyperion tonight."

A stealing crease worked its way across my brow.

"You haven't forgotten about tonight's DeLaney Constructs gathering for the new contract have you? The entire workload and their plus-ones will be there, Kady."

Shit, how could I have forgotten about that damned event? Liam had been organizing it for the last month. But, then again, I had been designing the interior of the house for the last month, so no wonder it had escaped me. "Of course I remember," I lied.

The distance closed between us, and my dried, withered lips were swiftly and accordingly slanted over by his soft, minty mouth. "Good," the small presses of his lips as he mouthed it against me was then removed when he drew himself away and reared up. The mattress shifted once again. "I have to stay behind tonight, so I'll send a car to pick you up at about seven and I'll meet you there."

"Okay."

"And umm," shrugging on his navy suit jacket, the plastic card twisted between my fingers. "Take someone with you today. I don't want you on your own."

When I suggested I call Liv and have her accompany me, the idea was swiftly overturned, with Liam's insistence that I avoid being snowed under by Liv and her God forsaken guilty conscience, which has been making a meal out of her for a while, it would seem. I needed to take time to relax and enjoy *myself*. Apparently, I deserved it.

"What about Laurie?" he proposed with an arched dark brow.

"Good idea. I'll ask her."

Once again he strolled toward the bed, the mattress swallowed his fists as he leaned into me and bracing his weight through straight arms. He planted a chaste kiss on my lips. "Good. Treat her to something, too."

"You are being awfully generous this morning, Mr. DeLaney," I teased with a sheepish grin.

He chuckled briefly. "Don't complain, Miss Jenson. I have one last request."

I had already responded with a quick, "Anything," before I even considered what this 'request' may be.

Seemingly ashamed, remorseful even, his head was lowered. "Could you please…" he wavered, drawing in another breath, I could feel the power he was striving to muster to push past his hesitancy as he faintly rolled his forehead across my own.

"Could I what?"

"Could you wear your sunglasses please?" he whispered, reserved and unsettled.

Wear my sunglasses? That was an unusual request if ever I did hear one. Nonetheless, I nodded my acquiescence and with a brief peck on the lips and a 'thank you', Liam left for work, leaving my house keys and large, Jackie-O styled sunglasses on the bedside unit.

It wasn't until I shunted myself out of the terribly alluring bed and made a beeline to the en-suite and gazed at myself in the vanity mirror, during which I patiently waited for the pressure and temperature of the shower to stabilize, did I notice why Liam made such a trivial request. My left eye was turning an ugly darkened purple, while the white of my eye had a minor red tinge. Yes… very large tinted lenses and a make-up artist's never ending supply of cosmetics was definitely going to be needed on that day.

Within fifteen minutes, my wet body was being rapidly toweled of trickling, warm droplets, when I caught sight of the round, red mark which coated my thigh; all it did was add insult to injury. The day before my body was a temple, unblemished, just as it always had been. And now, I had two screaming flaws, and all from one catalyst.

Nevertheless, I refused to let the happenings of the day before tarnish a new day—a day which was important to Liam and the business. So going about my business, I dropped everything that I needed into my red leather shoulder bag, when a piercing, double beep informed me of Laurie's arrival. For the second time in as many minutes, I checked myself in the full-length mirror. Sporting my red gauze blouse shielding a black camisole and tucked neatly into my black fitted pants and finished with red heeled pumps, I looked both casual yet sophisticated—something which I'd never have achieved without Liam and his tirelessness mission of: modify Kady's fashion sense. I was ever grateful that I listened, and he'd succeeded.

My bag was snatched from the bed, before I made a hastily retreat down the stairs and out of the door. Head hanging down, I slipped my shades on as I descended the front steps.

A very lively, "Good morning, sunshine," greeted me as I slipped into the cherry-red Honda. When the door was firmly shut behind me, my seatbelt was fixed into place. "What's with the Jackie-O's? It's not that sunny, you know."

Awash by a form of protectiveness and defense, I wrenched my gaze to the woman who made up for her lack of height by teasing and ribbing, and frowned. The only words the voice in my head could repeat was: '*It was my fault. He did what he felt he needed to do*'. Making an attempt to veer away from the subject, I flipped her off with the typical, 'migraine forming' excuse.

I thanked my lucky stars that Laurie was so down to Earth, that she actually believed me.

Laurie and I made a day of it. We talked, we laughed and we teased. We sat in a booth in a quiet bistro sipping a glass of wine and enjoying a light lunch, while watching other patrons and making up little scenario's, and possible conversational topics that they were engaging in. My hair was now comfortably on my shoulders, my layers flicked in every direction creating a shaggy-like look which bounced and swished. I loved it. Laurie opted for dark purple nails which matched her bangs, while mine were coated in a rich, glossy chocolate.

The only item left of the agenda, was to buy an outfit for that night's event.

It was 3:15 p.m. when we stepped through the royal blue door and into Marcela's Obsession. The bell sounded its inviting jingle as I closed the door behind me.

"Good afternoon, can I help you?" Behind the glass fronted counter, a middle-aged, impeccably dressed woman greeted us; the assortment of jewelry behind the glass sparkled as the light seared through and ricocheted off each gem.

"No, thank you. We're just browsing."

Up two narrow steps I climbed when I spotted exactly what Liam had said he wanted me to get, 'something that will stun everyone'. My jaw plunged the floor, and I was sure my specs would soon be joining it. The overly-large frames were tipped down onto the tip of my nose allowing me to examine the ensemble clearly, when a firm hand crashed onto my shoulder. "Wow!"

"I know. It's..." words failed me. One thing I knew for certain was that, whoever wore this dress would definitely have people stunned at something like tonight's event.

"You got to, Kady. I'm sure he would kiss your fucking feet if he saw you in that. Either that or turn into a puddle of mush before your very eyes." Damn, Laurie was swearing? She must have felt passionate about it, because Laurie very rarely swore.

Without thinking, I lifted my shades from the tip of my nose, to rest atop of my head and resumed examining the material and cut of the dress. The material was cold and a little rigid between my fingers, but as I inspected it further, I silently considered whether the mark on my thigh would be screened by its length. The last thing I wanted was something that ugly to be put on display.

"What are you thinking, Kady?" her gentle voice penetrated my silent musing.

My lips tipped and my lower lip found itself snared between my teeth. "I'm thinking…Liam is going to turn into a puddle of mush when he sees me tonight."

The release of her high-pitched, demented squeal had me laughing from my belly. I removed the hanger in a daze, checked the size and turned to face the woman bouncing up and down with a degree of excitement rivaling a child getting ice-cream, when she came to an abrupt halt. Her face fell and as her hand was raised to my face, I jolted on instinct. "What the fuck happened to your eye?"

Shit. How could I have been so damn stupid? I hastily fumbled with the frames which were still sitting comfortably on the top of my head, and attempted to pull the mask over my contusion. It didn't help though. Laurie batted my hand away and glared at me with rooted expectancy.

"Well?" her terse question bounced in the mute void between us. Allowing the silence to swell, it wasn't long before she jumped to conclusions as I strove to find a believable answer to her pushy query. "Did Liam hit you?"

Okay, so she wasn't jumping to conclusions as such, but it

was my responsibility to make sure she thought she was. "No, don't be so silly," a deceitful mirthless gurgle vibrated around the lump in my throat, the corners of my lips twitched as my overactive right hand motioned with the gushing of my words. "I tried pulling that damn front door open last night when you left, and it hit me straight in the face—" The conviction behind the words which were being rapidly strewing together was absent. Quickly becoming desperate to remove that shrewd scowl from her face, I would have thrown just about everything I had at her to deviate from the subject—Hell, I did. "It didn't happen to Pooh Bear's friends when they pulled him out of that honey tree."

Nope...nothing was going to thaw that expression from her face. Hazel eyes stared at me almost...pitifully, knowledgeably. It was an expression I urgently sought to remove myself from being under.

Setting my glasses back onto the bridge of my nose, I took the dress and approached the narrow steps. "Come on, I want to buy this dress before someone else comes in and decides they want it."

The footsteps from behind me were shadowed by her small cynical statement, "Funny. You didn't seem to have any problem with the front door this morning."

Blood boiled over in my veins, my heart was a steel drum pounding an erratic rhythm in my chest. My legs and hands trembled as I considered every avenue which I could take to stop people from jumping the gun and thinking the worst of my boyfriend—a man who had been supporting and looking after me for all those months, a man who wouldn't intentionally cause me any harm. A man, who with everything he had, even if it meant overriding his morals and values, would do anything to make me see the fault in my behavior, just to make sure that we survived as a couple.

As I handed over Liam's credit card to the sales assistant, I knew what I had to do.

Maybe if I began to believe my lies myself, others would believe me, too.

CHAPTER twelve

There seems to be no element of time when you study yourself in the mirror, and you're enthralled by what's staring back at you. In the bedroom, I stood at the foot of the bed, admiring myself before the Grecian themed, full-length mirror.

I turned left, I turned right, and I struck several model-worthy poses while pouting my lips. Pathetic, I know, but even so, I felt an element which had been lying dormant for so long slowly awaken: the sense of desirability. Everybody in the world wants to feel desirable, it's a fact. I think there's even a quote about it being an irresistible desire. And with each ticking minute that passed, that feeling was being revived.

The pencil-like leather dress was tight. It hugged me like a second skin, but it wasn't trashy or streetwalker material. It was classy, appealing, and something which, to me, screamed prestige. With long-sleeves and a slight plunging neckline, the sapphire necklace which Liam gifted me on our first anniversary was able to taking pride of place and rest peacefully on my chest. The peak of the reversed V at the front of the ensemble extended to my mid-thigh, allowing my long, toned legs to be displayed, but without fear of revealing the result of yesterday's incident.

Thick, bouncing, tousled blond locks rested on my shoulders, my newly-cut thin bangs scattered across my brow, and I was more than impressed with my mission to disguise my bruising eye with ample cosmetics. It wasn't even noticeable.

I was pulled from admiring my reflection by a blaring of a horn outside. Taking several steps around the bed to the bay window, I placed my knee on the padded bench and folded my body over to gaze down at the sidewalk. A black limousine was parked alongside the walkway, and a smile stole across my features. Gazing down at the chauffeur beside the car, his hands grasped and hanging at the front of his body, his head lowered, all I could sense was the degree of Liam's love for me. He may not say it often, but actions speak louder than words, and his were screaming at me.

Seizing my black and silver clutch purse from the foot of the bed, the slight protesting of leather sounded as I lifted my arm and I nestled my purse in-between my bicep and breast, and checked my reflection once more. The silver mirror of my peep-toe heels matched perfectly with the silver trimming of my purse. Flicking the light switch off as I exited, I dashed out of the room with an enormous grin, and headed down the stairs and out of the house, locking the door behind me.

"Good evening, Miss Jenson," the elderly man greeted and held the door open simultaneously.

"Good evening," I replied, slipping myself inside. When the door was closed I breathed in deeply. The fresh scent of the car mixed with the new leather of my dress was a heady combination.

As we pulled off, I dug into my purse and retrieved my cell. I punched in a quick message to Liam:

Liam, you have spoiled me rotten. I was expecting a cab.
See you shortly.
Love you xxx

A few minutes later, the handset chimed:

Liam: When was the last time I allowed you to get a cab? The lengths some people will go to in an attempt to pick up victims are deplorable. I'll see you soon.

Love you, too xxx

Liam, Liam, Liam…always worrying about me and my safety. Dropping my cell into my bag and clipping it closed, I grinned to myself. Why was I even moaning? It was an honor that he cared so much. The time to worry would be if he didn't care about me. It's nice to be looked after.

Thirty minutes later we were pulling to stop in Seaport, alongside a huge building with a red awning that had, 'The Hyperion' scripted in elegant cursive, silver writing. Peeking out of the tinted window to my right, I was still studying the structure when my door was pulled open. The leather protested as I twisted on the seat, dangled both of my legs out of the door, and unfolded myself to stand on the sidewalk, making sure my dress remained shielding what needed to be.

"Thank you," I muttered to the elderly gentleman.

Lifting his hand to his hat, he nodded, "Ma'am," then rounded the hood back to the driver side.

The light clicking of my heels on the ground echoed as I ascended the three front steps beneath the awning, with my purse tucked under my left arm.

When I pushed my way through the classy revolving door, I didn't expect to be drowned by that degree of a lavish elegance.

Greater than what it appeared outside, the thick, luxurious

blood red carpet with silver, swirling scattered patterns throughout drank in my heels with every step I made. A round, mahogany reception desk sat in the center of the lobby, while rounded couches were dotted around the expanse area. Bellboys meandered around with guests, guiding them to the bank of elevators.

I suddenly felt very self-conscious as I carefully made my way to the desk. After asking the young woman where I could find the DeLaney Constructs event, I was escorted through the remainder of the lobby, down a corridor to the far right and into one of the function rooms.

Stealing a deep, calming breath and exhaling through pursed lips, it was obvious that the butterflies in my gut were getting the better of me as I stood before the heavy, intricately carved double doors at the end of the small, elegant corridor. With my wits finally gathered, I pushed the door open, and was bathed by sounds of soft chattering and clinking of glasses as both architects, and the construction workforce of DeLaney Constructs, gathered together in their little groups, around the elegantly dressed round tables with their plus-ones. A subtle, golden glow was emitted from an elegant heavy crystal chandelier, which hung from the epicenter of the square, segmented mirrored ceiling, while the bar was situated at the very far left end of the room.

I spotted Liam the instant I traveled deeper into the room… could this even be classed as a room? I was sure many a wedding reception had happened in this very spot. Standing facing away from me as he conversed with his employees, his arms were waving around and gesturing as he spoke. I didn't need to hear what was being said to feel the passion he obviously felt about their topic of discussion.

One of the four men in front of him had said something which I couldn't quite hear, but the tip of his head in my direction, told me that he was informing Liam of my arrival. This was the moment that I found both exciting and nerve-wracking: his reaction to my makeover, as a result of his generosity.

Butterflies stretched out their wings in my stomach once again as I, taking well measured steps with swaying hips and weaving between tables, closed the distance between us. When Liam turned to face me, I smiled, my eyebrows rose as my eyes widened, seeking silent approval.

"Hey, Kady," the men I had never met before welcomed me. It filled and warmed my heart more so, knowing that they knew *of me*, even if I didn't know *of them*. Liam obviously talked about me while in their company.

"Hi," I replied quickly, and as I leaned into Liam to greet him with a kiss, my smile was wiped from my face. Wrinkles appeared quickly in the center of his brow, while his eyes caught fire and the familiar tick of his jaw worked overtime.

As the men continued to talk between themselves, Liam, with reservation, bent to kiss me on the cheek. Prickles spawned in my body when he whispered, "What the fuck is that?" into the hollow of my ear. As soon as he withdrew, lips were covering my own and a hand, which at that point in time was amassing my unease, roamed over my back. His brow tipped to brace against my own.

"I thought you would like it? It's classy, and—"

"This is what my money buys? You're lucky I'm obligated to stay here, because I swear to God…" his scathing statement weakened as he trailed off and I sucked in a harsh breath, thankful that he halted his words just then. With everything I had, I stopped myself from being overridden by fear of what he *would* do—what he *could* do.

"I'm sorry, Liam. I thought it would make you happy—"

Like a dictator, he held his head high and defiantly reared

back, making me feel inferior once again. These moments were vastly becoming common, yet I was still conflicted by how loving he was that morning, in comparison to who stood before me now.

I really needed to stop pressing his buttons.

The left side of my face was cradled in his hand. I couldn't command myself to look him in the eye. I didn't have a right to, not after I had done this—not after I had made him feel this way. But when he whispered his demand that I look at him, I peeked up at the God in front of me. If he commanded that I got down on my hands and knees to kiss and lick his feet in front of everyone in that very room, I would have without hesitancy, because at that moment, I was the lesser of us and he deserved my respect.

"You have made me happy." He was making me dizzy with his rapid mood changes, yet I couldn't stifle my moment of relief as I smiled, and each taut muscle in my body unclenched. My smile was mirrored, although unlike mine, his wasn't genuine. It was unhinged. It was wicked…it made me panic and fight for air, my muscles straining once again as I grew guarded.

The warmth and tenderness of his touch upon the side of my face soon became heavy. Blazing eyes alongside the sinister upturn of his lips prompted the butterflies in my stomach to attempt their great escape. "You managed to cover this," he finished, the tone of his voice a complete opposite of the demanding power behind his caress. I sucked in a deep inhalation, the air hissing as it passed my teeth and caught in my throat, while he bore his burdensome thumb into my injured cheekbone, his smirk spreading wider.

In a room full of approximately thirty or forty bodies, I was standing immobilized before Liam as he issued my punishment. Not wanting to cause a scene, I fought my body's instinct to retreat.

So what did I do?

I closed my eyes and breathed through the tenderness as he

continued to bore and roll his taxing thumb over the arch of my cheek.

To the people of the room, Liam was issuing a compassionate, ardent gesture and I, like a loving partner, was absorbing it, relishing it. In reality, I fell into the void in my mind where I could see past the pain, past the fear—the part of me where, only yesterday, I managed to find my escape…

As his hand swept away from my face and the pulsating of my cheek radiated into my eyeball and upper jaw, he told me to leave him and get a drink. While I made my way to the bar through the throng of individuals and white-clothed tables and chairs, I silently hoped and prayed to a higher being, that what just happened was the beginning and the end of yet another penalty for my foolishness and lack of respect.

I gestured to the young man behind the bar who was stacking numerous crystal glasses with a snowy towel draped over his shoulder. His black hair was combed over and stuck to his head with enough styling product, to surely be flammable. Having been given a three drink rule, I asked for a small white wine, when I overheard a faint yet crafty whistle resonate from beside me. Craning my head, I muttered an affronted, "Excuse me?"

The man in a crisp white shirt, navy suit pants and silver tie, lifted the glass bottle to his lips and took a draw before setting it back onto the dark wooden surface of the bar. "Sorry, it's just…" his piercing blue eyes greedily scoured my body as he shook his head with an appraising smirk. "Wow."

By the time my eyes drifted back to the bar, my wine glass sat waiting for me. Offering a measly smile, I wrapped my fingers around the beverage and raised it in a mock toast with an arched brow. "And that was the reaction I was expecting from the boss man," I muttered morosely before caressing the rim with my lips.

"I'm sorry to disappoint you, but I hear he's taken."

"I know." I freed the chilled glass of my grip and leaned into folded arms which were resting on the edge of the bar. Peeking back at the man beside me, I sighed, "I am she."

Incredulous widened eyes gaped back at me, his hand fisted into his light brown hair, causing it to stick up in an attractive, disheveled kind of way. His stubble-coated mouth curved as he offered a smile which dripped with ample embarrassment and showcased straight, white teeth. It was adorable. "Oh, Jesus Christ, I am so sorry. Here, let me buy you another drink."

"It's okay, no offence taken," I snorted as he gestured to the bar tender to get me another drink. Over the brim of my recovered wine glass, my eyes narrowed. "I haven't seen you around before. Are you new?"

The top of his glass bottle lingered on his full, pale lips. When he dragged it away, he nodded. "'Aye, just been signed for this Williamson contract. Who knows whatever's after that?" I smiled briefly at his accent. It was gentle. It was pleasant. It was enthralling.

"Well, let me be the first to welcome you aboard."—I held my hand out politely—"I'm, Kady Jenson."

Staring into ocean blue eyes, I saw the corner of his mouth twitch giving way to a tiny dimple in his left cheek, his shirt tightened over his chest as he breathed heavily. The rough skin of his palm grazed as he wrapped it around my own. "Walker."

"Mr. Walker, it—"

I was cut short by a low, deep chuckle vibrating from his throat. "No, Mr. Just plain, Walker," he corrected me.

"Walker," I tentatively tested the name on my pallet. "Unusual name."

"About as unusual as finding an Irishman in Boston, eh,

Kady?" I was completely thrown by the way my name fell from his mouth. The way his tongue rolled over the 'D', making it sound like 'Katy', was both warming and sensual. It made me smile—a genuine smile, one that touched my eyes and had the shy sophomore I was in high school, resurfacing.

"Fair point," I whispered then motioned my glass in a toast. "Well, welcome aboard, Walker. I am sure they'll find a good use for you."

An elegant clink chimed as the neck of the glass bottle in his hand collided with my wine glass. "'Aye, I'm sure they will, darlin'."

CHAPTER
thirteen

As Walker and I stood talking for a little while at the bar, my body shuddered and bristled. In the back, a sharp stabbing sensation followed by worrisome warmth told me that Liam was casting those menacing, silver daggers in my direction.

By the time I'd silently counted to eight, possessive arms came to snake around my narrow waist. I was drawn back against his immaculately dressed, hard body and a kiss on my temple was planted as he staked his claim on me. I'd never felt so out of sorts as I had done at that point. A ruse…that's what it was. And I knew better than to argue with it and cause a scene.

"Kady baby. I see you've met Walker, the newest of our construction team." To anyone else his tone would've sounded polite and normal. To me, the way he 'casually' dropped the position into conversation was a way to demoralize the man. Like he was a lesser of a man because of the line of work he was in.

I knew that feeling. I knew that feeling well.

My head craned marginally as I twisted into Liam's hold

and felt the throbbing heat of his neck against my face. "Yes, I have," I murmured then pulled my head free and gazed back at the Irishman who was casually resting his back against the wooden bar, his bottle of Bud grasped by the neck as he tipped it up to his lips. "And I think he will be an asset to the team," I smiled.

His pale eyes glimmered and a shy smile tiptoed across his stubble-coated mouth when his bottle was lowered from his lips. "You got a good woman there, Mr. DeLaney." An unnerving sensation rapidly followed his complimented words. My stomach roiled with hushed concern of how Liam would react to such an approval from another man.

The gush of air, which exited Liam's nose in a derisive snort, bonded to the side of my face. "Yes, *I* do." My middle was left bare when possessive hands fell away from my waist only to be replaced upon my upper arms. I was twisted to face him. "Baby, the wives are over there. I'm sure they're all desperate to know exactly how much that dead animal on your back has cost me." His cunning words were a subtle directive, one which would fall blindly to anyone in our company.

A tightlipped, dutiful grin spread across my lips. "Of course."

"Nice to meet you, Kady," the pleasant Irish lilt had momentarily halted my intention of turning away.

In Liam's mistrustful and wary company, I chanced a cautious glance at the Irishman and merely nodded. "You, too, Walker," I replied, and despite being reluctant, made my way toward the opposite side of the room, to be mauled by the plus-ones.

Albeit contrived, I maintained my level of politeness and sociability. Pleasant smiles, high-pitched giggles and intrigued arms were brushed along my body. Those women were vultures. You'd presume they'd never felt leather before, the way their fingertips swept over my arms and shoulders, and their cooing at the way the cut hugged my figure in a sensual although refined fashion, had bells ringing in my ears. All I wanted was to climb back under my rock and never come out.

Words of diaper changes, late night feeds and play dates, were blended into statements of vacations, new cars, designer clothing and someone called Marco who apparently, for a steep fee, can help you drop a minimum of seven pounds in a week. Their comments and topics of discussion seemed trivial in contrast with what contemplations were enjoying the carousel in my mind. Here they were, gushing over Marco and his wonder regime and drool-worthy, athletic body, while my thoughts consisted of: how not to make Liam angry with me, how not to fuck up, how to make things right for him and show him the respect he deserves without sticking my foot in it.

As oblivion sang out to me and my mind wandered over the edge of alertness, the volume of the extravagant housewives of the architects of DeLaney Constructs was barely processed in my mind. That's when I felt it.

While the mother hens clucked on about this and that, a laser beam was shot across the room, commanding my attention as I hung my head and focused on the remnants of golden liquid swimming at the bottom of my wine glass. Only it didn't make my body quake with fear, anxiety or dread.

Over the length of the room, I risked a peek and lifted sad eyes up to be met with the Indian Ocean studying me. His body was somewhat angled, his right elbow rested on the edge of the bar, a dark glass bottle once again, grasped loosely by the neck. The gaze made me feel heated, timid. It felt intense. It felt forbidden.

How one simple motion of his bottle being lifted in a toasting gesture could cause the bridge of my nose to sting and tears form in the corners of my eyes, I have no idea. But it did. When his pale lips tipped into a smile, I felt my heart lurch from my chest and a bead of sweat formed on the nape of my neck. It was too effusive, too unreserved, and the familiar bubble in my stomach and chest—the bubble which always made itself known when I could sense trouble on the horizon—taunted me.

The Irishman licked his lips and offered a deliberate wink; I had to drop my head. I desperately had to focus on something else before Liam jumped the gun, and suspected the worst.

Fifteen minutes later, everyone had taken their places at the tables. Headwaiters rounded us placing deep, white china filled plates at everyone's setting. Sitting next to Liam, I was caught unaware when he pushed himself out of his seat at the head of our table and tapped the surface of the glass with the edge of his fork. Until Liam opened his mouth, silence was governing the room.

"Good evening everyone," he began. "I just want to make a quick speech and then I'll let you get to your meals. I was lucky enough to have two loving parents who taught me to chase a dream. Who taught me that to make a dream a reality, you must first believe that it can be, and transform it into one. Well I had a dream: a dream that my buildings would have a place in the skyline. As Antoine De Saint-Exupery once said, 'A rock pile ceases to be a rock pile the moment a single man contemplates it, bearing within him the image of a cathedral'."

Awed by his words and how much he had achieved, I smiled up at him.

He lifted his glass in a toast. "To DeLaney Constructs and the finalization of the coveted Williamson contract, another blip to place on the map." Everyone followed suit, and as he lowered himself back into his seat with a rendition of 'hear, hear' rebounding around the room, I don't know what I was thinking, but I took a stand. Maybe I shouldn't have had that second glass of wine after all.

"Kady, what are you doing?" Dutch courage had me ignoring Liam's menacing whisper. Encasing his shoulder with my hand, I offered a rewarding, 'trust me' grin with a small wrinkle of my nose.

"I'm sorry, there's one little extra thing I would like to add to that, Liam," I said, an expectant silence governed the room anew as my focus remained fixated on the man to my left. "Firstly, I want to say that I am totally awed by your approach and by everything that you've achieved in such a short time. You've always believed in people, I can attest to that, and giving the opportunity to others and trusting them with your work, to make a dream come true…" I shook my head. "You're an amazing boss, Liam DeLaney—"

"Get him to give us a raise then, Kady," one of the construction workers called out, and a round of applause and catcalls immediately followed.

After rolling my eyes at the dark-haired man with the smart mouth, I lifted my glass in a toast and glanced over the table at Walker, who was sitting opposite me. "And I would like to formally welcome Walker to DeLaney Constructs."

"Thank you, Kady," the Irishman mouthed across the table and as I lowered myself back into my seat, I set a warm, pleasant hand on Liam's thigh beneath the table. With a world of wonderment in my eyes, I smiled at him, and as he smiled back, I knew that my words of admiration and applause had saved my ass from my earlier misdemeanor.

It was just after 11:30 p.m. when all and sundry began to file out of The Hyperion and into their cars to call it a night. Before folding myself into the BMW, I called goodnight to everyone in the parking lot, then allowed the combining sounds of protesting leather of the seat, alongside my dress, to caress my ears as I twisted to recover my seatbelt and drew it across my body.

Sliding in beside me and pulling out of the lot and onto the street, I watched the man at the side of me, closely. The passing streetlamps transformed the side of his studious profile into a rapid blending of oranges before being torn away by the nightly shadows. "Tonight went well," I muttered, approvingly. When he failed to respond, I set my hand on his thigh and issued a supportive squeeze. "Are you okay, Liam? You're being very quiet considering—"

"Considering what, Kady?" he barked, pulling his attention from the road ahead, to me. "Considering all my employees got a visual of Kady the Tart with you in that ridiculous outfit? Or considering I had to sit through hours of you flirting with *my* employees and sticking your fucking nose into *my* business yet again?"

My jaw dropped. I thought we were on the right track. I thought he had excused my mistake…I…

"Well?" he shouted, his enraged hands slammed against the steering wheel. "Gone fucking mute have you, Kady? What fucking button have I got to push to get that reaction from you, so I can use it next time?"

Loosely flailing my head in disbelief, I found myself unconsciously inching closer to the door at my right, placing as much space between myself and the demonic entity behind the wheel. "Liam, I wasn't flirting," I gasped, although spoke softly with great care and wariness weighing down my words of defense as my palm pressed against my chest. "I was being polite, just like I am to the people at the store, or Laurie or the people in the Doctor's Office. I really wasn't flirting."

"She wasn't flirting?" he scoffed. "She can't see the error of her fucking way even when it's being pointed. The. Fuck. Out. To.

Her." He was screaming as he scathingly drew out his final words. He was Goddamn livid. My breathing suddenly hit DEFCON 1. I felt the lamb and mint I hadn't long consumed crawl up my throat. My hands were shaking while the nails of my right hand found their way to the back of my left and scoured at the flesh as though attempting to strip away the harsh words and tone that I was having thrown at me.

Slamming on the breaks, I jolted forward; my hands parted and settled in my lap. "Get out."

Knitting my eyebrows together I made a silent pledge for him to not to do anything rash…not again. "Liam, please—"

The headrest took a beating as he tossed his head back and screamed blue bloody murder. "Get the fuck out of the car!"

"Liam—"

His hasty, heavy hand released my belt and then the door. Before I could register what happened, I was standing on the sidewalk with my purse under my arm, watching my boyfriend once again, speed off down the block, leaving me to make my own way back home in the light misting rain.

Three blocks I had walked in silence, swallowing back my sobs of anger, my sobs of regret. I may not have had a coat, but I was thankful to some degree that each droplet was slowly trickling down the material of my outfit, and not being absorbed by it.

In a dream world, focusing on my own shitty evening, bright headlights shone beside me. "Hey," I heard someone call and with squinted eyes, I turned my focus to the black and silver pick-up slowly moving alongside me. "Kady?" the acquainted brogue caressed my name, the 'D' once again being passed over. "What in Jesus' name are you doing out here in the rain?" he pulled to a stop, as did I. "Where's Liam?"

Through the shower, the empty street was scoured by my

squinted gaze, the orange glow from the streetlamps creating mini spotlights on the asphalt, while steel shutters of several stores were covered in heavy graffiti. "We um…" I dithered. I couldn't be truthful. My own words from that very afternoon rotated around my mind. *Maybe if I believed my lies, other would believe them, too.* But at that moment, the energy involved in maintaining a convincing lie, was nonexistent.

Walker told me to get into the car. Shaking my head I told him I'd be fine, that I needed time to think, all the while considering the extent of Liam's reaction, if he had knowledge that the employee he thought I was flirting with most of the night, was giving me a ride home.

"Where are you heading?"

The slight misting of rain was morphing into a steadily, increasing downpour. Right hand fisting into my hair, I called out over the rhythmic torrent, "Bricksdale."

"Bricksdale? Sod that, darlin', that's a thirty minute walk at the very least." Leaning across the console, the passenger door swung open. "Get in the car," he repeated.

A sliver of control spawned as I weighed up the scenarios of either getting attacked and possibly raped, or having the wrath of Liam on my case for accepting a lift from his employee.

Regardless of any looming ramifications, I made my decision.

I got in the car.

Most of the journey was made in silence. Every now and then I would feel a heated caress from the Irishman's eyes fall onto my flesh. I chanced a glance when we pulled to a stop and saw his focus flitting from the lights ahead, down to my thighs. It wasn't until I peeked down myself and noticed that the lights were shinning on the area of marred flesh from yesterday's incident, that I detected what he was regarding.

In the bench seat I shifted, and attempted to cover the mark as good as I could with a cross of my legs and knitted fingers hanging down.

"Can I tell you something?" he asked, breaking that ear-piercing silence.

I nodded, "Sure."

His hair was combed back by a swift motion of his hand, before tumbling to his throat, and slowly pulled and loosened at the silver necktie. Studying him as he licked his lips, his attention settled on me quickly before rapidly turning back to the road, as we pulled off at the turn of the green light. "The first day I met Liam, I walked into his office and he was all King of The World, or Doctor Evil minus the cat, whichever one. Either way he was sitting behind his desk, back facing towards to the door. When he spun around to face me, do you know what my first thought was?"

I shook my head, my perplexed scowl fixed firmly in place.

"I thought," he craned his focus toward me again. I was sure we were going to end up in some accident if he didn't keep his eyes on the road. "'Fuck me, it's Elmer Fudd.'"

"Elmer Fudd?" Again my head swung, totally missing the punch line.

"Oh, Kady, don't tell me you don't know Elmer Fudd. Give him a shot gun…let him hunt a rabbit…"

The scowl loosened at the same time as I dropped my head. "Oh, my God. Yes, I remember him now. I used to watch it when I was a kid; Walker, that's not nice." I tried to sound firm, but at that moment, my mind was holding up two profile shots side by side, and I couldn't disguise my amusement at the contrast, regardless of how bad it felt. A smile stole across my face as faint giggle vibrated from my throat.

"And there it is."

"There what is?" I asked dubiously, my gaze lifted up at Walker, his attention drawing from the road to me and back again.

"That amazing smile I knew you could crack." Feeling my cheeks flush, I hung my head again. "Just promise me one thing, darlin'."

"Depends what it is."

He chanced a glance at me again. "Don't tell the boss man. I really need this job."

By the time I muttered my compliance, he was holding his hand out to me. I eyed it cynically, as though one touch would be poisonous and near fatal. But I decided to take it anyway.

"Deal."

CHAPTER
fourteen

The house lights were out, but Liam's car was safely in the driveway when Walker dropped me off. I said thank you and wished him the best of luck on his first day at work, which happened to be the following day.

The slamming of the pick-up's door echoed through the night as I dropped onto the sidewalk, and made my way up the steps while rummaging through my purse to find my keys. The warmth of Walker's stare on my back, even when I was stood at the summit of the front steps, was ongoing. It was only when I pushed open the door and stepped inside out of the rain, that I heard him pull off.

Carefully, on the sideboard in the hallway along the balustrade, my clutch purse was set down. Braced by a steady hand, I slipped off my peep-toe heels before I began to advance the stairs.

"Who gave you the lift?" I started as the darkness spoke. Turning my head, I saw the silhouette of Liam's body, his arms crossed over his chest as he rested his shoulder against the right entranceway.

"Liam, you scared me," I rasped, my hand flying up to the center of my chest.

"Who gave you the lift?" he repeated himself, deadpan.

Taking a deep gulp of air, I readied myself for his reaction. "Walker did." When he didn't respond, I simply told him that I was going to go up to bed. It was well after midnight, and I was beyond shattered.

"Wait," my wrist was snared by a surprisingly tender hand, and before I could list what was ensuing, the darkness of the hallway was digressed as I was guided through the lower house and into the brightly lit kitchen. We stood on opposite sides of the island. "I know you're the one who made it, but,"—he lifted the covering off the platter, displaying three-quarters of the coconut cake I'd made yesterday—"Peace offering?" he suggested, brandishing a pout and puppy dog eyes. Still, all I could think of was that damned cartoon character. Walker was going to pay.

You didn't have to be an expert to realize that cake, past midnight, was a terrible idea. Even so, this was a peace offering. An olive branch. An apology. So I nodded. "Okay."

He went about the kitchen, opening cupboards and pulling out drawers before setting two plates, two forks and a knife in front of me on the island. He told me to cut us a slice while he fetched some glasses. I did as I was told.

As we were digging into the midnight treat, Liam muttered around his sponge, "You really did a good job on this, baby. What did you use?"

What did I use? It appeared I wasn't the only one who was clueless when it came to cakes. "Umm…" I swallowed before continuing. "Flour, sugar, coconut…"

Liam set his fork on the plate and strayed from the island, into the fridge.

"Eggs—"

"Eggs? I didn't know we had enough to make something of that size."

The fork lingered on my tongue for a moment longer than necessary before it was gradually pulled from my mouth. "They were large ones, so I only needed three. Why do you ask? Planning on returning the gesture?" I teased through a faint grin. His muscular form had shielded an object which laid in the possession of his left hand. As his body rotated away from the refrigerator and pushed shut one of the huge double doors, my grin was slowly morphing from one of amusement, to one of query.

Liam set out to retrieve another glass from the upper cupboard near the range in an eerie silence. When he assembled all three empty glasses in a line on the island, along with a glass bottle, a glass jar, and the cardboard carton, my heart rate began to pick up a staccato rhythm.

"Liam," his name was shakily drawn out. "What are you doing?"

His large, manicured hand dove into the cardboard carton and he removed a single egg, lifting it up between his fingers. "About this size?" he probed.

With a parched mouth, all I could do was stand there stock-still and nod my head while my guard was lifted.

The white casing was parted by his fingers as soon as a tiny crack appeared after being tapped against the rim of one of the waiting glasses. The gooey, transparent contents slithered its way into the tumbler while I whined his name again. Still, my blatant nerve-wracked tone was falling on deaf ears as he repeated cracking two more eggs, releasing the slimy substances into the remaining glasses.

"Everything in life begins with an experiment, Kady." The look of pure concentration veiling his features as he opened the large glass jar was terrifying. So chilling in fact, that it caused my body to be overridden by each jagged breath and pressing, suppliant words daren't pass my lips. "Here in this jar, we have my favorite. What is my favorite, Kady?"

I forced a swallow. And although I had lowered my head to evade the unhinged glazed coating of his hardened eyes, I could see in my peripheral vision that he was pouring the clear liquid into one of the egg filled glasses. This was too familiar. Immobilized by dread, it felt as though I was choking on my heart. I knew what was going to happen. I just hoped with everything I had, that my theory of what was about to transpire was in fact wrong.

"Favorite, Kady, now. What is it?" he raised his voiced, snapping his fingers impatiently in the air.

"Deviled eggs," I gasped in terror, the corners of my mouth trembled in sheer revulsion.

To combat my body's natural reaction of lifting my head as he applauded me with his 'good girl' praise was unviable. His jaw was set, his mouth curved more so, as terror carved its way deeper into my profile.

"Here we have one of your favorites,"—he pointed a cautionary finger at me and cocked his head—"So don't tell me that I don't think of you."

Think of me? How was that thinking of me? I should be thankful that something I enjoyed was going to end up with the same fate as Liam's remnants of deviled eggs? My stomach flipped and knotted, my face contorted as I studied him tipping, not a few drops of Tabasco sauce in the glass, but near enough a quarter of the bottle.

"Liam, please; you've made your point. Please, don't do

this." Tears of horror, alarm and distress accumulated in my eyes, testing the boundaries of the dam which I'd set in place. Blinking, the dam burst and the evidence of my panic were left to liberate themselves by tumbling over my lids and wetting my lashes.

"Don't do this?" Those three words were spoken mercifully, his eyes soft. Through his arms he braced his weight while grasping the edge of the island and dropping his weight through his hip. "Kady, you leave me no choice. Why should I listen to you when you don't listen to me? You never learn." And just like that, the demonic mask was shifted back into place, and that bloodcurdling smirk spread like wildfire across his shaven face. "Now, what could we use for experiment three?"

How could he be enjoying this? The upbeat tone in his voice, the expression of indifference on his face, it was like he was manic. I was his girlfriend, his partner, not some disobedient dog that needed punishing. The way his eyes had thawed along with his voice made me feel a shard of hope that he would relent and see what he was doing more clearly. But my hopes were shattered along with my heart as he continued with his torturous mind games.

Back facing me, he was rummaging inside one of the cupboards again when he called out 'yes' like he just stumbled upon some victorious notion. The entire contents of my queasy stomach rose as my body was inundated with dry heaves. "This will work perfectly…just as well you're not on a diet, right, Kady?" he stated, digging a dessert spoon into the tub of Crisco. With the pad of his thumb and an upturn of his lip, he glided down the surface of the metal, causing the fat to drop and push its way through the substance in the glass, like a baseball through slime. "I think we better mix this one up a little," with his words, he used his fork to whisk the egg and fat together before pushing all three occupied glasses in front of me.

Convulsions to a degree of which my body was unable to suppress, were prompted by the demented smirk he was exhibiting. Studying his torturous, vile creations ahead of me, horror, remorse and dry heaves were spawning each second. "Liam, please…"

He lifted his finger in the air to halt my words. "You have a choice."

Choice? I have a choice? He was going to let me choose? For a brief moment I found myself thanking the heavens. I couldn't withstand that scale of oppression. I'd do anything else, anything other than *that*. Dread, fear, revulsion, it was all pushed aside to make way for hope and gratitude.

A broadened smile and menacing eyes bore into me and took pleasure from my begging. His hand dug into his suit pants pocket. When he pulled it out, his large hand was masking, what I guessed, was my alternative. Setting it on the wooden surface of the island, I simply stared, silently willing his hand to move. A pack of Marlboro Red was uncovered with the removal of his hand.

What the fuck was this?

My hopeful expression faded into oblivion, and at that moment in time, I would have been more than willing to jump feet first into that void to reclaim it. My gaze scoured up to meet his face—his irrational, deranged face.

Unspoken optimism defeated, I shook my head as my brow knitted in sheer disbelief. He knew how I felt about smoking. Watching my granddad coughing and spluttering, while he fought for breath with an oxygen mask as he battled the final months of lung cancer because of those poisonous sticks, still haunted me.

"Liam—" I besought.

"Choose."

Salted droplets of misery and distress rolled down my cheeks and over my dried, cracked lips as I stood powerless with my head hanging low.

"CHOOSE!" he shouted, his enraged body physically shaking as he took possession and hurled the platter with the cake I delighted in creating, across the room. I jumped, drawing back from his formidable demand.

Within a split second of the din reverberating around the kitchen and dining room, my fingers were bound around the first glass. Tears came faster as I tipped the raw, slimy goo back, hurriedly. The vinegar tang was intense as the acid burned my lips as it settled into each crack of my parched lips. The quicker I got this done, the quicker it would be over, right?

With one down, two more to go, the pungent aroma of the Tabasco sauce scorched my sinuses, and although it hadn't even slithered down my food pipe yet, I could already taste it lingering in my throat, paralyzing my swallowing reflex and stripping me of breath. I thought the vinegar burning my lips was bad, I was very much mistaken. The blazing fire which smeared over my tongue and down my throat, as I pushed through on the task ahead, knocked all breath from my body. My ribcage screamed in protest as I fought with every ounce of strength I had to keep my stomach muscles clenched and hold the contents down.

But as my throat opened and my shoulders roiled, the dry heaves which was spawning in my body wasn't so dry.

Liam was already beside me. I could feel his smirk, and I heard it through his voice when he fisted his hand into the hair at the back of my head and wrenched my neck back. "Be warned, Kady," soft and enriched, his tone was totally uncaring and laid-back. "I have another three eggs in that carton. If you don't want to repeat this, I suggest you keep that down," he sneered.

I made damn sure to take heed of his words. I forced the regurgitated concoction back, and with the finishing line of this sick penalty just beyond one final mixture, I picked up the tumbler, and chucked it back. The lumps of fat sat on my tongue as I strove to force the lump-filled, slimy mixture down my gullet, the odd larger mass loitered and wedged in my throat. My ribs felt compressed, while my stomach contorted and pleaded for my body to expel the disgusting concoctions that lay assaulting it. In my mind, only five simple words were playing on repeat, 'I can't do this again'. With that repeating as my mantra, mind over body, the contents stayed put…at least for now.

Breathless and focusing intently on not throwing up, I dropped my head, screwed my eyes closed and allowed a moment of relief to flood through my veins. God I felt sick. "I'm sorry, Liam," I whispered after a beat. "Can I go to bed now please?" I needed to get away from that room, from that spot. For the first time that I can recall, I needed to get away from him and his torturous, sadistic means.

I lifted my head and fluttered open my lids, feeling the dampness of tears still coating my lashes, as my question remained unanswered and floating in the air between us. I didn't like what was glaring back at me.

Wave upon wave of goose bumps erupted from my body when I was met with him leaning over the island. His fingertips hooked around the bottom edge of the pack of cancer-sticks and were drawn closer to us. The wrapper was unraveled, the lid was flipped. One of the ten sticks was removed before Liam proceeded to dig into his back pocket.

"Liam, what are you doing? You told me to choose, I did. I did what you said…" Please, please dear Lord, don't tell me I did it all for no reason. Let that be the end of it. Please…

"Oh, no," he laughed, a V scored between his eyebrows as he stared at me with a look of pity in his eyes. He placed a lighter on the surface. "You misunderstood, Kady. I meant choose which one you wanted to do *first*."

My face crumpled then plummeted. I couldn't describe how I felt at that precise moment because I was being overthrown by so much. I felt nauseated, fright, sorrow. I felt a form of betrayal melding with stupidity.

"But, because you did such a great job..." he trailed off, his eyes glimmering. Yes, I did. I did as he said without question, and more importantly, I kept it down, if only just. I didn't have to study my reflection to know that I obviously looked like I was struggling to keep the contents of my stomach where it was. Maybe he would stop this. "I won't make you do this." His words were a life raft. As he enhanced his freed words with a brusque shake of his head, I slumped and drew in a liberal breath. I knew he wouldn't be so ruthless.

I opened my mouth to verbalize my gratitude, when his hand came up to cradle my face. I was leaning into his touch when he whispered on a smirk, "Not all of them, anyway."

What? I backed-up, pulling away from his gentle hold as his remark hit me full force in the face.

Each tear that fell from my eyes during the time it took me to complete his orders of chain-smoking five of the ten cigarettes in the pack, then having my lungs grated as both fire and chemicals burned and coated my chest, alongside the lightheadedness and ringing in my ears as vital oxygen in my brain was superimposed by the deadly chemicals in the smoke, had Liam smirking even more. He looked barbaric. Sadistic.

By the time I reached the third stick, the grating of my lungs had disappeared, the smoke caught in my chest and throat but I was no longer spluttering. My head was no longer spinning, and the ringing was not as loud as it once was.

By the time I reached my final stick, I peeked up at Liam and I was graced with his eyes, my Liam's eyes, green and blue speckled ones that displayed his elation, love and adoration toward me. Not sadistic, demonic, evil, merciless eyes that were being bored into me for the past twenty minutes.

Outing the butt of the cigarette, Liam's arms came crashing down around me. He held me tightly as I went emotionally numb in his hold. No tears left to cry, no fear left to cling onto, no love to help me through…just stillness. In that moment, I felt utterly stripped down. I secretly mused what on Earth I had left to carry me through my days, through my life. Pathetic. That's how I truly felt.

"You won't do it again, will you, Kady?" he asked amongst my hair.

Too exhausted to say a single word, I simply rolled my head across his chest in a silent 'no'.

"Good girl, because I don't like having to do this, baby. I really don't like it." Those words were the last to be spoken, as I was lifted into his arms and finally taken to bed.

"Liam," I called while rolling out of bed.

It was still dark outside. If it hadn't have been for the overflow of saliva swimming in my mouth and down my chin, I would have checked the clock for the time. But my stomach was rolling, my ribcage tightened with such force I was sure vital organs were going to get crushed.

"Liam," I called again, staggering into the en-suite beyond the base of the bed. I barely managed to flip the light switch before bowling over the toilet and allowing my stomach to be emptied.

I hated being sick. I feared it. And when the burning of

stomach acid affected my throat and nose and stopped me from catching a breath, all I could do was gasp and swallow continually in a feeble attempt to quell the paralyzing, fiery sensation.

I succeeded in shouting his name again, and within a few minutes, he was standing in the doorway of our bathroom, watching me as I drowned my face in the bowl and submitted to my body's heaves. "What?" he asked.

Seeking a window of opportunity between lurches, I lifted my face and transfixed my unsteady gaze on him. He was standing with his arms crossed, his eyes hardhearted. I noticed he was in his gray sweatpants and white T-shirt. I briefly wondered why he hadn't come to bed yet, while tears streamed down my cheeks.

"Please, help m—" My shoulders hunched, my body tightened while the remains of my gut were cast into the toilet. "Please, help me," I gasped between lurches.

"I'm in the middle of a very important phone call, Kady," he hissed then disappeared from the doorway back into the bedroom.

Phone call? At this hour? I didn't know what time it was, but I knew it was definitely late, or early, whichever way you look at it.

When he came back to the bathroom, my head was resting on my forearm, tears and sweat melded on my face as I heard his bare feet padding toward me over the tiles. "Here," he mumbled.

Gathering as much energy as I could physically muster, I pulled my head up and away from my arm. The pillow and tiny, thin comforter which he had thrown down on the floor was studied. The hefty sensation of abandonment crushed me both internally and externally. "Liam…"

"Self-inflicted, Kady. You wouldn't be in this state, had you not done what you did. Now, if you'll excuse me, I have a very important phone call to get back to."

"Liam, please don't leave me. I need you," I begged.

Nevertheless my beseeching words went unheeded and he turned on his heel, walked away closing the door behind him and left me to appease my stomach after such brutal assault, on my own.

The contents of the bowl were flushed. Falling back onto the pillow, I pulled the barely there blanket over my trembling body. Like an unmanageable canine, I curled up on the cold tile, adding my wrongdoings of the day to my ever growing list of delinquencies in a hope to have it burned into my mind, and avoid a repeat penalty.

For the remainder of that night, I licked my wounds and silently apologized for just being me.

CHAPTER
fifteen

May 2012.
Thirteen months before the accident…

Days blended into weeks. Weeks blended into months, and before I knew it, every moment of my day was shrouded by one objective: to make Liam happy.

After the dreaded night I spent laying curled up on the cold bathroom floor, I came to realize that, with each passing week you slip back into the comfort zone and old habits get reestablished. The relationship as it was would be fine once I had paid penance to Liam's standard. He would be happy because I'd fulfilled his demands and showed responsibility for my actions, and I would spend the following few weeks with both the memory of my punishment, and the behavior which caused the need for the vile act to be set forth, still freshly laid in my mind. Focusing intently on those two major factors helped me to see things from a different perspective. And so, every waking moment of my day was spent concentrating on those factors profusely, and in doing so, there was no reason for Liam to be overtaken by the demonic entity which I was used to seeing.

Each moment I spent observing my behavior: not speaking unless I was spoken to, making sure that if I was to buy clothing, it would be something that I knew definitively that Liam would approve of. Near enough everything on my rail in our closet, at that point, was the same just in a different color.

Some would consider my acts as a weakness, ones of a person who had to continually walk on eggshells. Did I consider it as such? No, I didn't. I was being mindful, I was being empathetic of what my partner wanted me to be, and I was making sure with every blurred day which passed, that I was remolding myself into someone he was proud of, and not falling back into the ways of the old Kady Jenson.

Time was mostly spent in the kitchen. Over the interval I had picked up quite a knack in baking. Nothing could describe the warmth I felt in my heart and the pride in my blood at seeing the huge grin I'd be rewarded with as Liam came home from work, kissed my temple and salivated over my next surprise creation, knowing full well that I had made it especially for him. In saying that, as much as I enjoyed concocting coconut cakes, lemon, chocolate etc., etc., I came to the realization that I was a moth, and the heat which surrounded me was my flame.

Following Liam's discovery of my act of self-harm, I'd come to an embarrassing conclusion. People tarnish the unknown and the misunderstood. No one could possibly understand how an act which provides pain could even help in that moment of dire urgency. I'd lost control, not in the act, but in the buildup. That act, that moment of insanity or weakness, it gave me back an element of control, I felt it the instant the heat penetrated my flesh. If I wanted to keep something which was solely mine—my own little secret, my own sliver of control—then enveloping myself in an atmosphere where little *mishaps* happen, would be the perfect way to keep my secret and draw a veil over the topic. I'm not going to lie; it was an aid, an aid which was vastly becoming a necessity. Granted, the gradual accumulation of blemishes over my thighs would probably disagree with the conclusion of facilitating.

It was a Thursday late afternoon and Liv and I were sitting at the dining table huddled over the swirling steam from our coffee mugs, chatting about random crap, but mostly, just catching up. It seemed like forever since we last had a decent, in depth talk and just enjoyed the company of one another. She seemed to always be busy with this new guy of hers.

When Liv's throaty voice traveled over the table, I was already drawing the ceramic from my lips, and lowering my mug onto the coaster. "Chick, can I ask your advice? And I mean I want total honesty."

This should be fun. One thing I knew was no matter what was said, nothing was going to sully our friendship. We may not have had the same beliefs and values but as adults, we respected that contrast. I nodded. "Shoot."

Her plump lips were caressed with a swipe of her tongue before her chest expanded then deflated on a troubling sigh. "Do you think I'm in the wrong for fucking that guy?"

The edge of my mug was unconsciously traced by my middle finger, as I concentrated distantly on the action and on my words. "The guy who is in a pretty stable relationship and using you as a mistress, all the while his poor girlfriend is the one preparing his meals and making sure he has a nice home to return to, after finishing his rendezvous with you?" the sardonic tone in my voice went unmasked as I spewed my words.

"There's no need to be so harsh, Kady. But yes,"—Peeking

up, I noticed her rolling her eyes—"that guy."

For a moment I pushed myself back in the white leather seat. A hissing, gargling sound came from my lips as I sheathed my teeth and sucked in a breath through the diminutive gap. "I think that there are plenty of men out in the world who are single. I also think—" drawing a pause on my words, with a scowl, I eyed Liv circumspectly. "We're going for brute honesty?" I quizzed.

The frantic nod of her head told me to continue.

Okay, she'd asked for it. "I think that you're being heartless and insensitive." Hazel eyes glazed as fire and affront shone through her panic. Opening her mouth to speak, I cut her off with the lifting of my index finger then pressed it against my lips like a tutor in kindergarten. She took my advice and grimly shut her mouth. "It's code. A woman shouldn't betray another woman like that. How do you think she's feeling?"

The slight snigger which followed the shake of her head triggered a form of incense which heated my blood and knotting my stomach. "It's not my fault she can't see what's happening in front of her eyes, Kady. Why should I feel guilty?"

"Because you're breaking up a happy home," was the simplest, most pungent reply I could mutter.

"If it was a happy home,"—she took another sip of coffee and swallowed before resuming with her head held high and conceited—"then he wouldn't have come to me in the first place."

Who was this woman sitting in front of me? She looked like Liv, but the Liv I knew for many years wouldn't stoop as low as that. Although a stripper, she demanded to be treated with respect. I couldn't understand why she would demoralize herself to the extent of believing she had conviction in being 'the other woman', like it was her right.

I was about to bite back on her last statement when I heard

the front door close and Liam came strolling through the bottom entranceway of the living room, into the dining room. He skimmed over my regard and focused directly on the woman opposite, her tousled brunette hair draped over her shoulders. "Liv," he spoke her name but made it sound like a question, as though silently asking 'what the fuck are you doing here'?

"Liam," she replied over the brim of her mug when she lifted it to her mouth.

"I wasn't expecting to see you here," The black leather and gold trimmed briefcase was set carefully down on the glass surface of the table as he turned to me, practically ignoring our guest. "Hey, baby," he muttered my greeting and as he pressed his lips to my forehead, I smiled, like it was an honor to have this PDA.

"Liam, how was work?" I asked like any dutiful wife would. My body was left cold when he strolled to the refrigerator and took out a bottle of mineral water.

"It was good. The final plans have been set, what was left of the old Williamson Estate is now knocked to the ground, so I can get the team in ASAP."

"That's brilliant news."

"Yes, it is. Which reminds me,"—my eyes followed him as he took well-measured strides from the corner of the kitchen island, back to my side and set a warm hand on my shoulder—"I think we should go out tonight, go and have a meal somewhere, make the most of things?"

Make the most of things? I had no indication of what he meant by that. As though he was noting my silent question, he answered, "With all the changes over the last few months, the move, the contract…us." His gaze drifted from my tightlipped, querying grin, to the woman whose boobs were spilling over the low rectangle-cut of her cream top. "Liv, are you up for it?"

"It's my night off, sitting home with a tub of ice-cream and shit TV, or going out with my two favorite people…" she flailed her head and upturned her lips. "No contest. Count me in."

My shoulder burned with Liam's expectant stare. "Well?"

Tipping my head back, I muttered apologetically, "I told Laurie that I would cal—" only to have my statement cut short.

"Invite her, too."

"What?"

"Invite her along." His gaze diverted from me, back to the brunette opposite cradling a mug of coffee in her hands. He finished with a cocky tip of his lips, "The more the merrier, right?"

As I rose from my seat, the legs protested and grated across the tiled flooring, and I hooked my hair back behind my ear. "Okay, well, only if you're sure though."

"I wouldn't say it if I wasn't sure." He leaned in and placed a chaste kiss on my lips. When he pulled back, he mouthed, "You deserve it."

Oh Liam. You don't half spoil me, I thought to myself with a smile, then excused myself to the foyer and dialed Laurie's number.

After a few annoying drills of the connecting call, I was greeted by her familiar buoyant tone. Once the brief small talk was over, I reiterated Liam's decision of going out for a meal, and that he extended an invite to her also, considering Liv was tagging along.

"Kady, I'd love to, but I kind of promised my cousin that he could pop over and order shitty food."

The small of my back rested against the sideboard against the stairs. "I'm sure Liam wouldn't mind if you brought him along as well. He did say, 'the more the merrier'," I answered while I folded my right arm over my middle.

"Really? Liam said that?" Her questioning tone and fleeting moment of disbelief mirrored my own. Nevertheless, I wasn't going to argue with him, his decisions, or begin an interrogation. It's those moves which had always landed me in Shit Street.

Once she finally relented, Liam craned his head around the doorframe. I covered the mouth piece with my right hand. "She asked where and when?" I whispered.

"Hamersley's Bistro, 8:00 p.m."

"Hamersley's at 8?" I relayed down the speaker.

"Hamersley's? Goodness, he is pushing the boat out. I'd be happy with a slice of pizza from Jasper's." our moment of amused snorting came to an abrupt end as I studied Liam and his dubious glare which he was throwing at me.

"We'll meet you there, Laurie. See you soon." With the handset set on its cradle once I ended the call, I turned my focus to the impeccably dressed man in the doorway. You'd never suspect he had just finished nearly twelve hours at work. "She said thank you, and they'll meet us there."

His pants pockets were slightly weighed down as his hands hung loosely in them. His lower lip was caressed by his tongue as he focused on his feet with each leisurely stride toward me. "They?" he questioned, his feet scuffing the wooden flooring with menacing strides, causing and my heart rate to increase.

Fuck.

"She was supposed to be spending time with her cousin, I'm sorry Liam. You said the more the merrier, so I just assumed that it would be okay to invite him along." Eyes screwed, I felt the wrinkles span across my forehead while my neck and shoulders gave into the weight bored upon it. My head began to fall forward and shoulders began to slouch. "God, I am so stupid, what was I thinking? I'm sorry—"

"Hey," my face was coated by his minty breath, while his hand rose to cradle my cheek. I suppressed the urge to flinch. When my head was coaxed upward to meet his scrutiny, I was chanced by soft, forgiving eyes looking back at me. "Please stop worrying. It is okay, I did say that, and I meant it—"

"But I had no right to assume it in the first place. Liam, please forgive me. I'm so, so sorry." His handsome, benevolent face was beginning to swim and distort as tears assembled and glazed over my pale blue eyes.

"I forgive you, Kady." As the words were freed from his lips, I felt myself physically lax, and when his mouth slanted over mine and his tongue dipped into my mouth as I gave him an opening, my tears dissolved. "Now go upstairs and get yourself ready," he breathed against my mouth when he pulled away. His warm, gentle hand lingered on my face, his thumb caressing the arch of my cheekbone. "Maybe wear that mint green blouse with those dark jeans. You know how much I love it on you."

"Okay," I nodded and stepped out of his clutch, his hand dropping from my face. I was rewarded with a small smack on the ass, when I turned on my heel to head for the stairs, and he went back to into the dining room to keep Liv company.

Liam and Liv filed into the BMW while I rummaged through my purse for my keys and locked the front door. Their hushed conversation was brought to an abrupt end when I slipped into the front passenger seat, and concluded with Liv playfully swatting his left shoulder from the back seat. "Okay, children, less of that, let's get going because I am starving," I teased lightly drawing the belt across my body.

Liam was just about to pull out of the driveway when his hand came down on my thigh. "You look gorgeous."

My heart melted. I took his advice and opted for my dark,

skinny jeans and pale mint, silk blouse with gold buttons and matching green heels. My hair was twisted and clipped into place, giving me nothing to hide behind, just how Liam liked it. Gazing into his eyes for an eternity, my lips tipped into a content smile. "Thank you."

"Okay, come on, enough with the mushy talk," the voice from the back seat griped, and I couldn't help but snigger. If only she knew how much I appreciated this degree of, 'mushy talk'.

"Why, Liv, making you jealous?" Liam teased, staring intently in the rearview mirror as he began pulling out of the driveway.

"Nauseous, more like."

I shook my head to myself, thinking that when she finds the man of her dreams, she will be the first to revel in 'mushy talk'.

It was 7:55 p.m. when we pulled up outside the restaurant and Liam handed the keys, along with a substantial tip, to the valet parking before linking out fingers together and leading us to the olive green entrance.

I scanned the area and peeked back at the man beside me. "What about Laurie? She's not here yet."

His warm, soft fingers had already begun to come loose around my own as Liv muttered, "We can go in and get a table, and you can wait for Laurie, right Liam?"

"Yeah, that's a good idea. Will you be okay with that, baby?"

Liv was already holding the door open when I smiled and nodded my acquiescence. I watched as they stepped inside, Liam's hand resting on the small of her back as he steered her into the warmth of the bistro, as I waited alone in the chilly breeze.

A stone rolled under my foot, as I sluggishly perused the area decorated with two green metal benches, potted ferns and the large green awning over the door. Lots of green, I thought to myself, and idly contemplated the chance of the interior matching the pallet of the exterior, when a bubbly, high voice shrieked, "Hey, girlie."

By the time I lifted my head, Laurie was bouncing her way toward me, her black hair was loose, tumbling past her shoulders, while the splash of cosmic blue dye spruced her bangs.

Cosmic blue...

Memories of my sister and her beauty mishap refused to stay dormant. As I strived to shake the thought out of my head, where it should no longer dwell, arms of the petite, pale woman, had by now encompassed me and were ruthlessly squeezing me like a ragdoll.

"Laurie, you made it," I strained returning her embrace.

"Yeah, sorry I'm late," she nudged her head into the direction she just surfaced from while holding me at arm's length. "You can blame him."

"'Blame me' says the woman who spent fifteen minutes admiring herself. That's love for you right there."

Showered by familiarity, I peeked up and watched as the man strolled toward the entrance. His brown hair was longer on the top and left slightly disheveled as he raked his hand through prior to letting it go limp at his side. The white T-shirt beneath his navy and caramel plaid shirt was exposed as his left hand sat peacefully in his beige denim pants pocket, trapping the one-side of the shirt behind his forearm.

"Hey, Kady, nice to see you again."

My eyes bulged out of their sockets, and my mouth went dry. I turned my attention back to the secretive woman beside me. "Walker is your cousin?"

"What?" her shoulders practically touched her ears. "You never asked."

"But, you're not Irish."

"Technically, it's only by marriage. My uncle married her

aunt," Walker clarified.

With an exasperated shake of my head, I gestured toward to entrance, muttering, "Six degrees of separation is everywhere you turn."

Shuffling into the warmth of the establishment, we were instantly drowned by pristine cream walls and bright white light from the hanging candelabras, the glow reflected off the surface of the surrounding mirrors and glass paneled doorways which lead into a more intimate, smaller dining area. Patrons sat at their crisp white covered tables, adorned with fresh white lilies in the center as glistening crystal glasses waited to be filled.

The maître d' led the way, weaving past scattered tables as we made our way through the bistro, where we emerged in the smaller dining area. Four spacious wrought iron candelabras hung from wooden beams, while a bar extended across the length of the right wall. Square tables were covered in the same crisp, white lining cloths and decorated with beautiful, white lilies just as they were in the larger room. This area may have been intimate; the glow may have been subtler, though it didn't lack elegance by any means.

My paranoia whispered taunting words when I sighted Liam and Liv, once again, in hushed conversation when we made our way to join them. He was smiling and nodding at something she had said, when his eyes became rigid as gestured toward us with a tip of his brow.

Rising from his seat as we neared, he snaked his left arm around my waist, drawing me into his side. "Kady," his barely audible voice became even fainter as his lips slanted over mine. The maître d' scuttled off back to his position by the time I lowered myself into the waiting seat.

"Laurie, Walker," he nodded his acknowledgement to each of

our little party as they took their places opposite.

"Boss," Walker responded, mirroring his nod. It still seemed strange hearing someone calling my boyfriend boss.

I introduced the Irishman to Liv, who extended her arm over the table for a friendly handshake, before she went back to focusing on Liam. "Shall we browse and order then?" she asked, handing us each a menu, and it was one of the best suggestions I had heard all day. I was famished.

Within minutes, the young waiter was signaled over to our table of five, with his notepad and pen in hand.

"We will have two of the grilled New Zealand venison, one of the deviled eggs with house smoked salmon and caper aioli, and two of the garlic roast chicken."

Liam had barely finished placing the order when I looked up at the young, smartly dressed gentleman and added, "Extra garlic—" The entire table fell into a deathly silence when my words were shadowed by Walker's reiteration. Our eyes locked across the table as shy smiles danced across our features. How could something so innocent, feel so illicit?

"Not another self-confessed garlic freak," Laurie jeered, her tone playful. Even so, her speech was merely a muffle in my ears as Walker and I continued examining each other. "How did I not know that about you?"

Flailing my head and lifting my shoulders, I was becoming somewhat nervous about the reaction this could prompt in Liam. Yes, it was a trivial chancing, but it was something that I had in common with another *male*. Taking into consideration that he thought I was flirting with his employee the last time I was in his company, I didn't like the chances that he would possibly twist something in that head of his, and insinuate I was doing it again. Or maybe I was and I just couldn't see it.

Either way, I wasn't going to continue standing on the railway tracks while I waited for Freight Train Liam to come hurling toward me. As a result, I tore my gaze away from the man smirking affectionately ahead of me and hung my head low. For my own peace of mind, I remained mute with my focus aimed into my lap while the waiter scurried off to the kitchen.

"So, Kady how's the baking coming along?" Laurie questioned over the table, placing her fork into her left hand and retrieving her glass of Shiraz, taking a welcome sip.

"Really well actually; you were right. It is relaxing." I craned my head to the man sitting at my right with that deviled egg on his plate dredging up some difficult memories. In spite of everything, I locked them back in the steel encased box at the back of my memory, and only focused on the behavior I demonstrated that monstrous night, which resulted in my fate. I wouldn't act that way again. "Liam's enjoying them, too." I forced a grin.

"You know, there are courses you can go on to further those skills, Kady."

"Further?" so much caution dripped from that lone word.

"There are plenty of courses which help teach the art of *actually* decorating them. They usually only run for a few weeks, but they teach you everything you need to know."

"You know," Liam interjected, pointing and waving his fork in a loose grasp, in Laurie's direction. "That is a really good idea."

"I don't know, I don't think I'd be very good around new people. I—"

"Kady, this could really open up some doors for you. I think it's an amazing idea."

"But what about—"

"No, don't worry your pretty little head over it. I'll sort out everything," he winked.

And just like that, I felt that same fisted, irate feeling consume me when I realized that, once again, I didn't have a choice in this. This wasn't a decision I could make, it wasn't a decision I was being *allowed* to make. What made it even worse: Liam was going to be the one forking out the costs for all of this…failure wasn't going to be an option. In that lapsing moment, I dreaded the consequences of if I did indeed fail.

The fork was carefully set to the side of my plate as my hand lifted to my throat. I couldn't sit there for a moment longer, I felt like I was being smothered, I couldn't breathe, I couldn't focus on anything other than being forced into something which should have been optional, instead, Liam had just made it mandatory. My head was fogging, my breathing ragged.

All I desperately wanted was to just slam my hands down on that crisp white table and tell everyone to back the fuck off, that it was *my* life, *my* options, and *my* fucking decisions. Oxygen caught in my throat, the buzzing in my ears made my vision shake. I had to get away. Urgently.

"I need to use the restroom," I excused myself, and slipped my clutch purse under my arm as I headed to the privacy of the ladies with one sole purpose.

I locked myself in one of the empty stalls, feeling like some fugitive. With the toilet seat lowered, I perched myself on the edge and folded myself over to frantically empty the contents of my purse over the cream tiled flooring, totally uncaring of the thunderous clattering. Cell phone…purse…cards…bills…

The inner-side zipper was hastily opened, and I yanked out a small, metal nail file and held it between my fingers like it was my lifeline—the silver edge reflecting the overhead halogens. Breathing still rough and my thoughts still clouded, I shunted myself from the toilet, undid my jeans and lowered them over my hips, down to mid-thigh.

Panic and alarm, trepidation and angst, so many overwhelming emotions surged through my body, making me physically tremble and heated tears gathered in my eyes. He took it away from me... again, and in the presence of our friends...

I didn't feel like a grown woman. Dammit, I was twenty-five but made to feel like a reduced being that needed her actions in life dictated at every turn. I needed it back; I needed something I had power over, something I could manage.

With that sole thought, that one purpose, I pressed the shiny hooked edge of the file against my thigh. But it didn't help. My head was still a haze of anger and resentment, so I pressed it in deeper. Still nothing I frantically sought was regained.

I needed, even just for an idle moment, to feel and salvage that sliver of control.

I felt the abrasion of the file slipping and grazing between the surfaces of my fingertips as I pushed the implement into my leg with exacting force.

Harder...

A slow burning and a somewhat bruising sensation began to encircle the area being gradually impaled.

Tears fell; yet, I pushed harder...

Stifling a whimper, I tipped my head back. There it was: that sharp stabbing sensation. The burning of my flesh circled around the skewer as I speared it into my thigh. It hurt like Hell—a raw, tender throbbing, which soon radiated down the tissue of my leg in regularity of the pulse in my neck. I'd reached my limit.

Breathe in...breathe out...in...out...slowly...methodically...

Gradually decreasing the pressure which I bore upon the tool with each stable and balanced inhalation, the racing, unsteady thoughts began to stabilize and regulate. I was drawn back; the pain was my lighthouse in the dark, overpowering tide of the stormiest seas.

My eyes closed as twin tears glided down my cheeks, and I sunk into my moment of tranquility and lucidity. My grip on the file released sending it plummeting and clattering onto the tile of the stall.

As I sat back in the privacy of the restroom stall, my head dropped forward. Concrete may well had been coating my arms with how weighed down they felt. While I sank back into the world around me, my feet tingling against the solidity of the ground beneath them, I felt, for a brief moment, serene, unperturbed and gratified that *I* was the one who had control, for that one diminutive moment.

CHAPTER
sixteen

"What happened, you get lost in there, Kady?" Walker joked as I rejoined our little party, taking my seat opposite him.

The tender wince and a soft catching of air in my throat were ignored, when Liam set his hand on the tender puncture of my right thigh. "You okay?" he asked.

Once I muttered that I was fine, *'I'm sexy and I know it'*, began to resonate from Liv's phone. God she really was self-assured. Damn…was I ever like that? She didn't bother excusing herself to take the call, she simply answered from the comfort of her seat, and I found my subtle gaze centering on Walker who was frowning at me for some God forsaken reason. It was as if he could see through my pretense, could notice that I had to take care of a need that was no longer optional for me. When I rubbed the nape of my neck with my left hand and offered a tiny, tightlipped grin, the creases in his forehead began to loosen and his mouth, coated in prickly scruff, began to lift as he nodded his head.

"Damn you, Benny," she hissed with a jab of her thumb on the 'end-call' button and stuffed it into her purse. "I'm so sorry. Looks like I'm going to have to leave you all to your devices. One of the girls is sick so I've been called in," she muttered rearing from her seat and shrugged on her little denim jacket.

"You need a lift?"

"A lift would be fantastic, thank you, Liam."

"You know, maybe we should all call it a night. It's getting kind of late anyway." I began to shift from my seat when Liam's hand crashed down on my shoulder, halting my intention.

"The night is still young," he smiled. "Here," the credit card was fished out of his wallet then placed into my palm. "I'll take Liv, you settle the bill, and you two,"—his gaze lifted to Laurie and Walker. Pointing his finger, he tethered them with an invisible line— "show my girl a good time. She deserves it."

Walker nodded his acknowledgment, "Boss."

"I mean it, if she's home before midnight, I'll know she didn't have a good time and you'll be fired."

The words Liam spoke had stunned me. I was in a wary yet slightly gratified daze. The clashing of silverware on plates and generalized chitchat that engulfed the restaurant, fell away, only to be replaced by a galling, muffled buzzing. My protective and possessive boyfriend was giving permission to the man, who was one of the reasons for his last vile deed, to show me a good time? Deep down in the pit of my gut and floating around in my mind was one query: was this some kind of test? I didn't know. I didn't know what the right answer to this conundrum was. Either way, I knew I was fucked.

As Walker held his hands up in a gesture of defeat and stated, "No need to tell me twice, Boss," Liam's tall body had already leaned down and planted a swift kiss on my head.

As I sat back in the padded chair, he towered over me, eclipsing me with his shadow. The seat he had occupied was tucked comfortably under the table, as he muttered, "Good. Enjoy yourself." Then, like a bat out of Hell, he began steering Liv out of the room. Once again, he failed to disguise his fingertips, which were gently caressing her lower back, before I even had chance to say goodbye to either of them.

During a brief lapse of utter madness, I felt a sizable degree of risk feasting on my vulnerability. 'Fuck it', was what the small voice in my head was whispering to me, while I watched Liam and Liv fade into the distance. When they were both completely out of sight, the whisper became more of a necessitating yell. Either way, I had no clue of what game Liam was playing, or whether the hand he had dealt to me was one of deception. I was filling my lungs to borderline bursting point, when I was struck with my epiphany. If this happened to be the, 'you do as I requested' game, then I was going to make damn sure I passed with honors.

"Who's for cocktails?" I bellowed a little louder than necessary.

Laurie glanced between me and her cousin, her eyebrows lifting considerably with a shrewd little wriggle. I'd be lying if I said it wasn't adorable. "How about a little karaoke instead?" she countered.

"Karaoke? You're kidding, right?" I scoffed. "I don't do karaoke."

"Oh, Kady, everybody does karaoke. The people that think they don't just don't realize it yet."

I still wasn't being won over. Singing was a big no-no for me. Singing in the privacy of the shower was about as far as I would ever go. Mainly because the crashing sound of the spewing water masked how bad I really was.

Walker pulled the cuff of his navy and caramel shirt up and checked his cuff-like watch. "Sorry to disappoint you, dear cousin, but Karaoke has been over for thirty minutes."

She hung her head like a child, with the word, damn, traveling on a moody sigh.

"But we could still go to McGinty's for a quiet drink. Would you be alright with that, Kady?"

I nodded, all the while thinking, McGinty's? Where the Hell was that and who the fuck was McGinty?

"Kady's in, what about you, misery guts."

Tried as I might, I couldn't suppress an amused snort. The directness which both Laurie and Walker engaged in was fascinating. I loved how they bounced off each other.

"A quiet drink?" she sneered. "Nah, you can drop me home on the way. Jesus, I never knew an Irishman could be so boring."

After settling the bill we left the bistro and filed into Walker's beloved pick-up. Considering Laurie was going to be the first to exit, she was taking her place next to the door, while I sat in the middle of the bench. I was so close to Walker that I could feel his body heat, I could smell his cologne. Every time he shifted the side of his body would graze against my own, and it filled me with…I don't know…it was something which I hadn't felt in a long time, almost…thrilling, daring. It was something I knew damn well I had to steer from, not because I questioned my fidelity; I would never cheat, or do anything that would be remotely considered as cheating, but because I questioned how Liam would perceive it.

I couldn't and wouldn't stick my head in that lion's den again.

We dropped Laurie off at the building I once called my home. She gave me a kiss on the cheek and told Walker that she would call him the following day, before slipping out of the truck. The door was slammed behind her, and we watched on for a brief moment, making sure that she got herself safely inside before pulling off.

"Have fun," she called, her voice echoing through the night.

A small distinct gasp, which I tried to mask, was torn from my throat when Walker stretched himself across the bench. His right hand was a hairsbreadth away from my thigh when he called out of the opened window, "We will once you get your arse inside."

She merited him with a hasty salute then disappearing inside her apartment building.

I found myself giggling in disbelief when Walker pulled into the gravel strewn car lot in front of McGinty's. "What's so funny?" he grunted, putting the truck into park.

"You know, for three years I used to live in that exact same building as Laurie, yet I never knew that this place existed just around the corner."

"Never knew this place…" he trailed off on a scoff, his opinion enhanced by the unimpressed shake of his head. "This is the best place in town. And that's not me being biased."

"Biased?" I queried. Granted it was left one-sided. Why I was even remotely peeved about that, I have no idea. I was used to my questions going unanswered by Liam, but by another? That was just plain rude.

He abandoned the truck with a rushed slam of the door. Before I even unclipped my belt and released the passenger side door, Walker was already at my side holding it open for me. I whispered my thanks while lowering myself from the seat, and shakily made my way over the gravel in my heels.

The display of Walker's thoughtful manners had an intense warmth heating my insides. I never would have thought that someone as…masculine as him would even bother with the chivalrous acts. Macho and chivalry were worlds apart in my mind. So when the green door of the bar was held open for me, and the gentle, warm tone of his voice offered a "Ladies first," my response was a simple, timid smile that made the erratic, pumping muscle in my chest billow.

A voice calling out, "Alright, son?" sounded through the vacant building. The source of the greeting was a man with silver hair hanging to his shoulders, going about his late night duties behind the green surfaced counter.

"'Aye," Walker answered with me trailing behind, making our way through the empty tavern and rounding a pool table as we went. It was impossible for his caressing fingertips over the green felt, to go unobserved. How he managed to achieve a degree of seduction in such an effortless act was perplexing, so much so, the act of drawing my attention from that hand was proving challenging. "I see it got delivered then?"

"'Aye, that it did, son. Arrived this afternoon. Now I just need to think of a place to put the fucking thing." The man's gaze swept up and down the length of the room, as did mine.

A small stage extended over at the end of the building to my left with a small dance floor below it. While dark, round tables and matching chairs were strategically placed for comfort, yet enough room to maneuver around them. Flashing lights of slot machines and an old fashioned jukebox at the right of the building caught my eye. There didn't appear to be a vacant spot anywhere big enough for the table to be rehoused. Keeping it where it was got my vote.

"Who's the pretty lady?"

"Da, this is Kady. Kady, meet my da."

"It's nice to meet you," I smiled, and when he flipped a towel over his shoulder, I shook his hand.

"You, too, Kady." It must have been an Irish thing, because

the 'D' of my name was transformed into a 'T' by the old man as well. It made me smile and hang my head.

He asked what he could get us while Walker lit up a cigarette and dragged an ashtray closer to him, stunning me for a brief moment, as my mouth went dry and my stomach flipped. The lightheaded buzzing and grating of my lungs which I had experienced only a few weeks ago when I was the one on the receiving end of those chemicals, was recalled as I studied him in an uncomfortable silence. I watched the smoke twirl and spiral as it left his mouth in a controlled exhale, before he ordered a bottle of Bud for himself.

I halted the old man after Walker order me a large white wine. "Actually, I'll have the same as Walker, please."

I felt Walker's cynical, yet comical gaze burning into me. I turned to face him and was met with slightly narrowed eyes. "Really?" he probed, drawing the smoking stick from between his lips before moistening them with a sweep of his tongue.

"When in Rome, right?"

The dimple on his left cheek and the lengthening of his throat, as he lifted his head back with a husky chuckle, was hypnotizing. With a sphere of butterflies in my stomach and the hugest, most sincere grin that my face has borne in a long time, I watched him flick the gathering ash of the tip of his cigarette into the tray before him, and then took a draw from his bottle.

"I didn't know you were a smoker," I mused, seizing the uncapped, dark glass bottle from Walker's father with a smile of appreciation.

He cocked his wrist, examining the burning stick held loosely between the fingers of his right hand. "'Aye, but only socially—" I smiled through my unease, my eyes drifting over the bar when he drew my attention again. "Sorry, darlin'. I didn't mean to make you feel uncomfortable," he lifted his arm to his mouth for one final draw on the tip before outing it in the ashtray and blowing the gathering of chemicals out on a shallow breath.

The mere fact that he drew an end to his act after sensing my unease made my heart billow under my ribs.

"Better?" he asked, smiling wide.

"You didn't have to do that. But thank you."

He tipped his head gallantly, wrenching the dark glass from his lips. When he gestured toward the pool table along my left, his eyes twinkled. "Fancy christening the table, Kady?"

"Excuse me?" My eyes were made wider in utter shock horror while I heard the old man behind the bar snigger.

"I meant join me in the first game of pool, on the table."

Air gradually left my lungs and I dropped my head with a tiny shake, awaiting his censure.

"My God, your mind is filthy, darlin'…" he was practically purring. By means of his forearm, he pushed himself away from the bar. The step he took toward me had my heart lurching into my mouth, while my nostrils instantly demanded a fresh encounter with his cologne. As my eyes scoured over the white T-shirt that was stretching across his broad chest, much needed oxygen had already caught in my throat. Eventually, our eyes had locked.

A moment of silent conversation was communicated through the Indian Ocean reflected within each other, until his narrowed into a clear, refreshing spring, "…I like it." The smell of beer, garlic and a hint of smoke, traveled on his whisper. The lopsided grin and roguish wink spawned exhilarating chills throughout my body, as he skirted me and graced the table.

"I, um…" oh God, this was both embarrassing and awkward. My train of thought came to an immediate standstill when I witnessed his beige, denim pants stretching over his behind as he bent down then stretched out over the felt.

When I failed to continue, my mouth suddenly bone dry thanks to my jaw slackening, he reared up, the plaid shirt hanging open appealingly, as he asked, "What is it, darlin'?"

Deep breathe, Kady, find the fucking words. I offered an abashed smile. "I don't know how to play."

"You've never played pool?"

I shook my head and rolled my lips over my teeth, shrugging my shoulders.

"Jesus. That's just unacceptable. Don't worry, I'll teach ya, darlin'." Another snigger from his father had Walker pointing at him and tilting his head down in a mocked warning. "Don't you start, Da," he chided, and went about putting the balls in the triangle.

"Okay, so, where's the stick."

He tried, I know he tried but he was doing an absolute awful job of concealing his amusement. Lifting his eyes up at me, those hypnotic hands slithered over the green felt, until they were braced on the cushion, bearing his weight as he smirked. "Stick?"

"Yes, the stick to hit the balls."

"This,"—he shifted and recovered the topic of discussion—"is called a cue, darlin'."

My jaw practically rested on my left shoulder as I simultaneously cocked my head and submitted to a noncommittal shrug. "It's made from wood and whittled into a long pole. It is, in all intents and purposes, a stick."

His thick, husky laughter was contagious. He finally shook his head, "I give up. Here, take your stick, darlin'." So I did with a triumphant grin. "Do you want to break?"

"Break what?"

The center of his upper lip was lightly grazed by his right

thumbnail. I watched as wry eyes widened from over his hand, while he clutched his stick in his left. "Never mind, I'll break."

It was suggested that I back up a little to avoid being hit as he began to fold his body over the table. Snared by absolute fascination, I studied him once I'd stepped around the corner of the table. The way his body fell so low against the surface and the look of sheer concentration in his eyes, while his tongue came to rest on his lower lip, was the most alluring sight I'd ever had the pleasure to witness.

Taking his shot, the white dispersed the triangle of colors sending them scattering over the table, still none of them fell.

"Okay, I didn't pocket any, so you're up."

"What one have I got t—?"

I shivered as he smirked. "Whichever tickles your fancy, darlin'?" That had my eyes glazed and my lower lip snared between my teeth. This man and his innuendos. And he said I have a filthy mind.

For a long while I scrutinized the table. Finally, I opted for a striped ball aiming toward the middle right hole, or pocket, whatever it's called. I peeked up at the man waiting on tenterhooks, his eyebrows lifted, and I found my attention being repeatedly drawn to his mouth as his right thumb once again, lightly scoured the center of his upper lip in thought. "Help me, I don't know how to…"

"Come 'ere," he mounted his stick against the wall then took position behind me. "Bend down," he ordered softly.

Cagily, I did as I was told.

"Lower…lower…"

"My God, this is embarrassing," I lightly protested, letting my head fall forward onto the felt. I felt exposed with my ass on full view for everybody. I knew the only people in the bar were Walker and his father and the lights were low, but still, I felt a wave of vulnerability crash over me.

"No, it's not. Here, stand back up."

An unsuspecting shudder journeyed through my entire body as I reared up, and felt his hand pressing between my shoulder blades, gently guiding me back down to the table below. His body was soon joining me, plummeting from his stance until he was hovering over my back. The warmth of his front sliced through my blouse, while his hand glided infinitesimally from my shoulder blades down the length of my spine. I had to work twice as hard to contain a whimper.

"Drop your weight through your hip," he sighed, his voice scratchy. My body didn't stand a chance as his softly spoken brogue sent a current of vibrations through me, causing my body to give birth to a ruthless shudder and my skin to prickle.

I did as I was told, slotting my right foot behind and effectively, in between his legs, and dropped my weight into my right hip.

Feeling the hardened skin coating his left hand as he aided in supporting the tip of the cue, had me gasping. "Focus on the balls," he purred from behind. "Imagine you're a lioness, Kady, that ball is your prey. You're getting ready to pounce, understand, darlin'?"

My swallow reflex was resisting thanks to that lump of desire lodged in my throat, as his right hand left my spine and came around me to hold my hand as I grasped the cue. "Yes," I rasped, trying with everything I had to focus on that damn striped ball instead of the weight and heat of the Irishman on my back, my leg between his, his arms around me, shielding me as the scent of smoky garlic and beer caressed and pasted onto my neck and jawline.

"Pull back," he guided my right arm back. "Tell me when

you're ready, darlin'."

I didn't ever think I would've been ready, but I said it anyway. When my words were freed in a sigh, he muttered the single word, "Softly," in my ear, and gently guided my right arm through to hit the white, which collided with, and sent my desired ball into the pocket.

"I did it," I shrieked, straightening my posture.

"'Aye, that you did, darlin'." He grinned, and then lifted his head to his father who was still arranging glasses behind the bar. "See, Da, told you I'm a good tutor."

The old man simply grunted before Walker turned back to me. "You get another shot. Just try not to pocket my solid, okay, darlin'."

It was bizarre. I probably should have felt awkward to a certain degree with the Irishman's choice of words and the way in which they were spoken. But I didn't. I found myself amused and desired, and I suppose some part of me, at least for tonight, felt like I was able to let my hair down.

Those dimples of his made an A+ appearance before I playfully back handing him in the gut. Feigning a wound and bowled over with a grunt, he looked adorable as I rounded him.

"You say I got a dirty mind."

"Takes one to know one, darlin'. Now, have you chosen your ball?"

Studying the table intently, I finally nodded pointing to the top left pocket. When I just stood there staring at the sphere like I was going to move it telekinetically, he chuckled. "Want another hand?"

"Please…"

Before I knew it, his heavy, hard body was shielding my back once again. In spite of taking position, I felt out of place, almost off center. As I attempted to get comfortable, I shifted my right leg less than an inch, but that inch was enough to cause my behind to graze along something that really shouldn't have been in my reach.

A faint gasp at the connection from behind had my body stiffening and cheeks heating. Damn, what was I saying? My entire body was heating, muscles in my belly fluttered while every hair follicle stood to attention.

I wrenched my head to my left to peek over my shoulder. The side of Walker's face so close that if I moved an inch closer, my cheek would have been brushed against that prickly scruff coating his jaw. "Shit, sorry."

Locking our eyes, he muttered something so direct, that I would never be able to look at a ball the same without that statement resurfacing. I would remember it, and the effect it had on my body, until my dying day. "When I said focus on the balls, Kady,"—his eyes fluttered shut for a split second—"I meant the ones on the table, darlin'."

Less than an inch away from his face, his body cloaking mine as he folded me over the felt, my ass unintentionally grinded against him again as I dropped my weight through my hip, anew. Ragged, unsteady breaths grated from my lungs. As my tongue swept across my lips, I felt them trembling.

How can so much be told, secrets and undisciplined desires, become blatant knowledge in one look? When glassy eyes fluttered down to his lips, I had to shake myself out of it. I'd be lying if I said what I felt at that moment didn't terrify me. It did. Because one man, one situation, and one measly statement, had me almost abandoning my morals.

Once I finally dragged my focus back to the game and took my shot, I totally missed sending it bouncing off the cushion.

That mishap caused me to spend the next four consecutive shots, studying Walker as he successfully pocketed his solids, and trying so hard not to be distracted by the calculating look in his eye, his tongue resting on his lower lip, and the way he looked as he doubled over.

I was sipping my beer when he finally fucked up on the shot. "Fuck. You're up, Kady."

With a deep breath I examined what was left of the stripes and solids. I was so going to lose this one. When I comfortably took my position, he asked if I needed any further assistance. Body bent, head down low, I pinned him with my eyes. His smirk and tiny gasp didn't go unnoticed. "I think I'll try myself."

"As you wish," he muttered composed, a smirk and a lopsided nod of his head rendered me speechless, while addictive tingles spawned in my body.

I took everything he'd taught me in such small time and steadily, I guided my arm through and successfully dropped the ball into the pocket. Complete concentration, I dropped one after another, after another until finally, only the black was left, torturing me with its impossible angle. How the fuck was this going to work? I couldn't even reach the white to hit it anyway.

"You alright there, darlin'?" he mocked me.

"How the Hell am I supposed to hit that?" I glared at him, pointing to the table. "I can't reach."

"As long as one foot is on the floor, you can climb on."

He had to be fucking kidding me. Accompanied by a dirty minded smirk, I made damn sure my right foot was on the floor, as I lifted my left leg and spread myself out on the felt. "I thought my days of climbing on tables were over with," I spoke harshly, but had to stifle the small snort which was brewing.

I was shifting and adjusting, but I'd be fucked if I could

somehow manage to find a position that I could use to my advantage. "Need a hand there, darlin'?"

Over my shoulder I peeked, half of my body spread out in invitation on the table like some playboy centerfold, and I couldn't help but think that I would feel less conscious knowing he was shielding me, rather than watching the very…provocative pose I had gotten myself in. "Please," I nodded.

Staying perfectly still, at that moment I felt as though I was about to be mauled by a bear. I sensed him behind me, standing between the edge of the table and my right leg. When he slithered up and over my body, every muscle from head to toe tensed and quivered inexorably. Every hard muscle of him was digging into me, my back, my behind. Even his burly arms which were concealed by his shirt were pressed against me, guiding me as I supported the cue. I took a deep, pacifying breath, his scent torturing me just as much as the weight, warmth, prominence, and the mere thought of the position we found ourselves in.

"Ready?"

I wish he would've stopped asking me that, because every time he did, my unruly mind was tethering the question to my slowly diminishing morals. I couldn't speak in fear of panting, so I simply succumbed to a nod of my head.

The callouses coating his hands were pressed against the soft skin of my knuckles as we pulled back in unison, and by God alive, it was the most thrilling, lust-filled motion that I had ever experienced in my life. I couldn't concentrate on what we were doing, our goal. My mind was too busy tossing images and tantalizing tidbits out to taunt me, to tempt me.

So I let him guide my arm through as though it was him taking the shot. Somehow the black fell into the pocket. As it did, all I could do was let my head fall forward, allowing the abrasion of the felt to press against my brow. It was either that, or I knew I wouldn't be able to resist the abrasion of the Irishman's scruff to caress my cheek.

CHAPTER
seventeen

It was 12:15 a.m. by the time we headed out of McGinty's. I'd said my farewells to Walker's father, only for him to order that I call him Carriag, and that I was to come back again soon.

I couldn't promise that I would. But I told him I'd at least try.

Twenty minutes passed in a gawky silence as Walker drove me home. I couldn't help chancing the odd glimpse in his direction. He looked so in control and defiant with his left hand casually grasping the wheel, while his right fisted into that hair, leaving it sexy and rumpled.

He offered a quick peek in my direction before turning back onto the road, as my left hand worked its way to the curve of my shoulder and neck, before rubbing at my nape.

I smiled. "Thank you for a fun night. It's been a long time since I…" I trailed off, my voice getting smaller and smaller while my head lowered for the briefest of moments before peeking back up. "Just, thank you."

"I suppose this means that I'll be keeping my job then."

The corner of my lower lip was nipped after a small giggle and a long, dreamy sigh. Letting my teeth drag across the plump flesh, I finally spoke. "Yeah, I guess it does."

When we pulled up outside the house, I noticed the only light which was on, was that of Liam's home office. He must have still been settling things on the old Williamson Estate. It felt like the project had been going forever.

"Here," Walker shifted causing the leather of the bench to squeal, and dug his hand into the back pocket of his pants. When he handed me a folded piece of paper, my brow instantly furrowed. "Just in case you need anything."

The twitching corners of my mouth gave way to a cautious smile as I studied his phone number. "Is this…" I peeked at him, the paper was caressed by my fingertips as though they sought to caress his face. I lost myself in his gaze, a shadow cast over the side of his face adding a little mystery. "Is this a good idea?"

A rumble of a snigger made my breath hitch, while he hung his head and his right thumb rubbed the center of his upper lip. When he looked up, his expression turned coy. "It's just a number, Kady. In case you want or need to talk. That's all. Nothing else."

I won't lie. I felt a small pang in my chest at his instance of 'nothing else'. And that pang alone should have been enough reason to scrunch up the number and toss it in the trash.

"We all need someone to talk to at some point, darlin'. Sometimes venting helps diffuse a situation before it gets out of hand."

His choice of words had thrown me. I didn't know what he was referring to, but I wasn't naïve enough not to know that there was a reference behind them. Slipping the paper into the side zipper of my purse, I said my thanks again for a fun night and ejected myself from the truck, placing a safe distance between me and temptation.

"Hey," I angled my head around the door of Liam's home office.

"Good morning," he grinned, pushing himself back into his seat. Was that a sarcastic statement or a happy one, considering I had done as I was told and was kept out until past this time? I didn't know, and that unknown bred a menacing shudder which turned my blood to ice. "I take it you were shown a good time?"

"Yeah, we had fun. Your night doesn't look so fun though."

"Ah," he lifted his arms and let them fall back to the arms of his chair. "It's been quite interesting actually."

"You always find interest in the most trifling of things. I'm going to bed. I'd really like for you to join me," I posed with a suggestive arch of my brow. If there was one thing I needed, it was that dull ache in my lower abdomen to be hit head-on and the sexual, pent-up frustration to be alleviated.

"I'd love to, baby, but I've got a lot that I need to get done."

I folded my arms over my chest and cocked my head. "And I can't draw you away from being master of the Boston skyline for thirty minutes?"

"Sorry, baby. Maybe tomorrow." Stunned after his rejection hit me in the face at full force, he went back to his work leaving me to saunter down the hall, to the bedroom…alone and very, very horny.

When I got there and out of my clothing, I slipped myself between the cool satin sheets. Thoughts of the night spiraled around my mind, the line between right and wrong blurring as each end of the spectrum was blended together. What started off as a small throb was quickly becoming an unbearable ache as I closed my eyes, the heat and heaviness of a certain someone still bearing upon my back.

My nipples strained painfully against the satin, my hands caressed at the heavy, tightening burdens on my chest before skimming down my sternum, my stomach, to the summit of my inner thighs. Back arched, I thrust my hips up as my hand plunged under the band of my panties and glided downward over my core, drawing a small gasp of pleasure from my lips. My middle finger swept along the damp heat and creamy slickness as my thighs fell further open, a current of desire and need shooting from the tip of my clit through my entire body as I shuddered.

What was I doing? What was I thinking? This was…it was… fuck it was nice…

Rough, baited pants were passing my lips while my pelvis gyrated under my touch. Slow fingers orbited over the swelling peak of my core at a leisurely pace, and it was exhilarating, feeling the evidence of what my private touch was instigating. All the while, a certain pleasant, seductive brogue was rounding my mind, his scent and his innuendos. Oh God, the feel of his body as I accidentally grinded against him, the bulge in his pants, the image of that final position we took atop of that table, teased my mind as I continued teasing my seeping core.

Eyes screwed tightly, I licked my lips, my hand relentlessly worked on fueling my body, my hips circled, my shoulder raised. I felt my wetness coating the material of my panties while I stroked myself inside of them, tiny bolts of electricity firing from that nub of nerve endings that the tips of my fingers were stimulating at an agonizing slow pace. I was in no rush. I needed an intense, body shaking orgasm. I knew it wouldn't be as pungent as the ones the man down the hall could give me, but I needed it as powerful as I could give myself.

'When I said focus on the balls, Kady, I meant the ones on the table, darlin',' his words tormented my mind as I envisioned his

scruff pressing between my thighs, his tongue taking the place of my fingers. With round, sweeping motions all I could focus on was the image of his tongue doing what I was doing to myself, tasting the juice of my core escaping at the mere fantasy of him here with me.

Sweat beaded on my brow and down the crevice of my spine, and soon, every muscle in my body began to stiffen and contract. My lower back and abdomen surrendered to the weightlessness of bliss as the pressure behind my touch gained, my speed rapid. I chewed on the edge of the comforter to stifle my cries as my body erupted, trembling and tightening as my synapses sparked and fired, then traveled through my entirety with heady jolts of bliss.

Breathless and wasted, I allowed my body to sink into the mattress, and as I spiraled down from my release, I was caught by a generous amount of guilt.

I just fantasized about another man, a fantasy that brought me to orgasm, when *my* man was less than thirty-five feet away. What the fuck was I doing?

Have you ever experienced those moments when you're caught between dream and reality. You know, those moments just before you flutter your eyes and prepare yourself for the day, when you forget everything? That's what I felt when I woke the following morning.

I was stretching my body, alleviating the tightness in my muscles and joints with a smile on my face, when I fluttered my eyelids and came face-to-face with that damn phone on the bedside.

That damn phone was the trigger to my shit awful day.

At some point during the early hours the thing had started ringing. It shocked me awake. Disorientated, I clambered over Liam's empty side of the bed and picked it up. It somehow connected to phone in the home office, and like some masochist, I deserted slumber and allowed myself to listen to the voices on the other end.

The voice of Liam…the voice of Liv.

"Liam, I'm not sure how that would work. We've pushed it a few times," she giggled, practically uncaring.

"Trust me, it'll be fine. Come on, we have to, Liv."

As the words played havoc with my mind, gut-wrenching tears sprang to my eyes while fury and betrayal became my morning wake up call.

"Good morning, Kady baby," Liam was standing in the doorway, already dressed in his light gray suit and blue shirt. The mattress swallowed in my hands as I pushed myself up to sit. "I brought you breakfast."

Breakfast, I inwardly scoffed. He thinks breakfast will help diminish a guilty fucking conscience?

The distance between us was closed. The bed plunged as he set the wooden tray on my lap and took a seat against the lower left post of the bed. I examined the contents of the tray: bacon, pancakes, scrambled eggs and ketchup, with a glass of orange juice and a cup of coffee, the full-bodied aroma traveled along the steam as it danced and spiraled into the air. At least there was no blood sausage or mushrooms on it this time. So I knew this wasn't a punishment breakfast at least.

"What's the matter, baby? You look a little pale."

Sitting in silence, I didn't dare look at him. I knew I'd break if I did. How could I have been so naive? I'd listened to her for hours gushing over this new man in her life. Her words continued a haunting tune in my mind as I stared blankly at the array on the tray. *'It's not my fault that she can't see what's happening in front of her eyes, Kady. Why should I feel guilty? If it was a happy home, then he wouldn't have come to me in the first place.'*

The mental fog began to lift. Was that the reason why Liam made it his mission to for all this time to keep us separated?

"Kady?" the voice laced with concern reeled me back. I lifted my head. "What's wrong baby? You're worrying me."

"What's going on with you and Liv?" The words tumbled unbidden from my lips. I couldn't suppress this. This was something that needed to be said, that needed to have place in the open air so we knew where we both stood.

His face fell and a scowl appeared. Usually, that expression of his would've had me cowering. But not at that moment. At that moment, I was making it my mission to find out exactly what the fucking Hell was going on behind my back, with someone who was supposed to be my best friend and my partner. "Excuse me?"

"You heard me. What is going on with you and Liv? And don't lie to me Liam. I deserve that much at least."

"Kady," he sniggered, which didn't sit well with the tight ball in my belly that was increasing as my adrenaline rose. "I have no idea what you're talking about. Why would you think there was anything going on anyway?"

I licked my lips and grit my teeth so hard I was sure one was going to chip. "Don't. Fucking. Lie to me!" I screamed. All logical thought sailed out the window to be replaced by sheer wrath. In a blur, the tray was picked up from my lap and hurled across the room, narrowly missing Liam's head, before smashing against the doorframe of the en-suite and crashing to the flooring. "I heard you on the fucking phone last night!"

Each unsteady, quivering breath had my chest heaving. I watched on as all dry amusement dissolved from his features to be superseded with sheer antagonism, while the severity of my actions was concrete at my feet, pulling me down as I crash-landed back to reality from my moment of sheer rage.

"No, no, no, no…" I shook my head frantically with each beseeching syllable that was drawn from my lips. Jaw sturdy and tight, eyes hard and uncompromising, with the swiftness of a hunting lion he jumped up, the back of his hand connecting at an angle across the left side of my face. The bitter, metallic taste seeped from my lip to my tongue as I fell backwards. Wild, brutal hands grabbed at my legs and yanked me back as I tried to escape from his clutches.

But it was a wasted effort.

He finally fisted his hand in my hair and dragged me out of the bed.

"Liam, no please, let me go, I'm sorry, I'm sorry—" I yelled as I struggled to find my feet all the while being pulled across the floor with my hand clutched at the back of my head, in a futile attempt to stop him from yanking a fist-full of blond hair out from the root.

I was hauled kicking and shouting to the end of the room where the food and drinks laid dispersed over the ground.

As if I was worshipping the chaos on the floor, I was positioned on my hands and knees before it, his hand still gripping forcefully in my hair while he stood behind me, my hips trapped between his legs. "If you had let me fucking explain," he hissed and unexpectedly, my face was being buried and scrubbed into the mess that I had created, like some puppy having her nose rubbed in its own piss after an accident. "I was talking to a client. He wants my company to design a casino. He said about life being short, and I said that we have to *live* life."

The fraught sounds of me spluttering and choking were masking his intimidating words. The heat of the coffee had absorbed into the carpet, and with each merciless plunge he made as he held me there, face first in the disarray that was supposed to have been breakfast, my face was getting burned. The fibers of the carpeting scoured at my flesh as he unrelentingly scrubbed me across it.

Finally, I felt his death grip leave my hair and my hips were no longer trapped between his legs. On shaky arms, I pushed my face away from the floor, tears streaming down my cheeks. Sobs escaped my throat as I spluttered the chunks of food which found their way into my mouth after his assault.

Liam remained in my peripheral vision. "This,"—he screamed, pointing at the remnants of breakfast—"was a fucking apology because I have to go on a fucking business"—his words were getting tighter as he reared up and out of view. Before I could intuit his next move, his leg came back and a swift kick in my ribs was issued upon me. I called out on a gasp, the tears coming faster and harder, making my stomach tense painfully. "Trip, and I won't be here,"—leg pulled back, my ribs suffered the brunt end of another ruthless strike. I bowled over struggling for breath, a face smothered with food, hot coffee and orange juice, while I supported myself on a shaky left arm. My right folded over my middle to the battered area seeking protection. "For your birthday next. Fucking. Week." As he punctuated the final two words, another two swift kicks were delivered.

Somehow as I fought for breath, I managed to cry out, feeling my lungs being compressed by the string of kicks while my ribs throbbed and smarted, drawing gasp upon gasp from my winded body.

When he finally moved away, my frame gave in and I fell to the floor in a crumpled heap. I watched through my tears as his hands raked back in his hair. I didn't care that mine was getting matted and dipping in the shit on the floor. I just held my ribs, crying inanely.

How he could've been be so composed after doing that, I have no idea. But he waltzed to the doorway like he had just given me a kiss before leaving for work.

He turned on his heel and straightened his tie, commanding one more thing of me before he left me a winded and damaged heap, at his hands, on the flooring of our bedroom. "Oh, and clean up your damn mess once you're done with the crying."

CHAPTER eighteen

15th May, 2012.
Thirteen months before the accident…

The week passed in a blur of pain relief, tiptoeing on eggshells and utter silence. Unlike past incidents, Liam never attempted to right this wrong. He never offered any affection or comfort. Striving to regain what we were before that day apparently wasn't on his list of endeavors, either.

With a bruised ego and equally bruised ribs, I continued to go about my daily duties, gasping and panting, wincing and scowling all the while I was doing them, but I did my utmost to remain the good little housewife. I didn't bother going to the emergency room. There was no point.

On hands and knees, I scrubbed and scrubbed at the stain on the bedroom floor. Six stain removal treatments later, and the traces of that monstrous morning were near enough erased. If only there was a solution to remove it from my mind, I thought to myself more often than once.

The silence that chased over the days which followed that

Friday morning, was temporarily disrupted when Liam stepped through the front door the following Thursday. He slammed it behind him, causing the walls to shake under protest, and me to jump out of my skin with the vacuum in hand, cringing as I did so, as I made my way up the staircase.

"What the fuck have you said to her?" he shouted, his face contorted like some demon was pushing to break free from his flesh. His briefcase plummeted to the hardwood flooring in the hallway. The thunderous din made me jolt farther, until I felt the rigid lip of the stair above burrowing into the back of my leg.

"What did I say to whom?" I shook my head, my heart beating faster than humming bird's wings while my body temperature rocketed, resulting in a bead of sweat filtering down my spine. "I haven't been out anywhere."

Liam wrapped menacing fingers around the balustrade and began to snarl. "Don't. Fucking. Lie. To. Me. Steinbeck just cornered me when I was getting out of the car."

Fuck.

My head dipped. I would have sighed, but my ribs weren't facilitating that level of ease at such gesture. "She came by earlier asking if everything was okay because she'd heard quarrelling. She'd knocked several times the last few days when you've been at work, Liam. I had to answer. I told her that I've had that bug. She said to make sure you look after me, and I assured her that you already were. That's all; I promise you."

I watched under nervous lids as his chest expanded with his deep intake of breath, for a moment, I envied him. "That better had been all, Kady. I swear. You think you're in pain now? That's fuck all, baby," he sneered.

I fought to suppress the evidence of fear in the form of tears, which was making my vision blur, at his words. Sniffling, I faintly nodded my understanding.

"Get back to what you were doing," he ordered.

His gaze was spearing into my back as I struggled to carry the vacuum up the stairs, I could feel it. I winced and subtly chanced a glance. Immobile, he was still firmly planted at the bottom of the case, the menacing hand continued to coil around the wooden balustrade. But it was the look of total indifference carved into his profile, which was the bitter pill to swallow.

Alone, my Tuesday alarm came in the form of the sweet sound of the birds' song outside my window. Liam had left the day before for his business trip to God only knows where. He didn't leave a number, didn't leave a hotel. Damn, I didn't even know what part of the country his trip was, or whether it was in fact, even in the damn country. Still, as he left in the cab, without so much as a 'goodbye' or a 'kiss my ass', I felt a brief moment of sheer reprieve.

For the first time in ten days, I curled up as well as I could in the bed and I allowed myself the time to sob, to grant my barrier of strength and persistence to crumble and disintegrate before my eyes. I felt sorrow, I felt manipulated and fragile as I filtered through every conflict that we'd had over nearly two years, and every warranted punishment that's been issued.

That night, I freed every single tear that I'd stored since the first time Liam had turned into the monster, which I shared my life with.

Steadily brushing the comforter back from my body, I reluctantly ejected myself from the bed and made a beeline to the en-suite. I avoided the mirror along my left above the basin, scared of what would be looking back at me. So after taking care of business, I stripped out of my Hello Kitty pajamas and stepped into the shower, hoping to feel a little more alive afterward.

Within fifteen minutes, I was out of the stall with a bath towel wrapped around my shivering wreck of a body. Ridding the large vanity mirror of steam, I stood before the basin in front of it and brushed my teeth, before studying my reflection intently. The split on my lower lip had scabbed up and mostly healed. At that point, it could easily be passed off as a cold-sore, for that I was thankful. My eyes were swollen and bloodshot thanks to my hours of irrepressible sobbing the night before, but what made me well up again, was how diminished the woman looking back at me appeared to be. Her sparkling topaz eyes were dim and lifeless, as though she had nothing to live for. She looked close to breaking; she looked so close to drowning in the deathly waters which were full of regrets.

Private regrets, private beatings…private knowledge.

The sight before me shimmered and swam, the bridge of my nose burned. Blinking, a tear escaped over my lid. "Happy birthday, Kady," I muttered into the mirror, the escaped tear being chased by several more.

I had pulled on a pair of faded jeans and a plain black long-sleeved T-shirt, once again, avoiding the full-length mirror as I did so. Looking down was another action I made damn sure not to accede to. I couldn't and wouldn't examine the battered area which coated the left-side of my ribcage, it would make it harder to disregard. It would make that incident a reality. And that was something I wanted so desperately to elude. I knew in doing that, I was eluding the part of my life which desperately needed confronting.

A knock at the door sounded through the house, while I was piling my hair on the top of my head in a loose knot. "Please don't be Steinbeck. Please don't be Steinbeck," I continued chanting my mantra as I strolled from the bedroom, down the stairs and to the door.

Holding my breath, I pulled it open and was greeted by an Irish speaking balloon, singing, 'Happy birthday'. Everybody sounds like an idiot when they sing that song, but Walker, however, managed to pull it off.

"Walker, you're off your tits, do you know that?" I giggled when his adorable smile appeared from behind the inflated foil after his melody.

He grabbed the right-side of his chest with his left hand which made me chuckle a little more. "Tits? Nah, these are called pecs, darlin'. Can I come in?"

I nodded and shifted to the side, allowing him entrance. "Take your boots off, I don't want any dirt trailed through," I ordered, and without hesitancy, he slipped off his boots and followed me through to the kitchen with an approving whistle.

"Damn, some house you got here, darlin'."

"Yeah, I guess," I sighed, thinking backing to the first time I set foot inside, and the apprehension and grief I felt as I considered the fact that it was indeed a blank canvas. The walls and rooms had no memories embedded into them. Now, all I wanted was to erase them all and start afresh with a new blank canvas, filling it with colorful memories, not menacing black ones. "Coffee?" I asked which earned me a swift nod.

Walker pulled out a seat once the birthday balloon was set in the center of the dining.

I made my way into the dining room, veering the island and set our mugs down on the coasters, pulling up my own seat at the bottom of the table.

I tried to let it go unsaid, but the question was killing me. "What the Hell is with the old man hat?" I teased.

"Old man hat?" he scoffed. "Darlin' this,"—right arm lifted, his fingers pressed against the lip—"is called a flat cap. There is no defined age when one can start wearing one."

I snorted, "Well, it looks ridiculous," which earned me an expression of pleading puppy dog eyes. God, he was adorable. I felt the coldness of the glass surface spear through my long-sleeves as I set my right elbow upon it, and braced my chin in my palm. "But you make it work," I concluded in earnest.

"'Aye,"—with a sip of his coffee, he arched his brow over the rim and swallowed—"That I do, darlin'."

Time lapsed in a companionable silence with Walker subtly perusing the area with inquisitive eyes as we sipped at our coffee. When they came back to set on me, I was staring at the balloon in the heart of the table. I couldn't help but inwardly consider how thoughtful he was. I hadn't received a phone call from anyone thus far. It seemed Walker was the only one making that effort to celebrate my day—a day, which after the events of the prior week and a half, I didn't even wish to acknowledge myself. So why should anyone else?

"I have a little something—"

"There's more?" I gasped, his hand dug into the inner pocket of his black leather jacket. "Walker, you have no idea how ecstatic I am over the balloon."

"Ah, fuck the balloon, here." I was handed a pink envelope, along with a small silver cardboard box. When I neglected to seize them and simply gaped at the offering with wide, cautious eyes, he pressed again in that irresistible brogue, "I said take it."

With a nonchalant scratch of my head, I licked my lips and accepted. "Walker, there's really no need. I'm twenty-six not six. Gifts for the birthday girl are no longer mandatory."

A permanent scowl took pride of place under his cap. "Shut up and open the damn gift, woman."

Snorting, I started on the envelope. A card with a pink bunny holding a bunch of glittery flowers was pulled out. Inside it simply read:

> *To Kady,*
> *Happy birthday, darlin',*
> *Hope you have a great day.*
> *Walker*

My first and only birthday card. The mere fact that he'd thought about me to take the time and look for a card, and wrote something so minor inside, was so meaningful. A card is worth a hundred gifts. "Thank you," I whispered, refusing to allow my striking tears to fall.

With a smile, he tipped his brow motioning at the silver square box lying in wait on the table. Carful hands slipped the cardboard case from the glass surface. It was small enough to fit in the palm of my hand, yet I held it delicately between my fingers. A gasp was torn from my mouth as I removed the flat lid and set it on the table ahead.

"I know it's cheap and nothing special, but—"

"Walker," I couldn't say anything else. My emotions were being wrung, well and truly wrung and those tears that I refused to free only a moment ago, spilled down my face, splashing onto my hands and blurring the silver bracelet which held only one, single charm: a teddy bear holding a shamrock.

"Kady, there's no need to cry. It's only something cheap and–—"

The reproach in his words instantly had me dragging my blurry vision up to his face. "Don't," I shook my head, more tears tumbling. "Don't find fault with this, Walker. You have no idea…"

choking on my words, he instantly lifted himself from the leather seat and lugged it closer to me. His arm around my neck, he pulled me into his chest to show comfort. I found myself taking it, simply by his scent alone.

For the first time in a long time, I felt acknowledged—acknowledged and accepted that I was a human being. One with feelings and with faults, yet I was still a person. I wasn't an animal that needed to be taught lessons. I wasn't a punching bag. I was an individual with needs, and in Walker's arms, I felt appreciated and accepted.

And that made me cry more.

I was blindfolded and escorted down the front steps and into the pick-up. Why he felt the need to blindfold me, I have no idea. Persistently probing, I was answered with, "It's a surprise, don't start." So I listened and complied like a good girl.

The difference between complying with Liam and Walker was, with Liam, it was under duress. I learned not to fight back because the consequences of doing so just weren't worth it. With Walker, I felt his enthusiasm…I felt safe.

As we came to a halt at a set of lights, I assume, I craned my blindfolded gaze toward the Irishman behind the wheel and asked, "Can we put the radio on?" I found it somewhat amusing how I couldn't see him, yet I could still tell he was smirking at me. I lifted my right arm, my newly acquired silver bracelet jingled as I pointed a chiding finger in his direction. I knew it was something that I wouldn't be able to wear when Liam was home. It wasn't something I could tell him about either. Another secret to add to my life. One which would evoke a happier memory, a contented feeling.

"Don't you smirk at me," I pouted.

"Fascinating, are you sure you can't see?" his tone was laced with glee.

"Trust me; I cannot see a damn thing. Now, can we put the radio on?"

"What's the magic word?"

I sighed. A small sigh, but a sigh nonetheless before tipping my head back defeated. "Please oh the amazing, Walker; can we have the radio on?"

His buoyancy was contagious as his rumbled laughter echoed in the tight space between us. "A simple 'please' would have done it, darlin'."

The speaker crackled as he brought it to life. I rested back into the seat, patiently tapping my fingertips against my thighs. It's funny how time-consuming things seem to take when you can't see the world around you.

"Kady, can you do me a favor, darlin'?"

"Hmm…" I rolled my head in his direction, still waiting for those damn lights to change.

"Look to your right and give a smile and a wave."

"What?" What kind of request was that?

"Just do it," he ordered softly, so I did. I felt a total idiot blindly staring out of the window waving at someone I couldn't see, but he found it comical, the ass.

Finally pulling off, I slumped back into the bench seat, listening to a man's husky voice warbling about not waiting for a hero to save us. I smiled, dwelling in the hollows of my mind, unconsciously valuing the reference, as it was drawn from the speakers.

At long last, we came to a stop. The sound of the leather of his jacket protesting as he flopped back into the seat and twisted after turning off the ignition, had me drawing my blinded attention toward him.

"Are we here?" I asked warily.

"Yes."

When nothing followed, not a sound, not a movement, I sensed the creases on my brow deepen. "Walker?"

"Hmm…"

"Can I take the fold off now?"

"Not yet," his voice was barely an octave over a breathy whisper.

A few seconds ticked past before I whined his name again.

"Yes, darlin'?" he replied.

"Why are you so quiet?" *Why was I whispering?* "What's going on?"

"Shush…I'm just taking a moment," his words were sweet, enriched and velvet soft. If they were edible, I'm sure they would've had the consistency of heated caramel.

Isn't it bizarre how even blinded you can still sense when something it placed in your line of sight? How your other senses heighten. I licked my lips, and though I felt the warmth of his hand a few centimeters from my cheek, I didn't move. Inside I was trembling with longing and pleaded for him to make that single connection. Outside, I played dumb, and allowed him to continue with whatever it was he was going to do.

All too soon, the shadow and presence of his hand was lowered from my face. "Okay," he gasped, fighting for composure. "Stay there and I'll help you out now, darlin'."

"Can't I just take off the damn blindfold?"

"Umm…actually…no."

One word was wrenched from my throat as the door slammed shut, "Bastard."

My elbow was grasped by the calloused hand, and I was guided through a parking lot. When we stepped away from the spring breeze and into an echoing surround, I whispered again if I could take the covering off. I was simply told, "Not yet."

"Two for an hour," I heard and although I had a cloth over my eyes, I felt them widen. A few moments later, my left arm was warmed by his heat as he stood beside me. "Ready, darlin'?"

"Two for an hour? Walker you better not have taken me to some seedy—" He laughed so hard that it was an unfeasible task to laugh at him. The moment of joviality came to a premature end on my behalf, when a brief gasp past my lips. My ribs throbbed and tightened, still, I fought beyond my moment of tenderness and blindly backhanded him in the gut. "Don't laugh at me," I pointed.

Stunned and embarrassed, the heat in my cheeks was unmistakable as I heard a female, softly spoken voice say, "Excuse me?"

Who the fuck was that? I flailed my head, scouring my sightless observation around the area. "I'm sorry," I muttered to the people of wherever it was I was currently standing. Now I was getting disorientated, I think I had spun in a circle three times before I halted. "Jesus Christ, Walker,"—I stamped my foot like a spoiled toddler in the market—"Take this Goddamn thing off me."

"Oh, my God, Kady," he was panting. The Irish bastard was laughing so Goddamn hard he was panting, the fucking asshole. "That was hysterical. Come on." His friendly hand surrounded my own as I was shakily led through a set of doors.

Walker's heat collided with the nape of my neck as he stood towering over me from behind, his fingers in my hair, weaving under the fabric depriving me of my sight. "Ready?"

"Yes, take this thing off me."

My lids unsealed when the material was unraveled. Feeling my retinas burning from the brightness drowning the room was the cause of my squinting. I scanned the area. A sea of trampolines over the floor and angled against the walls stared back at me. "Where are we?"

"Sky Zone. I thought it'd be fun. Trampolines aren't just for kids you know."

I smiled a brief smile as Walker shrugged out of his leather, slipped out of his boots and climbed up onto the bouncy masses. His hand was opened and extended to me, readying to help me up. "You go ahead and make a fool of yourself first while I watch."

"But—" the expression he flashed at me was adorable. He looked like a youngster having his toy taken away.

I shook my head unfazed. "Nope, only fair after what you did to me out there," I gestured to the double doors along my left side. My voice may have given the impression of sardonic gratification, yet it betrayed me. In reality, guilt flooded my veins and clutched painfully at the beating muscle in my chest. He'd surprised me for my birthday, and here I was, making excuses to not participate. The painful truth was: I didn't know how on Earth I was going to survive flouncing around like that with my injury. It was challenging enough just laughing.

"Fine, but I will be dragging your arse up here, you know."

I spent a good twenty minutes watching him as he flounced across the springy surface, tossing himself against the trampolines positioned against the walls into backflips and side flips, and any other flips he could throw himself into. I was enraptured and smiling like a lunatic.

"Come on, darlin'. Get your arse up here." He was making his way toward me. I knew it wasn't a good idea. I still couldn't laugh without my ribs smarting. But his lively air and the effort it took to get me here made me push on.

I shrugged out of my denim jacket, toed off my shoes and took hold of his hand as he helped me up. "Is this even safe?"

I questioned attempting to find my feet while being led into the center. I couldn't bounce. I couldn't walk. It was more like a pathetic skipping crossed with a shuffle.

"Of course it is. Kids have these in their backyards for Christ sake." He studied me as I continued with my new shuffle-skip. Lips twitched a handful of times before he lowered his head, his shoulders juddering.

"Charming," I made no effort at all to mask my deep disapproval. When his head came back up, tears were trickling down his face while I stood glaring.

"Oh, darlin', I'm not laughing at you," he panted.

My eyebrows met my hairline. "You sure as Hell weren't laughing with me either, because I'm not laughing."

"You would have, darlin' if you could see yourself."

Hands held, he told me to follow his lead and began to bounce softly, the surface remaining graced by our feet. We did so in unison, and before long, I was getting into the swing of things while reveling in his boyish demeanor. I let my hair down, lived for the moment and allowed my minute of happiness with him to chase the sinister clouds of the previous week away, as well as the physical discomfort. It was actually fun.

An animated shriek was ripped from my lips as I began to gain a little height. His hands had subtly worked up my arms, until they rested on my shoulders as we supported each other, clinging onto one another as our feet sunk into the elastic, before tossing us back into the air. "That's it, Kady. Higher?"

"Higher?" I posed it as a question, but as animation took over, I suppose it sounded more of an agreement.

I hadn't noticed what he was going to do, until it was too late.

His large hands left my shoulders and a pain-enthused cry was forced from me when he grabbed at my ribcage. I stopped bouncing instantly, suppressing my body's natural instinct to crash down onto my knees, and fought for a lungful of air while the discomfort that seared through my body made me nauseous. I was folded over, my right hand instinctively reaching for the source of pain.

Immediately drawing an end to his own eager springing, he spoke my name in earnest, "Kady?" His hand supportively pressed against my shoulder, his own tall, muscular form doubled over to examine me. "What's wrong, darlin'?"

"Nothing," I gasped and rolled my lips over my teeth halting my spontaneous cries and begging for the throb to ease. "I'm fine."

"No, darlin', you're not. What's the matter?"

I lifted my head, allowing his concerned features to disappear from my sight as I closed my eyes and sucked in an appeasing breath. "Nothing, Walker. Just leave it. I'm fine." I punctuated, only to be greeted with a staunchly shake of his head, his lips tight, his brow tighter, as fluttered my lids open.

"You've been panting—"

"Walker, we're on a fucking trampoline, of course I'm going to be panting," I hissed scathingly.

"And you've been wincing. Don't lie to me, Kady, I'm not stupid. I have noticed," his tone was one not to dare mess with. I'd never witnessed him display such level of concern, of determination. I had to stop myself from crying then and there.

"It's nothing," I pressed.

The bottomless inhalation he drew in from his nose as he lowered his head echoed around the room. When his eyes lifted, I was pinned by their blue flamed intensity, alongside his ticking jaw.

He wasn't going to let up and leave it be, was he?

For a moment, silence suffused. I was staring him in the eye, restrained by his gaze, pleading that he'd fail to see my doubt and reservation float to the surface. So intent on not allowing anything to be uncovered with simple eye contact, it didn't even register to me when a sneaky, quick hand came to grasp the hem of my T-shirt and was recklessly lifted under my protest.

"Jesus Christ, alive," he gasped almost winded by the sight. Unknowing what to do or say, I merely screwed my eyes wanting to jump into my imaginary time machine and travel back in time five minutes. "Kady—" The arch of my cheeks were freed of the long lashes that lay fanned out across them, as I hesitantly opened my eyes when my name tumbled from him. He was still staring at my discolored flesh.

"I'm fine, it's nothing." Trying to back away on a trampoline was a nightmare, I was unsuccessful, but I tried. My black T-shirt was gathered in his hands, his stunned inspection continued to linger on me. The look on his face, the crumpling of his brow, the narrowing of eyes and twitching of lips was sheer torture.

Examining eyes drifted from the injured area for a brief second as he gulped, "Fine?" In return, his heated, enraged scrutiny was replaced on my exposed flesh. "This is not fine, darlin'. This couldn't be further away from fine if you tried. Wh–what…" Even the warmth of his fingertips set and tracing the border of the marred area had me cringing. "Darlin', please…"

I was licking my lips when he looked me in the eye. Worry, alarm, confusion…it was all there staring back at me on the bobbing waves as they shimmered before me…for me. If only he knew the reason why, I thought to myself.

If I began to believe my lies myself, others would believe me, too.

"I'm okay," I breathed with faux conviction, forcing my lips into a wistful smile. The lone tear seeping down my cheek, however, was surely betraying me. "Can you take me home please?"

He nodded his head in agreement, releasing the material in his grasp, taking extra care to cover me up. "Sure."

We sat for minutes in the pick-up alongside the sidewalk outside my house. The silence was stifling. I didn't want this. This was a sure way to lead into something that I didn't want, something which I couldn't handle: pity. Living each day of my life knowing that someone out there who knew me was actually pitying me, was the worst punishment I could receive.

Walker was rubbing the pad of his right thumb down the center of his upper lip when finally, silence was extinguished. "Kady—" In the periphery of my vision, I saw him turn to face me while my ears were graced with the creaking of his leather jacket. The same courtesy was repaid as I wrenched my head in his direction. And there it was…pity. Unspoken knowledge. A knowledge which I knew if admitted, would be the final nail in my coffin.

"Don't—" I halted his words as he opened his mouth to say something.

"Don't what, darlin'?" he gasped, affronted. "Don't worry about you? Don't care about you? I wouldn't be fucking human if I saw something like that on someone I fucking care about, and not be fucking concerned."

The tartness of his words had me hanging my head and my fingers unconsciously began to rub the tiny teddy bear on my bracelet.

Under his breath, he chided himself. Before I knew it, he shifted along the bench, closing the distance, and my head was coaxed up by the insistence of his finger under my chin. "I care about you, Kady. I'm sorry that I come from a family where affection and respect is mutual and given freely and basked in.

You don't do this to—"

Somehow, I succeeded to choke out the word, "Stop," before he went any further with that statement and there was no turning back for me. Vision clouded and drowning with repressed tears, I watched as his gorgeous, caring face scrunched into a scowl as he shook his head, baffled. "Don't look at me like that or say another word."

"Why? I just want to help." A rolling tear from under my eye was brushed away by a gentle, tender hand before he cradled my cheek. He grimaced, a gasp ousted, as his thumb traced the relics of my split lip and I could see in his eyes he was putting two and two together. I never in my life wanted someone to come out with forty-three so badly.

I was unsure whether it was my own tears I was fighting to curb that was making the depths of his eyes shimmer, or whether they were shimmering as he curbed his own emotions.

I think over time, you become, not accustomed per se, but you can understand in your own little twisted way the reasons for why you deserve the beatings. You make excuses for their behavior, it's easy to discount, easy to justify in your own way. But when an outsider sees it, acknowledges it…you can't hide from it any longer.

"I ask you not to say anything, because if you do, you'll have a way of finally convincing me that I didn't deserve this, and then I have to accept the reality of what *this* actually is."

Shifting in the seat, I went to pull the release of the door when Walker asked if I wanted him to join me and watch a movie, maybe order some takeout. But I knew it was the pity talking. I shook my head, muttering, "I just want to be on my own," and ejected myself from the truck, slamming the door shut behind me.

"Kady," I tuned on my heel as he called my name, that tongue of his rolling over the 'D' yet again. I was getting used to being called Katy by him now. As I looked back I saw he was stretched over the seat, left arm resting on the steering wheel. "Happy birthday," he called, his voice journeying from the lowered window.

Peeking down at my right wrist, and the silver bracelet which adorned it, I smiled. "Thank you," I breathed, before making my way up the front steps and into an empty house to spend the remainder of my birthday fighting a voice that was screaming for my attention.

Its name was, Truth.

CHAPTER
nineteen

The remainder of the evening I spent puttering around the house, polishing, tidying, anything I could think of to stop myself replaying the conversation Walker and I had engaged in while in the truck, along with that tempting voice whispering obscenities of how stupid I was for not listening to it when it only wanted to help me. I cooked some pasta and covered it with a generous helping of cheese, which I was surely going to pay for. Still, the time was ticking at a snail's pace.

It was 8:45 p.m. when I decided to run a bath. We'd lived there for five, nearly six months, yet the tub still went unused. I should've known it was going to be a mistake as soon as I had begun running it. Draining the oils under the faucet, I watched dazed as it fused with the cascading water, the foamy bubbles materializing almost immediately.

I'd slipped out of my clothing, lowered myself into the foam and rested my head back against the side, allowing the diminutive bobbing and swaying of the waves to manipulate my heavy arms into weightless limbs. It was when a void in the bubbles appeared as I gathered them in my arms, giving me an unobstructed view of the sight I had avoided placing my eyes on for quite some time, that had my lungs ripped of breath.

Bronzed flesh colored with a plastering of black, purple, reds and yellow, caused my stomach to constrict and my heart…my heart was shattering. I knew because I could feel the splinters it was leaving in my chest as I recalled that Friday morning, just eleven days ago.

How can someone who says they love you, do that to you? The voice in my head whispered, while the voice of denial and justification told me, that if he didn't lash out after my accusation, it would have been a sure sign that my insinuation was indeed one of fact.

The knot in my gut was weighing me down. To avoid from drowning, I stepped out of the tub. If only I could have admitted that it wasn't water I was going to drown in.

Body wrapped in the warmth of a fluffy towel, I made my way through to the bedroom and into the walk-in-closet. It was when I started tugging on some pink yoga pants and a red camisole that I heard a faint beep. What the fuck was that? Listening intently, I heard it again. It appeared to be sounding from Liam's rails.

I began rummaging through his suit jackets, the beep got louder as I approached his black Armani. My eyes widened in surprise as my hand dipped into his breast pocket and my cellphone was fished out. I'd been wondering for days where it had been hiding. And it was beeping because the battery was almost at zero.

I strolled down the stairs and surfaced in the kitchen, where I pulled the spare drawer open that housed the chargers and odd bits and bobs. The batteries continuation of its dramatic demise ceased when I hooked it up to the charger. I pulled up a message informing me of one voice message. With the handset connected to the charging cable, I dialed my voicemail.

"Kady, its Mom. I'm sorry to call *again* but we've left message after message and still haven't heard back from you, and we really need an answer."

Perplexed, my brow knitted as I continued listening to my mom sniffling at the other end.

"I know that you and Brittany aren't talking, but you're not kids anymore. You're grown adults, so I'm not going to force you both into a room and not have you leave until things are back to normal…"

Damn right she wouldn't.

A crippling sigh from the recording had my lips set in a firm line. "Kady, she's promised she'll stay away from you, just please. She had two grandchildren and loved you both dearly, but you were her first…"

Wait…what? A tremor surged from my knees, up my thighs and hips. I had to lean back onto the unit to maintain holding the weight which was physically crushing my body.

"You'll regret it if you don't say goodbye."

Goodbye? My breathing caught. I held my breath, like the longer I held it, the longer time would pass without hearing the words which followed.

"Your Nan's funeral is next Thursday. Why am I telling you this? I've told you on every one of the messages I've left when it is, so you already know. I'm sorry; I'm all over the place. Kady, you didn't come when I told you she was sick. You didn't have a chance to say goodbye. Don't let this chance pass. I love you, Kady."

In a daze, I ended the call and set it on the counter. Isn't it funny how when the world crumbles away at your feet, the only thing you can hear is the air passing your ears as you fall into oblivion. I knew for a fact I hadn't had any phone calls when I had my phone. Dammit, I hadn't had any voicemails. The only time those calls could have been made was when my handset went missing.

Liam?

Deceived, that's what it was. I felt deceived and confused, enraged, lost, and…

Endeavoring to keep my feet firmly planted on the ground and disallow it to crumble farther, I ran to the sink. Everything in my gut was evacuated before I could halt its progression up my throat.

My head misted over while my stomach flipped, my nails bored into my palms as my fists grew tighter. I couldn't make heads or tails of anything; it was like I wasn't really there. It was a dream, a nightmare, none of this was real. I was waiting for the ground which was swallowing me whole to spit me back out and solidify under my feet. But it wasn't. I was tumbling, freefalling down a chasm with jagged edges, scraping myself on those painful pieces of rock, but still, my body wasn't physically in pain. Adrenaline was overriding everything.

Frantic, I recovered my purse and hastily opened the side zipper. With Walker's number between my fingers, I focused on dialing the number, anything to put my hands to another use which wouldn't include me smashing up the place.

"Walker?" I was panting.

"Kady? What's the matter, darlin'? Everything alright?"

I shook my head, although I knew he couldn't see me. My mind was blurred, dense and screaming. "Where are you?"

"McGinty's. What's the matter?"

"I need to see you. Now."

"Okay, just calm down. I'll come over, give me a few min—"

"No, stay there. I'm leaving now." I hung up, leaving my phone on charge while I gathered my purse, slipped on my flats and scampered out of the door.

"Hey," I flagged down the passing cab while making a hasty descent down the steps. He pulled over, allowing me to slip inside. I told him where to take me and offered twenty dollars tip if he could get me there in less than fifteen minutes, and another ten if he didn't talk to me.

Safe to say, he earned his thirty dollar tip.

The back of my left hand was red, scrapped and on fire by the time I arrived at McGinty's. I barged through the door, spotting Walker at the bar outing his cigarette as he turned to face me, creases marring his brow. Frozen, his large body turned to stone as I charged amongst the throng of people obstructing the walkway, and threw myself at him, wrapping my arms around his neck while standing on tiptoe and permitting his neck to muffle my sobs.

I felt one hand in my hair, resting at the back of my head, while the other was set between my shoulder blades. "Jesus, Kady. What's happened?" When I failed to answer, I heard him ask, "Da, can we go out back?" Carriag must have agreed because next thing I know, I was being steered from the rowdiness of the bar, into the calmness of the back room. "What's happened?" he pressed again, the sound of him locking the heavy door echoed behind us.

"My nan. I haven't been able to find my phone for days. I found it in one of Liam's pockets in the closet. I had a voicemail from my mom saying she's been trying to get in touch with me," the words spewed from my mouth at a frantic pace and I saw he had trouble keeping up. "My nan's dead, Walker, and Liam has been intercepting all of my messages and calls so I didn't know."

His muttering of "Jesus Christ," was shadowed by careful arms gathering around me, taking special care not to touch my ribcage, while he drew me into the consoling warmth of his chest. It was only the feel of his heart drumming like a brass band against my cheek that managed to appease my sobbing. "I'm so, so sorry, darlin'. Is there anything I can do?"

My own breaths were ragged when I pulled away. My hands, already fisted into tight balls at my sides, began to gather into my hair. Like a cornered animal, I studied the small, dimly lit room we were standing in, but not actually taking anything in. "I–I..." tears came harder, my chest was tight, my heart thrumming as adrenaline thwarted my system. "I can't do this...I...I can't think, I can't breathe, I feel like I'm suffocating on so much rage, so much..." My words trailed off, only to be molded into a lengthy grief-stricken roar. Before realization could halt me, a balled, bloodless fist, rapidly connected with the white painted brick wall. Twice.

The shooting pain of the joining surged from my knuckles up my arm into my elbow as it trembled in both shock and temper.

"Kady, enough!" For the first time since meeting him, he actually shouted at me. His demand had me stopping dead, but I still couldn't comprehend and extinguish the wildfire which seared through my entirety making it impossible to breathe. My body was swelling and heating with so many conflicting emotions. I couldn't deal with this. I needed to stop that swelling; I needed to release it, to breath, to free myself of The Devil behind my emotions.

I needed to feel numb.

He stepped toward me, his jaw sturdy, his head held high. I'd not seen him like that before, he was virtually...domineering. That look in his eye, he knew...he knew just like he'd known what I had done in the restroom of Hamersley's that night less than two weeks ago.

My lips trembled. "Help me."

Sucking in a deep breath, his head remained held high, his shoulders back. "Turn around, hands on the desk."

I didn't question him. He knew how he could help me, what I needed, that was blatantly clear. So I did as instructed.

My head hung low focusing on the swirling patterns of the wooden desk, my palms flat against it. He tugged down my yoga pants in one swift motion. But I didn't care. I knew he knew…and I trusted in his judgment. Through rough, rutted breaths I heard the wrenching of leather, before he stated sternly, "This is just to help you, Kady. You tell me when to stop. I need to be able to trust you to tell me when to stop. Do you understand?"

I nodded. "Please, just fucking do it!" I screamed my hysteria, my body temperature so high I was certain I was going to self-combust, while the desk brooked a beating of my right hand in sheer desperation. Tears of irritation and displeasure seeped from my eyes as oxygen lingered in my throat. "DO IT!"

Then, with a catching of his breath, the sound of his belt slicing through the air followed by the bite of it as it connected with my backside had me stiffening. The polished surface was gripped forcefully by tightening hands. My face contorted on a whimper while another sharp bite, followed by another, had me breathless. Still, I wasn't even close to what I needed. I continued to shake with adrenaline, tears of confusion and frustration bled from my eyes, the wooden surface underneath me catching each splattering. The swelling of emotions was nowhere near alleviated, and in those moments, the fraught urgency I felt alone, would've been enough to sway me to do something dangerous just to relieve them within a heartbeat.

"Harder, please, Walker, Harder…"

With heavy, ragged breaths and a menacing grunt, he stood

aside, and the dividing of air was the loudest I'd ever heard in my life. Whatever air I successfully managed to gather in my lungs between lashes was ousted on a pleading yell as the power behind his belt intensified upon my command. Winded as the sting radiated across my ass cheeks in a form of welts, up to my throat, hands which braced my weight tautened, and my head was thrown back, while every muscle in my body tensed beyond any strength they'd ever endured.

The blissful place I had frantically sought was found thanks to the man behind me. During each stabilized pant as my breathing regulated, the lashes, although lessened in power, continued. Each thrashing now dispensed, my body sank into, practically unresponsive as I stood, hands braced on the desk without so much as a tensed muscle after each additional belting. My limit was found and reached. Walker knew that without so much as me telling him, and now, like a pro, he was reeling me back, working me down, leveling me out…prolonging my feeling of clarity, of emotional numbness…of bliss.

My own blissful oblivion.

When tears ran dry, I closed my eyes, my inhalations shallow and even. The sound of leather clattering to the floor was shadowed by Walker's own heavy gasps. Unmoving, my head remained hung, the swelling gone, my head no longer aching, just…silence.

Flinching wasn't an option when I felt calloused hands clutch my hips, and turned me around. I was practically catatonic when we sunk to the ground, Walker cradling me in his understanding, reassuring arms, his legs open, as I avoided any pressure on my behind and positioned myself on my hip in between them.

Into his heaving chest I nuzzled, while relaxing fingers twisted in my hair.

"Thank you, Walker," I whispered, my voice low and smooth,

my gratitude bountiful.

"Shush, don't speak. Just savor it. Savor that numbness, darlin'." And oddly enough, I understood exactly what he meant.

"I don't want you to be left on your own tonight, darlin'." Walker's concern was broached while we were in the pick-up, drawing the seatbelt across our bodies.

For the first time since that afternoon, I sniggered ironically.

"What?"

"Funny enough, I was about to say, I really don't want to go back home."

One word was posed that had my head rearing up and our eyes locking over the bench. "Mine?"

I couldn't say anything. The simple faint nod of my head was his indication, and with a grin, he promptly pulled out of the gravel lot, and headed west.

Just by the dilapidated buildings, the graffiti surrounding the area and the not too distant sound of sirens, I knew that this was a bad part of town. And I didn't even need to work years on the force and get promoted to detective for that one.

Putting the truck into park, I perused the area. A basketball court surrounded by a metal fencing along my right, and what looked like a never-ending row of run-down, dark terraced properties, some with boarded up windows, others with yet more graffiti, spanned along my left. The corner building was tall, bay windows stacked above one another. The scorch marks on the exterior were evidence that the structure had seen more than one fire in its time.

"The Pavilion. Home sweet home," he murmured with a somewhat derisive undertone in his husky, lilted voice.

I wasn't going to lie. A name like that and a structure like this, really should be immeasurable miles apart. But, I kept that to myself and flashed him a wistful smile.

"Come on, in we go."

Inside the small entry hall, my heart lurched. With each flight of creaky stairs we ascended, and each vandalized wall with X-rated doodles and certain curse words scrolled, my heart eventually gave up lurching, and merely sat clogging the space in my throat. Walker really lived here?

When we graced the third level, I was startled by shouting from beyond the door to my right. "Ignore those, they're always at it. You learn to block it out eventually." If I was the one living here, I didn't think I could ever ignore an argument which was that heated. I meekly followed up behind him, my hands forgoing natural instincts to clasp hold of the balustrade that looked ready to crumble at any moment.

The green door ahead of me stated that I was standing outside apartment 4b. Walker slipped the key in the lock, twisted it and gave the bottom of the door a swift kick, before the door swung from the frame. As he went inside, I lingered just on the threshold. I finally took a cautionary step inside, when the side lamp next to the couch chased the shadows of the apartment away, and closed the door behind me with a press of my back.

"Welcome to the humble abode," he teased, his hands gestured to the surroundings that were the living room then fell deeply into his denim pockets.

The plain boards protested under my feet with each step I took. The mismatched furniture, the barrenness of the cracked and crumbling walls, the chipped gloss on the windowpane of the bay window, everything was… rundown, worn. But it didn't matter, because it was Walker's place, and even though it wasn't much and wasn't as glamorous as some properties, he managed to make it a home—his home, a home without fear.

Motioning to the sofa, he told me to have a seat before offering me a drink. I nodded. "Too late for coffee, I'm afraid, darlin'. Beer okay for you?"

"Sure," I snorted. With a playful bow, he made his way down the small hall to the right as I strolled toward his couch along the back wall.

The lamp on the side table to the left of me created a muted glow, one which could be deemed as almost romantic. The gap in the right corner beside the bay window piqued my interest; I noticed the neck of an acoustic guitar. Being nosey, I shimmied across the dark cushions, the springs groaned and twanged like a harp being played by unskilled hands, as I did so, and pulled free the instrument.

Bracing it on my lap, I admired its simplicity while my fingers caressed the strings. When Walker finally advanced from the corner, he set my bottle of beer on the coffee table separating the couch and a ragged, chair facing the sofa.

"You play?" I asked.

He nodded his head, taking a slow draw from his bottle.

"Any good?" I grinned, my brow arched.

He sheathed his perfectly straight white teeth with his lips, before his right thumb came up to rub along the center of his upper lip in that adorable, shy way that never failed to have me smiling. "I think it would be biased if I answer that, darlin'."

Stroking the orange wood, I plucked one of the strings and nipped my lower lip keenly as it vibrated. I lifted my gaze and came face to face with adoring, enraptured eyes studying me. "Will you play something for me?"

After a beat, the bottom of his beer clanked as he set it on the coffee table. He took position on the chair opposite after taking possession of the neck of the instrument. "What do you want me to play?"

I shrugged. After the night I'd had, damn, after the week I'd had, anything would have been a welcomed distraction. "Something soothing."

I watched as the cogs behind his eyes turned, his lips pursed with thought. Finally he nodded, and got himself comfortable, perching himself on the edge of the seat and shifting his legs apart slightly. He began to play a soft tune. He was good. Real good.

What I didn't expect was for his mouth to open, freeing yet more of a talent that went unknown.

"Just give me your hand,
Just give me your hand,
And I'll walk with you,
Through the streets of our land.
If you give me your hand,
Just give me your hand,
And come along with me.
By day and night,
Through all struggle and strife,
And beside you, to guide you,
Forever my love.
For love's not for one,
But for both of us to share,
For our country so fair,
For our world and what's there."

"Wow," I gasped with a stunned, unmasked grin. "That was…" I shook my head, his shy smile dancing across his mouth. "That was beautiful. I've never heard that before."

"It's an old Irish folk song. My ma used to sing it to me."

"Used to?" The curious tone of my voice had Walker's head tipping forward. "She died when I was seventeen."

"Oh, Walker, I'm so sor—" My sympathies were cut short as his tall, muscular form was hastily lifted from the chair, allowing him to slip the guitar back into its designated corner.

"It's alright, darlin'." He swapped the chair for the empty space beside me on the couch. "She's always with me. Right here," right arm crooked, he pressed his palm against his heart and smiled. "You look tired, Kady."

I yawned. The last thing I remember was saying thank you.

"What for?" he asked with narrowed, skeptical eyes.

"For caring about me."

A broadening smile along with the warmth of his hand cradling my cheek, I was promptly lost in the bottomless depths of The Indian Ocean. "Forever and a day, Kady. I promise."

CHAPTER
twenty

The following morning, as I straightened out my limbs, arched my back and fluttered my eyelids, two questions in my mind were found to be contending for the entitlement of first to be answered: when did I get into Walker's bed, and why was I looking down on myself? Or up at myself, whichever way you want to discern it.

"She's awake." A soft, familiar brogue sounded from the right of my feet. Eyes being rubbed to within an inch of their lives in sleep removal, I peered down at the doorway. Walker was leaning against the doorjamb, his hair all wet and unkempt from his shower, while the shape and broadness of his body was presented by the hugging of dark jeans and a black tank top. He looked utterly divine—especially with that dark scruff coating his mouth. "I have coffee," he added, practically forcing his speech through a shy smile.

Bringing the coffee mug to his chest, he began gradually strolling into the room.

The springs inside the mattress squealed as I sat myself up, muttering a sleepy, "Thank you," while seizing the mug of happiness from his clutches. As the bitter taste of Heaven slipped down my throat, the black wrought iron bedframe squeaked when he lowered himself onto the edge beside my feet. Embarrassment chased my lustful ogling of his muscular arms. It was the first time I had seen them, and the tribal sleeve tattoo ran down his left arm, whereas a large, Celtic-styled cross lay covering his right bicep.

"Should I even ask why you have a mirror on your ceiling? You're not just an Irishman are you? You're hiding some kinkiness under that exterior," I giggled; although, I'd be untruthful if I didn't admit I felt some sort of spear voyaging through my heart at the mere contemplation of Walker being intimate with anyone, especially in the bed I was currently occupying. It was stupid and immature, I knew that. Still, it didn't stop me.

He tipped his head back on a small, husky chuckle, the prominence of his Adam's apple eliciting unexpected effects from my body and my mind. A vision of me setting my mug on the bedside table, pushing myself up onto my knees and gliding my tongue from the hollow of his throat, up and over to his jawline, and through that facial hair, was killing me. "You're still new to all this, Kady. I'll explain it one day."

"Wow," Pouting, arching my brow and bating my eyelashes in unison, I lowered my coffee, "You're being very…Yoda-ish this morning."

"Yoda-ish? That's a new one for the Oxford dictionary. I umm…" Walker dropped his focus to his hands and momentarily trailed off as he wrung his fingers in his lap. "I thought we could go out for breakfast."

"Go out? Walker, I am far from suitably attired to be going

anywhere, let alone somewhere with patrons."

"Don't be silly, darlin'." The bed groaned its irate noise, which could rival nails down a blackboard, as he shifted and plowed into the walk-in-closet, which was more of a cupboard, at the foot of the bed. After a little delving around he said, "Here," and in his grasp, hung a white Lonsdale sweater.

He had to be kidding me. I had never been one for brand-named sportswear, even in my own house. I certainly couldn't go out wearing it, unless I was going for a run, at least. Returning back to his position as he perched himself, once again, on the bed, Walker handed me the sweater. The cautionary glare I was directing upon the material, contrasting with the hopeful gleam in his eye. "Kady, you could be wrapped up in a potato sack and still look gorgeous, darlin'."

I sighed loudly with a flail of my head in defeat. "Fine, you win, I'll wear it. But first, I have business to take care of." I fumbled around with the comforter until I'd finally unbound myself from the gothic-styled bed, only to have Walker halt me with a warm, passionate grip around my wrist.

I had no idea where my yoga pants were. I stood before him, under his intense scrutiny in only my panties and camisole, but I didn't care. For some reason, I felt that what we shared together the night before—although nothing sexual—had brought us closer together and strengthened our friendship. It was almost like it had bonded us.

So with a shudder at the single contact of Walker's fingertips brushing and tracing over and around the oval and circular silver scars coating my thighs, I merely peeked down and studied him, studying me.

Did I feel at all embarrassed like I had with Liam? No, I didn't, far from it. Did I feel ashamed of how I had defaced my body as

I sought an outlet? No, I didn't, because at that moment, the only person in the world who understood me, was the one who's fingers were caressing my flesh. I didn't feel an ounce of pity, of shame, or disgust coming from this man, but understanding, support and attachment.

When he peeked up at me, I was smiling down at him, my heart and body swelling, but in a good way. Gazing into his eyes, I could see it all, all his emotion, all his fondness. A universe of understanding looked back at me. And the barrier I had placed up before me and my own secrets, to remain masked by everyone in my life, was lowered. At least, it was lowered for this person.

With Walker, I could truly be myself.

Forty-five minutes later, Walker was holding my door open like a gentleman, as I lowered myself out of the truck in front of the red and yellow diner.

"Walker, I'm really feeling uncomfortable in my state of sloppy-dress, here," I griped for the eighth time since leaving his apartment, burrowing my hands into the oversized pouch pocket on my abdomen. Yesterday's pink yoga pants, a pair of flats, a certain someone's five times too big Lonsdale hoodie and disheveled blond hair piled in a knot atop of my head with the odd, windswept tendrils escaping and framing my face, was not the most gracious state of dress.

"Jesus Christ, Kady, you look gorgeous. You got that natural beauty about you, stop grouching."

The proffering of his hand went overlooked with a small shake of my head, and an apologetic, tightlipped smile. I simply followed behind his towering physique, while replying teasingly to his previous statement, with, "Yes, sir."

"Morning, Walker." Behind the counter a pretty woman tugging her high set ponytail even tighter, before refilling a patron's mug of coffee, greeted him.

As I combed my gaze around my surroundings, I came to the conclusion that the Diner had that 1980's, milkshake after school, kind of feel to it. I liked it.

"Mornin', Tiff," he answered.

"Take a seat; I'll be with you in a moment."

"'Aye, whenever you're ready." He waved her off when we slipped into the comfort of red pleather bench seats of one of many booths along the perimeter.

"An old flame?" I pestered, taking possession of one of the menus.

"Who, Tiffani?" he snorted. "She owns the place, darlin'. I'm always here, can't get enough of their breakfasts."

"Tiffani's Diner?"

"'Aye, well, I'd be a little concerned if it was called Tiffani's Diner, and the owner was a fat balding guy called, Shamus, wouldn't you?"

Certain that a simple amused chuckle would be unfeasible, but more like a, 'roll on your back while clutching your side and clapping like a demented sea lion' kind of hysterics, I fought to maintain my poise. With a collected shake of my head I resumed the task of scouring through the menu.

"I'm sorry about that, busy morning today," Tiffani chuckled, looking a little windswept while she brushed, what I could only presume was clammy palms, down her retro yellow waitress dress and red waist apron. Notepad and pen in hand, with a smile and deep composed breath, she waited for our order.

"I'll have my usual, Tiff, and for the lady…"

"I'll just have a strong coffee and the waffles with maple syrup, please."

"Sure thing; won't be too long." She smiled again, and

scampered off to the kitchen.

I was amidst people watching from the window along my right, and toying with one of the sachets I had pulled from the caddy, when I eventually summoned the courage to ask something which had been playing on my mind.

"Walker, how did…" When I chanced a glance over the table, he was toying with his own little sachet while studying me. "How did you know what I needed last night? How did you know what would help me—"

"Is that really a question you want an answer for?" There he was, the little green guy with big ears surfacing from him again, and I'm not taking about a leprechaun either. "It wasn't that difficult, Kady. I knew it the night at Hamersley's."

"But how—" I scowled.

"You rush from the table like a mare that's been startled by a snake in the reeds, and you come back looking practically serene."

The heaviness and brute honesty of his words had my head dropping forward. If it was so blatantly obvious to him, was it that obvious to the others? "I'm so weak," I sighed.

"Weak?" The sole word was gasped from across the tabletop.

I raised my head with a sullen look burned into my features, and met his staunchly fixed expression from under ashamed hooded eyes. Griping pleather drilled into my ears when he shifted to the edge of the bench, his body virtually folded over the white table separating us.

"Kady, I like to think that people like us are as strong as they fucking come. A man goes to work, gets stressed out, has a game of golf over the weekend and all is right with the world. But for us, we let things mount up. We're strong enough to keep adding and adding to the pile of shit that fills that damn balloon, and after a while, we just can't take no more. A puncture in that balloon isn't going to help, we need to gut that sucker open and release all the shit that we, as strong motherfucking people, managed to accumulate and conceal."

"But why? Why does it work that way? How—?" That is what I wanted and needed to know. Why? Why did it work that way? I knew most of it was down to sheer control, but why would someone who was emotionally hurting, need to physically hurt themselves to feel better? It didn't make any sense.

He shrugged his shoulders. "Who knows?" Weighed sighs and perplexed expressions filled the time lapse, before he finally spoke again. "Kady, I want to ask you to do something for me, and if you say yes, it means you're going to have to make me a promise."

Intriguing. "Go on."

"When you feel that way again—and I am straining the *'when'* because it isn't a case of *if* anymore. Your mind has already processed that in doing this to yourself you're able to get instant relief, so it is a matter of *when*—you'll come to me. I don't care if it's at 4:30 in the morning or if Liam is beside you, you make an excuse and you come to me."

I did a pretty shit job at masking my confusion. His speech was full of passion and seemingly desperate. With furrows in my brow and a minute cock of my head, I pursed my lips. "That's a strange request, Walker."

"Kady," he rubbed his forehead with his left hand, virtually exasperated, before going back to his sachet with a heavy droop in his posture. "It's easy to lose control, and I don't want you to lose it."

"Lose control? I—"

"I'm going to ask you a very personal question, darlin'. What's your method?"

Without a second thought, I tossed his question back at him.

"Well, I didn't see any lacerations on your body, so I know you're not a cutter."

How did this conversation get so deep, so quickly? He really wanted to know? Me sharing something, a secret which was mine, and mine alone, a dark and dirty secret full of so much sin, was something that I couldn't even contemplate. I didn't want to share this. But it was Walker, and he knew me and how my twisted, warped mind was working, better than I did. This was all so new to me, and by the way he talked and explained it, he was obviously talking from experience. Good God alive, how can someone be experienced in the art of self-harm? It was twisted.

The sphere of apprehension cleared from my throat with a loud grunt. I licked my lips. "Heat," my voice was scarcely a whisper over the clattering of cutlery around us.

I watched on as his eyes widened and glimmered. Rays blazed in through the window to my right, casting a stream of light across the table and brightening his already ridiculously bright eyes. "Heat, like wax?"

"Heat, like…" damn this was hard. In sharing this with him, I was sharing my soul. I dropped my head to focus on the table distancing us, unable to look him in the eyes when I bore myself to the only man in the world who understood me. "Heating metal, or anything that's there really."

The moment I sought his gaze, I discovered his eyes twinkling with knowledge. He nodded his head pensively, "Makes sense. Okay, this is just an example, okay." His statement was enhanced by the firm gesture of his hand. I'd felt his calloused before, but I never really saw the physical damage to the skin over his palm until then.

I nodded.

"One day, you will have stored so much in that body and mind of yours that the simple blistering steel on your skin, won't help alleviate it quick enough. You will be in so much emotional pain, so much fury inside of your body, that your judgment will be clouded by sheer greed and desperation. You won't see the consequences of your actions because all you need is to gut that swelling open and free yourself of that anger, and emotional suffering." He spoke with his features set in a hard, uncompromising fashion, The Indian Ocean darkening as his head tumbled forward slightly, yet they still possessed the intensity to pin me in my seat from the opposite side of the table.

He spoke like he had experienced this before. It was scary.

"That day, is the day you will cross a line and lose utter control. You won't go for a spoon, you won't care about reaching your limit and reeling yourself back, you'll push that limit to get instant relief. You might set yourself on fire."

I scoffed, "On fire?" That was too farfetched for me to stifle any forms of disbelief.

"Example, Kady," he chided before resuming. "My point is: if you set fire to yourself, your brain registers that within a millisecond you're free of that emotional, pent-up frustration. The next time it happens, you'll remember how quick it was to free yourself. You'll no longer abide by your body's limits, Kady; you'll keep exceeding them, overstepping them. You'll have no respect for them or your body, and one day, you'll wake up not recognizing who you are."

"You speak like you've faced this before." A wistful smile was offered from my side of the booth, before I narrowed my eyes perceptively. "Have *you* ever lost control?"

His head lowered, but his eyes remained lingering on me. "Yes," he admitted bluntly, and the flow of air caught in my throat at his admission. "And it's something that I can't escape from—

something that is always there and something which I have to focus on, when I need my next form of relief. I'm not proud of it. But that is something that I don't want you to go through, darlin'."

"You just admitted to losing control with yourself, how do I know you wouldn't lose control with me?" Fair question, I thought.

"You have just shared with me the darkest, and probably the biggest secret you will ever have in your life, Kady. Do you trust me?"

"Yes," I replied without a second of hesitancy, because I did. He was right. I just shared a piece of my soul with him. I did trust him, probably more than a certain someone.

Our moment was broken when the waitress came with plates in her hand. "I have Walker's usual, and waffles. I'll get your coffees now." She set the large white plates down on the table and returned back to the counter.

Gathering my hands in his as he extended his arms across the table, the look of undiluted restraint burned brightly in his eyes. "Please, Kady. I want to help you. Let me help you. Let me be your anchor."

When Tiffani came back with our beverages, I couldn't shift the voice in my mind which kept telling me that, I was new to all this, by the looks of things, Walker knew damn well what he was talking about. I knew I'd be safe there. I knew he would keep me safe, I'd never doubt that.

As my answer was conveyed by a simple nod of my head, a smile tiptoed across his face.

In his clutch, my hands were lifted up to his mouth. "Thank you, Kady." He kissed the back of my hand with a sigh, his callouses grazed my palm as his scruff grazed my knuckles. "Thank you."

CHAPTER
twenty-one

It was four hours after leaving Walker's company when Liam strolled through the front door. This was the moment which bred my anxiety, my fear. The mere sound of the front door closing behind him had me struggling for vital breath amidst the heavy blanket which fell above me, storing all negativity that was surging its way through my system, retaining it as it frantically sought an outlet.

The sound of his footsteps had me quaking. In that moment, I idly pondered how it was possible for the soft sounds of feet padding over hardwood, to be both gentle and menacing.

Behind the kitchen island, I stood immobilized staring down at the cellphone that had caused so much heartbreak just last night. A soft, cheerful whistle wafted through the house, the lively melody was shaded by a not so lively man.

I didn't venture a look at him. I kept my regard fixed firmly on the handset on the oak surface of the island, my hands gripping lightly at the ledge, upholding my weight through locked arms.

Seeing him in my peripheral vision at the dining table, I granted the much needed breath I drank in, to surpass the penetrating sense of foreboding. I wanted to cry. I wanted to break. I wanted to just run far, far away and live, or not live, the rest of my life without this sickening, fisted ominous feeling in my gut and my chest—the same one that was the foundation of my everyday life.

It was consuming.

Liam was consuming.

"Well, this is a warm welcome if I must say," he sliced the silence with his cutting words, his tone one of derision.

This wasn't going to go down well. I think I dwelled for those full four, lonely hours on how I was going to advance this hurdle, and how I was to fare with the ramifications afterwards. I still hadn't called my mom back. There was no way on this God's green Earth, was I going to fail to attend my Nan's funeral, however, I wasn't going to provoke Liam by jumping straight in and demanding. I had to try and take the right steps.

If only I knew what the right steps for this problem were.

Gripping hands turned white and cold as the blood of my knuckles ceased with the increasing pressure initialized on the island ledge. A shudder spawned as I felt him prowling toward me. The heat of his glare practically stripped the flesh from my bones.

"I go away on a business trip to land a contract so I can buy my girlfriend clothes, cosmetics, make sure she has a nice house, and extravagant meals," by this time, he was on the opposite side of the island, mimicking my pose, yet, a contrasted mirror image—him angry, me desolate. "And I don't even get a 'welcome home, Liam', or 'Do you want a coffee, Liam'. Even better, 'I have made you dinner, Liam'," he hissed.

"Why didn't you tell me?" His former words fell on deaf ears as I lifted my rapt stare from the handset and studied the man who was more like a stranger. His dusky blue shirt was undone at the collar, the spider's web pulsing on the left side of his neck. A hand was removed from the wooden edge, only to be raked back through his brown hair, making it slick back before falling to the side. "Why didn't you tell me about the phone calls? Why didn't you tell me about the voicemails?"

I swear I saw the mist from his harsh outbreath leave his nostrils. Brow crumpled he muttered, "What the fuck are you talking about?"

"My nan, Liam. Why didn't you tell me?" My jaw was working at a million miles an hour as I dragged the words out through clenched teeth. The fury I felt in those few minutes were nothing in comparison, to how I felt that morning I accused him doing something with Liv. A stranger could have sensed that this was the calm before the storm. Pearl Harbor was about to be rivaled.

He shook his head with a dumbfounded look, which only served to stir my anger more so. "What about your nan?" He was doing a damn good job at keeping up his pretense that was for sure, nevertheless, all it did was outrage me more.

"This," I held the handset up in my right hand. Pressing the little green button, I pulled up my voicemail and pressed call before handing it to the idiot opposite me.

Time always has a way to mock you when you try to make a point. But it was when Liam drew the handset from his right ear, looked down at it, then at me and said with a snigger, "There's nothing there, Kady," that time froze completely.

"What?" I glowered, my finger lifting to point at the piece of tech in his possession. "There is a voicemail from my mother on there, saying about all the messages she left, that my Nan was sick and I missed my chance to say goodbye, and that the funeral is next Thursday. I didn't get any of those calls or messages, Liam. Now stop lying to me!" I shouted, the island taking the brunt end of my rage as I thumped the underside of my clenched fist upon its surface.

"Kady," he freed an incredulous chuckle, which was shadowed by an even more incredulous grin as his mouth quirked. "There is nothing in this voicemail box. Here,"—the phone was handed back to me over the island—"if you don't believe me, listen to it yourself."

Not so steady hands reached out to seize his offering. Glaring at him with my heart threatening to explode from my chest, I redialed my mailbox and listened carefully to the robotic-like voice sounding down the speaker.

"You have no new messages…main menu, to listen to your messages, press one…"

I pressed one.

"You have no new messages…main menu, to listen to your messages, press one…"

I pressed one again and again only to have the same message relayed. I pulled it from my ear, giving it a little shake. I don't know why, but it seemed like the right thing to do, shake some sense into it or something, I don't know, but when I lifted it to my ear again, and pressed that damn button once more, the same message was communicated.

My frantic state on the opposing side of the kitchen was studied by Liam with an imperiling, sanctimonious smirk plastered across his face.

His expression alone spoke volumes. It revealed a notion, an act so devious I couldn't comprehend. My heart ceased in its cavity, my veins were chilled from the ice streaming through them. He had just fucking deleted it…

"No…no, no, no," I muttered, flailing my head. My hands were shaking, while internally, I felt every organ, every nerve tense and jitter. I knew there was a message on that thing. I listened to it myself last night, and five times during the prior four hours before Liam's return. It was on there. It was definitely there.

I was seething. The icy blood in my veins thawed and boiled as anger stewed deep in my bones. Erratic pants were clouded by my panic, my frustrations and despair. Seeing Liam's face carve into a blood-curdling sneer wasn't helping.

I was breathing, I could feel my lungs filling to capacity, yet my chest wasn't registering any air which had passed, allowing the lingering stifling sensation to sit and brew in my chest. Muffled ringing in my ears caused everything to fall away. I was dreaming. I had to be. No, not a dream, this was nothing but a nightmare, a nightmare which I could wake from, if I did something to shock myself out of it.

Dazed and provoked, I scanned the room in utter desperation; Liam's voice was nothing but a distant hum. I don't know why, but once again instinct took over, and I pulled one of the drawers open hastily and retrieved one of the steak knives, one that had a jagged, shiny blade. The cold wooden handle took its place between my fingers as I concentrated profusely on shocking myself enough to wake myself from this terror. Swiping against the bronzed flesh of the upper inside of my left arm, the serrated edge burned prompting a gasp to be wrenched from my throat. The warmth and trickling of the velvet, crimson fluid down my arm, was followed by another sharp slice, which brought my tears into full flow.

This had to be a dream, because Liam merely stood observing me in my hysteria. If the last incident he witnessed was anything to go by, then he wouldn't just stand there watching, that I knew.

After the sweeping of the fourth slash and salted tears robbed me of my vision, I came to realize, I wasn't dreaming. Lines had been crossed, deceitful, conniving lines which no human in possession of empathy and compassion would cross. Nothing was going to wake me up from this, and the part of me that accepted that knowledge, just wanted to take the knife I held in my hand and slice right into the pale blue pipe running up my wrist, and drag it upward. That was the same sorrowful part of Kady Jenson, which just wanted to watch the emotions, the anger, frustration, grief, and confusion bleed out of her in the fusion of liquid rage.

When I eventually stopped, I wailed in my desperation.

"Kady," I was pulled back by Liam's velvet, husky voice drawing out my name. He held out his hand, "Give me the knife, baby," he requested as though talking to a child with a razor blade, while utmost concern and love veiled his tone.

Deadened and crushed, I inertly handed him the blade, feeling my lips wither with every conflicted, chaotic gasp that passed them. When the wooden handle was clasped in his right hand, a shudder paved its way up my spine and down my legs as I saw his features, which were concerned and cautious only a breath ago, now hardened with a demonic mask. The left corner of his mouth lifted in an evil sneer, his green and blue speckled eyes hardened in a fashion that dared to be challenged with.

"No, no, no, Liam, don't—" I yelled out, but it was too late. The cutting edge of the knife was pressed into his left palm as he closed his fingers around the steel and sliced downwards. Blood instantly flowed from the incision to trickle and pool on the flooring, while the knife fell from his grasp and clattered to its fate.

"Kady," he sighed with his hand open, offering an unobstructed sight of the wound. "Look what you did."

Huh? "Wh–what, I did? Liam, I di—"

"I was only trying to help you, Kady," his brow crumpled in his desolation, his eyes watering. "Why would you run at me like that?"

"Ru–run, I...I, didn't do anyth—" I couldn't string a sentence together if I tried. My jaw unceasingly dropped open like it was no longer attached to my body. During the spell of flailing my head as I strove to recall exactly what had transpired, my chest heaved. All the while as I attempted to make heads and tails of the situation, my lips were twitching.

"Kady, you're sick. I want to help you, but this is twice you've attacked me."

"T–twice? Atta—?" Was I missing something? I frantically perused the area as I filtered through my memory bank, striving to seek and add together these disremembered moments. But it was nothing but a cold, blank canvas.

"You're a self-harmer, Kady baby. But you're not only a danger to yourself anymore; you're a danger to others...you're a danger to me."

"No...no...no...no...I haven't gone for you Liam. I would never attack you. I know that message was on my phone, and—"

"Kady, you heard it yourself. There is nothing on that phone. And you just struck me because of it." Even though his calm, collected and convincing voice traveled to my ears, my brain was frantically absorbing the words he spoke, while I untiringly hunted for the missing acts he was referring to, but the void was just that...a void.

"You're delusional, Kady. I can't ignore this anymore. You need actual, psychiatric help."

Did I? I didn't think I did, but then again, how would I know if I did? Was I blacking out? A nauseating sphere of remorse and turmoil sat and spread through my body as I peeked down at the laceration in the center of Liam's palm.

"Liam, I…"

"I'm sorry." He took me in his arms, held my head against his chest and softly swayed us both, his shirt damp with my tears. "You've been under so much stress lately. It shouldn't have gotten this out of hand. But we'll get you better, baby." He planted a kiss on my head, and I swore I heard the smile in his voice as he added, "I'll get you the best treatment and medication that money can buy."

Three hours later, I was sitting in a ball in the corner of the living room feeling like a fragile little girl in a complete catatonic daze, while Liam and the emergency shrink sat on the couch along the way.

"So, how long as she been like this, Mr. DeLaney."

"It's been a few months." He sounded like he was underwater, or I was underwater. Fuck, was I even here, or was I in a bath with my head submerged listening to him talking to me on a normal day? "She began self-harming but after a while, she began acting almost… delusional."

"You say delusional, what do you mean exactly? Could you give me some examples?"

"Nearly two weeks ago, I surprised her with breakfast in bed…"

I listened to the muffled voices, my eyes incapable of crying anymore tears. Heat coursed through the back of my left hand as my nails grated at the flesh over my knuckles, burrowing deeply as if to remove the thing that was causing me to act this way, and bring harm to those I loved.

"She woke up convinced that she heard me and her friend talking on the phone early hours in the morning, and accused me of sleeping with her."

"And you hadn't been—"

"Of course not. I was having a business call. Even so, I'd never stoop that low. I wouldn't like it if she did it to me. Anyway, the next thing I know, the tray with hot food and coffee was hurled at my head. It's lucky I'm a fast mover."

"And today?"

Watching the flesh of my left hand scoured by my nails, I found the changing in color, the light bronzed glow of my skin, turning white with pressure then red with burning irritation, somewhat hypnotic. I continued focusing on the mass of distant, clouded voices.

Liam sniggered. "Her grandmother has recently passed, and she just lost it. She was convinced that there was some message on her phone, when I listened, the voicemail was empty, and she flipped. She started cutting herself and when I struggled to get the knife from her, she turned on me. I held my hands up to protect myself, but it was no use. It could have been my eye she had out."

I hung my head while relics of tears I didn't know existed, seeped from my eyes. Was that really what happened? How come I don't remember any of this? For God sake what is wrong with me? My God, Liam, I am so, so sorry.

"Mr. DeLaney, we all deal with grief in our own personal ways. Obviously, this is Kady's way, and denial plays a big part in the eventual form of acceptance. Considering she has suffered… umm…unstable moments, I think it would be best, not only for her own safety, but for the individuals who she groups with, if we take her in short term for assessment. We can begin a course and observe her reactions with medication that will help relieve the tension and stable her a little. Does that sound okay with you?"

I sat in that ball, my knees pulled up against my body wanting to protest with every remaining bit of strength and perseverance that I had. Nonetheless, the voice of justification and denial told me that I had no right. It told me that this has gone too far, and that Liam was right: I did need help. Next time it could be worse.

"Yes, please, do whatever needs to be done to make her better. I'm just sorry I didn't notice the warning signs sooner. All of this could have been avoided."

"Mr. DeLaney, you can't post blame on yourself, you're getting her the help she needs now. That's the important thing. Do you want to press charges?"

Charges? Oh, God…oh, God…

"No, that's not necessary," he muttered, and I found myself releasing the breath I had stored in my lungs at the mere noting of that question.

Lost in oblivion with the fiery overlay plastered to my left hand, I was pulled from my ball in the corner of the living room, and escorted out of the house, down the steps, to the sidewalk.

"Can I just say goodbye to her?" Liam asked the male shrink who must have nodded, because I was soon swallowed up in Liam's arms, his mouth an inch from the hollow on my ear. My body shuddered at the absence of concern in his voice, which was only to be replaced with haughtiness and a somewhat scathing tone, "There's no point in demanding that you're not crazy. They won't listen. All the crazy people say that they're not."

Feeling dead, his arms fell from around my mentally fragile body before I was folded in the car. The seatbelt was drawn across my body by the shrink while I remained motionless, totally inert, just focusing on the grating of flesh, as we pulled away from the sidewalk.

I'm not crazy…I'm not crazy…I'm not crazy…my mantra was repeated after every tree we passed along the tree lined streets.

Eventually, I sank back into the seat and rested my head against the window to my right as we journeyed to Pinewood Institute.

Who was I kidding, Liam was right: all the crazy people say that they're not.

CHAPTER
twenty-two

Days in Pinewood Institute were like reading the instructions of a shampoo bottle. Lather…rinse…repeat. Although, this was more of a: wake up. Have your pills. Have your breakfast. Sit in the dayroom. Wait for your appointment. Get summoned by the orderlies for your appointment. Talk to the shrink or in my case, sit and stare into oblivion, it's easier that way. Nothing can be misconstrued. Words can't get put into your mouth, and at least you remember not saying a word. Go back to the dayroom. Have your food. Take your pills. Go to bed, and repeat.

    The first two days I was less than compliant. I never needed to take medication in my life, not for mental illness anyway. Mental illness…those words are like an ugly brand, a brand that divides you from the world of people. It makes you feel alien. Yet, you can walk down the street and bump into someone; you don't know whether they've had a breakdown, suffered depression, acute anxiety, bipolar…delusions. I sniggered to myself, delusional… if I was on the street now and bumped into someone, I think my entire day would consist of questioning if it actually happened.

Was Liam right? Was I in fact delusional? A fixed false belief that is resistant to reason or confrontation with actual fact…he said I attacked him. He said I was the one who cut him.

For the days in which I was a patient of Pinewood, I fixated on how I felt and the events that occurred which led to that dreadful confrontation. Everything was like a dream. I was in a dream, a nightmare—a trancelike state. I remembered back to when I was seven. I had a dream where I was running, running so fast my feet would barely touch the floor, and before I knew it, I was jumping like The Incredible Hulk all over the place. When I woke the following morning, I attempted it. Because sometimes, to realize that it was only an act of a dream, you need cold, hard evidence.

Maybe the same thing happened with Liam and me. Maybe I did attack him but dreamed I didn't. I had to take the three inch laceration on his palm as my cold, hard evidence.

I *did* attack him.

I *was* delusional.

Despite the fact I loathed being kept prisoner by four stark white walls and the black and white checkered tiling beneath my feet, and only the sounds of mumbling and the occasional obscenity being shouted out, I was thankful to Liam for one thing: he sought the help I obviously needed, but couldn't appreciate that I needed. It could've been so much worse. Liam could've been in the hospital, and I could have been in jail with a criminal record for assault…or even worse.

Sitting in stark white pajamas, I gazed out the window of the dayroom, silently studying a flower swaying in the breeze. Because of the strictness of daily routines, the days were vague and indistinct as they blurred into one, and I was heedless of the significance of the day…until I peeked up at the clock above the dayroom entranceway, 'THUR' displayed above the clock face.

I turned back to the window. The only evidence of the spring breeze was the movement of the single flower amongst the fresh, plump grass shoots of the garden.

Tears threatened, burning the bridge of my nose and my right hand unconsciously came to meet my left as it rested on the windowpane. Mining my nails into the skin, I pulled so tightly, so ferociously, I swore I felt a familiar warm liquid oozing from the indentations beneath them. A part of me hoped I did.

Only two thoughts brought me comfort in my state of despair. That breeze was my Nan's spirit. She was watching over me, keeping me company, helping me tap into a hidden strength, and not leaving me alone in the scary surroundings like Liam had. And the fact that Walker had requested to see me.

I thought I was dreaming when the orderly approached me that morning, the sound of the soles of her flat shoes squealing and sticking to the polished flooring. I tore my melancholic stare from the window as she knelt in front of me and asked if I was feeling up to having a visitor. When the name Walker slipped from her mouth as a whisper, for the first time in eight days of being locked up, I felt hope. I felt an unfamiliar smile steal across my face and as I nodded my answer, she disappeared back to where she came, leaving behind a sliver of faith which I had long ago forgotten.

Eight days I had been locked up there. Eight days without a visitor. Eight days to attempt to see sense. Eight days to hit reality with a bang and accept what I had done and somehow, allow the professionals to get me better. Even if it did mean that I was dosed up to the eyeballs with anti-depressants and tranquilizers.

"Kady," the woman in white scrubs was standing over my shoulder as I slowly and cautiously craned my head around to face her. "It's time to go down to the visitors' room." The warm and friendly smile she displayed helped me find a little energy of what I had left, to rear up from the seat and follow in her wake.

She steered me through the echoing corridor. It seemed as though those black cameras were stationed at every corner of the institute, always keeping an eye on you. The way they sometimes shifted angles and the grating noise as they did so, did nothing for my paranoia. Still, I was glad to escape the ramblings along with sudden cursing and shouting from the other patients.

Patients? It felt as though we were inmates…

My fingers found and toyed with a loose thread dangling from the bottom of my pajama top, as I stepped into the small, white painted room and took the seat next to the window. The breeze had picked up some, sending tulips bowing as though they were worshipping each grass shoot they were sitting amongst.

"Hey." I jolted at the sensation of a hand on my shoulder, the legs of the chair grated under protest. "It's okay," the familiar voice told me, as I redirected my rapt attention from the garden beyond the window, to the man skirting my body and taking a seat in front of me. He offered a wistful grin, his brown hair as sexy and disheveled as always, yet his attire was immaculate. A crisp white shirt tucked neatly into navy suit pants. "How are you feeling, darlin'?"

I merely stared at him, unsure of what to say, what to do. I couldn't open my mouth because if I did, my dam was going to break. Walker gazed at me with a bountiful compassion that I knew damn well I didn't deserve. I was the one undeserving.

Hanging my head low, I felt the wrinkles of stretching skin gathering when I pulled my eyebrows in and downward. I swept my tongue over my parched lips and sniffled. "I went for him, Walker," I finally admitted, sorrow and regret mixed with overt perplexity encased my tone, as I pulled my head back and met his caring gaze.

Seeing his broad shoulders sagging and his face tumbling on his outbreath was another kick in my gut. "Kady," he shifted to the very edge of the seat, my knees caught between his thighs. He took my hands in his warm, calloused possession.

"I attacked him, and I can't even remember it."

Although the walls were thick, you could hear each and every tortured soul. Night after night the screams were my lullaby. And I knew this was going to be a big confrontation, hearing the screams, the banging and smashing from down the hall, in the room that only a few moments ago, I was in.

"Oh my God," the woman gasped; still I held my head low.

The next thing I know, I saw Walker in my peripheral vision looking up at the door behind me. "It's okay, we'll be fine," he said.

Strengthening sounds of commotion vibrated through the room as the door opened, and soon faded to a degree which was easier to disregard if you were familiar with such things.

"Kady, listen to me," now we were alone, his voice was somewhat pressing. "You did not attack him. Do you understand me? You did *not* attack him."

Flailing my head in a fraught attempt to shake his words from my mind, I muttered 'no' over and over. Eight days I'd had to realize and acknowledge the verity of my actions. I had just come to accept it—acceptance is the first step of getting better—and now Walker was making me question myself all over again. I couldn't allow him to do that.

"You didn't attack him, Kady. You're not that sort of person; you don't have a combative bone in your body."

"How do you know, Walker? People live next-door to rapists and child abductors, but they always say the same thing, 'We never realized, it's come as such a shock, he/she was such a lovely person'."

His features turned sturdier with his resolve. "No, Kady, that's enough. You didn't do what he's made out you've done."

Faintly shaking my head, my overthrown words were unfettered as a whisper. "Then why would he say it?"

He breathed a troubling, vexing sigh. "I don't know, but we're working on it—"

"We? Whose we?"

He smiled, one that sent shivers up my spine as I witnessed the degree of his determination. "Let's just say, the FBI has nothing on me and Laurie at the moment."

The flower bowed down into the grass once more as the breeze intensified for all but a second. "Today was the funeral," I muttered, the vision before me awash with a painful, burning accumulation of warm droplets of grief over glassy eyes. I heard the snarl emitted from Walker's throat, one that screamed knowledge and clarity. Still, I found myself lost in the visual of the dancing flower, and in the barrenness of my own dark mind. "I didn't even get a chance to say goodbye and now I never will."

Craning my head to Walker as he answered me with silence, I silently cursed the tear which had escaped and was being pursued by countless more. "He deleted my voicemail, Walker. The one from my mom and everything else after that is a complete blur."

His minty breath collided with my face. Leaving my hands on my lap he halted himself from chewing on his chewing gum while his gentle, tender touch rose to my face. My tears were dried by his thumbs before he pulled my head closer to him, until our brows were resting against one another. "Please don't cry, darlin'," he whispered. I swore I heard him sniffle before he repeated his plea. "Please don't cry."

When he finally drew his head from me, my brow felt cold and bare, Walker's hands were still framing my face. The look in his eyes as he searched mine…that look was teeming with anger and fortitude, like a parent who was about to lift a car off their child. "I need you to listen to me, Kady. Do you remember the night you stayed with me on your birthday?"

I nodded.

"Do you remember breakfast at Tiffani's the following morning?"

I nodded again.

"I told you to make me a promise, and you did. I told you that I wanted to help you and to let me be your anchor. Do you remember that?"

"Yes," I whispered through the lump in my throat.

"So I am going to be your anchor. Say after me, Kady: I didn't attack, Liam."

"No, I'm not saying that. Refusing to believe it is why I'm here, Walker. I'm not saying that. I did attack him. I did. He has the cut to prove it, I'm a nut-job, I'm delusional—"

"Yes Kady, you are delusional. You're delusional because you believe his lies, his deceits, his fabrications call them whatever you want, it all comes to the same thing." His breaths came in tiny, shallow, uneven gasps, while my mind was haunted by the mere intensity of his eyes as he bored them into me. He was riled, that was clear. "Kady, you told me not to say anything to you when I saw your ribs. I'm not doing it any longer, I'm not keeping my mouth shut so you can continue with this twisted world that he's made you believe you deserve. I'm done."

"No, no, no," head shaking, frenzied, my own inhalations were sucked up into my lungs in wild, pleading pants. I tried to shift away from his hands which were framing my face, but it was fruitless. He was determined, and I was terrified of the truth he was compelling me to listen to.

"He is abusive, darlin'. You are in a physically and psychologically abusive relationship, Kady. That is the truth and you know it, you just deny it over and over. But look where it's got you, darlin'," His words of truth were hitting me full force in the face.

I had known this, I had known it for a while, but justification and plausible deniability always won hands down. Countless tears swept down my cheeks at his words, and I watched as his own eyes began to shimmer and glaze.

"You're in this place, taking medication you don't need, questioning your own sanity, Kady, this isn't right. You're worth so much more, darlin'." He faltered for a brief moment, but when he spoke again, his voice was both pained and sincere, "I can't offer you the world at your feet like Liam can, but if you were mine, I would offer you a world of happiness, a world of safekeeping and respect where you wouldn't have to walk on Goddamn eggshells. I'd never treat you the way he has."

I couldn't keep listening to his truths. I needed him to stop. "Walker, you have to stop, please stop."

"Repeat after me, Kady: I didn't attack, Liam." When I remained quiet for an age, and twisted my head a margin to peer back at the flower on the lawn, his insistent hands which had been framing my face for an age, tugged me back, holding me steady to focus on him and the words he spoke. "I don't have time, Kady, please, repeat it—say it, say: I didn't attack, Liam."

"I didn't attack, Liam," I whispered just to shut him up.

He shook his head before tipping it forward to brace himself on my brow once again. "Do you trust me, darlin'?"

"Yes."

"With trust, comes belief. You didn't cut him. Say it, Kady, please—" his voice shattered beneath the straining of his unrelenting words. "Just say it, say it for me, say: I didn't attack him."

"I didn't attack him."

"Again…"

"I didn't attack him." He told me to repeat it once more, and with each time I repeated it, I felt a little resolve filter into my statement.

"I want you to do something for me. Tell the shrink whatever you think he wants to hear, simple yes and no in the right places. Slip the pills under your tongue, I don't care where you put them just don't take them, you don't need them. Do you understand?"

I nodded.

"One more thing,"—my eyes fluttered closed as his thumbs skated over the arches of my cheeks—"cling onto this conversation. Hold on with everything you have, keep replaying it and keep remembering these words. Don't lose yourself, Kady. I couldn't bear it."

When I opened my eyes, his brow was creased and lips quirked. Staring blankly into his eyes, his left hand fell from my face, to pinch the bridge of his nose.

I heard the handle of the door behind me squeal as it was pushed down, and a slight breeze filtered into the room. "Is everything okay in here?"

I saw him nod as he glanced up and put the orderly at rest as he assured her. "I gotta go. Keep remembering," his words came tersely and he set a quick, chaste kiss on my forehead before quickly shunting himself from the seat in front of me, and left.

The coolness of her flesh journeyed through the fabric of my pajama top as she wrapped her hand around my upper arm and guided me once again on shaky, lifeless legs back to the dayroom.

The chairs and tables were set as they normally were, the TV on mute, while a woman sashayed from each black tile, avoiding the white ones, to the softly emitted music from the radio. There was no evidence of an uproar, everything was as it was. And once again, I was alone on my seat, gazing longingly out of the window to my left; there was no evidence of any visitor. No staff saying goodbye, I didn't even hear the door close.

The transition was done so quickly, too quickly for my head to acknowledge. That alone prompted the worrisome thought in my mind: was Walker even here in the first place? Or was it just the mere voice of denial manifesting in the form of the only person I could truly trust, in a bid to sway me back after I admitted defeat?

Like the saying goes: the truth is hard to swallow.

CHAPTER
twenty-three

"There she is," I heard his voice echoing from the furthest end of the corridor, beyond the painted iron gateway and check in desk.

Being escorted down the corridor, I couldn't stifle the fixed, overawing sense that I was being escorted down The Green Mile and the bald, coffee skinned mammoth beside me, discharging me into the arms of the person who put me in here in the first place, was more like the guard walking me to my fate…my death.

Axle, as we came to name him, never cracked a smile, and he was one strong bastard. In my first two uncooperative days, it only took him, and him alone, to pin me down on the old, thin mattress covering a squeaky metal frame as the nurse stabbed me with that Goddamn needle full of liquid relaxant.

However, peeking up at his towering, beefy form at my right as we approached the gate to the outside world, he was grinning down at me. It was like watching a dog walk on its hind legs. That alone bred an inward giggle.

"Kady baby," Liam mouthed while Axle opened the gate, the loud groaning and squealing of old hinges journeyed down the hallway. It felt like I was being freed from prison. *Out of one, into another,* I thought to myself as I stepped over the hold.

In an instant, Liam's arms crashed around me, swallowing me whole with a tight embrace that had me tapping out on his arm to loosen up. Finally, arms outstretched, he held me at length, giving me a once over perusal. "I'm so happy to have you back," he grinned and placed a kiss on my forehead.

I couldn't bring myself to smile; I couldn't reciprocate his level of eagerness at getting me home, or leaving this place. I didn't know what it was, but it was something about spending just over two weeks locked up, drugged to the eyeballs that had me realizing how vulnerable I had been. Even worse, people who knew me on the outside saw my vulnerability before I did.

"Mr. DeLaney, here is Kady's medication." Liam took the bag handed to him by Axle. "She *must* take them. I can't stress that enough. The stabilizers will keep her mood exactly that… stable, so there should be no repeat of her aggression or anxiety. The tranquilizers are to be administered if she grows agitated and distressed. The doctor will continue with a follow up appointment which will be sent to you."

Liam nodded.

"The tranquilizers will knock her out, so Kady," turning his beefy attention back to me, I couldn't help but notice the rolls at the back of his neck over the white scrubs. "There is to be no driving or operating machinery once you have taken them, you understand that don't you."

"Yep, I've already heard it. No need to lather, rinse, repeat," I joked, my mouth caving in to a lopsided grin.

I was gestured to the gate, "Go on, get outta here, girl."

Tossing the friendly giant a wave and a forcing a smile over my shoulder, I did what I was good at: I did as I was told.

Hand in hand, we made our way through the entrance, down the steps and into the parking lot. The sun was beaming, the breeze light and refreshing against my flesh. Breathing in deeply, I delighted in the scent of wildflowers from the patients' garden which housed the odd scattered benches, as it drifted along the gentle breeze. I peeked back at the structure, which was now growing smaller as we moved further away.

It was a strange feeling. It wasn't a place I'd particularly want to visit at the best of times. I most definitely didn't want to go there against my will. But, for just over two weeks, that place had been a little haven for me, a place where I could hide away, lick my wounds and discuss how to get better. In Pinewood, I was surrounded by other patients who were in the same boat as me, who were vulnerable and couldn't see it.

Now, I was being dragged away from that distorted form of security, where no judgment was passed, back into a world full of people who do nothing other than pass judgment, criticize, and frown upon the sick and diverse…

That scared me.

"Come on, baby, in we get," Liam held the silver door open as I stood stock-still in the gravel driveway frowning at both him and the car.

"What happened to the BMW?"

"Oh, we needed a new car; Liv needed a car, so I bought this and gave her the BMW."

My eyes widened with blatant cynicism, my jaw fallen open. He did what? "You gifted her with a BM-fucking-W?"

"It's okay, I got you a gift too, baby," he smiled a little too happily. His gifts were one thing I had learned to have great apprehension about. Either, it wasn't a nice one or it was going to come at a price. "But you need to get in the car."

Fixed in place was the wide grin on his face. So much hesitancy stewed in my body. I was unsure how to cope with the ever changing colors of Liam DeLaney's attitude. If I was to be truthful, I was on tenterhooks in his presence, and my paranoia knew that dreaded fact. In spite of my worries, I reluctantly did as I was bid and slipped into the Mercedes.

Thirty minutes of deafening silence proved too much for the man at my left. A hand, which I grew used to cringing from, crashed down on my denim-clad thigh, causing me to jolt with the expectancy of an uncongenial, harmful touch.

"Hey, why are you so jumpy, baby?"

He thought that was jumpy? That flinch had nothing on how the beating mass in my chest was functioning. Lips moistened with a sweep of my tongue, I faintly shook my head. "I…umm…I…"

"For God sake, Kady, what's the matter?" My body quailed at the sound of his scaling voice as my mind worked overtime. He was going to blow his fuse if I didn't talk.

Out of one prison, into another, the small voice in my mind echoed.

"I'm just feeling like a burden."

"Burden?" his attention was torn from the road ahead, to me then back again.

"I couldn't see that I was sick, Liam. You could, and I'm sure everybody else could. I…I just feel like I'm spreading my wings again, entering the big wide world, and knowing how people judge and frown upon people, I just…"

"What?"

I shook my head once more then redirected my observation to the people and buildings flying by outside my window. "Fuck it.

I just want to go home, snuggle down, not answer questions, eat when I want to, or don't want to, and just enjoy not having to be on a routine."

When I was told that there was going to be a problem with my daily preference, my blood instantly turned to ice, my heart ceased to beat in my chest. Instead, the throbbing came from my eardrums, spawning a compressed sensation in my head. "What do you mean?" I asked with a great deal of caution.

He flashed a shrewd grin in my direction, his eyes glimmered with secret knowledge…a secret knowledge which I had great trepidation over. "I told you, it's a surprise."

Once we took the first right turning bypassing Bricksdale Square, I was told to fetch the flight mask out of the glove compartment. My timid refusal was countered by Liam's presentation of an evil, demanding sneer. I'd been out of Pinewood for less than forty-five minutes, Liam had already raised his voice once and in conjunction with that expression he was honing, I knew that fighting back would cause me to be more fearful, than doing what he instructed. So, I conceded, recovered the black satin flight mask, and put it into place, making sure my vision was completely absent.

When the ignition was shut off, I was told, "Stay there, I'll help you out now," before hearing the sound of the driver side door slamming shut. It's amazing how your other senses become more in tuned when one is removed. "Come on, baby." Although his voice was at a normal octave, I still jolted at the loudness of it as he took my hand and aided me out of the car.

Led down the inclined driveway, I felt the smooth and evenness of the sidewalk under my feet. Liam's arms coiled around my middle from behind, while I heard a small jingle, which would probably have gone unnoticed, had my removed sense of sight been present.

The air ousted at his murmuring over my shoulder, sent my body into a mass of goose bumps. "Okay, you can look now."

Butterflies in my stomach were attempting a not so stealthy mission to break free. No words could describe how distrusting I felt at that moment. I knew how downright brutal Liam could be when he wanted.

Flight mask removed, I fluttered my lids while reacquainting myself with the bright light of day. "Oh my, God. Liam what is this?" I rasped. Stagnant, all I could do was study the black Audi SUV with a huge red ribbon planted on the roof, while Liam swung the keys in front of my face.

"Surprise," he sang merrily. All I could do was shake my head in disbelief, and silently wonder what price this car had come at, not in actual money terms, but in the sense of what truly matters. My sanity? My bruised ribs? A lifeless person who lives with a caged lion and is full of mistrust? "Do you like it?"

"Do I like it? Liam, it's an SUV. You didn't have to do this." Despite my words, I was hit by that boulder of reasoning. I knew exactly why he made this grand gesture. I could see it now. It was clear…so very, very clear. Just like the morning after he first set upon me, his attentiveness and generosity were evident just like they are now. He was feeling guilty, and this was his way of making it up to me.

His way of redeeming himself, for lack of a better term.

The approaching sound of slippers shuffling over the paving stones of the sidewalk was interrupted by a flamboyant calling of, "Coo-ee." Internally I cringed at the shrill voice of our overemphasized, attention-grabbing neighbor.

In unison, our concentrated focus upon the mammoth car parked along the sidewalk, veered towards Mrs. Steinbeck, who was rapidly advancing, her arms already opened, and her hefty chest swaying. "Kady, it's fantastic to have you back with us. I'm so sorry for your loss." Everything that woman said was conveyed with such an overdramatic air. God help you if she ran over your puppy, she'd manage to turn that news into some cheesy Chicago worthy production. I could actually imagine the jazz hands, too.

She pulled me down to kiss me on the cheek and I stiffened. This was part of the reason I didn't want to come home. If she knew I'd been carted off to Pinewood, I was sure the entire neighborhood and the ones adjacent knew, too.

When she let me go, I nodded with a timid whisper of, "Thank you."

"If there is anything I can do for either of you, you know where I am. My door is always open for this block,"—she peeked down at the watch wrapped around her thickset wrist—"Oh my goodness, is that the time? I have to run or I'll be late for the neighborhood meeting." And she turned away, shuffled back along the walkway with a wave over her shoulder and calling back, "I mean it, my door is *always* open."

I couldn't move. My body was like stone, my gaze distant as I stared blankly on the gray paving stones. "You told her? You know the entire block is already aware now that you're sharing your life with a nut job?"

Liam's hands were set on my upper arms. My vision blurred as he twisted me around to face him. "I told her that you were in D.C. for your Nan's funeral. I wouldn't tell anyone what you did or where you had to go. I don't want people to see you in a different light. It's our secret. Okay?"

Gratitude flowed thick and fast at his words. I loathed that my Nan's funeral was used as a cover-up for my absence. However, keeping my stay at Pinewood under wraps was considered necessary.

With a grin and a motioning of his head in the direction of the lavish car beside me, he returned to his previous topic with a muttering of, "And that's not all, baby." As his left hand opened, he waited patiently for me to accept his offering.

It was when I lowered my gaze that had my legs turning into concrete, and my heart exploding.

With a gentle finger, I reached out to trace the screaming red scar in the center of his palm. It was big, spanning from between his thumb and index finger, to the outside of his hand, right across his lifeline. Fault, shame and remorse flew from every direction of my body before clashing together and forming a world of indignity and regret in my chest. Tears threatened. "I'm so sorry, Liam."

"It's okay, baby—" he soothed while tipping my head up with a gentle finger under my chin.

"No, no, it's far from okay; my behavior was far from acceptable. I don't know how I can make this up to you."

"Just promise me one thing—"

"Anything," I gushed without disinclination, because that's what he deserved. He maintained that right to ask anything of me, after what I'd done. I should be offering him the world as repayment for his injury, his endurance, and for the help he sought for me.

"Just promise me you'll take your medication. They wouldn't have prescribed them if you didn't need them, Kady."

I nodded willingly. This I knew. "I promise."

I had hoped that to some extent, I'd feel a level of relief when I stepped into the house, away from prying eyes and whisperings of compassion and sympathies. I couldn't have been more wrong. The sound of clattering and humming coming from the kitchen had me unnerved and a thick form of dread flowed through my veins like honey. I didn't want to be around people. Still, as being steered into the kitchen with a warm hand on the small of my back had revealed, I obviously didn't have a choice in the matter.

"Chick," Liv shrieked then bounded toward me with her arms spread. I stood inert, allowing her to hug me with my arms flush against my sides before pulling away. "It's so good to have you back. How are you feeling?"

How was I feeling? Hmm…let me think about this one. Nope. No words in my vocabulary were expressive enough to describe how I truly felt. Rolling my lips over my teeth and rolling my eyes heavenward, I merely shrugged my shoulders and shook my head.

"Well, here's something that'll cheer you up. Ready?" the lively tone in which she spoke, was enough incentive to hear her out with a small, tightlipped smile. "We are going for a picnic down at…" she held her finger in the air, and with a wide-eyed pose like she was about to reveal the bonus ball on the State Lottery, added, "Castle Island."

"Castle Island, as in the beach?"

"And you,"—Liam opened my hand and deposited the keys to my new, glossy black Audi SUV in the center—"are going to drive."

It was a sweet gesture, that I couldn't deny, but the scowl in which was embedded into my profile was betraying how I truly felt. I didn't want to go anywhere; I just got back from a sixteen day holiday in the metal house. I wanted to sit, relax, stuff myself with ice-cream and watch crap TV. I didn't want to go to a beach, and I most certainly didn't want to drive—new car or not.

"I don't know, I—"

"Oh, come on, Kady, it'll be fun. Catch some sun; you're looking a little pasty." The back of Liv's hand splayed across my brow as though checking for a fever. Annoyed, I swatted her away with a disapproving cluck of my tongue and a full-on grimace.

Well, I'm awfully fucking sorry for that, but let's see if you come out with rosy red fucking cheeks after you've been where I was left.

I held my tongue, breathing deep and slow to alleviate the ball of anger progressively forming in my body. I closed my eyes, and pushed my snappy words aside in a desperate bid not to free them.

"All I want to do is—" drawn to a premature end was my statement as I was twisted around to face Liam, who was looming over me.

"Kady, it will do you some good. You've been cooped up in that place for over two weeks. Stretch your legs, find your bearings again. A little bit of Vitamin D will do you some good; it'll make you feel better."

I sighed and screwed my eyes shut. Why wasn't anyone listening to me? Why was I getting treated like a child…again? Behind my closed lids, a familiar burning of salted moisture made itself known. "I just—"

"Liv has gone to all this trouble of preparing a picnic and getting your beachwear ready, plus we have your pills if you need them."

Yes, that was a fantastic selling point.

With loosened skin furrowing along my brow, my eyes remained firmly screwed, as I finally succumbed to peer-pressure and muttered one word under duress, "Fine."

Forty minutes in the SUV, the boats bobbing up and down along the waves as they came into shore were just visible along the horizon as we approached the parking lot of Castle Island. Beach and park in one, who could complain about that? Apparently, I could…secretly anyway.

I dropped out from behind the wheel in my small denim shorts and my oversized black sweater which fell off my shoulder. The round markings stared back at me as I peeked down at my thighs. But I didn't feel any shame. I'd come to accept that my method of releasing all my pent-up frustrations made me a stronger person, just as Walker had told me. I wasn't ashamed of them anymore. They were a part of *me*. They were *my* story. A story of what I had been through, a story that told how I was delivered from those troubled times and a constant reminder that at some point in my life, I did have a form of control.

Settling down on a blanket along the white sands of the shore, I was digging into a ham sandwich, when Liam stuck a devilled egg in front of my face, asking if I wanted a taste. My stomach contorted, my pulse began an unexpected race as the scent alone evoked that disturbing memory of a punishment which, although past, was brought back into the present. He let out a throaty chuckle barely audible over the crashing waves with his head tipped back, as he taunted me with that haunting recollection.

Laughing at his secret misuse. It was kind of sadistic.

When Liam pulled himself together, he glanced over at Liv and flashed her a smile, not a typical smile, but one that displayed a undisclosed awareness, almost intimate. I had to squeeze my eyes tightly and redirect my focus on my breathing, which was slowly but surely becoming erratic. Why was I so jealous?

"Don't tell me off, but I got another surprise for you."

More? It was becoming too damn much now. He must've a: really felt guilty, or b: whatever was going to ensue throughout the day was going to be horrific. Arms curled over his head to meet the neckline of his long-sleeved T-shirt that he'd changed into before we left the house. I came face to face with a large eagle tattoo on his left forearm and a Chinese symbol over his heart, when he whipped it off. "You know I've always wanted this one," he motioned to the bird of prey on his arm before pointing to his left pectoral. "And I finally got your name done, Kady."

My eyes widened. After everything, he really had my name tattooed on his body? I had my own personal mark over his heart? The mere fact of such a permanent declaration physically warmed me from inside out. "My name?"

Briskly nodding his response with a wide grin, all I could do was toss myself over the blanket, wrap my arms around his neck and lay a kiss on him that was more passionate, more feverish than what we had experienced in a while. It was as if the tide had come in and washed all the undesired, torturous memories out to sea.

On that beach, it felt as though we were gifted with a new blank canvas. Although, I still couldn't shift the tiny whispering of paranoia and foreboding in the back of my mind.

Before I could register what was happening, Liv was giggling as I was wrapped up in muscular arms and hauled down to the splashing waves, the white foam settled on the wet sand as the water retreated.

My feet sunk into the shore as soon as Liam set me down on my feet, the cool seawater washing over them, when we were out of earshot. "I'm sorry for everything, Kady," he spoke in earnest, "I'm so, so sorry. I'm going to change, I promise. This is the start of a new beginning for us, if you'll still have me."

Fisting my hand into his hair, my body rose up onto the balls of my feet as he slanted his lips over mine in a warm, loving kiss. "I can't lose you, baby. Will you still have me?" he asked when his lips left mine, his forehead resting peacefully against my own.

I had spent four years with this man, I couldn't throw it away. I needed to give him this chance. I owed it to us. I smiled, "Of course."

"Come on, up you get," he demanded with a shit-eating

grin, pulling away and skirting my body to face away from me, indicating for me to jump on his back like I used to do when we first started dating.

He caught his arms behind my knees as I clung like a baby chimp around his neck.

"Don't let me fall," I giggled when he began to pick up the pace back to the woman, who most probably, was beginning to feel like a third wheel.

I was laughing like a lunatic, and spluttering as the wind tore through my loose hair, sending it whipping and flying across my face. I only just heard Liv shout, "Smile," before I was blinded by a blue flash.

The pair was unusually quiet, with Liv busy burying her feet into the cold depths of the beach, while Liam's head tilted back, gazing up into the sky with his aviator glasses in place.

"I fancy ice-cream, anyone else want one?" I asked over the crashing waves.

His rapt focus on the powder blue, cloudless heavens was torn away as both turned in my direction. He smiled. "Ice-cream sounds fantastic."

The golden grains were dusted off my backside as I shunted myself up from the sand. "One mint chocolate chip for Liam, and,"—I narrowed my eyes at Liv. With her brunette hair in a loose side braid, tiny white shorts and red halter bikini bra on a beach, she looked ready for a damn photo shoot. "Strawberry?"

"Always strawberry, with sauce, and one of those flake thingy's too if they have them."

"Yes, Ma'am," I gave a small salute, before grabbing my purse and heading up the embankment to the ice-cream parlor.

It was while I was waiting and watching the middle-aged man scooping the ice-cream into cones that my stomach began to flip and my nerves were scattered for some God forsaken reason. The constriction in my chest was impossible to ignore, I felt as though I couldn't breathe, and the panic which hardened at the suffocating sensation just made me worse. My legs felt like they were about to give away, so my right hand came quickly to my aid, resting on the counter, halting my imminent crumpled fate.

Steady breathes, Kady…steady breathes…

One…two…three…repeat…

One…two…three…

I concentrated solely on making my outbreath longer than my inhalation, just as the doctor instructed, to stop myself from hyperventilating and kill the ringing and compression in my head.

I handed the man the money for the ice-creams and made a hasty retreat back to the beach. At least with Liam and Liv, I knew I'd be safe if anything happened. Like passing out.

Down the paved slope I tread with two ice-creams in one hand, and one in the other, while my purse was nestled under my arm. The measly wave I offered went unnoticed. They were drowning in their conversation; Liv's hand rose to meet Liam's cheek then lowered to his left pectoral.

What the fuck?

Even in the distance, I could hear her discerning, throaty, one cigarette too many, giggle leave her chest. What caught me completely off-guard were Liam's arms snaking around her waist, his hands set on each ass cheek that was barely covered with the tiny white shorts she was wearing. He pulled her into him, his lips crashing down to her as she tipped her head back to reciprocate.

I was standing no more than eight feet away, my breathing coming in short, and frantic pants. The sand sucked me under, proving too weighty for me to even lift my legs to close the remaining space between us. I tried to shout, instead, my words were unfettered as a quavering, mistrusting sound as my voice box jittered. "Wh–what the Hell is this?"

The cavorting twosome relinquished each other and gaped at me like they'd been caught with their hands in the chocolate cake, despite the fact that they were told it was forbidden.

"Don't just stand there. What the fuck was that?" I challenged once again, sensing the anger stirring within the depths of my soul but for some reason was incapable of liberation.

"Chick, I'm so sorry, I wanted to te—" at least she had the decency to look contrite about it, but before she could continue, her words were halted by the dismissive wave of Liam's hand.

He took a steady step towards me, while Liv threw a frown at his back. "Kady," drawing out my name like I was an errant child about to fly into a full blown hissy fit in the local store, he continued with his right palm raised towards me, his head cocked. "I don't know what you thought you saw, baby, but nothing is happening."

"Nothing…h–happening…?" I grimaced, "Are you fucking kidding me!" The inner me begged to be released, to scream and demand answers, but she was under wraps. Instead, I stood there like a lemon once again, being compelled to question my sanity as my hands went numb and the ice-creams fell into the sand. "I saw you both. You were caught red handed with yours on her ass, your lips on hers,"—I pointed at Liv over his shoulder—"Don't you dare tell me—"

Despite my desire to move away from him, my legs and mind refused to join forces, and the distance between us continued closing. "Baby, I promise you. Nothing happened. Maybe it wasn't a good idea coming here today. You just got out of that place after suffering paranoid delusions. This is obviously too much stimulation for you, Kady. I'm sorry, baby. Here take one of your pills."

"I don't want any fucking pills; I want the truth, Liam."

Liv opened her mouth, a little groan of protest ripped from her throat. The rational part of my head was happy that she wanted to say something. Maybe the truth. Validate what I just fucking saw, because I knew what I saw with my own two eyes. I think.

As soon as that husky groan was freed, Liam quickly flung his left hand back in her direction and held it there, a wordless motion to get her to shut up. "Kady, listen. You're getting yourself into a state. You're agitated. Nothing happened, baby. It's all in your head. Maybe they shouldn't have let you out. Maybe we should take you back."

Take me back to Pinewood? No way. I just got out. I wasn't going back. No chance. I'd drown myself first.

"A few more days might help," he added, his voice velvet soft caressing my flesh.

The mere notion of going back to the looney bin was enough to overshadow the incident I just witnessed. If Liam decided that I should go back, I knew there was nothing I could possibly do to stop it. He could sign me in and leave me there, no problem. I shook my head frantically. "No, Liam. I don't want to go back, please. Please, don't make me go back."

He was standing right in front of me, towering over me and smelling like Liv's expensive perfume. Or did he? I fisted my hands into my hair in exasperation, my eyes burning with salted moisture. What the fuck was wrong with me?

The pill bottle was drawn out of the back pocket of his shorts, with the greatest concern reflecting in his eyes. Opening the lid, a pill was tipped into the palm of his hand. "Then take your pills, Kady. You need them, baby. You promised me that you'd take them." He presented it like Lucifer offering an apple to the starved. In his eyes, coercion overturned his concern and glinted like silver blades.

Wearily, I eventually took it from his hand, popped it in my mouth and down my throat before being swallowed up in his arms. I didn't fight back. I allowed his warm and hard muscle to offer comfort. "I'm sorry, Liam. I really thought that I saw—"

"Shush, baby, it's okay now. But you owe Liv an apology, too."

Sniffling, I apologized to Liv from over his shoulder.

She simply nodded with a displeased look on her face.

"Can we go home now please?"

He kissed the top of my head. "Of course we can. I'll drive; you can sleep in the back. Liv can sit shotgun."

The journey back home was only a forty minute drive. Nevertheless, I was in and out. I swore at one point, I saw Liam's hand resting on Liv's thigh as I fluttered my lids open. The tears came, as did more questions, so many questions. Eventually, I slipped back into slumber.

What was wrong with me? What was wrong with my mind? I didn't know what's real anymore…why couldn't I just be normal.

Normal.

What is normal?

CHAPTER *twenty-four*

6th June, 2013.
The day before the accident…

For over three hundred and sixty-five days, I had concentrated profusely on throwing myself in to distraction. Three hundred and sixty-five days…twelve months…it seems so long. It's not.

The days, well, my days at least, were blurred, distorted. They were filled with unspoken qualms of what was real, and what wasn't.

During those twelve months, four weeks were spent back in Pinewood, dosed back up to the eyeballs, dwelling on why my mind worked the way it had been. I had never been a troubled child. There was no history of mental illness, delusions, depression or anxiety. Nevertheless, I guessed my rap sheet was a mile long with medications and statements from Liam recounting a few vital moments where I had blacked-out and been a danger to him or myself.

Incalculable times I had seen both Liv and Liam, in less than compromising circumstances. Seeing them kissing in the car, making out in my kitchen…walking in on them in my bed. At least, that's what I thought I was seeing. Bursting with rage, I'd fly off the handle, shouting obscenities and demanding explanations. Without fail, Liam like a white knight absent sword but armed with my tranquilizers, would come to my aid, alleviating that hurt and anger as he talked some sense into me through my delusional haze.

In the end, I came to realize I was merely visualizing something that I feared. So when my fear and paranoia played with my mind, I'd screw my eyes tightly, wishing it away. Then I'd down the pills myself and go to sleep. Everything was always better after that.

When I wasn't locked up like the nut-job I was, Laurie's advice was taken. Not only did I enjoy baking cakes, but I was able to use it as a diversion, something to concentrate on to mellow my mood without the need of further pills, considering Dr. Oleman discontinued my anti-depressants. And although it took a while for me to feel enthusiastic about it, I finally resigned when Liam went ahead and signed me up for decorating courses to further that skill.

I'd stand back and study the edible masterpiece which I created, and I would be overflowing with a sense of achievement. Nothing compared, however, to the sense of achievement unlocking when your customer is in awe of what your hands have accomplished.

It was when Laurie dropped into conversation about a unit going to waste in Bricksdale Square, and the element of how unemployment rates were still a problem, that Liam's statement from the night I met Laurie flicked in our heads.

See, that's why it's more fulfilling being your own boss.

With Liam's help, we signed a joint lease and Ent-icing was established. Everything was down to him. He made it possible.

And we owed him for that.

Over time, business trips for Liam went from once every few months, to practically once a month, every month. Did it bother me how it used to, being left without my partner from anything from two nights, to five nights? No. Not one bit. Why? Because each time he was away, I felt a sense of normalcy returning. I was able to forget about all the shit that went on in my relationship, down to the deep, dark places of my mind, and focus on being me. Kady Jenson.

That and the fact of, I wasn't ever truly left alone. I had my business partner who had grown to become one of my best friends, and her cousin by marriage, who was also my anchor, Walker, and he was doing a great job of being that anchor.

There were times over the year when the familiar boiling rage sat in my chest and gut, radiating its heat and hatred throughout my body, and I'd call him for help. Sometimes he'd take me to his apartment and give me what I needed. Switch, spank, lash, even use my 'favored method' as he heated a blunt blade and pressed it against my thigh, or have me lay face down in his sheets and pour hot wax down my spine.

I remembered him straddling the backs of my thighs as I called out when my flesh was pasted by the steady streaming of scalding wax, its intensity delivered fire on sensitive skin, while it cooled and extinguished the brutality of haywire emotions under my surface. In dire circumstances where I would have freely tossed myself out of the pick-up on the highway, if that is what it would take to bring an end to the frustrations and rage inside of me, there was no other option but to pull into an abandoned parking lot or a field, bend me over the truck and improvise.

It's difficult to understand and accept that there was no sexual gratification in what we were doing. It was purely for relief, an outlet in which he worried about my ability to lose control. It was a factor, and that factor had brought us closer. It was a safe way to obtain my release.

Unlike Liam and his aggressive and degrading ways, Walker would never lay a hand on me until I begged; even then he would ask if I was positive that it was what I wanted. The way he would scoop me into his arms and hold me as I sat silently in his lap, telling me to savor the detachment I felt, the detachment which I craved, after he had given it, was the most intimate feeling. In some ways, I liked to think it bonded us in a way that was sacred to *us*.

Despite all of that, despite how I felt about Walker and our unique bond, as I was looking at myself in the mirror of my bedroom, in an empty house, considering Liam was on another trip, I couldn't help but silently curse the Irishman to Hell.

Donned from head to toe in a white, knee-length pencil dress with a suit jacket, a black wig in the style of a bob hid beneath a white pillbox hat as I slipped on a pair of white gloves, I shook my head and sighed.

I was going to kill him for this.

My focus was torn away from the woman in the mirror when a beep of the truck horn blared through the night. I made my way around the bed, set my knee on the bench in the bay window and peeked through the heavy, satin embroiled drapes. Signaling for one more minute, I drew myself away from the windowpane, fetched my white clutch purse off the bed, and made my way outside.

He was already standing at the bottom of the front steps when I pulled the door closed, locking it behind me. "I am going to kill you for this," I chided, my silver bear jingling on my charm bracelet as I pointed a scolding finger at his black suited and booted form.

That small chuckle, which he tried to suppress, was very poorly stifled. "Is that anyway to talk to the thirty-fifth President of the United States, darlin'?" he muttered with faux affront. He crooked his arm for me to link as I stepped carefully down the last step in my white heels.

"An Irish President of the United States, that has to be a first."

"Will you two shut up and get in the car already? I don't want to miss the karaoke." I turned to the source of the irritated voice and gasped, before sheathing my teeth with my lips. "What?" Laurie asked shifting to the center of the bench, as Walker gallantly pulled open the passenger door.

"Stay Puft? Really? For Historical Characters Night?" I slipped inside.

"Don't start, it's a classic. Tell her, Walker."

Being caught between two distinct outlooks voiced by two women, he wasn't stupid. Hanging his head with a grin, he faintly shook it from side to side somewhat defeated. "I'm pleading the fifth on this one. Sorry, cuz."

Laurie scowled adorably as Walker slammed the door shut behind me, and rounding the hood to slip in behind the wheel.

The entire journey to McGinty's, I couldn't help but stare and offer the small not so secret snort of amusement at the woman next to me. Even so, she earned credit for improvisation. With her tight-fitted white T-shirt topped off with a blue traditional sailor's collar and red neckerchief, teeny, tiny white shorts, little white sailor's hat and a pair of what appeared to be cut-off sleeves of a white sweater, she looked like a very hot, Mrs. Stay Puft, one which was in desperate need of a tan.

"What?" She hooked her overly long, blue block-dyed bangs behind her ear.

"Nothing it's just…" my words faded with a shake of my head.

"I bake cakes right? Cakes are sweet and delicious…like marshmallows, so it's all very obvious." Her voice was just as sweet as her costume.

"I just don't understand how you could make something like that, look…hot," I shrugged.

Sounding some sort of mewling noise like she just spotted a litter of puppies, her hand shifted to my knee, and offered a little thank you squeeze.

The familiar sound and vibrations of the truck going over the gravel parking lot of McGinty's had the butterflies in my stomach startled awake and fluttering to attention. "You girl's ready?" Walker asked, putting the truck into park and removing his keys.

One word flew from my mouth instinctively, and had both of them gaping at me with Cheshire cat grins fixed firmly in place, "'Aye."

Before I knew it, the words, "Jesus Christ, woman," was being grunted by Walker. He didn't hide the fact that my slip of the tongue had caused him to need rearranging in his pants.

Mrs. Stay Puft was already a mile ahead of us as we strolled casually through the lot, my clutch under my right arm, while I linked my left under Walker's elbow. "You look gorgeous," he complimented.

I answered with a snort. "I haven't been to a costume event in years. I kind of feel ridiculous."

By the time I had finished, Walker had come to a standstill, and I was swiftly turned around to face him, my arm still trapped in his crook.

Although his hair was now in a side parting, which should have made him look ludicrous, he looked breathtaking. I don't know what it was, but seeing someone who was always dirty and rugged in construction gear and heavy boots, turn suave when sporting a tailored black three-piece suit with the little silver handkerchief in his breast pocket, silver tie and black dress shoes…it made every part of my body tingle. It made my heart beat harder, faster. It made a secret part of me, apart that only I knew, want to risk everything and live in a reckless, impulsive moment.

"You are beautiful, Kady Jenson. You could be dressed from head to toe in white designer, or in a potato sack. Either way, you're gorgeous. You need to start believing it. That is another duty I'm adding onto the role of 'Anchor'—"

I frowned.

"To make you realize how gorgeous you are, and what you're worth. Shall we, Mrs. President?" he motioned with a sweep of his hand to the entrance. I nodded, and he led me inside.

We strolled arm in arm through the masses of Elvis', Cleopatra's', 1920's gangster's and a load of other discerning costumed clientele, until we reached the bar. The pool table which was usually sat between the entrance and the bar was lacking. I'd come here enough times now to know that Carriag always made sure that there was enough room whenever he organized an event, which would pull additional punters in. And that pool table, which held delicious memories that kept me warm on more than one lonely night, took up enough space for at least an additional five bodies.

An older, huskier Irish lilt traveled from behind the bar. "Come on fellas, let Mr. and Mrs. President through."

Two Elvis' and a Frank Sinatra gathered their beverages before fleeing the counter, freeing up space for us to approach.

"Carriag I have no idea what possessed you to come up with this event, but you're going to want to hope that I get amnesia and forget the entire thing." I teased, slipping myself up onto one of the recently unoccupied stools with Walker at my side.

"I thought it'd be different,"—the white cloth draped over his shoulder rose as he shrugged—"And truthfully, it's the closest I'm going to get with rubbing shoulders with the stars. What can I get you, Jackie?" he asked, scouring my upper body with a sparkle in his eye. I held no reservation that he was a ladies man back in his day.

"Hey, Da, take that look away from my wife."

Wife? To say my heart failed to cease in my chest at that statement, and that the air I had just sucked in didn't catch and burn in my throat, would have been the biggest lie in the entire history of mankind. I knew we were dressed up, having fun while portraying famous historic characters, but that lone word…and coming from Walker…

I had to blink back tears which were threatening to spill and plaster a faux, dazed smile over my face. It made me giddy, and for the first time in so, so long, I sat with my head held high, feeling like I was protected…claimed. I felt like I belonged…even if it was just a pretense.

Even if it was just for one night.

"I'll have a white wine please, Carriag." I chanced a look at my dashing, JFK, who was lighting up a cigarette beside me. "And a beer for my, Mr. President."

It was fair to say that the night went smoothly. We laughed, we teased, we let our hair down…and unconsciously, we found ourselves falling into the act of the couple we were posing as. Linking arms, physical contact, fond glances, timid smiles…

When you step into the shoes of a couple who you are impersonating, a couple who happens to be husband and wife, it becomes more than a costume. For that night, Walker was my husband. I was his wife. The verity of that notion making my blood tingle and my hairs stand on end was something which scared me. Love, attachment, lust…it was all rising to the surface, making its presence known. But it was only an act right? Those feelings had to be present to make the pretense believable.

We were acting out a scene, a scene where those feelings had to flow naturally, a scene which, through no fault of my own, was clearing the fog away from hidden feelings that I had possessed, but ignored for so long.

I suppose, I didn't see it crossing any lines in our relationship, because for that night, we *were* that couple, and it was expected.

I was sitting on one of the chairs surrounding a round table. Short of Walker, Laurie, Carriag and I, the bar was empty. I surrendered to my body's demands and tipped my head back, when Walker seized my right foot, slipped my white heeled pump off and began massaging at the sole of my aching base. Still vaguely aware of Laurie and Carriag chatting about something or other by the bar, it was Walker's skilled, yet calloused-coated hands which tore the satisfying groan straight from my throat.

Fighting to kick start my reserved energy to lift my head straight, I watched the grin on Walker's face spread to his eyes. "Is this your way of apologizing?" I asked.

Less than impressed when Laurie and Walker ganged up on me, and dragged my ass up onto the tiny stage to join in with their rendition of 'Mustang Sally' over the karaoke, I cursed like a sailor, and was told he would make it up to me. Behind the bar, Carriag merely laughing at my feeble attempts of protest, and not coming to my aid as I was hijacked by his son and niece, was something I was going to damn well remember.

"You can't tell me you didn't enjoy it, darlin'." I was very much aware of his rough, workman hands skating over my instep, caressing my ankle and skating up my calf to behind my knee as he shifted to the edge of his seat, practically leaning into my personal space with his legs parted. "I've been telling you for over a year that I was going to get you up on that thing—"

The heat radiating from his eyes evaporated every drop of saliva I had, making my lips wither as my lungs fought for vital breath. My gaze combed over his profile, landing at his luring, pale lips.

"—And I did, darlin'," he added, before shimmying back into the opposite chair, and resuming the sweet, pleasurable sensation of his thumbs massaging into my sole.

I tipped my head back once again, silently praying for the Lord to help me as I handed myself over to the blissful sensations he prompted in my body, which also happened to torture my mind.

"Son," Walker halted the pleasurable, circular motions, I felt him shift beneath my foot, so I knew he was craning back to look at his father. "I'm going to take Laurie home, could you two lock up for me?"

"'Aye, no problem."

"The keys are behind the bar. Goodnight, Kady," he and Laurie called in unison.

"Night both, thanks for a fun night." And as they left, I was left wondering what it was about being left alone in private with someone of the opposite sex, that makes it so…tempting? The barriers lower, and that persuasive seduction, that appeal, the charging between you and that one person, the mutual attraction, the excitement, the thrill, need, longing and desire…it's impossible to stray from. It's impossible to ignore.

"I'm getting a beer; do you want anything, darlin'?"

"No, I'm fine," I yawned.

"Very well," his voice was somewhat strained as he reared up from the chair ahead, relinquishing my foot of his touch. The sound of his dress shoes over the dark, hardwood flooring reverberated around the room as he made his way to the bar behind him. Damn, it was such a sexy sound.

As he did so, I lifted my ass from the seat, slipped back on my shoe and in an attempt to wake myself up, I headed over to the jukebox.

Perusing the choices displayed, I smiled to myself and bit my lip as I made my selection. The soft intro sounded from the box, my index fingers danced to the rhythm against the glass before I turned my body to be met by Walker on the customer side of the bar, his left palm shifted from the bottle of Bud and laid flat against the emerald surface. He looked phenomenal, casually standing there in his three-piece suit, his hair combed over, the dark scruff coating his mouth and eyes so piercing, I could feel the warmth radiated from them as he speared his gaze into my body.

I slowly closed the distance, arching my shoulder, swaying my hips and playfully manipulating my body into small, timid dance moves, which earned me a shy, affectionate smile.

"I had no idea you liked the Jackson Five," he said, leisurely pushing himself away from the counter. He treaded deliberately and with purpose toward me, until we finally met in the middle. The soft, timing sound of his shoes scuffing across the flooring made every muscle in my body spasm with pleasurable and addictive force.

"I love them, and Michael. Playing their music was the only way my mom could get me to sleep at night when I was a kid."

We were standing toe to toe, chest to chest. His intoxicating cologne graced my nostrils, while, with hands at our side, our fingertips found their way to each other. I peeked down at our hands when I felt a small tug on the links of the silver bracelet.

His small smile was heard through the sigh of approval. "I can't believe you wore this," he said, the bear being caressed between his thumb and middle finger.

I stole a look up at his gorgeous face, a smattering of hair around his mouth, and gazed aimlessly into The Indian Ocean, an ocean I could happily be stranded in. I licked my lips. "I don't get to wear it as often as I'd like, but I will wear it whenever I can. Now, Dance with me?" It was a statement, but somehow, longing hijacked my words and posed it as a question.

"What kind of man would refuse his wife?" Oh, we were back in character. That was making it so much harder.

Smiling, Walker coiled his arm around my waist, my right hand placed in the warmth of his palm, while my left caressed his muscular bicep. Rhythmically swaying, we gazed into one another's eyes as we lightly serenaded each other. I could never stay quiet while listening to the Jackson Five, so as I mouthed, "Just call my name," Walker surprised me, coming in directly after, his rugged, perfect indie style voice shadowing mine with the words, "And I'll be there."

We were bathed by lyrics which were meaningful to us, to our relationship as his head dropped and his brow fixed against my own, his breath warm and enticing as I felt his exhale against my lips. Although it went unsaid, I think we both realized that this song was in fact, our song, and always would be.

Swaying in each other's arms he breathed my name, making it sound like Katy, once again.

We both had our eyes closed when I replied with, "Hmm…"

"Leave him. Leave, Liam." We came to a pause, my eyes sprang open and I was greeted with a shimmering tide, the waves proving too much as a lone tear escaped over Walker's eyelid.

"What? I–"

"I told you before, Kady, when you were in Pinewood. I wouldn't be able to offer you the world at your feet like Liam can, but if you were mine, I would offer you a world of happiness."

Pinewood? That means…I furrowed my brow, the creases carved into my forehead like a sculptor had just carved into my flesh as if I was his next marble project. "You…you were there? You actually came to see me?" Although a year had passed since my first break, we never spoke about it. For so long I had considered that moment to have been another delusion in my head.

"Yes, darlin', I was there. I saw you and I told you to not give up. I had no choice but to leave the way I did because seeing you like that killed me."

I sagged in his arms as the song began again on its repetitive cycle.

"Kady, that outfit on your back, one article of clothing in your closet may cost more than a month of my rent, but I have a little saved up, we could move away, somewhere Liam won't ever find us, somewhere I can keep you safe…somewhere where we can be together and you don't have to worry about beatings, or punishments.

"I hate knowing what he's doing to you, how he's treated you, but unable to do anything about it because of the ramifications *for you*, Kady. I can't save you from him while you're still with him, darlin'." He closed his mouth with a loud exhale through his nose.

"I can't do this Walker. I can't…" I had no idea what I was attempting to say. His declaration had completely thrown me.

My body was left cold as his hands were removed from my waist and my right hand. Instead, they held my face, coaxing my gaze upward to maintain eye contact as he searched my eyes. "Since the first day I laid my eyes on you, I was snared. You're the classy uptown girl and I'm the downtown guy, I don't have much to give. But I give you me, Kady. Please..." He glided his thumb pad over my lower lip while my breath caught in my chest. "Kiss me..."

In that moment, the guilt I felt was abundant because I wanted to, I wanted to so badly, but I couldn't just up and leave Liam, even though I was still waiting for him to change back into the caring man that he was at the beginning, the man he promised that he would give back to me on the beach, not the monster that he still shared his body with. And with everything that he had done with Ent-icing and my medical bills...I owed him.

My own tears were making their escape, leaving warm streaks down my cheeks. "I can't. I'm no cheater, Walker—"

"Look me in the eyes, Kady, and tell me that you don't feel anything for me."

A spell passed in silence, yet the music continued in the background. Isn't it strange how you can enjoy a song when you're happy, yet the lyrics have a profound meaning when you're torn? Eighteen months had passed. Walker had been right there beside me through the obstacles I'd faced and that alone strengthened us—strengthened my feelings. It was time to admit defeat. "I can't," I sighed.

"Then you're already cheating on him, darlin'."

Terrified by his words and my feelings, I ripped myself away from his hands with a step backward, and I tore out of McGinty's like a tornado in a trailer park. I had no choice. I had to remove myself before I gave up entirely, and ran back inside, into the arms of a man who, regardless of his own emotions, had been, and will continue to be there for me...to care for me without asking for anything in return. No matter what my decision may be.

CHAPTER *twenty-five*

The sound of the alarm clock tore me away from a night of vivid yet disturbing dreams. Disturbing dreams caused by a disturbing end to a rather fun night.

The brunt end of my exasperation was delivered upon the alarm as I hit it full force to get it to shut the Hell up. Today was Friday. Today was the day that Liam was due back home. I didn't know how I felt about it. I hadn't missed him. In actual fact, I found I had grown somewhat relieved when he went on each business trip. That was the part of me that was slowly finding her independence again. The part of me that felt marginally normal… whatever that was.

With an arch of my back and a pleasant groan, I kicked the comforter off my body and made my way into the en-suite, whipping my negligee over my head as I went, and headed for a shower.

In and out within ten minutes, I set about hastily blow-drying my shoulder length blond hair, fixed my face with a little makeup and, considering it was dress down Friday, tossed on a pair of faded jeans and a white blouse, before heading down the stairs.

It was when I was halfway down the staircase that I sighted a folded piece of paper having been pushed through the mailbox, and waiting on my hallway flooring. With a bemused frown set firmly in place, I descended the final few wooden stairs and bent to retrieve the note. Unfolding it, it simply read:

ENT-ICING, 8:45 a.m.

No name, no please or thank you. Just a simple directive. Instinctively, I twisted my left wrist upward, considering my watch face was always displayed on the inner side of my arm, and checked the time. It was already 8:25 a.m. It was too early for this, I hadn't even had my morning coffee, and by seems of things, it was going to remain that way until I located a coffee shop.

I shoved my feet into a pair of black heeled boots with a great sigh, then fetched my car keys out of the bowl on the sideboard under the balustrade, and headed out.

"Good morning, Kady," a voice called as I derived the front steps and made my way to the driveway along the right of the house.

"Morning, Mrs. Steinbeck."

"I was going to ask," her voice was shadowed by the sound of her famous shuffling of slippers as she approached. I began to wonder if she actually owned decent shoes. "Is there any way you could do my granddaughter's birthday cake? It's in two weeks and my daughter has left it awful late, no one can fit her in."

I pulled open the door of my Audi SUV and slipped inside. "I'll have to check the schedule, Mrs. Steinbeck," I called through the open door. "But I'm sure that shouldn't be a problem. Just pop into the shop when you're not busy so we can take the details."

"Perfect. Have a lovely day, Kady."

"You, too," I called, my voice shaded by the sound of my door slamming shut. The seatbelt locked into place, I started the ignition, pulled out of the driveway, and headed to Bricksdale Square with my mystery note.

Within fifteen minutes, I was pulling up outside of the pink awning, with the gold scripted words of 'Ent-icing' upon it. Dropping from the car, I peeked around. The shop was still closed. The bustling sounds which usually came from the Square were near nonexistent. Only the proprietors of the surrounding workplaces were bustling in and out of their stores, preparing for opening hours.

It was like a fucking Ghost Town and that was enough to unnerve me.

I was inspecting the note again, studying the handwriting as carefully as possible. For a fleeting moment I considered it to be Liam with one of his surprises, but it wasn't his writing. It was when my thumb glided over the ink when I jumped as an old-fashioned public payphone incased in a silver surround a little down the way of Ent-icing, began to toll. Within eight steps, I was at the phone and lifting the receiver.

"Hello?"

"Madison Avenue, ten minutes."

I didn't recognize the voice, it was terse and sounded muffled, however, before I could ask who it was I was speaking to, they hung up, leaving me in the lurch and confounded as I sped back to the car, and headed south to Madison.

Slipping from behind the wheel after I put the car into park at the sidewalk, I checked the time again. At nearly 9:00 a.m., my irritation was mounting. It was far too early for this type of activity. I didn't like it one bit. I hated games especially games that felt like scavenger hunts.

With each ticking second, I was preparing myself to personally send the person pulling the strings behind this one, to Hell, considering I still hadn't had my first caffeine fix of the day.

I scanned the block left to right then checked my watch again. My heart was thrumming in my chest, my head was spinning and my stomach was moments away from expelling stomach acid onto the sidewalk.

A person wearing a black baseball cap with the lip down low, practically concealing his face, was heading straight towards me. His black hoodie looked a little too extreme considering the sun was blaring down on us, casting shadows of the buildings behind me, onto the street.

"Hey, watch it," I chided when he ran into me head on, sending me staggering backward.

"Sorry," he muttered, forcing a newspaper into my hands before subtly continuing down the block.

I took a moment to unfold the Boston Times I had just been forced with. A note was safely placed into the crease. In red marker it simply read:

VENUE 129,
MIDDLE BOOTH,
READ ME...

This was getting beyond a fucking joke now. But at least I'd finally have my coffee. So, again, I did as instructed and headed to the barista around the corner.

I slipped into the middle booth with my mug of happiness, having ordered a skinny latte, and began to read the paper as instructed. I was moments away from rivaling a tantrum of a toddler in a toy store when I overheard a familiar chuckle—a chuckle that sounded like one too many cigarettes had been drawn upon. Peeking over the pages ever so slightly, I was face to face...

well, face to back, with Liv and Liam standing together at the register.

My stomach flipped and adrenaline gushed when I heard him tell her, "Go and get us a seat, gorgeous," and with a playful swat on her backside, they both smiled merrily as she walked away. The wall of my booth vibrated behind my back as she slipped in behind me, clearing her throat.

What the fuck was going on? I felt like a spectator.

The pleather padded barrier behind me shook again as Liam slipped in the booth with the person who was supposed to be my best friend.

My face was disguised by the paper while the masochist in me was found to be intently listening to the twosome. It was when the sound of wet, passionate kisses sounded that I scrunched my face up and screwed my eyes shut, questioning what the fuck was going on around me.

"Thank you for an amazing week, Liam," said Liv. I could imagine her sweeping her fingertips up and down his arm. I had to fight the instant reaction to confront them there and then.

"You're worth it. I'm glad you enjoyed it, but regardless, I still don't think I've had my fill of you just yet." His words were cut by a soft suggestive groan and another wet kiss. I felt sick. I had to stop listening, but for the life of me, I couldn't tear myself away. I could feel my heart beating in my stomach.

"Liam," the barrier shook again, the material squealed so I knew she had shifted. "I think we should tell, Kady. It's not fai—"

"Hey, don't you worry your sexy little head over a thing. Things are going smoothly, Liv. Why ripple the water? She doesn't suspect a thing." I overheard a derisive snort. I sensed his statement wasn't yet finished when Liv interjected.

"Liam, the time will come when she'll start suspecting.

We've been caught by her too many times now. You can't keep forcing those pills down her throat and telling her it's just another delusion, or having her sent back to that God awful place just so we can have time together."

Tears flooded my cheeks. What…? He's…they've…I'm not crazy? Is that what all that meant? Everything that I was convinced I'd witnessed, was true? I'm not delusional? My mind was being played with like a ball of yarn by a dangerously, sadistic wild cat?

Lowering the paper, I forced myself to pick up my coffee and hoped that a sip would gift me with a further degree of understanding.

"Liv, baby, if we continue this way, then we all get what we want." With that coaxing tone laced through his words, he virtually sounded like The Devil himself. It was a tone I was unfortunately, more than familiar with.

A sharp shooting pain surged down my right arm. My hand befell to numbness while my grip became nonexistent, sent my mug clattering to the table, the warm liquid gushed out coating the table and seeping to the brown tile.

"What the fu—" Liam choked on his words as I stood from the booth and glared at both, my partner and my best friend. My lip curled upward, incessant tears wet my face as I shook my head. "Kady," he gasped.

I peeked over at Liv as I flailed my head in disgust. She was pushed back in the pew with a satisfied grin plastered over her oval face. Liberation sparkled and lit up her almond shaped hazel eyes.

"I can explain, Kady baby."

The shake of my head intensified. Words were floating around my mind, that Devil on my shoulder urged me to free them, but I couldn't bring myself to. They stuck in my throat as fear of ramifications restrained the need of my own liberation. With a gasp laced with disgust and betrayal, I fled the shop, wishing I had fled the moment that they came in through the door.

In that moment, I realized that the saying is true: ignorance is bliss.

It was like the universe was crying out alongside me. The pain, the betrayal and heartbreak was something which I couldn't avoid, and I knew deep down in the marrow of my bones that regardless of how many lashings I was given, regardless of how hot the metal was or how quick the impact would be if I drove the SUV into a wall, nothing was going to numb this pain. No physical pain was going to detach the emotions which were feasting and surging through my body, rendering me an emotional, pent-up wreck.

After everything that we had been through over the years, after feeling like his prisoner more times than I could count, it was ironic that it was down to these feelings, the ones which spawned after truth was finally revealed, which felt like my captor.

My boyfriend had been shagging my best friend, and I had caught them at it, more than once…but he was drugging me all this time…this situation was something I couldn't fathom. Not for one measly moment.

The pedal met the floorboard as I sped through the Boston traffic. Droplets crashed onto my windshield, the speed of the wipers nowhere near quick enough to eradicate the glass of the tiny diamonds which led into streaks down the surface, masking my vision.

I finally pulled up opposite the building site, my car taking a beating from the incessant downpour as each ruthless, heavy drop crashed onto my roof making the car vibrate. Usually, such sound would send me into a state of repose, but not today.

Today, Mother Nature was channeling my emotions.

God help the people of Massachusetts.

I exited the car, taking an idle amount of infuriation out on my door as I slammed it shut behind me and ran across the busy road. Horns blared, tires screeched and the glow of headlights was unsteady as drivers veered around my oblivious, wrath-fueled body.

By the time I had made it to the building site across the way, my white blouse had already clung to my flesh and turned transparent. The sludge of the site caused my heels to sink and with each step, the soles of my boots would slip out before my heels were drunken in by the dirt once again.

"Where the fuck is he?" I shouted over the crassness of catcalls being issued by the workload at my inappropriate state of attire, to a middleweight man, his dark curly hair peeping out from under his hard hat.

"Where's who?"

"Well, I know where your fucking boss is, so who else would I be talking about?" I chided.

It seemed as though each anger-lined word caused the battering of rain to come harder. Droplets fell into the muddy puddles scattered across the construction site, while my form stood between the rain and the ground and caused me to be speared by each icy collision as they crashed onto my skin. The man simply pointed behind me to the white cabin, and I wordlessly stomped off the site, and into one huge confrontation.

"You're a fucking asshole. You motherfucking cunt, how could you do that to me?!" I screamed after he muttered my name, following the slamming of the cabin door, with an element of surprise.

Rearing himself from the chair behind a table scattered with designs and blueprints, he guardedly made his way around, fisting his hands into his brown hair. When he had finished, the lengthy locks stayed stuck up in a sexy yet disheveled fashion.

"You couldn't have just told me? You had to send me on a motherfucking wild goose chase?"

"You're telling me, if I just came out with it, you would have believed me, darlin'?" And there it was: my confirmation. I had known as soon as I sat down in that booth and they walked in, that Walker was the one behind all of this. But hearing it, hearing him telling me that he had planted all of this, is beyond treacherous. What did I get from this new information? The truth, yes, but also heartache…heartache and utter humiliation.

There was no longer any distance between us, and his warmth did nothing for my freezing, soaking wet body. I wanted to lift my hands and let loose the anger and adrenaline that was holding my rationality prisoner. But I didn't have the energy. And almost immediately, despair showed its presence in the form of liquid seeping from my eyes and down my cheeks.

"You're sick," I sighed in contempt.

My words wounded him that was palpable. Contrite, he hung his head, focusing on his dirty, heavy boots, his lips rolled over his teeth, while his eyebrows pulled in. When he lifted his head after a silent moment, he was nodding faintly. "Maybe…" his brow rose, an ocean of apologies gazed back at me. "But it was something you needed to discover for yourself. I just gave you a hand."

The concoction of emotions had me trembling. I couldn't focus on anything. A stern finger caught my chin and tipped my head back when I began to let it fall forward, completely crushed. The chilliness of my body was cloaked by his heat and had me quivering with unthinkable expectation as we stood at the door.

Vision distorted, I sniffled. "I don't know what to do now."

His head dropped. Staring into each other's eyes, I breathed in his masculine scent, my slim body dwarfed behind a shield of muscle as his hips held me in place. The sound of the lock twisting was shaded by three directive words which came heavy, indulgent and the thickest that I had ever heard his Irish brogue. "Don't fight it."

Before I could bring an end to the situation, I felt his hands caressing my hips, and I found myself lifting my head to meet him when his lips crashed down over mine. Wandering and grasping hands matched our tongues dance and explored one another with seductive strokes and squeezes, as we gave an outlet for eighteen months of hidden desire. Abrasive yet intoxicating, the scruff shadowing his mouth was practically indescribable, and I wasn't going to attempt to describe it. I washed all logical thought from my mind and concentrated on sheer carnality.

This kiss was nothing like what Liam and I had shared, this was obsessive, wild and needy. Lips working against one another, our mouths opened farther, giving entry to a lustful circus which was surely becoming the best show on Earth. The minty heat of his breath masking the relics of his smoking was swallowed. His tongue gliding and circling my own was heady. Yet, the feel of his hard body towering over me, pinning me against the door as he invaded my mouth, while both of us succumbed to feral, eager groans which were swallowed by one another, was even headier.

"Walker," I breathed against his lips which were coated with evidence of our hunger, "we can't do this…" I panted. Still, my body was betraying my words. I kept thrusting my head back, meeting his lips and fisting my hands through his hair until I was at the nape of his neck, drawing his tongue deeper and further into my mouth.

"Why?" he panted.

"Not here…Liam…he'll come looking for me…" each gap

between words was filled with wet, feverish kisses.

"Mine?"

That lone word had me pulling my lips away, breaths coming in wild, short pants. I gazed back and searched the ocean in his eyes.

He had been there for me. He had understood the way my mind worked before I did…he was my anchor, and the anchor was getting cast. At that point, I wasn't adrift at sea any longer. I knew what I wanted.

I nodded, "Yours."

I don't know how we managed to pull it off, but somehow we got away from the site without questions being asked. Walker took his pick-up while I tailed him in the SUV.

We parked outside the Pavilion and the moment we stepped foot into his apartment on the fourth floor, we were ravishing each other all over again. My saturated blouse was peeled off my body with greedy hands, leaving me in just my black bra, jeans and heeled boots. Walker's plaid shirt soon met mine on the floorboards. I worked to remove his white tank top. To my surprise I was instantly halted with him breathing the word 'no' against my mouth, so I continued to wrench his mouth onto me with a forceful, pleading grip at the back of his neck.

Feverish fingers bored into the flesh behind my knees, and my back was rapidly glided up the wooden surface of the door behind me, my legs bound on instinct around his hips.

Down the corridor, we blindly stumbled. I was set down onto the mattress, the springs of the black, wrought iron bed squeaking as it bore our weight without warning.

Walker was cradled between my thighs, his lips leaving my mouth to work down my jawline, my neck and collarbone, until the silkiness of his tongue brushed over the swell of my breasts as they rose and fell rapidly, with one fluid sweep.

Tilting my pelvis upward, the ache which was beating at my core was thrust against his stomach with a long, beseeching whimper.

Every muscle in my body tensed when finally, Walker slithered down the span of my body. I appraised him as he reared up, shoulders back and head held high like a man who knew what he wanted—like a man who had known and waited for months, for the exact right time to take what I was finally ready to give.

The blue veins in his muscular arms were thick and throbbing, the stretching of white material which covered his torso dipped between each abdominal and emphasized his pectorals. The tribal sleeve covering his left arm and the large, intricate Celtic cross on his right bicep were on full view. My twenty-seven year-old vocabulary was lessened as I stared up at him. He was sexy as fuck, plain and simple. As my gaze swept lower to land at the bulge in his workpants, my erratic breaths quivered in anticipation.

He took my foot and unzipped my boots in turn, before releasing the button and zipper of my jeans and peeling them, along with my panties, down my legs. Sheer hunger burned in his eyes as he stood back as studied me, toeing his boots and freeing himself of his filthy workpants and boxers.

Fuck!

I was blatantly staring at most probably, the most intimidating cock I had ever seen. Thick and veiny, I gasped as I considered how the fuck he was even going to fit. But at that moment, even if I was ripped in two by this mammoth of an Irishman, it would be the most pleasurable of deaths.

My jaw fell open when he approached the side of the bed. Opening the bedside unit, he pulled out a foil packet, ripped it open, and watched me with weaving hunger and amusement as he rolled it over himself. "It's okay, darlin'. I won't hurt you. I'd never hurt you." I didn't contemplate for a second that he ever would.

With my head on the pillow, Walker slipped between the sheets with his tank top still on. Rough hands caressed the length of my body, my thighs falling open the lower his touch went, until finally, the tip of his finger swept across the tip of my clit. Electricity and vibrations shocked my nerves into surrendering to the delicious sensations he was prompting, while my hips bucked, forcing his finger to slide down my core and into the wetness of my very depths.

Hearing him gasp was one thing, but seeing his expression as he eyes fluttered closed, blatantly savoring that moment, when his finger slipped inside of me had a groan ripped from my throat. Inner muscles clenched and throbbed as they wrapped around his fingers, drawing him deeper inside of me as he continued to work on my frenzied body.

The springs of the bed squeaked again as he rolled over and shielded my body. Fingers circling, he left his mark on my inner walls as he readied me for his length. Ever so slowly, he eased himself inside of me, stretching me, filling me, owning me as he pushed in further until he was buried to the root. Each decadent inch in both length and girth had my head thrown back and keening as I licked my lips.

Burying his face in the crook of my neck, my head rolled back, my eyes closed as I allowed the wave of sensation to wash over my body, and set my nerves on fire as I adjusted to his invasion—his blissful, satisfying invasion.

He stilled when I was fully impaled. When he lifted his head, I saw his lower lip trembling and I *felt* his entire body trembling above me as he held himself. "Fuck, Kady," he gasped, "Jesus

Christ," was the last words he breathed before he began to move rhythmically, gliding in and out of my body like we were made for each other, hitting that delicious pinnacle inside my core that repeatedly tore moan after pleasurable moan from my voice box.

When his tongue dipped back into my mouth, swallowing my cries, my body was already joining his in its trembling fervor. Hips grinding upward, I was meeting him thrust for thrust when my gaze landed on the mirrored ceiling. I watched the sheets pooling and shifting as the space between my parted thighs was filled by his muscular physique, pulling his hips back and gradually rocking back into me.

Seeing him working his body against mine, feeling the tingles and pleasure as he worked with me, and hearing the evidence of such pleasure with moans and labored breaths, along with the sounds of the deed itself, the fluidity as he pushed through my slickness and the protesting groaning of the wrought iron bed as we moved in unison, was sensation overload.

The prominence of his shoulder blades shifted as he bore his weight through his arms at either side of my head, dragging himself back before gently lunging again.

A familiar, long sought-after tightening in my pelvis radiated through my lower back, and tingles shot down my hips and legs, making my toes curl as he drove into me at some glorious angle that had his shaft gliding down the smoothness of my core, sweeping over my highly sensitized clit, before burying himself to the root in my depths once more.

Walker cried out as my muscles constricted around him, his eyes screwed shut as heavy, jagged breaths were pasted against the others face.

"God, Walker, fuck, fuck…" I whimpered and I swear tears were threatening. Under the sheets, my back bowed, my hands glided down his back before settling on each of his ass cheeks, feeling the muscles tense beneath them as his gentle rocking turned into powerful, feverish drives.

"Jesus, Kady," he called while sheer greed and desperation spawned and my hands pressed into his behind further, drawing him into me, filling my already filled body as much as he could.

With a yell and a rapid gasp, he stilled, his body shuddering above me as I convulsed beneath him, my walls squeezing around him as we worked our lust-fueled possessed selves down from release.

I felt his fingertips gliding across my hairline, but all I could do was concentrate on having my heart rate return to normal while he braced his heavy body atop of me.

When he rolled over, I was taken in his arms, a kiss planted on my head. I snuggled against his chest, hearing his heart drumming against my ear and breathing in his manly scent.

Everything else faded away as slumber took me prisoner.

CHAPTER
twenty-six

It was the invasion of a soft golden glow, eradicating the shadows behind closed lids, which caused my eyes to flutter open. My body felt like I had been hit by a ten-ton truck. Stretching my limbs and cracking my back, a not so foreign sound of metal and protesting springs stirred and sounded beneath my body.

Fuck…

As soon as I came face to face with my naked body reflected in the ceiling, and the snowy white sheet pooled and creased around me, I forced myself into a seated position like it was going to halt the guilty conscience which I could feel manifesting in my bones.

"She's awake," the thick, seductive voice sounded from the bedroom doorway just beyond my feet. "I brought you coffee."

I'd already gathered the sheet around my body, holding it knotted in the center of my chest with my left hand. I was frantically searching for my clothing when he began prowling into the room, his black sweatpants resting low on his hips, his broad shoulders and defined lines framed by his white tank top.

Assembling my scattered attire, I hastily shoved my legs into my panties and jeans and quickly set to work, making myself presentable. "I can't stay, Walker. I have to go."

"Go where?"

Pulling my hair free of the collar of my blouse and with a frown marring my brow I breathed, "Home."

"Home? Kady—"

"No, Walker..." I held my hand up in a bid to halt his words, but it was a fruitless indication. Instead, he curved around my body, rested the mug of steaming liquid on the bedside and placed me under his undivided attention.

Two oceans met and melded into one as calloused hands freed my face of stray tendrils, before cradling both my cheeks. "He doesn't deserve you, Kady. You heard yourself what he's been doing."

"Walker—" I objected.

"I don't have much, darlin', but I have a little saved. I can clear it this weekend, we can leave Sunday night. I have a friend in Chicago who owes me a favor. We can be there before early hours Tuesday morning, and we don't have to look back. A new life, for *us*."

When I failed to interrupt his statement, the hopeful smile spanning his face caused an intense warmth in my heart.

"What do you say, darlin'?" he asked, his eyes hunting mine with such urgency, that all I could do was hang my head with guilt.

I didn't know what I wanted. I didn't know anything. The last twelve hours I had discovered that over a year of my life has been centered on nothing but total lies. To make matters worse, they were lies told by two people I had trusted for years.

Walker muttering the word, "Please," had me lifting my gaze. His face grew closer to my own, and soon after, the tip of his nose was grazing down the length of mine, his forehead pressed against me. My lips were sought by his, and instinctively, my treacherous body began to reciprocate.

I couldn't do this…

Pooling every ounce of strength, I finally dragged myself away from his lips and his clutch. "I can't Walker. I'm sorry," were the last words I battled to free as I skirted his body and with hurried strides, left the apartment.

As I descended the second flight of stairs of the Pavilion like a bat out of Hell, I heard his strangled bid to stop me. When I refused to stop, I knew that his lingering words were ones I had to keep reminding myself of when I got home. "You know the truth, Kady. You're stronger than him. He can only hurt you if you give him the ammunition. Stay strong. Stay angry."

I was on autopilot as I drove home. I couldn't remember getting from point A to point B, through the amassing of erratic thoughts in my head, colliding against my skull like they were in some pinball machine.

I felt as though I had lost myself. Liam may have remolded me into something he desired, and that therefore caused me to lose aspects of myself. But the one moral that always remained, the one belief I had always upheld was my ability to be faithful. I wasn't a cheater. Only now, unfortunately I was. I had lost myself entirely.

After pulling into the driveway alongside my home, the home where each wall should be painted black with the sinister memories that lay inside each of them, I noticed that Liam's car was also parked in the driveway, yet each room of the house was shrouded by darkness.

When I stepped over the threshold, I closed the door firmly behind me, unzipped my boots and left them at the bottom of the stairs by the sideboard, and through the darkness, I treaded up the stairway.

Into the master bedroom I went and flicked the light switch to my right, eliminating the shadows which dwell in their corners. I gasped and my hand lurched to my chest when, through the golden glow, I encountered Liam sitting on the bench seat in the bay window on the opposite side of the room. His legs were spread, his arms folded across his chest while his jaw was firmly set.

"Where've you been?" his tone was even and baleful. It sent a shiver up my spine when I realized which direction this confrontation was headed.

"Out."

"She was out," he mocked. Rearing himself up slowly and menacingly from the seat he took a deep breath, and watched me like a hawk as I strode to my side of the bed and placed my purse down on the mattress. "Was it good, Kady?" he probed. His hands now nestled in his pockets, his stance radiating hostility.

"Was what good, Liam? Finding out my boyfriend has been having an affair for over a year with someone who was supposed to be my best friend? Or finding out he's been hand feeding me medication which I don't need and causing me to question my own fucking sanity?" Although my voice was full of resolve, internally, I was shaking and cowering away like an abused child.

Liam hung his head for a fleeting moment on a derisive snigger. When he looked back at me, his eyes displayed a look both indestructible and tormenting. He began to prowl around the foot of the bed toward me. "I meant being the Irishman's whore? I can smell him all over you," he snarled.

Deep breath, Kady...deep breath...

"Well, at least I'm not denying it like some people."

He scoffed before his voice altered into a hard and

authoritative timbre. "How dare you talk to me that way; you are my girlfriend—"

Walker's words revolved around my head like a guiding light. *You're stronger than him. He can only hurt you if you give him the ammunition. Stay strong. Stay angry.*

"No, Liam. This,"—I drew an invisible line between our gradually nearing bodies—"hasn't been a relationship for a long time. It's time for me to wake up and admit what it truly is. This is nothing but an abusive relationship: emotionally, mentally, and physically. I am not your lapdog. Not anymore, I refuse to be because I am worth *more*. Now, if you'll excuse me…" My legs were barely capable of sustaining my weight for much longer. My entire body from head to toe was vibrating.

I avoided his body and began to make my way to the en-suite, when I felt his hand in the back of my hair. His nails scraped across my scalp leaving a burning sensation in their wake, which quickly subsided when my face was ruthlessly rammed into the wall. Instant pain shot through my head, my vision was drowning as tears sprang. Yanking my head back after impact, he brutally shouted through clenched teeth, "How dare you disrespect me!"

My eardrums rang, the volume of his voice enhanced the pain radiating in my head as my vision shook. My face was driven back into the solid barrier before I was tossed to the end of the bed, landing in a dazed, crumbled heap on the floor. Blood seeped from the gash on my forehead and trailed down the side of my face like warm velvet.

As he pointed a scornful finger at me, I watched the demon break free. "You're nothing without me," he derided.

I had to fight back. I had to fight back. Keep hold of that anger, Kady, I told myself. He abused you…

"No!" I eventually roared, "You're nothing without me, do

you know why, Liam? Because you're an abuser, and an abuser feeds on their victims weaknesses. No more, Liam. No fucking more!"

The deranged grin on his face and that look in his eye broke through my resolve. On the floor at the foot of the bed, I was a quivering wreck. "No? Really?" he sneered, and before I could make for my escape, he was already pulling his arm back. The blow of his brutal fist across my jaw, followed by another directly upon my mouth had my lip split. My instant reaction was to trail my tongue across my teeth, just to make sure he hadn't knocked any out.

As my forehead and my lip wept warm crimson liquid, I forbid the salty tears to weep from my eyes. He'd enjoy that too much.

The ache in my jaw was tremendous. But I wasn't going to cower away. I couldn't. No more.

Like a cockroach scurrying to the nearest sofa when blinded by light, I'd crawled on my hands and knees away from the foot of the bed. My face prickled by the trickling of blood as it flowed from my wounds. After a dazed, futile attempt of pushing myself up onto my knees to stand, blood droplets falling to the ground, a powerful arm clutched around my middle and I was hauled back into his squatting body.

"You forget everything I have done for you. You think you can free yourself of me that easily, bitch? Well, let's see about that shall we?"

When I heard a familiar rattling sound emerging from out of his back pocket, and my gaze landed on a familiar small bottle when he held it in front of me, I willed myself to struggle in protest with every power I had, just to free myself.

"No, no, no, no…" The grip behind his immobilizing clutch grew stronger as my arms and legs flailed.

"It's okay, Kady baby," he strained, yet his tone was almost placating. Popping the lid free with his thumb, he fished out one of the blue pills before my struggles sent the bottle, and the remaining contents, scattering across the carpet.

Merciless, he held me by the jaw like a dog, coaxing my jaw open. With my lips rolled over my teeth, I shook my head frantically to avoid his intentions.

My hands rose to his in an attempt to pull him off me. "Stop fighting me, Kady," his strained voice vanished, and with my throbbing jaw snared in his right hand, the pill was concealed in his left palm as he balled his fist.

My face contorted in agony as with everything I had, I forced myself not to gasp or yell at his winding strike upon my ribcage. But I couldn't take this beating silently. Not with the force behind the second battering of my ribs. I gasped. And as my mouth opened to catch vital air, Liam's fingers were rammed down my throat, placing the tablet on the very back of my tongue.

I gagged. My shoulders were heaving, my arms and legs thrashing in my desperation.

Still, Liam held my head back against his shoulder, forcing my mouth shut and rubbed my throat. "You'll feel better after a nice sleep, then all this…" I'd fought against it for too long, and soon after, the motion of his fingers rubbing over my throat prompted my swallowing reflex. Body turning lax from wrangling for what seemed like an eternity, I was finally let go.

When he stood, straightening out his attire and dusting himself off, he delivered a swift kick in my injured ribs. I doubled over with a pain-enthused cry, feeling his eyes boring into me. I felt that deranged, sickening smirk plastered over his face as he watched the result his assault had on me. "…Will be better, and we can go back to normal. Now, if you'll excuse me, I have to wash your blood,"—he motioned to his hands—"and the remnants of Liv's pussy juice off my cock. You stay there until I've finished. Understand?"

I simply nodded and panted through the winded sensation as I shielded my ribs in my right hand.

"Good girl."

Time drifted as I concentrated on my breathing. The door to the en-suite was ajar. Only the sound of cascading water from the shower and Liam singing, *My Girl* was heard.

You can't live like this, Kady. When will enough be enough? When he puts you in the hospital, or when you end up in the damn morgue? You need to get out of here.

Those words were my mantra. They were repeated ferociously and impassioned until I found the strength in my trembling body, to push myself up onto my feet. I reached for my purse on the bed with my gaze transfixed on the en-suite door, before tiptoeing out of the room and down the stairs while Liam continued to sing a song, which I'll most probably never have the courage to listen to again, for as long as I live.

After thrusting my feet into my boots, I staggered out of the house, carefully closing the front door behind me and down the steps to my car.

My ribs smarted as I battled to fill my lungs with a purifying breath. I was sitting in the driver's seat gazing up at the house. Anyone who passed could see that my bedroom light was on. If only they knew what just happened in it.

We never truly comprehend how many houses we pass each day that mask domestic abuse, be it mentally, emotionally or physically. There is never one group worse than the other. It affects us all the same, and like a rock dropped into water, it's only so long before ripples form…

I knew that my decision and my strength to leave him were sure to cause ripples before too long.

I had to get out of there before he realized I was missing...

The seatbelt was drawn across my body, the engine roared to life as I slammed the door shut and speedily backed out of the driveway and down the street.

A red light had me pulling up opposite Bricksdale Square. I rummaged through my purse for my cellphone as I waited. Pulling up my contacts, I scrolled for his number and pressed the green button. The handset was stationed in the hands-free dock as I waited for him to answer.

"Hello?"

"Walker?" I gasped.

"Kady? What's the matter, darlin'? Is everything alright?" Throughout everything that had happened that day, after how I left him less than an hour and a half ago, he was still worried about me. That notion made the corners of my mouth lift. The stinging of my split lip drew a wince from me.

"Yes," I answered.

"What's the matter?"

Pulling off as the light turned green, I gushed, "Yes, Walker. My answer is yes. I'll leave with you."

His heavy sigh vibrated and rustled over the speaker. I was driving with blooded streaks down my face, and a thick, split lip, but the sound of sheer relief coming from him had me smiling. "Really? You'll..." he trailed off like he could see I was nodding my aching head. "Where are you? I'll pick you up."

"No, I'm in the car; I'm on my way to you."

After a beat, my name fell from his lips sounding like, Katy. My stomach started to tie itself in knots. Bells were ringing loud and clear in my ears. Each breath I made, I endeavored to listen to over the muffled buzzing.

"Kady? Are you there?"

All at once, my body began to feel very, very heavy; it was almost like I was sinking further into my seat. My heart was aching and racing a rough, jagged rhythm, while haziness hijacked my vision. "Yeah, I'm here." I discovered just about enough energy to form the words, although they vibrated and lingered in my head like an echo. My eyelids grew heavy, I felt myself slipping. "Walker, keep talking to me," I slurred.

A long, appreciative groan left his throat while I overheard him flop back into his seat. "You don't know how happy you've made me, darlin'. Kady…I–I love you. I've loved you since the moment I first laid eyes on you."

Everything felt like I was on the cusp of unconscious. Deep breaths were drawn into my lungs, as I contended with that potent urge to let my head fall forward. Although I couldn't feel my legs and lights beyond my windshield were distorting and dancing, I smiled at his words while my eyes surrendered to a protracted blink. "I lo—"

The car was sent spinning. Repeatedly slamming on the breaks, endeavoring to end the rapid rotations, I was forced back into my seat by sheer G-Force alone, as a result of the trucks impact hitting the side from the juncture. Nothing was going to stop it. That I knew.

An eternity had passed before everything was brought to a standstill, yet it was all over before I could decipher through my clouded head what was happening.

I was tipped onto my side watching the events unfolding horizontally through partially closed lids. The commotion of tires screeching and horns blaring were distant as the traffic came to a standstill, and I observed the world around me resuming in slow-motion.

"Kady? Kady? Talk to me, darlin'. What's happened?" his fraught voice traveled over the speaker.

When I tried to call out to him, a groan took place of his name.

"Kady—"

My body was heavy…

"Kady—"

My head was aching…

"Darlin', talk to me, please. Where are you, so I can come to you?"

Focusing on the sound of his voice, I was calmed by the notion of, if those few moments were to be my last, I wasn't alone…as my anchor, he was there with me, holding onto me for as long as he could, just as he'd always promised.

I reached out for the handset as though reaching for his hand, alas, my arm was too heavy. Energy was one thing I didn't have.

Energy and time.

That I knew.

"Kady, can you hear me, darlin'? Kady—"

I let the lingering sound of his voice calm me, as I was taken by darkness…

EPILOGUE

I ran like I was striving for first place in the Boston Marathon. The downpour had eased, and the water which had seeped through the satin material of my emerald dress, warmed my body like a wetsuit.

At the end of the tree-lined street, I hailed down a late night passing cab. When he came to a stop, I yanked open the door and slipped into the sticky backseat. His beady eyes examined me through the rearview mirror, an expectant look on his face.

"I don't have any money—"

"Do I look like I give free lifts lady? This is a cab. No fare, no ride."

My wrist slipped through the cuff of my Rolex. "Here," I passed it through and dropped it into his palm. "It's not a fake I can assure you. Just please, can you take me to the Pavilion?"

After a brief moment of studying the gold watch, he smiled like his winning numbers had just been announced, and pulled off.

I had no idea how long it was before we came to a stop outside the dilapidated structure for the second time that night. Pulling the release on the door, I voiced my thanks in frantic gasps before slamming it shut and knocking on the bay window to the right of the communal entrance. When the baldheaded man peeked out of his drapes, I waved my hand in the universal language of, 'come here'.

"Second time tonight, lady," he muttered disapprovingly as he opened the door, allowing me entry.

"I know, I'm sorry. It's the last time, I promise," I called back as I sprinted up the creaking steps, overlooking the cries and shouting coming from the passing apartments. Ignoring the stench and the pornographic graffiti which lined the shabby walls, I only focused on one thing…on one person…

Chest heaving, my ribs ached and lungs burned and grated with each pant. I knocked fanatically on the green door.

"Alright, alright," I heard him call; still, his acknowledgment didn't stop my incessant knocking. "Wha—" Hard, exasperated eyes thawed as soon as he saw me standing there in the hallway beyond his threshold. "Kady…"

Hanging my head, I drew breath after breath, pushing past the pain in my heart, lungs and throat as the starvation of oxygen tortured my body. From the ground, my gaze scoured the length of his frame which was clothed in a tight black tank and gray sweatpants.

"I remember," I panted.

Cocking his head, he dropped his weight through his hip, his arms folded across his chest while he braced his shoulder against the doorway.

My own desperate gaze hunted his eyes with as much intensity as he had shown earlier that night, when he begged with me outside McGinty's to tell him what I remembered after serenading me with our song.

I swallowed harshly. "I remember everything…"

The End.

BONUS *scene*

~ *Walker* ~

The floorboards groaned and creaked with every step I took as I paced from the coffee table to the front door of my apartment. My hands found their way into my hair, my nails scraped across my scalp as though attempting to hunt and rid the voice which had haunted me since that morning, out of my Goddamn mind.

How the fuck could he do that?

How the fuck could someone do something so sadistic to the person they say they love?

Don't get me wrong, I've done some fucked up shite in my time, shite that my Ma and Da wouldn't be fucking proud of, but still, I was taught to treat people with respect. So that's one thing I make sure to do. Even that sick, twisted bastard. Does it come easily? It did, until I saw through their perfect fucking relationship, until I saw the marks he purposely left behind on her perfect flesh.

I snatched the pack of Marlboro's from the coffee table as I paced back for what seemed like the millionth time in twenty minutes. Usually only a social smoker, I'd rarely have a cigarette unless it was outside a pub, but at that moment, I needed something to focus my hands on for as long as fucking possible.

Flipping the pack open, I took out a stick, pressed it between my lips as I tossed the remnants onto the table, probably getting lost to the pile of chaos spread across it. The smell of gasoline escaped the Zippo lighter as I flipped it open, struck it against the material of my thigh and lifted it to light the cigarette.

Like a fucking saboteur in WWII France, I lurked around the corner listening to the vile things he told his coworker inside the office. The vicious and toxic words haunted me as I sucked back and held the chemicals in my lungs, while helplessness mocked me. I hadn't felt that level of weakness since I was seventeen and watched my ma as she gave up the fight. The one thing I needed her to keep doing, she fell to. And after this last stunt Liam had organized, I knew without a shadow of fucking doubt, this would be what Kady finally fell to.

Well, fuck you, Liam DeLaney you fucked up bastard.

Kady needs someone to protect her, that should fall under her partner's responsibilities, but that was never meant to be. How can the one person you spend your life with find pleasure in crushing the life and soul of someone so heartened and beautiful? How can a man find pleasure in abusing his woman?

I paced again, taking drag after drag of the cigarette, my thumb instinctively flicking the butt as I felt both agitation and rage simmering in my blood. No man should lay an abusive hand on a woman for his own liking. And no man should purposely cause their woman to question their own sanity.

My hand balled into a tight fist as I passed the door, the hasty thumping on the opposite side ricocheted around my cold bare walls, making me jolt. All I wanted was to punch something or do something to take this shitty feeling away. With the amount of anger festering inside of my body, I wouldn't doubt for a moment that I could send the already cracked wall crumbling to its end.

"About fucking time," I complained under a weighted sigh after yanking the door open, then resumed with my wild pacing, taking another draw from my Marlboro.

"Sorry it took me so long," she apologized, closing the door behind her with more poise than I could ever muster at that point. "What the fuck has happened?"

The floorboards turned into cement, causing me to pause mid-stride. On shaky legs I turned to face the woman who had been there for me in my time of need, the woman who never once judged me for my escapism, but was there to help clear me up afterward. Letting my head drop, I outted the cigarette in the glass ashtray. My warm, smoky hand met my mouth as though I was going to be sick, still she didn't once touch me. She knew beyond all reason not to.

"Walker? Talk to me. What's happened?"

"He…he…" My thumbnail scoured down the center of my upper lip as I tried desperately to find my voice beyond the lump in my throat. This kind of shite you expect to see in some sick thriller movie, not in actual life, and certainly not to someone you know. Shaking my head, I drew my hand away and lifted my gaze to meet red block-dyed bangs. "He's had her put into Pinewood."

"What?!" her eyes widened, and even I could notice her jaw tighten as the shriek rang loudly in my ears. "So that's why she hasn't been taking my calls."

Motionless, I could just find the energy through the resentment and anger…anger, no, this wasn't anger—this was fucking fury, and shook my head. "I knew something wasn't right, I could feel it in my damn bones."

I fished for the pack not giving a flying fuck about the stack of papers being knocked from the table in the process. For a blinding moment, those papers were Liam DeLaney's head and the table was his shoulders. I drew out another cigarette and lit it. The silver smoke danced and swirled weightless and aimlessly into the air as I took a deep draws and blew it out between tight lips.

"How the Hell did you find this out?" Laurie asked, taking up the brown chair and dropping her purse to the floor.

The floorboards were wearing with how frantic my pacing was growing, but I couldn't stop myself. I needed to try and burn out the adrenaline along with the ball of mixed emotions which were wreaking havoc on my body. "I went to his office to ask about my paycheck. He wasn't in a meeting because the door was open, but he was talking to another one of the architects. I was going to leave it, check back later but the guy asked if Kady was getting better now that she was in Pinewood, and I couldn't move." The tip of the cigarette glowed ruby red as I took another draw.

"Better?"

Under my fucked up exterior I felt every organ attempting to escape my body. I didn't blame them, I wanted to fucking escape it, too. "He's saying she attacked him with a knife, Laurie. A FUCKING KNIFE!" I shouted, and regardless of how hard I tried, I just couldn't breathe. I wanted to protect her, but despite that ever growing need, I realized that I couldn't. And that ripped the heart from my chest and shredded it into a million pieces. I can't protect her, without make it worse *for* her.

FUCK!

The boiling of my blood was the hottest I'd ever felt, the thumping in my head, the ache in my heart; the helpless and sickening twist of my gut was going to kill me. I tried distraction. The smoking stick between my lips was evidence of that, but it wasn't helping in the slightest. Nothing was helping. It may have been years, but once again, I felt the weight of that label, the one which screamed 'failure', smothering me. I failed my Ma when I left, and now I was failing Kady, too.

Dragging it from my lips, I muttered, "I can't do this," more to myself as I quickly outted the cigarette in the ashtray. I didn't care that the glowing cherry separated from the stick and was a potential fire hazard as I reared up, and like a startled charger, I hurtled down the hallway, booting the leg of the table as I did so. "I can't fucking do this, Laurie!" I yelled.

"Walker, come on. We can do this together. You've been doing so well. We knew these moments would come, remember just breathe. You need to breathe," The sound of Laurie's footsteps trailing me down the hallway came to a sudden end when I slammed the bedroom door closed behind me, then twisted the lock. "Okay," she said, reluctant. "Five minutes, Walker. If you're not out by then, then I'm coming in. I'll kick the door down, so help me God, Walker."

I didn't bother answering. As a matter of fact, the selfish part of me, the part that I'd been trying for months get under control since pulling myself out of the fighting scene, wasn't even listening to what she'd said. For a while, those fights were my back-up, they gave me what I needed, without the need of myself adding to the canvas of my self-mutilation.

When I sat my arse on the edge of the bed, the old iron springs groaned and squealed, while a black candle was taken from the beside unit drawer, the lighter pulled from the back pocket of my jeans. Once the wick was set alight, I doubled over and scrambled to find my safe box from under the bed. The moment I held that box in my hands, although my heart was jittering and my arms shook, I felt safe, I felt control.

Placing it on the bed beside me, I flipped open the lid. Razor blades, penknife, glass shards and a broken porcelain ornament with a deadly pointed edge stared back at me. I stopped falling. The items that lay in that box were my safety net, catching me from the lumbering feelings that I was desperate to rid myself of. The ones I urgently need to escape from.

It's strange how something like this can be named a safety box. I think only people who function in this way can understand the reason why it has such an inapt name.

The objects in the box shuffled as I drew the small, sharpened knife and set the case onto the planks of my floor, before yanking the white T-shirt from my body. Have you ever been so angry that all you want to do is cry but just can't? That's how it feels every time, and each time that need grows more powerful than the last. Nothing makes sense when your head is cram packed full of rage. You need something to shock you into thinking clearly before you lose utter control. And losing control to this is the only way to stay one step ahead. It's the only way to stay somewhat in charge.

Fuck that saying; *never make a permanent decision based on a temporary emotion*; this was the quickest route to stability for me.

Absorbed on the implement, I watched its edge glow a burnish orange from inside the flickering flame, before lying back onto the bed. I watched the man in the mirror above me as my head sank into the pillow. A man filled with so much hurt and so much grief that all he can do is mutilate his body to feel a measure of normalcy.

Silver stripes, blemishes and the hideous weathered flesh mocked me from the mirror. I hated looking at myself. I hated having to watch as I caused my own destruction. But there was no other choice. I'd lost complete control already in my life; this was my way—the only way—to ensure I didn't push those boundaries and lose it again. Focusing on that permanent reminder, the damaging result that the lack of control could cause, was the only way I could keep myself focused, and remain on that very edge instead of hurling myself from it, in a brief second of desperation.

A deep breath was sucked into and held in my lungs while the heat of the blade was felt as I paused idle a hairsbreadth from a section of unmarked flesh. Clamping my teeth together, I lowered the blade. Slowly slicing the cutting edge down the hideously marred flesh, my face screwed tightly as I breathed through the pain while the sharp burn spread on each side of the growing laceration.

Only when the pain struck was I able to free myself, my mind and body of the rage and helplessness I was being strangled by. I wasn't only slicing through my flesh; I was slicing through that overwhelming surge of adrenaline, and allowing myself to be carried back to my body's natural balance. It was a way to feel control in a situation where control was nonexistent.

The warmth of the blade, the burning of the scored wound alongside the seeping of lifeblood had me steadied, numb. Watching and feeling the fury bleed from me brought a form of life—of inner peace, and as the clouds shadowing my judgment began to dissolve, I could focus on the most important problem: how to get Kady home.

Sitting on the old chair with wooden arms opposite the sofa with a green medical kit resting in her lap, her warning tone hit me like a brick wall as I surfaced topless from the opening. "You're lucky; I was just about to kick down the damn door." Laurie may be a foot shorter than me, but Jesus Christ could she give me a telling off.

She looked up at me as I ran my hand through my hair and

rubbed my neck.

That was another thing I loved about Laurie, she never stared. She never just looked at what was standing in front of her. She saw *it*—she saw *me* as a man, and each time she was totally unfazed by the tales of pain and release that stood in her presence. Had it be anyone else, they would've stared at the train wreck in front of them with cold, assessing stares, completely repulsed by the spreading of chaos over my body.

"Come on," she tapped her thigh as though summoning a canine as she often did. "Let's get you cleaned up."

I didn't care about the blood oozing from the gash or the fact that it trickled down my skin as I walked toward her, swiping my cigarette pack along the way. I was sparking one up while Laurie carefully slipped her hands into a pair of latex gloves and ripped open the antiseptic wipe.

"Fuck," I hissed, the smoke leaving my mouth in a rushed cloud. That wipe stung like a bitch.

"Really?" she peeked up from the seat. "You can handle doing that, but a wipe is painful?" her directness of the situation amused us both, and with a look of concentration, she went back to cleaning the stream of blood oozing down my torso as I held my head back to the ceiling. "So have you got any ideas about how we're going to get Kady back home?"

I wish I did. Short of coming up with a prison break plan and helping her escape, I had no idea how to move forward with this one. What I did know with undeniable fact was I had to see her. Kady meant everything to me, and knowing what he was doing to her and that I was powerless to stop it, was killing me. No way on this God's green Earth would she ever attack him, I'd bet my fucking life on it.

"I need to see her. That's the only thing I can think of right now. I need to make sure that she's alright."

The largest Band-Aid in the box was torn open and placed over the four inch laceration, with Laurie's gentle fingers smoothing down the edges. "I knew all along something wasn't right. I've had a bad feeling about that man for months," she said softly, her attention still directed at dressing yet another one of my self-inflicted wounds. "You could try calling the institute, maybe they could help. Other than that, you know whatever you need, I'm always here," hazel eyes peeked up at me from the seat.

"That's why I fucking love you. Where's my phone?"

She made a disapproving, whinnying noise as I stepped back from her touch and grabbed for the cellphone on the table. Holding the handset to my ear, I shushed Laurie with a wave of my hand and asked the operator to put me through to Pinewood Institute.

"Good morning, Pinewood Institution," the depressed voice greeted me after several rings. By that point, Laurie was standing on tiptoe with her ear against the phone, eavesdropping.

"Hi, I wonder if you can help me. I have a friend that has been admitted. Her name is Kady Jenson. I was wondering if I could come and visit her."

"Are you on the approved visitation list, sir?"

Pulling away, Laurie mouthed, "Visitation list?" with a frown.

"Um…no, I'm not—"

"I'm sorry, sir, but there's no way I can authorize the visit unless you're on the list…"

A small hand came up to cover the speaker, "Ask them to ask Kady if she will see you."

I nodded and licked my lips.

"Couldn't you ask Kady yourself if she'd see me? I really need to see her. Please…Just tell her that Walker wants to see her."

Seconds, that felt more like fucking minutes, passed before

the voice muttered, "If you'll hold for a moment, sir. I'll see what I can do." Then the line went silent. "Hello, sir—"

"Yes."

"Kady has agreed, but the visit will have to be supervised."

I heard my sigh of relief crackle down the speaker. I didn't care how many people would have to be in that room. All that mattered was that I got see her. "That's fine. Can I come in this afternoon?

"You can come by at 3:00 p.m., and please bring identification with you otherwise I can't let you in."

"Thank you. I'll be there," I sighed before ending the call. I could feel my face falling and a scowl spreading when I looked down at Laurie. Was I being selfish? I knew I had to see Kady, and make sure she was alright. After everything that had happened, it seemed only Laurie and I were the ones in her corner, attempting to support and comfort her from within the shadows. Going to see her that day was really only going to benefit me. It was for my own peace of mind that I could help her keep fighting through this. But what would the consequences be for her if Liam discovered I'd been there to see her…

"Hey, wipe that look off your face. She agreed to see you. And I can promise one thing: we'll find out what's going on, Walker. You know we will."

I put the truck into park and stared up at Pinewood Institute. My heart feeling as though it was going to explode in my chest at any second, knowing that my Kady was in there, somewhere where she didn't need to be, being force fed medication that didn't need to be administered.

Dropping from behind the wheel, I slammed the door shut and made my way through the silent grounds, passing the small garden which was situated beyond the entrance steps, with a colorful array of flowers and benches. It had that contrasting peaceful quality which screamed that this was a garden of an institute, and that alone was enough to cause a fire in my blood.

How the fuck he could put her in here, I have no idea.

"Good Afternoon, may I help you?" the woman behind the registration desk asked, looking up at me with uncertainty.

"I'm here to see Kady Jenson. I called in this morning."

Her skeptical look deepened.

"If you check on your systems you'll see that she agreed to see me."

Fixing her glasses into place, she focused on the computer screen and clicked on the mouse a few times before asking for my name and identification. My wallet was pulled from my navy pants pocket, and I tapped my foot impatiently as the woman behind the desk studied my driver's license. Finally, she smiled back at me.

"Perfect, if I could ask you to sign in please, Mr. Walker," she muttered and twisted the visitor's book around for me to sign. Mr. Walker…that was enough to send a chill across my flesh and up my spine. Still, I did as I was bid. This wasn't about me and my issues. This was all for Kady. "And for the patient's safety, can you hand over your wallet, cellphone, any shoelaces and your belt please. You can collect it all when you leave."

With everything dropped into the tray at the desk, I was buzzed through the door and escorted down the corridor, past a large room with ranting patients until I was outside a visitation room. The camera above the door watched my every move.

When the door opened, I felt my heart plummet to my stomach when my gaze traveled from the female orderly sitting in the corner with her hair pulled into a tight bun, to Kady.

Clothed in white pajamas, she was sitting at the far end of the room, gazing out of the window like a grounded child watching her friends playing in the fresh air, while she was forced to stay indoors. Lost to a world of her own, she didn't even acknowledge my being there as I stepped across the checkered flooring. So when I set my hand on her shoulder, only to have her jolt so forceful at my touch, that the chair scraped across the flooring and the orderly shifted to make her way toward us, my heart shattered. Offering a soft gesture to the woman in scrubs, I muttered, "It's okay," before focusing back on Kady, and the woman cautiously dropped back to her seat.

Kady knew I'd never harm a single hair on her head. That being said, her need for release is something I understand. You need pain; you need to hurt physically to end the emotional hurt, to lower your adrenaline. There is a world of difference between what I had done to her, and the way Liam forces her to live. My intentions were to keep her safe from herself. His was to degrade and make himself feel powerful.

When you seek detachment and numbness through pain for an emotional release, you're aiding someone, I was aiding her. When you beat up, degrade and cause physical, emotional and mental harm of your own freewill…that is abuse. That night when I held Kady in my arms after inflicting the pain she needed, I reassured her; I made her feel safe after I submitted to her requests. I never once made her feel scared of me. Liam is the exact opposite, the sick cunt.

"Hey," I muttered, as I took the vacant seat ahead of her. "How are you feeling, darlin'?" Moments passed where my question went answered. I didn't recognize this person in front of me. She wasn't the Kady Jenson I came to know and have a deep attachment for. Instead, a hollow shell was staring back at me. The want to take her in my arms and carry her away from all the shite she had been living in, and offer her a better one, was that greatest

I'd ever felt.

She hung her head defeated. "I went for him, Walker." When she pulled her gaze back to me, my heart died in my chest. Her face was pale, her eyes dim and lifeless, confused beyond all comprehension.

Her name was a painful muttering as I shifted myself to the edge of the seat, her knees snuggled between my thighs as she wrung her fingers together in her lap.

"I attacked him and I can't even remember it."

Unexpected, a commotion was heard from outside, the orderly rose from her chair quickly and peeked out of the small glass window of the door. "Oh my God," she gasped.

"It's okay, we'll be fine," I reassured her as she nodded her head and dashed out of the room, leaving us alone.

"Kady, listen to me, you did not attack him," I stressed, my hands wrapping around hers. "Do you understand me? You did *not* attack him."

Her bedraggled tresses were swept across her face when she shook her head with unending mumbles of defeat and denial. A mass grew in my chest and practically strangled me at seeing her so brainwashed. I pressed again. "You didn't attack him, Kady. You're not that sort of person; you don't have a combative bone in your body."

"How do you know, Walker?" she challenged. "People live next-door to rapists and child abductors, but they always say the same thing, 'We never realized, it's come as such a shock, he/she was such a lovely person'."

My God, what the fuck had that bastard done to her? It took every strength and effort to pool each ounce of determination I possessed, and stop myself from crumbling in front of a person who was once strong enough to endure such abuse, but had since been diminished to such a manic state. I simply grinded, "No, Kady, that's enough. You didn't do what he's made out you've done."

The sternness in my words had her frozen. With a faint doubting shake of her head, she frowned. "Then why would he say it?"

More than anything in the world, I wished I could have told her the answers which she deserved. She didn't deserve to be confined by these four walls; she didn't deserve to be abused the way she had been for God knows how long. "I don't know, but we're working on it—"

"We? Whose we?"

A small wistful smile stretched across my face, and I prayed that the grit behind my words would bring her a form of comfort. "Let's just say, the FBI has nothing on me and Laurie at the moment."

After a moment, she returned her rapt gaze back to the garden beyond the window. I studied her silently and when she whispered, "Today was the funeral," it was like I was hit by a fucking freight train, and the fog was lifted. I wouldn't put it past the fucker. Every abuser breeds on control, they strive for it, what a perfect way to keep that control than by having her locked up, depriving her of her right? "I didn't even get a chance to say goodbye and now I never will," she added, a tear escaping over her eyelid.

I was sitting in silence, stringing each piece of new information together in my head to try and see the bigger picture.

"He deleted my voicemail, Walker. The one from my mom and everything else after that is a complete blur."

Tearing my hands away from her, I set them on each side of her face, my thumbs catching and drying each droplet of despair as they fell. I hated seeing her cry, so I coaxed her forward and halted chewing on my chewing gum, as I pressed our foreheads together. "Please, don't cry, darlin'," I whispered struggling against my own tears. "Please, don't cry."

When I pulled away, I searched her eyes and asked if she remembered the conversation in Tiffani's the morning after her birthday, when she agreed to let me be her anchor. With each desperate word, I hoped that I'd find a sliver of strength in her eye. That was what she needed at that moment in her life. She needed someone she could trust to help her find and grasp hold of reality. When she nodded, I told her, "So I am going to be your anchor. Say after me, Kady: I didn't attack, Liam."

"No, I'm not saying that. Refusing to believe it is why I'm here, Walker. I'm not saying that. I did attack him. I did. He has the cut to prove it, I'm a nut-job, I'm delusional—"

Jesus fucking Christ. I shut up when she asked me to, but I couldn't stand on the sidelines and watch him drag her down any longer. "Yes, Kady, you are delusional. You're delusional because you believe his lies, his deceits, his fabrications call them whatever you want it all comes to the same thing," I gasped, pointedly. "Kady, you told me not to say anything to you when I saw your ribs. I'm not doing it any longer, I'm not keeping my mouth shut so you can continue with this twisted world that he's made you believe you deserve. I'm done."

I felt the power of denial behind my hands as she shook her head, frenzied, and pled with me not to burst her delusional bubble that she had been cooped up in for God only knows how long. Enough was enough.

"He is abusive, darlin'. You are in a physically and psychologically abusive relationship, Kady. That is the truth and you know it, you just deny it over and over. But look where it's got you, darlin'."

How was it possible to feel like the bad person just by stating the truth? Witnessing the untold tears as they spilled down her face at my words, caused my eyes to water and a lump the size of Ireland to clog in my throat.

"You're in this place, taking medication you don't need, questioning your own sanity, Kady, this isn't right. You're worth so much more, darlin'. I can't offer you the world at your feet like Liam can, but if you were mine, I would offer you a world of happiness, a world of safekeeping and respect where you wouldn't have to walk on Goddamn eggshells. I'd never treat you the way he has."

The more she begged for me to stop, the more I had to keep pushing forward. She knew this. She'd known it for a long time but always justified it. And right at that point, it was my job to make her see sense if it was the last thing I did. I knew from the very moment I laid my eyes on her, and saw the forced and sad look in her eye, that I wanted nothing more than to make her smile. Now it is me, the person who wants to keep her safe, the person who would travel through Hell and back for her, who's the cause of her sadness. More than anything, I hated that the tears which were falling were as a result of my voice, of my words. But they were words that needed to be heard.

"Repeat after me, Kady: I didn't attack, Liam." When she stayed quiet, I repeated myself again.

"I didn't attack, Liam," her voice was a small, unconvincing whisper.

Sighing, I braced my brow against hers again. "Do you trust me, darlin'?"

"Yes."

"With trust, comes belief. You didn't cut him. Say it, Kady, please—" I couldn't hold myself any longer. My voice was already splintering and the chaos outside had seemed to die down. This needed to be done quickly before that damn orderly returned. "Just say it, say: I didn't attack him."

"I didn't attack him." There's my girl, I couldn't stop the relieved twitch of my lips. I told her to say it again and again, and with each time I could feel a little more belief in her voice.

Telling her not to take any pills, and to just say yes and no in the right places with the shrinks, she agreed with a nod of her head. "One more thing,"—I glided my thumbs over the arch of her cheekbones as I took a breath—"Cling onto this conversation. Hold on with everything you have, keep replaying it and keep remembering these words. Don't lose yourself, Kady. I couldn't bear it." In that moment, all I could imagine was losing her. To not have the chance to look into her eyes, breathe her scent, hear her voice. I would have gladly slipped a knife into my gut and twisted that sucker at the mere thought of having to live that nightmare.

Rolling my eyes, I knew I had to get out of there. I was Kady's rock—her support. I couldn't let her see me like that.

A gust of air as the door opened traveled through the room as the rather flustered orderly came back. "Is everything okay in here?"

Glancing up, I nodded, "Yeah," before dropping my head back to Kady. "I gotta go. Keep remembering," I muttered abruptly, pushing past that lump in my throat as I pushed myself from the seat. When I took a brief moment to press a kiss against her forehead, I felt the creases of my brow deepen. And as I made a hasty retreat past the member of staff, the hate for Liam in putting her in there in the first place, ignited my blood. But it was the hate directed toward myself because I had to leave her there, that slaughtered me.

The steering wheel of my truck was what saw the brunt end of my frustration. Once I allowed the threatening tears to finally see freedom, I breathed my private apology to Kady, then sucked in a breath and reached for my phone. Dragging up Laurie's number, I hit call.

After a few rings, I was greeted with, "How is she?"

"An absolute fucking mess, she's been fucking brainwashed. It was like watching those monkeys forced to watch war and conflict on the fucking television over and over again."

"Fucking Hell, I had no idea she was going to be that bad. So what do we do?"

I tossed my head against the headrest. Opening my mouth, I was quickly interrupted, "We can't confront Liam about this, Walker. It'll put her in more danger."

"She's already in fucking danger, Laurie!" I yelled, as an enraged sob found its escape. "God, I said I would help her. I was supposed to protect her. How could we not have seen this at the beginning? How—"

"Walker, stop! Calm down, breathe. Searching for ideas when you're in a state isn't going to happen."

I said my silent thanks to the heavens that Laurie knew how to calm me the fuck down, and then took her advice. With my eyes shut, and without a sound, I counted to ten and concentrated on my breathing. One thing I knew for certain: Liam and Liv were up to no good. I remembered back to the night at Hamersley's a few weeks back. Their hushed conversations, eye and physical contact, the way he left with her with that shrewd grin plastered all over his sickening face. That is something that can't be hidden from another man. It's rooted into us, we know how we work.

I could only hope that my crazy arsed idea would work, too.

"Laurie, I think I have an idea."

The Dark Evoke Series
Transending NIRVANA

Sneak Peek...

CHAPTER
one

~ *The Dark Evoke Series, (#3) Sneak Peek* ~

A rumbling, "hmmm," coming from in front of me pulled me from slumber. Fluttering my eye lids, the sun charred through the window, creating a thick beam in the halfway point of the room and over the bed. Walker was sound asleep, his thick, black lashes fanned out over the arch of his cheekbone, his full, pale lips more tempting than an apple in Eden.

The rumbling noise which pulled me back to reality was released again, alongside a momentary furrow of his brow. He looked adorable. The snowy white sheet pooled around his hips, showcasing the band of his gray slacks, while his upper body remained visible. I smiled as I remembered the way we coiled around one another and spent hours simply kissing. Some people wouldn't understand how heady that is, participating in something so intimate, so intense, yet not lead into sex or masturbation. It shows constraint, it takes you on a journey like no other; it holds you steady at that peak of bliss and never wanes.

It was phenomenal.

With his right hand snug under the pillow, his left settled on my hip, I observed the destructive scarring on his left pectoral. The lump of sympathy clogging my throat was swallowed harshly as I cautiously shifted and brought my right hand up to it.

Last night, with the combination of impassioned kisses, he allowed me to feel him. My fingers slipped over each jutting gash, each round blemish. Still, as soon as I made my way to hover over his heart, my intention was halted.

This was the one which held his most anguish.

With the tip of my middle finger, I kept vigil, and with extra care not to wake him, I softly traced around the edging of withered, pale flesh. His chest rose and dipped with each steady breath, and as I began to take the journey into the midpoint of the mutilation, the flesh feeling somewhat like leather against my fingertip, Walker stirred. His lashes left the arch of his cheek as they fluttered open.

"Morning," I smiled, discreetly lowering my inspecting hand.

"Mornin' indeed, darlin'."

I giggled and bit my lip while he rubbed his eyes.

"What's so funny?"

"I never thought that your voice could sound any sexier, boy was I was wrong? Sleepy Walker's voice is something else entirely."

Shifting his body closer, he seized behind my right knee and hooked it over his hip. "I'm glad I could please you. How long have you been eyeing me for?"

I rolled my eyes and added an additional serving of over dramatics to my voice. "Oh, I don't know…too long."

Tiny, stirring circles were being traced on my thigh when his lips covered mine. I didn't care about morning breath, all I cared about was that after so long, we were finally here, the point we secretly longed to be at. It was almost surreal. When we pulled away, I licked my lips and rolled my head over the pillow. Peeking up at the ceiling, I muttered, "You never did tell me about the mirror."

"Not today, darlin'." The circular motions on my thigh came to an abrupt end when I redirected my attention back to him. His sleepy features turned hard and angry in a blink of an eye. "You're starting to bruise," he whispered almost apologetically, while I winced as his hand lifted to brush across my wounded cheekbone.

A snort of absurdity left me as I shook my head.

"What is it, darlin'?"

Looking him in the eyes was an impossible task while being besieged by embarrassment. Instead, I focused on his Adam's apple and took a deep breath. "I can't believe how much I let him get away with. I can't believe how much I changed in my outlook and how much I justified what was happening." When an encouraging hand cradled my face, his thumb settled peacefully at the hollow behind my ear, I peeked up and wistfully continued, "How sickening is it that my instinctive thought just then was, 'I'm used to it'?"

Words were halted as he breathed my name with a combination of hurt and anger hardening his ocean eyes into ice. "I'm going to fucking kill him for this."

The scary part was, I felt the determination behind his words. I didn't for one moment think he wouldn't do it. Over the time we had spent together, Walker had proved to me on more than one occasion that he would do anything to insure I was safe, to ensure my wellbeing was maintained.

The secret part of me was terrified because I knew that getting away from Liam wasn't going to be as easy as any other breakup.

Liam DeLaney had connections, he had money, and what's more, he had the determination and the sick, twisted views and judgments that I knew he would put into play, just to get me back. But I kept that knowledge to myself.

That was another attribute I was used to: secret knowledge.

"Don't, it's not worth it."

"Don't go back," he said while his fingers combed through my hair.

I scowled. My voice barely a whisper as one word fell from my lips. "Never."

He smiled and that sexy as fuck dimple stopped by to say 'good morning'. "Well then, today, darlin' is your first day of freedom."

I didn't have the heart to tell him that I wasn't entirely sure of that statement. So I merely filled my lungs and plastered a smile on.

That was another thing I was good at.

About the Author

Raised in a creative family, witnessing one another expressing themselves through creativity, albeit musically or through a form of literature, it was only a matter of time before my passion for devising characters and their unique stories in their own world, began to form and grow. From there the seed was sown and flourished into a young girls dream.

Throughout the years I have often toyed with the idea of pursuing this path, yet unknowing where to begin. There are so many routes in this day and age to help get from A to B, that the dream was both tangible and terrifying. So with that, and after a few months of kicking myself into gear thanks to a certain someone, I decided to self-publish, and that decision was most probably one of the best decisions I have ever made.

I am a mother of a 6 year old son who knows how to keep me on my toes, self-confessed garlic freak and coffee addict. If I'm not writing I'm constantly thinking about writing and can be found either chasing my son around, with my nose in book or being creative in the kitchen.

In writing this series, it was my intent to not only evoke the same feelings in the reader which they would experience while watching a friend or a loved one in the same situation as Kady, but to also give an insight as to how the victim of domestic violence perceives the situation from the insiders perspective, and why is isn't easy to just leave.

One thing I ask of you when writing a review is to please be sensitive with how you approach the topic of domestic violence. Thousands of people live this way, with hundreds unaware that they are in fact in an abusive relationship. Abuse isn't just physical. And while I am aware that this story will most probably be a topic of controversy, and may have had you, as the reader, frustrated, I hope that I was able to portray and demonstrate the sensitive matters in which the mistreated party is subjected to. Furthermore, I hope that it brings a deeper understanding as to why getting out of the situation isn't as easy as saying the words, 'Just leave him/her'.

There is a saying which I have carried with me since writing this series: 'Place a frog in boiling water, it will jump out. Place it in simmering water and it will sit there and boil.'

To both women and men of domestic violence. It can get better. You hold the power.

I read every comment, every review, message and email that I receive, so please feel free to connect with me. I have thoroughly enjoyed experimenting with my writing style, and demonstrating the different foundations which relationships are built upon. Each page and each chapter I write, I am learning more, not only about my characters, but about myself. As long as I maintain this journey, perception, astuteness and knowledge will never cease.

Other books by V.L. Brock

~ Impulses ~
~ Seeking Nirvana: The Dark Evoke Series (#1) ~

Made in the USA
Charleston, SC
13 June 2015